EXILED FROM EARTH

"The stars!" Lou shouted. "That's our answer, Bonnie. We can turn this orbiting prison into mankind's first starship!"

FLIGHT OF EXILES

"Think of your children, Val," Larry said. "The geneticists will be preparing your children for that death-world down there. They'll be sulphur-breathing, gorilla-sized monsters!"

END OF EXILE

"If you're really our priestess, set an example for everyone. Lead us now through the mattler-transmitter, or we'll all die!"

THE EXILES TRILOGY

BEN BOVA

The complete deepspace adventure now in one magnificent volume

THE EXILES TRILOGY
BEN BOVA

THREE NOVELS

BERKLEY BOOKS, NEW YORK

This Berkley book contains the complete
text of the original hardcover editions.
It has been completely reset in a type face
designed for easy reading, and was printed
from new film.

THE EXILES TRILOGY

A Berkley Book / published by arrangement with
E.P. Dutton and Co., Inc.

PRINTING HISTORY
EXILED FROM EARTH
Dutton edition published 1971
FLIGHT OF EXILES
Dutton edition published 1972
EXILES FROM EARTH
Dutton edition published 1975
THE EXILES TRILOGY
Berkley edition / June 1980
Fourth printing / March 1982

ISBN: 0-425-05714-3

A BERKLEY BOOK ® TM 757,375
Berkley Books are published by Berkley Publishing Corporation,

CONTENTS

EXILED FROM EARTH

In alphabetical order:
To Gordon R. Dickson and Harlan Ellison
with thanks and caritas.

(1)

The General Chairman paced across the soft carpeting of his office, hands clasped behind his slightly stooped back. He stopped at the wide sweep of windows that overlooked the city.

There was little of Old Messina to be seen. The original city of ancient churches and chalk-white houses bleaching in the fierce Sicilian sunlight had been all but swallowed up by the metal and glass towers of the world government—offices, assembly halls, hotels and residence buildings, shops and entertainment centers for the five million men and women who governed the world's twenty-some billions.

In his air-conditioned, soundproofed office atop the tallest of all the towers, the General Chairman could not hear the shrill voices of the crowded streets below, nor the constant growl of cars and turbotrucks on the busy throughways.

At least we saved some of the old city, he thought. It had been one of his first successes in world politics. A small thing. But he had helped to stop the growth of the New Messina before it completely choked and killed the old city. The new city had remained the same size for nearly thirty years now.

Beyond the fishing boats at the city's waterfront, the Straits sparkled invitingly under the sun. And beyond that, the tip of Italy's boot, Calabria, where the peasants still prided themselves on their hard-headed stubbornness. And beyond the misty blue hills of Calabria, shimmering in the heat haze, the sterner blue of the sky was almost too bright to look at.

The old man knew it was impossible, but he thought he saw the glint of one of the big orbital stations hovering in that brilliant sky. He worked a forefinger and thumb against the bridge of his nose. It was one of those days when he felt his years.

He thought about his native São Paulo, how it spread like a festering sore all the way from the river to the sea, flattening hills, carving away the forest, bursting with so many people that not even the Population Control Center's computers could keep track of them. No sane man would willingly enter the heart of São Paulo, or any large city on Earth. No human being could live in the teeming guts of a city and keep his sanity.

How hard they had worked to save the cities! How hard they had worked to make the world safe and stable.

And now this.

The desk top intercom chimed.

"Yes?" The Chairman automatically switched from the Portuguese of his thoughts to the English of the world government.

His secretary sensed his mood. Her face was somber instead of showing its usual cheerfulness. "They're here, sir."

Nodding, "Very well. Send them in."

Six men and two women filed into the spacious office and took seats at the conference table. The women sat together up at the end closest to the windows, next to the head chair. They carried no papers, no briefcases. Each place at the table had a tiny intercom and viewscreen that linked with the central computer.

They are young and vital, thought the Chairman. *They know what must be done and they have the strength to do it. As soon as all this is settled, I shall retire.*

Reluctantly he took his place at the head of the glistening mahogany table. The others remained silent, waiting for him to speak. The only sound was the faintest whir of the computer's recording spool.

He cleared his throat. "Good morning. Last Monday we discussed this situation and you made your recommendation. I asked you to consider possible alternatives. From the looks on your faces, it seems that no suitable alternative has been found."

They all turned to the stocky, round-faced Minister of Security, Vassily Kobryn. He had the look of an athlete to him: tanned skin, short, wiry brown hair, big in the shoulders and arms.

Shifting in his chair self-consciously, Kobryn said, "I see I have been elected the hatchet man." His voice was deep and strong, with barely a trace of a Slavic accent. "All right . . . it *was* my idea, originally. We looked at all the possibilities and ran each case on the computers. The only safe way is to put them in exile. Permanently."

"Siberia," one of the women muttered.

"No, not Siberia." Kobryn took her literally. "It's too heavily populated. Too many cities and dome farms for an effective exile. No, the only place is the new space station. It's large enough and it can be kept completely isolated."

Rolf Bernard, the Minister of Finance, shook his head. "I still disagree. Two thousand of the world's leading scientists . . ."

"Plus their wives and families," the Chairman added.

"What would you prefer?" Kobryn snapped. "A bullet in each of their heads? Or would you leave them alone and let them smash everything that we have worked for?"

"Perhaps if we talked with them . . ."

"That won't work," said Eric Mottern, the taciturn Minister of Technology. "Even if they tried to cooperate with us, you can't stop ideas from leaking out. And once this genetic engineering idea gets loose . . ."

"The world is turned upside down," the Chairman said. He spoke softly, but everyone heard him. With a sigh, he confessed, "I have also been thinking about the problem. I have also tried to find alternatives. There are none. Exile is the only permissible answer."

"Then it is agreed. Good!" said Kobryn.

"No, not good," the General Chairman said. "Very far from good. When we do this thing, we admit failure. We admit fear—yes, terror. We are terrified of a new idea, a new scientific discovery. The government of the world, the protectors of peace and stability, must stoop to exiling some of the world's finest minds. This is a horrible state of affairs. Truly horrible."

(2)

Lou Christopher leaned back in his chair and put his feet up on the desk: his favorite position for thinking. In his lap he held a small tablet and a pen. Although he was both worried and puzzled, his face showed neither of these emotions. He was frowning and looked more angry than anything else.

Through the plastiglass partition that made up one wall of his small office, Lou could see Ramo, the Institute's main computer, flashing its console lights as it worked.

"Come on, Ramo," he muttered to himself, "get it right this time."

Lou tapped the pen on the tablet and watched the little viewscreen on his desk. It was blank. Then...

"I'm sorry," Ramo said in a warm baritone voice from the overhead speaker, "but the possible permutations are still three orders of magnitude beyond my programming instructions."

"Three orders!"

"I can proceed with the existing matrix, or await further programming." Ramo's voice sounded neither worried nor puzzled. Not happy nor angry. He was simply stating facts.

Lou tossed the pen back onto the desk and slammed his feet to the floor. The tablet fell off his lap.

"Still three orders of magnitude to go. Lou shook his head, then glanced at his wristwatch. It was already nine A.M.

"I'm waiting for instructions," Ramo said calmly.

You and your instructions can both... Lou caught himself, realizing that the computer wasn't at fault. There were millions upon millions of branching pathways in the human genetic code. It was simply going to take more time to get them all programmed properly.

Shrugging, he said, "Okay, Ramo, looks like we've got a full day ahead of us."

Ramo said nothing, but somehow Lou felt that the computer nodded in agreement.

Lou got up and walked out of the office, past the computer's humming, light-blinking main console, out into the hall. He got a cup of water from the cooler, gulped it down as he looked out the hallway window at the New Mexico morning outside. It had been barely dawn when Lou drove to the Institute. Now it was full daylight, bright and cloudless.

Half the gliders have already taken off, Lou thought glumly. *I just won't make this race. Better call Bonnie.*

Tossing the plastic cup into the recycling slot in the wall, Lou went back to his office, plopped tiredly into his cushioned chair, and punched the phone button on the desk top.

"Bonnie Sterne," he said. "She's not at home, you'll have to use her pocket phone."

It took a few seconds, then Bonnie's face appeared on the viewscreen. Behind her, Lou could see people bustling around in a crowded room. *She must be in the Control Center,* Lou thought. Sure enough, he heard the muted thunder of one of the big gliders' takeoff rockets.

"Lou! When are you getting out here? I've asked the judges to postpone your takeoff time, but..."

He put up his hands. "Better tell them to scratch me. Can't make it today. Probably not tomorrow, either."

"Oh no." Bonnie looked genuinely heartbroken. She was blonde and had light gray eyes, but the finely-etched bone structure of her face always reminded Lou faintly of an Indian's. Maybe it was the high cheekbones, or the cast of her eyes. Maybe she had some Apache blood in her. Lou had always meant to ask but somehow never did.

"Isn't there any way you can get out of it?" she asked. "Can't some of the other programmers do it?"

Lou shook his head. "You know they can't. I'm just as sorry as you are. I've been working toward this race all year. But Kaufman needs this stuff by Monday. The whole Institute's depending on it."

"I know," Bonnie admitted, biting her lower lip. Lou knew that she was trying to figure some way....

"Listen!" she said, suddenly bright again. "Why don't I come down and work with you? Maybe we can finish the programming in time for taking off tomorrow...."

"Thanks, but there's not much you can do. It looks like I'll have to work all night, at least. So I won't be in much shape for flying tomorrow."

Her expression dimmed once more. "It's just not fair. You have to work all weekend ... and this is the biggest race of the year."

"I know. But genetics comes before racing," Lou said. "You have a good weekend. See you Monday."

"All right. But it's really unfair."

"Yeah. So long."

"So ... oh, wait! There was a man out here looking for you. Said he was a Federal marshal."

Lou blinked at her. "A what?"

"A Federal marshal. He wanted to see you."

"What for?"

Bonnie shook her head. "I thought marshals were only something in Western stories."

With a grin, Lou said, "Well, we're out in the West, you know."

"But he said he was from New York."

Shrugging, "Well, if he's looking for me, I'll be right here all day."

"If he comes around again, I'll tell him."

"All right." Suddenly curious, Lou asked, "Did he say what he wanted? Why does he want to see me?"

"I don't know," Bonnie replied.

After Bonnie signed off, Lou plunged back into work, doing intricate mathematics problems with Ramo's help and then programming the results into the computer's memory banks. When he looked at his watch again, it was well past noon. He walked down to the cafeteria and took a sandwich and a steaming cup of coffee from the automatic dispensers. The cafeteria was practically empty: only a few of the weekend clean-up crew at the tables.

The scientific staff's out enjoying the weekend, Lou grumbled to himself. *Well, guess they can't do much until I finish programming Ramo.*

He took the plastic-sealed sandwich and coffee back to his office. As he got there, he saw Greg Belsen standing by the computer's main console, watching the big display viewscreen there as it flashed a series of colored drawings and graphs at eyeblink speed.

"What are you doing in here today?" Lou asked.

Greg turned and grinned at him. "Thought you might be lonesome, old buddy, How's it going?"

Lou jabbed a finger toward the viewscreen. "See for yourself. We're still three orders of magnitude off."

Greg gave a low whistle. "That close?"

"Close? It soundes pretty blinking far to me."

Greg laughed. He had an infectious giggle, like a ten-year-old boy's, that was known throughout the Institute. "You're just sore because there's still more work to do. But if you stop to think of where we were six months ago, when you started this modeling program . . ."

"Yeah, maybe," Lou admitted. "But there's still a long way to go."

They walked back into Lou's office together. Greg Belsen was one of the Institute's bright, aggressive young biochemists. He was just short of six feet tall, slightly bigger than Lou. He was lean and flat-gutted from playing tennis and handball, two of the favorite, socially useful sports. Like Lou, Greg had straight dark hair. But his face was roundish and his eyes brown. Lou had more angular features and blue eyes.

"Is there anything I can do to help out?" Greg asked, taking the extra straight-backed chair in Lou's office. "I know you wanted to get to those glider races today. . . ."

Lou sank into the desk chair. "No, there's nobody around here who can program this stuff into Ramo as fast as I can. And Kaufman wants it for Monday morning."

Nodding, Greg said, "I know."

"Is it really that important?"

Greg smiled at him. "I'm not a geneticist, like Kaufman. But I know this—what you're doing now, this zygote modeling, is a crucial step. Until we have it down cold, there's no hope of genetic engineering in any practical sense. But once you've taught Ramo all the ins and outs of the human genetic code, the way is clear. We can be turning out supermen within a year."

Lou leaned back in his chair. "Yeah . . . that's what Kaufman said."

"You're the crucial man," Greg said. "Everything depends on

you . . . and your electronic partner."

Not bad for a kid from a hick college, Lou thought to himself.

"Well," Greg said, getting up, "if there's nothing I can do to help, I can at least get out of your way. Guess I'll go see how Big George's doing."

Lou nodded and started to sort through the papers on his desk.

With a grin, Greg added, "Maybe I'll take Bonnie out to dinner . . . seeing's how you've stood her up."

"Hey! Hands off!"

He laughed. "Relax pal. Relax. I don't go poaching. Got a few girls of my own, hidden under rocks here and there."

"Hmph," said Lou.

"But if you can tear yourself away from Ramo for an hour or so, might be a good idea for you to take Bonnie out for dinner. The kid's worked just as hard as you have to get your glider ready for this race, you know. Be a shame to leave her alone all weekend."

"Yeah," Lou agreed. "Maybe I will."

But as soon as Greg left, Lou went back to work. He didn't think about Bonnie or flying or anything else except matching the myriad possible permutations of the human genetic code and storing the knowledge in Ramo's magnetic core memory. It was late afternoon when he was startled out of his concentration by a hard rap on his office door.

Looking up from his paper-strewn desk, Lou saw the door open and a hard-looking, thick-bodied older man stepped in heavily.

"Louis Christopher, I have a Federal warrant for your arrest."

(3)

With mounting anger, Lou asked a thousand questions as the marshal took him from the Institute in a black, unmarked turbocar. The marshal answered none of them, replying only:

"My orders are to bring you in. You'll find out what it's all about soon enough."

They drove to a small private airfield as the fat red sun dipped toward the desert horizon. A sleek, twin-engined jet was waiting.

"Now wait a minute!" Lou shouted as the car pulled up beside the plane. "I know my rights. You can't..."

But the marshal wasn't listening to any arguments. He slid out from behind the steering wheel of the car and gestured impatiently toward the jet. Lou got out of the car and looked around. In the lengthening shadows of late afternoon, the airfield seemed deserted. *There must be somebody in the control tower*. But Lou could see no one around the plane, or the hangars, or the smaller planes lined up neatly on the edge of the taxi apron.

"This is crazy," he said.

The marshal hitched a thumb toward the jet again. Shrugging, Lou walked to the open hatch and climbed in. No one else was aboard the plane. The four plush seats in the passenger compartment were empty. The flight deck was closed off from view. As soon as the marshal locked the main hatch and they were both strapped into their seats, the jet engines whined to life and the plane took off.

They flew so high that the sun climbed well back into the afternoon sky. Lou watched the jet's wings slide back for supersonic flight, and then they arrowed eastward with the red

11

sun casting long shadows on the ground, far below. The marshal seemed to be sleeping, so Lou had nothing to do but watch the country slide beneath the plane. They crossed the Rockies, so far below them that they looked more like wrinkles than real mountains. The Mississippi was a tortured gray snake weaving from horizon to horizon. Still the plane streaked on, fast enough to race the sunset.

The sun was still slightly above the horizon when the plane touched down at JFK jetport. Lou had been there once before and recognized it from the air. But their jet taxied to a far corner of the sprawling field, and stopped in front of a waiting helicopter.

The marshal was awake now, and giving orders again. Lou glared at him, but followed his directions. They went out of the jet, across a few meters of cracked grass-invaded cement, and up into the plastic bubble of the copter. Lou sat down on the back bench behind the empty pilot's seat. The marshal climbed in heavily and sat beside him, wheezing slightly.

Over the whir of the whizzing rotors and the nasal hum of the electric motor, Lou shouted:

"Just where are you taking me? What's this all about?"

The marshal shook his head, slammed the canopy hatch shut, and reached between the two front seats to punch a button on the control panel. The motor hummed louder and the copter jerked up off the ground.

By the time the helicopter flashed over the skyline of Manhattan, Lou was furious.

"Why won't you tell me anything?" he shouted at the marshal, sitting beside him on the back bench. He was leaning back with his burly arms folded across his chest and his sleepy eyes half closed.

"Listen, kid, the phone woke me up at four this morning. I had to race out to the jetport and fly to Albuquerque. I spent half the day waiting for you at that silly glider race. Then I drove to your apartment, and you didn't show up there. Then I went to your lab. Know what my wife and kids are doing right now? They're sitting home, wondering whether I'm dead or alive and why we're not all out on the picnic we planned. Know how many picnics we can afford, on a marshal's pay? Been planning this one all year—had a spot in the upstate park reserved months ago. Now it's going to waste while I hotfoot all across the country after you. So don't ask questions, understand?"

Then he added, "Besides, I don't know what it's all about. I just got the word to pick up you up, that's all."

In a softer voice, Lou said, "Well, look... I'm sorry about your picnic. I didn't know.... Never had a Federal marshal after me before. But why can't I call anybody? My friends'll be worried about me. My girl..."

"I told you, don't ask questions." The marshal closed his eyes altogether.

Lou frowned. He started to ask where they were going, then thought better of it. The copter was circling over the East River now, close to the old United Nations buildings. It started to descend toward a landing pad next to the tall graceful tower of marble and glass. In the last, blood-red light of the dying sun, Lou could see that the buildings were stained by nearly a century of soot and grime. The windows were caked with dirt, the once-beautiful marble was cracked and patched.

Two men were standing down on the landing pad, off to one side, away from the downwash of the rotors. As soon as the copter's wheels touched the blacktop, the cabin hatch popped open.

"Out you go," said the marshal.

Lou jumped out lightly. The marshal reached over and yanked the door shut before Lou could turn around. The copter's motor whined, and off it lifted in a spray of dust and grit. Lou pulled his head down and squeezed his eyes shut. When he opened them again, the copter was speeding down the river.

Sun's down now, Lou thought. *He'll never make it in time for his picnic.*

The two men were walking briskly toward Lou, their shoes scuffing the blacktop. One of them was small and slim, Latin-looking. Probably Puerto Rican. The breeze from the river flicked at his black hair. The other somehow looked like a foreigner. His suit wasn't exactly odd, but it didn't look exactly right, either. He was big, blond, Nordic-looking.

"Please come with us," said the Norseman. And sure enough, he had the flat twang of a Scandinavian accent. "It is my duty to inform you that we are both armed, and escape is impossible."

"Escape from what?" Lou started to feel exasperated again.

"Please," said the Puerto Rican softly. "It is getting dark. We should not remain outside any longer. This way, please."

Well, they're polite enough, at least.

Inside, the UN building looked a little better. The corridor they walked down was clean, at least. But the carpeting was threadbare and faded with a century's worth of footsteps. They took a spacious elevator car, paneled with peeling wood, up a dozen floors. Then another corridor, and finally into a small room.

"Dr. Kirby!"

Sitting on a sofa at the other side of the little room was Dr. John Kirby of Columbia-Brookhaven University. He was in his mid-fifties—white-haired, nervously thin, pinched face with a bent out-thrust nose that gave him the title "Hawk" behind his back.

"I'm sorry," Kirby said. "I don't seem to recall..."

"Louis Christopher," said Lou, as his two escorts shut the door and left him alone with Dr. Kirby. "We met at the Colorado conference last spring, remember?"

Kirby made a vague gesture with his hands. "There are always so many people at these conferences...."

Lou sat on the sofa beside him. "I gave a paper on computer modeling for forecasting genetic adjustments. You had a question from the floor about the accuracy of the forecasts. Afterward we had lunch together."

"Oh yes. The computer fellow. You're not a geneticist." Kirby's eyes still didn't seem to really recognize Lou.

"Do you have any idea of what this is all about?" Lou asked.

Kirby shook his head. He seemed dazed, out of it. Lou looked around the room. It was comfortable enough: a sofa, two deep contour chairs, a bookshelf full of tape spools, a viewscreen set into the wall. No windows, though. Lou got up and went to the door. Locked.

Turning back to Kirby, he saw that the old man's face was sunk in his hands. *Did they drug him?*

"Are you okay?" Lou asked.

"What...oh, yes...I'm all right. Merely...well, frankly, I'm frightened."

"Of what?"

Kirby fluttered his hands again. "I...I don't know. I don't

know why we're here, or what they want to do with us. That's what frightens me. They won't let me call my wife or even a lawyer...."

Lou paced the room in a few strides. "They grabbed me at the Institute. They wouldn't let me call anybody, either. Nobody knows I'm here." Back to the door he paced. "Why are they doing this? What have we done? What's it all about?"

Abruptly the door opened. The same two men stood in the corridor. "You will come with us, please."

Kirby started to stand up. But Lou said, "No I won't. Not until you tell us what this is all about. You can't arrest us and push us around like this. I want to talk..."

The Norseman pulled a needle-thin gun from his tunic. It was so small that his hand hid all of it except the slim barrel. But the muzzle looked as big as a cannon to Lou, because it was pointed straight at him.

"Please, Mr. Christopher. We have no desire to use force. You are not technically under arrest, therefore you have no need for a lawyer. However, you are wanted for questioning at government headquarters in Messina. It would be best if you cooperate."

"Messina? In Sicily?"

The blond nodded.

"But... my family," Kirby said in a shaky voice.

"They have been informed," said the Puerto Rican. "No harm will come if you cooperate with us."

With a shrug, Lou headed into the corridor. The Norseman tucked his gun back inside his tunic. The four of them walked slowly down toward the elevator, their footsteps clicking on the bare plastic floors and echoing off the walls. When they got to the elevator, the Puerto Rican touched the DOWN button and instantly the elevator doors slid open.

This building's empty except for us! Lou realized.

He stepped into the elevator, then whirled, grabbed the Puerto Rican and hurled him into the Norseman. They went down in a tangle of arms and legs, shouting. Lou punched the DOOR CLOSE button and yelled to Kirby:

"Come on!"

Kirby stood frozen, his jaw hanging open, as the doors started to slide shut. The Norseman was still on the floor, but he had pushed the Puerto Rican off and was reaching for his gun. The doors shut. Lou pushed the GROUND button and the elevator started down. He could hear somebody pounding on the metal doors at the floor above.

On the ground floor he tried to retrace his steps back to the corridor landing pad outside. He got lost in the corridors, finally saw an EXIT sign, and banged through the doors. It was full night outside, dark and damp-cool, with the ripe acrid smell of the garbage-choked river a sudden shock to Lou's senses. The city was almost completely dark; only a few lights shone, mostly high up in skyscrapers where people had their own power generators and had barricaded themselves in for the night.

He heard footsteps and flattened himself into the deeper shadows along the wall.

"Shall we turn the lights on?" The Norseman's voice.

"And attract every gang of pack rats on the East Side?" the Puerto Rican answered. "You don't know this city very well. He'll never live out the night alone. Either he'll come begging at our doors inside an hour, or he'll be dead. No one can get through a night on these streets alone."

"My orders are to bring them to Messina unharmed," said the Norseman.

"You want to search for him? Out there? You'll be killed, too."

They said no more. Lou could sense the Norseman shaking his head, not satisfied, but not willing to risk his own skin against the city streets. Lou heard a door click shut. He slid along the wall carefully and found the door he had come through. It was locked from the inside.

He turned away and looked at the city again with new understanding. He was alone in the city.

And the night had just begun.

[4]

Lou hunkered down on his heels, resting his back against the rough wall, and tried to think. He could bang on the door until they came and got him. Then he'd be safe enough. The Norseman might jab him with a sleeping drug, but probably nothing worse. Then they'd take him to Messina. But why? And where was Bonnie? Had they taken her, too?

And why should he let them pull him around by the nose, Lou asked himself with mounting anger. They had no right to take him here. *Who do they think they're pushing around, a frail old professor like Kirby?*

But—out here alone in the city! Lou remembered his high school days in Maryland, when the best way to show you had guts was to sneak into the city at night. Of course, you always went with your friends, never less than a dozen guys. And now that he thought about it, Lou realized that despite their loud claims of bravery they never went deeper than a few blocks into the outskirts of Baltimore. Then back to the friendly hills of Hagerstown, as fast as their cars could take them. And still John Milford had been killed on that one trip. Lou remembered tripping over his mutilated body as he ran for his car that night. It still made him shiver.

And this was New York, the heart of it at that! The closest place to civilization and safety was the old JFK jetport, out on Long Island someplace.

If I can get to the jetport in one piece, Lou reasoned, *I can get back to Albuquerque. Maybe Bonnie's waiting for me there.*

But how to get to the jetport?

As he sat there wondering, Lou heard the distant whisper of a

17

turbocar. He paid no attention to it at first, but gradually it grew louder and louder. A car! In the city, at night. *Can I get it to stop for me?*

No doubt of it, the whine of the turbine was much closer, coming this way. Lou got up and walked across the blacktopped courtyard, heading for the sound. Far off to his left he saw a glimmer of light. Moving toward him! He ran to the railing that bordered the courtyard. There was a sunken roadway beyond the railing, and down below Lou could see the lights of the approaching car. The roadbed was patched and rough, but apparently some cars still used it.

Lou leaned over the railing and tried to wave at the speeding turbocar. It roared right past him, making his ears pop with the scream of its engine echoing off the walls of the sunken throughway. A puff of hot, grit-laden, kerosene-smelling air blew into his face.

Maybe if I get down to the road I can get somebody to stop and pick me up.

In the darkness left by the passing car, Lou could barely make out a pedestrian bridge spanning the road, down at the end of the courtyard. He trotted to it. A wire screen fence blocked access to it, but Lou scrambled over it like a kid sneaking into a playground after it had been closed for the night.

He crossed the bridge and found himself on the sidewalk of an empty city street. *There's got to be a stairway down to the road someplace along here,* he told himself. He started walking along the street. In the darkness, he stumbled over a bottle and sent it clattering across the pavement. The noise made the city's silence seem more ominous. Lou got up and went on, keeping his eyes on the roadway. The city seemed deserted. But Lou realized that there were people all around him, by the tens of millions. Most of them were barricaded in for the night, terrified of those who roamed the dark. And the rest...

Another car raced by, coming up the other way. Lou didn't bother waving. The driver couldn't see him from down on the road. Besides, Lou was beginning to understand that no driver in his right mind would stop to pick up anybody in the heart of the city. It was enough of a chance to drive through the East Side. If the car should break down or have an accident...

Maybe if they see I'm wearing a flight suit, Lou tried to

convince himself, *they'd stop for me.*

"Goin' somep'ace?"

The voice was like a knife through him . Lou jerked around, startled. A scrawny kid, dressed in rags, was grinning toothily at him.

"Goin' somep'ace?" he repeated.

"Uh . . . I'm lost. I'm trying to find my way. . . ."

Another voice called from the darkness across the street, "Whatcha got, Pimple?"

"Buck in a funny suit, sez he's losted."

A trio of kids stepped out of the shadows and crossed to where Lou stood, frozen.

"Funny suit," said the one in the middle, the shortest of them all. None of them came up to Lou's shoulder. They were all wearing rags, barefoot, gaunt, scrawny, with the hard, hungry look of starving old men set into the faces of children.

The one in the middle seemed to be the leader. He eyed Lou carefully, then asked, "Got a pass?"

"What?"

"Yer on Peeler turf. Got a pass t'go through?"

"Well . . . no. . . ."

The leader broke into a cackling laugh. "Humpin' right you ain't! Nobody gets a pass, 'cept from me, and I don't give 'em!" All four of them laughed.

Then the leader asked, "How much skin on ya?"

"I don't understand. . . ."

"Skin, leaves, pages, paper, bread. . . ."

"Oh, you mean money," Lou realized. He shook his head. "Nothing. I don't carry . . ."

Something exploded in the small of his back. Lou sagged down to his knees, pain screaming through him. The leader stepped up in front of him. Lou had to look up now to see into his hard, glittering eyes.

"I . . ."

Smiling, the leader rocked back deliberately and then swung his fist into Lou's mouth. One of the other boys kicked Lou in the chest and he toppled over backward gasping for breath, his mouth suddenly filled with blood, tiny bright lights flashing in his eyes.

He felt their hands on him, ripping open the zips of his suit, tearing at the fabric. They rolled him over, face down on the filthy sidewalk. They pulled off his boots.

They were talking among themselves now, muttering and giggling. Lou's mouth felt numb and puffy. His back and ribs flamed with pain when he tried to move, but he forced his breathing back to normal, fought his way back up to a crouching position.

"Honest buck, ain't cha?" the leader said, grinning. "No skin, tol' truth. But boots is somethin' ta howl for. Big fer me, but I'll stuff 'em with paper or somethin'."

Lou stayed in his crouch and rubbed at the fast-caking blood on his chin. The four boys were ranged in a half-circle around him, looking very big now as they stood over him.

"Okay," said the leader. "How we gonna get rid of 'im?"

The kid on Lou's left flicked a knife open and started giggling.

Lou uncoiled and slammed straight into the leader, bowling him over, and raced away. He pounded down the darkened street, rounded a corner, and ran as fast as he could, blindly, away from them. Something sharp bit into one bare foot but Lou kept going, heart pounding, sweat pouring all over him.

"A hunt, a hunt!" he heard someone shouting from behind him.

And then the leader's unmistakable voice, "Peelers! A hunt!"

Other voices shouted up ahead, and from a side street too. Lou pulled up short. There was an alley to his right. *Dead end, most likely.* He walked, slowly and quietly now, past the alley and toward the corner of the street up ahead. He could feel himself trembling. The pain was buried now beneath the fear. From down the street he heard the scrabbling sounds of barefooted kids walking swiftly toward him.

"Try that alley," somebody said, half a block behind him in the darkness.

Lou turned the corner and started running again.

He lost track of time. Minutes and hours blurred together. Lou only knew that he was running, hunted like a rare gazelle—or more like a meat animal being chased by a pack of wolves. Whenever he stopped, he heard their voices behind him, off to the side, ahead, out of the shadows, everywhere.

He tried to get into the buildings, but the doors were locked.

Many of them sealed with heavy metal screens. Some were electrified, and Lou picked up a handful of burned fingers before he stopped trying the darkened doorways.

"Hey, head 'im off . . . don't let 'im get across the avenya!"

Lou looked up ahead. There were lights glowing a few blocks up the street. One of the main avenues, still lighted? Lights meant civilization, and civilization meant safety. Lou started running toward the lights.

"Hey, there he goes! Get 'im!"

Feet were pounding behind him, getting closer. From around a corner, two boys appeared, knives in hand. Lou swerved out into the middle of the street. When they raced to meet him, he cut back again in his best touch-football style. One of the boys slipped trying to reach him, and Lou planted a running kick on the other one's midsection so hard that the kid bounced halfway across the street.

The lights, the lights. He had to get to the lights. They were right behind him. A knife whizzed past his head and clattered on the trash-strewn pavement. Lou's lungs were in flames, his heartbeat a deafening roar in his ears. Something grabbed at his waist. He swung around and backhanded viciously. A little kid, no more than eight or nine, spurted blood from his nose as his head snapped back from Lou's blow. He looked afraid and angry and surprised, all at once. Lou grabbed him by the hair and pulled him off, tossed him into the next teenager coming at him, and then sprinted out into the brightly lit avenue.

"Hold it!" roared the leader. "Stop. Don' cross th' line."

Lou stood in the middle of the broad avenue, chest raw and heaving, ears bursting with the hot drumfire of his pulse, legs shaking with fatigue. The kids of the gang bunched together on the sidewalk.

"Good run, funnyman," siad the leader. "Lotsa luck." Then he raised his hand.

Lou saw a knife in that hand, saw the leader snap it forward in a quick throw, saw the knife fly through the air toward him. He jumped back, toward the far side of the street. The knife hit point first on the blacktopped street and stuck there, quivering. Now the other boys were slowly reaching for their knives, getting ready to throw.

Stumbling, nearly unconscious from exertion, Lou backpedaled and then turned and staggered to the pavement on the other side of the avenue. Back away from the lights into the shadows of a doorway. The kids merely stood on the opposite sidewalk, laughing and standing there, as if waiting for something to happen.

A pair of hands grabbed Lou's arms. "Whatcha want, pinkey?"

Lou never thought he would do it, but he fainted.

(5)

Lou woke up. He was in a room, on the floor. A single, naked bulb up in the ceiling glared at him. A half-dozen kids were standing around him. Black kids. Another gang.

He pulled himself up slowly to a sitting position. Every part of his body ached horribly.

The only furniture in the room was an antique wooden school desk and chair, battered and carved with hundreds of initials. On the wall behind the desk was some sort of old poster showing a huge lion leaping through a ring of fire. The top of the poster had been ripped away. Lou could make out the words...EST SHOW ON EARTH, APRIL 15 to 29. It didn't make any sense to him.

And then he focused on the black man sitting at the desk. He was immense, the biggest man Lou had ever seen. He must have weighed three hundred pounds or more. And he wasn't fat: just huge, giant muscles on a mountainous frame. He looked completely out of proportion to the rickety desk as he sat squeezed in behind it, looming over it and Lou. The only clothing Lou could see was an open vest. His black skin gleamed in the glare of the overhead lamp. It was hard to tell how old he was; he could have been in his early twenties or ten years older.

He was talking to one of the other boys, ignoring Lou's puzzled stare.

"...only way's gonna be to give 'im back. Otherwise the peace 'tween us an' the Peelers gonna get busted wide open."

"He's ours," the other boy answered hotly. "They lost 'im an' we got 'im. Makes 'im ours, right?"

The boys muttered agreement.

"You want the Peelers comin' up here after 'im? Ready to fight the whole pack of 'em? Tonight? 'Sides, he ain't got nothin' on 'im, he ain't *worth* keepin'!"

Lou realized they were talking about him. "Hey, wait a minute...."

"Shuddup, pinkey!" A toe nudged his tender back. Lou winced and closed his mouth.

"Naw, wait," said the giant, looking down at Lou. "Know where you are, white man?"

Lou shook his head.

Smiling from the desk, "You're in the secret headquarters of the Top Cats. I am N'Gai Felix Leo, president of the Top Cats. You may call me Felix, for short." Felix spoke very slowly and carefully, in precise English, for Lou. The way a teacher would speak to a backward child.

"Apparently," he went on, "you stumbled into our turf when the Peelers were chasing you a little while ago. We are now discussing whether we should give you back to the Peelers or deal with you ourselves."

"Deal with me?" Lou echoed.

"Kill ya," snapped a tall, lanky kid.

Felix shook his head and grasped the edges of the desk in his massive hands. "Zonk, whyn't you keep shut?" he said to the kid who had spoken. Turning back to Lou, "You can't stay here. You can't join our gang, for obvious reasons. If we let you go free, the Peelers would take it as an unfriendly gesture and they might start a war with us."

"Them whitesheets," Zonk muttered.

"My friends don't like to admit it," Felix said, his voice rising ever so slightly, "but we are in no shape for a war against the Peelers. They outnumber us badly, and they can call in a half a dozen other gangs as allies."

"An' we c'n get all uptown to come on our side!" Zonk shouted.

"Yeah, an' turn the whole city into a battleground?" Felix countered. "Been enough o' that, you fool. We gotta work out somethin' better... least, 'til we're strong enough t'stand up t'the Peelers."

"Look," said Lou, "all I want is to get to the jetport before the police block it off...."

"Police?" Zonk flashed. "Helmet heads? After you?"

"Not the tac brigades . . . Federal marshal . . . and some world government people. . . ."

They all stared at him blankly; none of them had the vaguest idea of what Lou was talking about.

Except for Felix. "Why are they after you?"

Lou shrugged. "They won't tell me."

Zonk laughed. "Since when the helmet heads tell you why they crackin' your skull? They jus' *do* it, tha'sall! You find out later in the hospital . . . if you make it that far!"

"If I don't get to the jetport before dawn, they'll probably be waiting for me when I do arrive," Lou said.

Felix shook his head again. "You're not getting to JFK either before dawn or after it. We can't let you go, the Peelers would get sore at us."

"You're just a kneeler!" Zonk yelled. "A chicken, scared o'them damn Peelers!"

Felix's face went unimaginably hard. His eyes slitted, like a cat's. Slowly, ponderously, he rose from his chair and stepped out from behind the desk on legs the size of tree trunks. Zonk glanced around at the other boys, then backed away a step.

"We been friends," Felix said as he advanced like a tide, engulfing the room. His voice was low, menacing. "So I'm gonna give you one chance t'take back that mouth. *Now!*"

"I . . . I . . . I'm sorry," Zonk stammered. "I got sore. . . ."

"Am I a kneeler?" Felix was towering over the skinny boy, scarcely a centimeter away from him. He seemed to surround Zonk.

"No . . . no, you ain't."

"Am I afraid of anything or anyone on this Earth?"

"No. Nothin' or nobody."

Before he could even think of what he was saying, Lou heard his own voice call out, "Then you're not afraid of helping me get to JFK."

Everybody froze. The room went absolutely silent. No one even breathed, it seemed to Lou. Least of all Lou himself. He sat there on the floor, the other boys ranged around him staring open-mouthed, with Felix off to one side, back turned as he confronted the petrified Zonk.

Very, very slowly, Felix turned toward Lou. The grimy

floorboards squeaked under him. His face was still as flat and hard as the face on the lion in the poster.

"What did you say?"

I'm dead either way, Lou told himself. Aloud, he answered, "If you're not afraid of anything or anybody, then you're not afraid of helping me get to the jetport. Tonight. Now."

Felix stared at Lou for a long moment, grim, unblinking. Then slowly his mouth opened and he began chuckling. The chuckle deepened into a laugh, a strong laugh that shook the room. The other kids started laughing, too.

"You're something, white man . . . really something, calling me out like that." Felix roared laughter and went back toward the desk. "You got guts . . . not much brains, maybe, but plenty guts." He dropped back on the chair so hard that Lou felt sure it would crack under him.

Felix shook his head, still laughing. "So you're trying to *dare* me into helping you. That's a jolt, a real jolt."

Lou got to his feet. "Okay, so it's funny. Either help me or kill me or let me go. Take your pick."

Waving a heavy hand, Felix said, "Man, you must have some black blood in you someplace. You got guts, all right. Look . . . if I let you go, you'll get killed before daybreak, y'know? If I help you, it'll start a war. But . . . shoot, baby it's going to be hard to kill you when you got the guts to dare me."

He turned to Zonk. "Go get us a car."

"You gonna . . ."

"Man wants t'see JFK," Felix said to them. "I ain't seen th' place myself for years. You ever see it?"

Zonk, wide-eyed, shook his head.

"You ready to fight a war when we get back?"

Zonk nodded. So did the others.

"Okay . . . get a car. Maybe we'll stop uptown on our way back, bring down some reinforcements. Show th' Peelers they gotta think twice 'fore they start a war."

"Now you're talkin'," Zonk said, and he headed for the doorway.

The car was an ancient two-door, crumbling with rust, dented, upholstery ripped, automatic guidance long wrecked, lights defective, radio gone. But it ran. It shook and rattled and whined, but it ran.

They were sputtering down the throughway, air shrilling through ill-fitting windows. Zonk was curled up on the back seat, sleeping. Lou wanted to doze off, too. He ached from his scalp to his bare feet. One foot was throbbing from a cut he had picked up somewhere. But he couldn't sleep. His insides were still as taut as a scream of terror.

They had gone across a bridge, and now the throughway was elevated. The horizon in front of them was just starting to turn gray. The buildings here seemed to be lower and not as closely bunched as back in Manhattan.

Felix was jammed in behind the wheel. He laughed softly. "Man, some people sure lucky. You got guts all right, but better than that, you got luck."

Lou looked at him. Somehow, in this flat, cold gray of early morning, Felix seemed different.

"Still haven't figured it out, have you?" Felix asked him.

"I don't understand...."

He squirmed around in the too-small bucket seat and glanced over his shoulder at Zonk, who was still sound asleep.

Then he said to Lou, "You think you just talked your way out of being killed by a teen pack? Just like that?" He laughed.

(6)

Lou stared at Felix, who merely chuckled to himself and said no more. Then the towers and hangars of JFK became visible in the predawn glow. Felix pulled the car off the highway and onto an access road.

"What's the matter?" Lou asked.

"Better get ourselves prettied up if we expect to get past the gates at the jetport."

They pulled into the parking lot of an automated, all-night shopping center. Felix woke up Zonk and the three of them walked to the shoppers' mall. Lou's foot was throbbing painfully.

The mall doors were locked, but there was a tiny security unit set into the wall beside them. Lou told his credit number to the receiver grille and let the camera photograph him.

"This credit number is from Albuquerque, New Mexico," said the shopping center computer, impassively. "It will require several moments to check it."

Felix said, "We'll wait."

"If the police are really looking for me," Lou worried out loud, "they'll have my credit number and picture pulled from the file and . . ."

"Sorry to keep you waiting," the computer said without a trace of regret. "Your credit check is complete. You may enter and purchase whatever you wish, up to a limit of ten thousand dollars."

Felix beamed. "Just what I've always wanted . . . a friend with a good credit rating."

The mall and shops were deserted. Felix waved Zonk off to a

men's clothing store and, with his hand firmly on Lou's arm, headed for a drugstore.

"You're really limping. Need that foot taken care of."

"Back in the car," Lou said as they walked through the open doorway of the drugstore, "what'd you mean...about me talking my way out of being killed?"

Felix laughed again. "Oh that. Well...you're lucky, but not the way you think. Never wonder why the Top Cats are being led by a guy my age? I'm over thirty, you know."

"What are you talking about?"

"Sit down here," Felix said, "while I get some stuff for that foot."

Lou sat in the plastic chair and found himself facing a dispenser-wall of medical supplies. Felix walked slowly down the wall, finding what he wanted in the display windows and touching the buttons that sent the goods down into the receiving bin. He came back to Lou's chair with his hands full of antibiotic sprays and plastic spray bandages.

"Listen," he said as he squirted a disinfectant over Lou's blood-crusted foot, "I'm a teacher. Work for the office of Rehabilitation. Trying to hammer some sense into these kids. Only way to do it is to join them, lead them, try to bring them around slowly. I been in there, in the city, for more than a year now. Got them to set up boundaries between turfs. Trying to get them to think of more than sex and wars. I figure it'll take another ten to twelve years before they start acting as civilized as Stone Age tribes."

"They don't know..."

Felix laughed. "Shoot, man, if they knew, I'd be just as dead as you ought to be!" Then his face went grim. "Some of the other teachers have been found out. What happened to them isn't pretty."

"But why do you do it?"

Shrugging, "How should I know? Can't just leave the kids in there by themselves. Too many generations have done that. Every year they get worse off and worse off until they're where they are now. *Somebody's* got to help them. We owe them something. They didn't turn into savages by themselves. They were pushed. And unless somebody starts pushing from the other direction, those kids are going to keep on killing, keep on dying."

Lou said, "It'll take a hundred years before kids like that become civilized."

"So we'll work a hundred years," Felix snapped. "Took more than a hundred years to let the cities fall apart like this. It's worth a century to rebuild them. Because if we don't—if we let those kids keep breeding and festering like they've been for the past century—pretty soon they're going to burst out of the cities and overrun everything. The Mongol hordes will seem like a Chinese tea party compared to what they'll do."

Lou shuddered.

"But it's more than that," Felix went on. "Those kids deserve a chance. They never asked to be born into that jungle. They never got a chance for anything better. And they'll never know anything better unless some of us get off our rumps and try to help 'em. Those kids are the future, y'know. What good's all our high and mighty civilization if we lose those kids? What use is all this technology and science if we're breeding cavemen in the cores of the cities? If we can't help those kids make their own future better, we don't have much to look forward to, I can tell you that."

"You ought to be a Congressman, or a minister," Lou said.

Felix laughed.

"And all that talk about killing me...."

"Oh, that was real all right," he said. "I was trying to figure out some way to get your white hide out of there. But I wasn't coming up with any answers. Looked like I was going to let them take you out...."

"You'd've let them?"

Another shrug. "Couldn't figure out what else to do, until you started talking tough. Gave me the out I needed."

"Well...thanks, I guess."

"Don't mention it," Felix replied, grinning.

Within half an hour, Lou was walking with hardly a limp. He showered, shaved, and put on a disposable summer suit and loafers that he picked out at the clothing store. Felix and Zonk had outfitted themselves, too. Felix went in for grander tastes, complete with cape and boots. Zonk leaned toward electric colors and the latest, form-fitted, sprayed-on styles.

"You look almost decent," Felix said to Lou. "Mouth's still swollen and you've got a nice blue lump coming along over your eye. But you'll be okay."

Felix drove them through the main gates of JFK just as the sun showed itself over the distant skyline. The white-helmeted security guards at the gates eyed the battered old car, but let it pass. Up the sweeping ramp of the once-grand terminal building they went, with Felix steering carefully to avoid potholes.

He stopped in front of the terminal and Lou got out, then ducked his head back in and put his hand in Felix's huge paw. "Thanks. For everything. And good luck."

"Nothing to it," Felix said, grinning. "Hope you make out okay." Then he turned to Zonk and said, "C'mon up front. Le'see what jet planes look like up close."

The clattering car drove off. Lou stood there for a moment in the growing light of dawn watching them disappear down the other side of the ramp. Then he turned and went inside the decaying terminal.

The first flight that connected with Albuquerque wasn't until seven. An hour to wait. His insides fluttering from hunger as much as nerves, Lou went to the autocafeteria and had powdered eggs, reconstituted milk, and a man-made slice of something called protosteak. It tasted like plastic.

No one stopped him or even noticed him as he went to the flight departure lounge, verified his ticket on the jet, went aboard, and took his seat. The plane was ten minutes late getting away from the terminal, and Lou expected each second to see the same Federal marshal come up the aisle and clap a hand on his shoulder.

But finally they were airborne. As soon as Lou heard the wheels pull up, he fell asleep.

He woke up with a start when the flaps and wheels went down again. Out the window he could see the familiar flat greenery of the New Mexico irrigated farmlands. Off in the distance, Sandia Peak stuck its rocky brown mass up in the sky.

I wonder if Bonnie's home. Maybe she never left for Charleston. Then another thought hit him. *What if they're waiting for me when I get off the plane?*

The plane landed and taxied up to the terminal. Lou put

himself in the middle of the ninety-some people who were getting off and tried to look invisible in the crowd. He stayed in the crowd until he was well into the terminal, then headed straight for the exit, looking over his shoulder a few times to see if anyone was following him. No one. Outside in the blazing sunlight, he wondered if his car was still in the parking lot. *Better leave it alone.* He waved for a cab, and one pulled away from its parking stall and glided to the curb where he stood.

Inside, after he firmly shut the cab door, Lou told the autodriver, "Genetics Institute."

If Bonnie wasn't picked up by the police, she'll be at the lab. And Dr. Kaufman and the others . . . they'll help me.

The cab drove out away from the city, into the farmlands, along one of the main irrigation lines. For the thousandth time, Lou tried to puzzle out why the police wanted him. The Federal marshal said he was under arrest. The Norseman at the UN building said he wasn't. But they were going to take him to Messina. Why? *Better check with Greg at the Institute and see if he knows a good lawyer.*

Finally, Lou could see the familiar white buildings of the Institute. Almost immediately, he could tell that something was wrong.

The place looked deserted. The parking lot was empty. Nobody was walking around outside. Nobody was visible in the big glass-fronted lobby. And as the cab pulled up to the outer fence, the gate did not slide open automatically.

Lou looked at his wristwatch. It was still on Albuquerque time; he hadn't changed it. It said nine-thirty.

Why is it . . . wait a minute! What day is it? Sunday or Monday? I took off . . . it must be Sunday, got to be.

He thumbed the window button down and felt the heat of the outdoors invade the cab. To the gate control box he said, "Code one-five, Christopher. Open up."

The gate rattled open. The cab drove smoothly up to the lobby door. Just to be safe, Lou gave a phony name and credit number to the cab's simple-minded computer. It had no camera equipment and therefore no way to check on who its passenger really was.

As the cab drove away, Lou stood squinting in the brilliant sunshine. For a moment, a flash of fear knifed through him.

Even for a Sunday the Institute seemed utterly deserted. Usually there was *somebody* around.

"Well," he said to himself in a deliberately loud, firm voice, "I can hide out here until some of the staff shows up tomorrow. Or maybe I'll call Greg or one of the other guys...."

The main doors into the lobby were locked also, but Lou's name and code symbol were enough to open them. He stepped into the quiet, cool darkness of the lobby; the sun's glare was screened out by the polarized windows. He hesitated a moment, then walked through the open doorway and into the building's main corridor. His footsteps against the plastic flooring and the whisper of the air conditioning were the only sounds he could hear.

First thing to do is call Bonnie, he thought, *find out if she's okay.*

His own office was down at the end of the corridor, next to Ramo, the big computer. Suddenly Lou realized, *Not even Ramo's making any noise!* Usually, the computer was humming and chattering electronically; it was almost always working on something, even on weekends and late at night.

Lou looked through the glass partition that surrounded Ramo. The computer was silent. No lights flashing on its main board.

"Ramo, you awake?" Lou called.

From a speaker in the ceiling overhead came Ramo's baritone voice. "Yes, Lou. I'm fine. What can I do for you?" A single row of lights on the main board flickered to life.

Lou breathed a relieved sigh. "You were so quiet.... I thought somebody had shut you down."

"All programs are completed at present." Ramo answered.

"All programs? What about the zygote modeling calculations?"

"That program was temporarily shut down by Dr. Kaufman."

"Shut down? Why?"

"I don't know."

Lou stood there watching the flickering row of lights, uncertain, feeling something like panic forming in the pit of his stomach. He fought it down. "Okay ... uh, get Bonnie Sterne on the phone for me, will you? Her home phone."

"Shall I place the call on your office phone?" Ramo asked.

"No . . . I'll be in the cafeteria. Anybody been in today?"

"No one. Except for Big George, of course."

Shaking his head in puzzlement, Lou went back up the corridor and turned down a side hall to the cafeteria. His head was throbbing with pain, and despite his nap on the plane he felt dead tired. And hungry.

Lou was surprised to see Big George sitting in the cafeteria, eating a huge plate of fruit salad.

Big George was an eight-year-old mountain gorilla, taller than Lou, even in his hunched-over, ground-knuckling posture. No one had weighed him for several months, since he playfully ripped the big scales they had used out of the wall of his special quarters. His face was all ferocity—fanged mouth, low beetling brow, black muzzle, and blacker hair. His arms could reach across the table without his ever getting up from the chair he was sitting on. The plastic chair itself was sagging dangerously under his weight. It was hard to believe that Big George was a gentle, even a timid, animal.

"Who let you in here?" Lou asked from the doorway.

"Let myself in, Uncle Lou," George whispered. "Got hungry. Nobody here to feed me. Opened the pen gate and came in for food."

Lou went over to the selector wall and punched buttons for a real steak dinner. "You mean nobody's been around to feed you since yesterday?"

"Nobody, Uncle Lou." George stuffed half a cantaloupe into his toothy mouth. Big George was one of the Institute's great successes. The geneticists had managed to give the gorilla a large measure of intelligence. George tested out to the intelligence level of a human six-year-old. It seemed that he would not go any further. The surgical team that worked with the Institute had altered George's vocal equipment so that he could speak in a harsh, labored whisper. It was the best they could do.

Lou carried his steaming tray to the end of the table where George was sitting. He was glad of some companionship, but it was best to give George plenty of room. Not that he was dangerous—just sloppy.

Looking up at the ceiling, Lou called, "Hey, where's that phone call, Ramo?"

"There is no answer," came the smooth reply.

"She's not home?"

"Evidently not," said Ramo.

"What's her phone say?"

"Nothing. No reply whatsoever. No forwarding number, no request to leave a message."

Lou stared down at his steak. Suddenly he wasn't hungry anymore.

"Ramo!" he shouted. "Where is everybody?"

"All of the scientific staff has been taken into custody by Federal marshals," Ramo said calmly. "Everyone else has been sent home."

Before it could really register on Lou's mind, George growled, "Somebody coming in the hallway, Uncle Lou. Strangers."

"Federal marshals," Ramo said. "I was programmed to call them when you returned to the Institute."

(7)

Lou stood up, hot fear burning through him. "Federal marshals?"

"They have locked all the doors and are searching the building for you," Ramo said without emotion.

"Uncle Lou, I'm afraid," George whispered.

"How many of them are there?" Lou asked Ramo.

"Twelve."

Big George pushed off his chair and shambled over to stand beside Lou, so close that Lou could feel the warmth from his great hairy body. George was terrified. *But the marshals don't know how timid he really is. They might shoot as soon as they see him.*

"Is the door to the courtyard locked?"

"Yes," Ramo answered. "All the doors are."

There were footsteps in the hall now; Lou could hear them. He turned to George, snuffling fearfully beside him.

"Can you knock that door open, Georgy?"

"I can try, Uncle Lou."

Lou patted his massive shoulder. "Come on, quick."

George scampered toward the door, accidentally knocking a chair clattering out of his way. From out in the hall a voice called:

"Hey... hear that? In here, quick, unlock it!"

George was loping across the floor in full stride now, knuckles and big splayed feet slapping the tiles. Lou had to run to keep up with him. George didn't stop or even slow down at the door. He simply crashed right through, his bulk and speed tearing the lock right apart and knocking both doors off their hinges with a blood-freezing shriek of ripping metal.

Lou was right behind him in the sudden glare of the sunshine.

"George . . . this way!"

Now Lou took the lead, through the courtyard and out the access tunnel toward the back lot. Stopping, he pointed to the stand of trees off behind the parking area.

"You . . . get back . . . to your pen," he panted. "Safest place . . . for you. They won't bother you . . . in there."

"But Uncle Lou, I want to go with you," George argued hoarsely. "All the nice people went away. These new people scare me."

Lou took a deep breath and said, "They won't hurt you. And you can't come with me right now. But I'll come back for you."

"When?"

Lou could hear shouts out in the courtyard.

"As soon as I can, Georgy."

"Promise?"

"I promise. Now get back to your pen and be a good boy. And don't be afraid, they won't hurt you."

With a troubled look, the gorilla moved off toward the trees.

Lou sprinted for the parked cars. The lab's electric wagons were lined up in the first row, and Lou knew their ignition locks were keyed to a simple voice code. He slid in behind the wheel of the first one in line.

"DNA-RNA," he said as he pressed the starter switch.

The electric motor hummed to life. *Never be able to outrun turbocars in this thing,* Lou told himself. A man in a gray business suit ran out onto the parking lot. He had a gun in his hand. Lou grabbed the steering wheel, kicked off the brakes, and slammed the accelerator to the floor. The wagon lurched feebly, than started to gain momentum. Lou drove straight at the man. He jumped away and fired. Lou swung the wagon away and then cut back for the access tunnel, dived through its shadow, raced through the courtyard and past another handful of jumping, shouting men, into the front tunnel and out past the main lobby.

The front gate was rolling shut, but Lou knifed the wagon through it and sped down the highway in the curiously quiet acceleration of the electric motor. He picked up the car radio microphone and called:

"Ramo, this is Lou Christopher. Over."

"I recognize your voice pattern, Lou. Over."

"Basic program zero, Ramo. Suspend all housekeeping functions until further notice. Maintenance and repair mode only. Execute. Over."

"Executed. Over."

Lou grinned as he raced down the highway, one hand on the wheel. "Very good, Ramo. Now suspend all communications until my voice pattern orders resumption. Understood? Over."

"Understood and prepared to execute," Ramo said tonelessly. But somehow Lou felt the computer didn't like to shut itself off.

"Execute. Over."

No answer. The computer was completely shut down. All the doors that were locked would remain locked until some of the Institute maintenance men could be brought in to open them manually. The front gate would stay locked too, and it was strong enough to keep the police cars inside even if they tried ramming it. All the lights, the air conditioning, everything, was off. *Have a pleasant day!* Lou thought grimly.

He eased off the accelerator and coasted down the highway at the legal maximum speed. No sense getting picked up by a traffic patrol. His insides were fluttering, now that he had enough time to think.

How long can I keep running? Where to now? Not my apartment. Ramo said everybody on the scientific staff was arrested. Did they take Bonnie, too? And why, why, for God's sake? What's going on?

He shook his head. It was like a nightmare. It couldn't be real. Police don't just march into a lab and arrest everybody. That was something out of the Dark Ages. People have rights, there are laws....

And then he remembered New York, and realized that in some places the Dark Ages still existed.

As he drove toward town, Lou switched on the radio and dialed to the police frequency. Plenty of chatter, but nothing about the Institute or himself. *Why not? Why aren't they calling for help? Or at least spreading an alert to pick me up?*

As if in answer, Lou saw a highway patrol cruiser gliding up behind him on the outside lane. He knew that the electric wagon could never outspeed a cruiser; the turbine-driven police car could even lift itself off the ground and literally fly on an air cushion for short distances, doing several hundred knots. But the cruiser zipped right past him, and the two white-helmeted officers in it never even looked at him.

Maybe the police aren't after me, Lou said to himself.

Another part of his mind answered, *Somebody is.*

But not the police. Then who are they?

A few minutes later he found himself driving past Bonnie's apartment building. *Got to stop someplace. Got to have some time to figure this out. Even is she's been picked up, I can still use her apartment. And if she's free, I can find out what's going on from her.*

He drove the wagon halfway across town, parked it in a public garage, and then took a cab back to Bonnie's. He gave the cab another false name and credit number. In the lobby of the apartment building, he told the door-computer:

"I'm a friend of Miss Sterne's, apartment 27-T."

"Name, please," the computer's flat voice replied.

"Roy Kendall," Lou lied, naming a mutual friend who lived in Denver.

"Miss Sterne is not in at present. I am not programmed to admit anyone."

"Miss Sterne has left special instructions under Code V for visitors."

The computer hummed to itself for a second. Then, "Mr. Kendall, you may be admitted." The door clicked open. Lou stepped through and went to the elevator.

He had to go through the same routine with the lock computer at Bonnie's door, but here the code symbol was SF for special friends. Finally, the door popped open and Lou stepped into Bonnie's apartment.

Shutting the door carefully behind him, Lou looked over the single room. Nothing seemed disturbed or moved. The closet next to the foldaway bed was open, and there were some clothes draped on a chair in front of it. Lou poked into the kitchenette alcove and found a pot of coffee still plugged in and warm. *Bonnie was here this morning. Or at least, somebody was here.*

He took a bottle of milk from the refrigerator and downed half of it. He was just putting it back when the front door opened.

Bonnie stood in the doorway, open-mouthed with surprise. "Lou!"

She ran to him and threw herself into his arms. She felt warm and soft and safe.

"Baby, is it ever good to see you," he murmured into her ear as he held her. "You even *smell* great."

"Lou, what happened to you? Where've you been? We heard . . . Oh, Lou, your face!" She reached up and touched his swollen jaw. It hurt, but Lou didn't mind at all.

"It's a long story," he said, still holding her tightly. "For a while there, I didn't think I'd ever see you again."

He kissed her, and then she gently pulled away. For the first time, Lou noticed she looked tired, strained.

"What's been going on?" he asked. "Why's the Institute been closed? Ramo said . . ."

"You've been at the Institute?" She looked startled.

Lou nodded. "Yep. Nearly got caught by a squad of guys who claimed to be Federal marshals."

"They *were* marshals," Bonnie said.

"But what's this all about?"

Bonnie went toward the sofa, by the windows on the other side of the room. Lou followed her there.

Sitting, she told him, "The first I heard about it was yesterday, at the glider races. There was a Federal marshal looking for you. Then, when I got back to my apartment, there was another marshal waiting for me. I had to go with him to the Federal courthouse. Practically everybody in the Institute was there!"

Lou sank back in the sofa, realizing now why Bonnie looked strained.

"They let some of us out after a few hours," she went on, her voice trembling a little. "But we were told not to go back to the Institute anymore. It's been closed down."

"Closed?"

Nodding, "Permanently, they said. I had to report to the employment center this morning. That's where I've been all day. Lou . . . what are they doing?" Her voice was starting to rise now, her tiny fists clenched. "Why did they close the Institute? What is it? What?"

He took her by the shoulders. "Hey . . . ease off now," he said softly. "Take it easy. You're okay. Nobody's going to hurt you."

"But they brought in Dr. Kaufman, and Greg Belsen, and just about all the scientists. All the technicians, all the secretaries and clerks . . . everybody!"

"But why? Did they give you any reason?"

She shook her head. "Nothing. Nobody seemed to know anything. They were just following orders." She reached out and touched his jaw again. "But what happened to you?"

"I got away." Lou told her about his night in New York, and this morning's visit to the deserted Institute.

"What are you going to do now?" Bonnie asked.

"I don't know," he admitted. "I'm about ready to cave in. Only had a couple hours' sleep on the jet. . . ."

Bonnie stood up. Brushing a blonde lock from her eyes, she said, "I'll fix you some lunch and then you can take a nap."

She went to the kitchenette alcove and started touching buttons on the control keyboard. Lou slouched on the sofa, already half asleep.

"Lou . . . it's like the world's coming apart, isn't it?"

He looked up at her. "Whatever it is, it's bigger than the Institute. They had Kirby from Columbia at the UN building. They were going to take us to Messina. . . ."

"The world capital?"

Lou nodded. "I guess the world government's behind this. And they've got the Federal people here on their side. But why? What's it all about?"

Bonnie took a pair of steaming trays from the cooker and placed them on the low table next to the sofa. She sat on the floor, next to Lou's feet.

"Lou . . . if the world government is after you—then there's no place for you to hide!"

"Maybe," he muttered, leaning over the trays and picking up a fork.

Bonnie said, very softly, "Maybe the only thing you can do is give yourself up. After all, if it's the world government, it must be something terribly important, whatever it is."

"But what are they up to?" Lou demanded. "Why yank us in like we're criminals? Why haven't they told us what's going on? They haven't called in the local police. And they're sure not giving us any chances to exercise our constitutional rights."

Bonnie didn't answer.

They ate in silence, and then Lou stretched out on the sofa for a nap. He dreamed of being chased through the streets of New York by gangs of kids and uniformed policemen. Somehow the streets became Messina, but the gangs still pursued him. And from a balcony above him, Felix leaned heavily on a frail railing, huge and black, booming laughter at the chase.

He woke up shouting. Bonnie was beside him, her hands on him, stroking him. He sat up.

"They . . . I . . ."

"It's all right," she said soothingly, "it's all right. You were dreaming. Look, you're in a cold sweat."

Lou ran a hand over his eyes.

"Bonnie . . ."

She looked away from him and said, "Lou, while you were sleeping, I was thinking hard about this whole thing. You can't run away forever. You were lucky to get away last night without being killed. Sooner or later, they'll either catch you or you'll get hurt or killed."

"Yeah, I guess so. But what else . . ."

Bonnie's hands were clenched together in white-knuckled tenseness. Her face looked bleak.

"Lou," she said, "I don't want you to get hurt. I . . . while you were asleep I called the courthouse. There are four marshals outside in the hall. They've come for you."

"You *what!*" Lou sprang up from the sofa.

"There's no other way out of here," she said There were tears in her eyes now as she stood beside him. "Please, Lou . . . let them take you in. They promised that nobody's going to hurt you. Please . . ."

Lou stared at her. "Federal marshals, the world government, the Institute closed . . . and now even you, even you, Bonnie. Nobody in the world is on my side. Nobody! In the whole world!"

"Lou, please . . ." She was crying now.

The door opened and they walked in. Four of them. Big-shouldered, tight-lipped. Wearing plain, dark business shorts and tunics. Armed, everybody knew, with needle guns and more.

"Louis Christopher. I have a Federal warrant for your arrest."

"Nobody in the whole stupid world," Lou muttered loudly enough for only Bonnie to hear.

[8]

In a way, Lou felt almost glad that his running was over. It was like the time he had an inflamed appendix, but didn't know it. For weeks he nursed the sullen pain in his abdomen, worried over it, but told no one. Until he nearly collapsed at the Institute and some of the other computer engineers physically dragged him to the clinic. From then on he didn't have to make any decisions. And he found that he didn't worry, either. The doctors did the deciding, and the worrying.

Now Lou sat in the back of a car, surrounded by Federal marshals. All the decisions were out of his hands. He stopped worrying, almost without realizing it. He was far from being happy, but for the time being he had nothing to worry over.

They drove to the jetport, past the terminal building, out to a sleek, white, twin-engined executive jet parked well away from all the hangars and commercial planes. The sky-blue insignia of the world government was painted on its tail.

Standing beside the plane, next to the open hatch, was the Norseman Lou had narrowly escaped from at the UN building.

He looked Lou over carefully as the Federal marshals escorted him to the plane.

"I see you made it through New York and then some," said the Norseman. "Congratulations. We were afraid you'd be killed."

Lou said nothing.

"Please, Mr. Christopher, my job is to bring you safely to Messina. No more adventures, eh? We'll only have to come and get you again."

He gestured toward the hatch. With a shrug, Lou climbed

into the plane. The Norseman followed him and locked the hatch shut, then went forward, into the control compartment. The jet was luxuriously furnished with big, deep swivel seats at the four forward windows. Back of them there was a couch on one side, and a full-sized desk on the other, complete with viewphones.

The Norseman re-emerged from the control compartment. "Pick any chair you like. This flight is exclusively for you."

Within minutes they were airborne and streaking supersonically across the country. They landed briefly at New Washington for fuel, then headed out across the Atlantic with the setting sun at their back. Lou slept as the plane sped into the gathering night.

The Norseman woke him when they were ready to land. It was black and moonless outside, and the only lights Lou could see below outlined a landing strip. Once on the ground, Lou was taken to a waiting car and driven away from the airfield. The Norseman sat silently beside him while two swarthy men spoke Italian to each other up in the front seat. All Lou could see was the narrow strip of road lit by the car's headlights, but he got the impression of hills and farmlands and wind-tossed trees swaying out there in the darkness. It was warm outside, and the night had that special softness that comes from the sea, very different from the desert of New Mexico.

Before long they drove past a gateway that was flanked by two live guards. After a few minutes more, the car pulled onto a driveway that swung up to an ornately decorated entrance, lit by antique lanterns. It even had an awning overhead to keep off the sun and rain. It was hard to tell how big the building was, but in the darkness it gave the impression of rambling on hugely. A *villa*, Lou guessed as the car stopped in front of the entrance.

The Norseman got out first and held the car door open as Lou slid along the seat and stepped out. From far off he could hear the sighing roar of the sea rolling in on a beach.

"This will be your home for the time being," the Norseman said, pointing to the baroquely carved door. "I believe you'll find many of your friends there."

He stood there while Lou slowly, hesitantly, went up the stone walkway and tried the door. It opened at his touch. Lou looked back and saw the Norseman smiling and nodding at him.

"Your job's done now, is that it?"

"Yes," he answered. "You were the last one on the list."

What list? Lou wanted to ask, but he knew that he wouldn't get an answer. He stepped into the entryway of the villa and the door swung shut by itself behind him. Lou knew somehow that it locked automatically. He didn't bother to try it.

He stood alone in a wide, long hall. At the far end a grand flight of stairs swept in a gentle curve to the next floor. There were heavy doors of real wood on both sides of the hall, and the walls were lined with paintings. Portraits, mostly. Old and original. A stately grandfather's clock back by the stairs chimed once. One A.M.

Lou walked down the hall slowly, his footsteps echoing on the intricate geometry of the parqueted floor. No other sound—no, wait. Voices, muted, from behind a door. He went over and opened it.

A half-dozen men were sitting around a table in the middle of the room. It must have been a library or study; books lined the walls except for a pair of French doors that stood open at the far end of the room. Their filmy curtains billowed softly in the breeze coming in off the sea. The room was dimly lit and most of the men at the table had their backs to the door and to Lou. One of them looked up.

"Lou! They dragged you in finally."

It was Greg Belsen.

Now the others turned to face him. They were all from the Institute: Ron Kurtz, Charles Sutherland, Jesse Maggio, Bob Richardson. And at the head of the table, Dr. Adrian Kaufman, Director of the Institute. Dr. Kaufman was a handsome, vigorous man, with strong leonine features topped by thick gray hair. But right now he looked very weary and unsure of himself.

"Christopher," said Dr. Kaufman, frowning slightly. "What on earth are you doing here?"

Despite himself, Lou grinned, "It wasn't my idea to come, believe me."

Lou walked to the table. There were no more chairs in the room, so he remained standing.

"Why did they bring you here?" Dr. Kurtz asked. He was about Lou's age, but his bushy brown beard made him look older. "So far the only people here are the scientists."

By *scientists*, Lou understood, Kurtz meant geneticists and biochemists.

"That's right," Dr. Maggio agreed. "Only the technical staff has been brought here. They let the secretaries and others go free."

"I am on the technical staff," Lou reminded them.

"But as a computer engineer, not a geneticist," said Dr. Kurtz.

"Or biochemist," added Dr. Richardson, a biochemist.

"Maybe the people who arrested us don't know the difference between computer engineers and geneticists," Lou said, feeling anger simmering inside him. "Maybe they just had orders to bring in the whole technical staff. They sure didn't stop and ask to see my diploma."

"Well," Greg Belsen said, "there goes the neighborhood. If they start letting computer people in, God knows what'll happen next."

The scientists all laughed. Lou realized that Greg was trying to smooth over the rift between the scientists and himself. It was an old wound, this caste system. Under ordinary circumstances at the Institute it hardly ever became noticeable. But here, in this strange place, it surfaced immediately. And it hurt.

Dr. Richardson changed the subject. "Does anyone have any idea of why we're here?"

"You used the word 'arrested,'" Dr. Kaufman said to Lou. "As far as I know, no one has arrested us. We've been brought here against our will, true enough. But no one has charged us with a crime."

"More like being kidnapped."

"I was arrested by Federal marshals," Lou said. "No charges, but they were ready to shoot if I tried to get away. And the Institute's been closed permanently, I found out."

"*Permanently!*" The word went around the table like a shock wave.

"I don't get it," Dr. Maggio said, frowning. "Who's doing this? And why?"

"It's pretty obviously the world government," Richardson said.

"But why?"

"Because they're frightened out of their wits over genetic engineering. They're afraid of what might happen when we succeed."

"I don't believe that."

"Oh no? Well, take a look around you."

Greg Belsen said, "The real question is, what are we going to do about it?"

"What can we do?"

Looking down at the polished tabletop, Dr. Kurtz mumbled in his beard, "Try to get out. Escape."

"How?" Sutherland asked. "Where to?"

Lou said, "They chased me all across the country and back. It may be the world government that's doing this, but they had plenty of Federal marshals helping them."

Dr. Kaufman folded his hands over his midsection. "We're several thousand miles from home, on an island where we'd be very quickly spotted as strangers. Even if we escaped from this villa we wouldn't get very far."

Lou had a sudden thought. "Maybe we don't have to get far. Just to some newsmen. Whoever's behind this, they're trying to keep it quiet. They didn't even notify the local police when they were chasing me. And I didn't hear a word about the Institute's closing on any newscasts."

With a sarcastic grin, Sutherland answered, "So you volunteer to go over the wall and find us a newsman. And he'll tell the world we've been kidnapped or something."

"Something like that," Lou snapped.

"So what?" Sutherland replied. "Suppose the newsman believes you. Suppose, even, he gets to broadcast the story and the world government doesn't stop him. What happens? Some government officials say that he's wrong, he's sensation-mongering. They say that we're a small group of scientists who've been brought here for a special project. End of story. The world doesn't care about twenty-five scientists. We're not news. We're not important people—like Tri-V stars or soccer players."

"Now wait, Charles," Dr. Kaufman said, his eyes brightening. "Christopher may have something. After all, they *have* tried to do this quickly and quietly. Maybe some publicity would break up this whole affair...."

Sutherland made a sour face. "Look at it objectively. We're just a handful of scientists...."

"Oh!" Lou remembered. "They got Dr. Kirby, too."

"Kirby? From Columbia?"

Nodding, Lou answered, "They had him in New York. They were taking him here."

"But he's not here in this villa."

Sutherland waved a finger at them. "You see? There's more to it than just us. I thought so. We're only a part of a bigger picture. And the world government is behind this, whatever it is. Publicity isn't going to hurt them. Either they'll clamp down on any news about this, or they've already figured out what to tell the newsmen."

"Then what can we *do*?" Kaufman demanded.

"Nothing." Sutherland shrugged. "We wait and see what happens. That's all we can do."

Dr. Richardson suddenly asked, "Say, what about Big George? Is he..."

"I saw him this morning...yesterday, that is," Lou said. "He was scared, but I guess somebody's taking care of him. I hope..."

"They can't stick him in a zoo," Greg said. "He'll die of loneliness."

"Or fright."

"Maybe we can ask..."

The door from the hall opened and Lou turned to see Mrs. Kaufman standing there, her portly frame tightly wrapped in a nightrobe.

"I finally got the children to sleep," she said to her husband. "Are you coming up soon?"

With a sigh, Dr. Kaufman answered, "In a few minutes, dear."

She nodded and shut the door. Lou stood there by the table, open-mouthed.

Greg said, "Didn't you know! The wives and children were brought here too. For every married member of the staff. It's a family affair."

[9]

Greg let Lou bunk in with him, in a spacious bedroom on the top floor of the villa. They left the air conditioning off and the balcony doors open. The murmur of the surf quickly lulled them to sleep.

The morning was bright and cloudless. Lou found some clothes in the bedroom closet that fit him: a gaudy disposable shirt and a pair of shorts. It was warm enough to go barefoot.

"There's a Sicilian house staff that will get you more clothes. All you have to do is ask," Greg told him as they went downstairs. "And, man, can they cook! We may not know why we're here, but they're sure treating us right."

The morning was spent exchanging rumors. They were being drafted by the world government for some ultra-secret project. No, there was war brewing between the United States and China and the world government was pulling out the top scientists on both sides to save them from being killed. Nonsense, war is impossible with all nations disarmed; the world government wouldn't allow a war to break out. The *real* story is that there's an epidemic of unknown origin at the Mars base, and we're going to be sent there to find a cure before it wipes out everybody on Mars. Nuts! My brother-in-law's at Mars base and I just got a lasergram from him last week.

The rumors and speculations spiraled hotter and wilder as the sun climbed through the morning sky. But nobody mentioned the simplest explanation: that the government had decided to prevent the work on genetic engineering from being completed. That was too close to home, too plainly possible and painful to be mentioned.

Just before lunchtime, Lou was prowling along the patio that looked out to sea. Several of the older men and their wives were sunning themselves. Lou just couldn't sit still. There had to be something he could do, *something*.

Greg came trotting up the stone stairway that led from the patio to the beach, down below.

"There you are," he said to Lou. "Listen, I've been exploring. Down at the bottom of this picturesque cliff is a picturesque beach. And some of the younger wives and older daughters have found some very picturesque swimming suits and are frolicking on the beach. Beautiful scenery. Including the boss' oldest daughter. How about it?"

The memory of Bonnie stabbed into Lou's mind. "No... thanks. I don't feel like it."

Greg shrugged. "Okay, suit yourself. I'll be down there chasing... uh, the waves. If anybody's looking for me."

"Sure." Lou turned and started pacing the length of the patio again, trying to think of something useful to do. But he kept seeing Bonnie, crying, scared, and desperate, more afraid of Lou's own anger than anything else, he realized now.

I ought to try to get in touch with her. Tell her it's okay, I'm not sore at her.

He got up and went into the house, looking for one of the housekeeping staff. Instead he found Kaufman and Sutherland.

"Have you seen Greg Belsen?" Kaufman asked. "They've just told us there's going to be a meeting to explain what this is all about, and we can bring three people. Where is he?"

Lou was about to answer when he remembered that Kaufman's daughter was on the beach. "Greg's... uh, he was here a while ago. I don't know where he is now."

Sutherland made a sour face. "The car's right outside, they want us now."

"I'll go," Lou heard himself say.

"You?"

"I'll sit in for Greg."

"But..."

"Unless you want to look around for somebody else."

Kaufman glanced unhappily at Sutherland, who was eyeing Lou's vivid shirt and shorts. The two older men were also in sports clothes, but their colors were dark and conservative.

"I could change in two minutes," Lou offered.

"No time to change," Kaufman said. "The car's waiting for us. Come on."

With only a slight grin of satisfaction, Lou went with them to the car. There were two men in the front of the car, both wearing brown uniforms without markings of any kind. They both looked dark, swarthy. And they said nothing.

In the back seat, Sutherland frowned as the car pulled away from the villa. "What do you think this is all about?"

Dr. Kaufman shook his head. "Whatever it is, it will probably be more fantastic than any of the rumors that have been going around."

They drove for nearly an hour down a winding dusty road. Most of the time the road threaded between hills, and there was little to see except the greenery whizzing by. But once in a while they would top a rise and view the sun-dazzled sea stretching off on one side of them, and rich fields of olives and citrus groves on the other side.

Thick clouds began to pile up as they drove on, and by the time they passed the gate of another old villa with its uniformed guards standing at attention, the clouds towered darkly overhead, grumbling and flickering with lightning. It seemed almost as dark as evening, although it was still early afternoon.

There were dozens of cars parked in front of the villa's main entrance. And inside, the old house was filled with men and women, milling around aimlessly, buzzing with conversation.

Lou, Kaufman, and Sutherland stood just inside the front door, gaping at the unexpected crowd.

"That's Margolin, from the Paris Academy," Dr. Kaufman said. "What's he doing here?"

"And Liu from Tokyo," Sutherland added.

"Look . . . Rosenzweig . . . and there's Yossarian!"

"My God, all the top people in the field are here."

Lou recognized some of them, the best-known geneticists and biochemists in the world. He saw no other computer engineers, though.

"Adrian!" called a frail, little man with wispy white hair. "I knew they would bring you here, too."

Kaufman turned and recognized the old man. Both shocked and delighted, he went to him, hands outstretched.

"Max...they brought you in on this."

Then Lou realized who he was: Professor DeVreis, the elder statesmen of the world's geneticists, the man who had taught the leaders of the field, like Kaufman, in their university days.

Dr. Sutherland joined them, and soon the three of them formed the nucleus of a growing, grave-faced, head-shaking crowd. Lou stood by the entrance, alone now.

"Do you know any of these people?"

Lou looked up to see a tall, gangly, lantern-jawed fellow his own age standing beside him. He was wearing a baggy suit with full trousers and the kind of shoes that you only found in northern hemisphere cities. At second glance, Lou could see that he was trying hard to look calm and unfrightened.

"I don't know many of them personally," Lou answered. Then he pointed out several of the scientists.

His new companion shook his head worriedly. "Geneticists? Biochemists? Why am I here? I'm a nuclear physicist!"

He spoke with a trace of an accent that Lou couldn't pin down.

Now Lou felt equally puzzled. "If it's any consolation, I'm a computer engineer. Um...my name's Lou Christopher."

With a toothy grin, he took Lou's offered hand. "I am Anton Kori. I'm from the University of Prague."

"And I'm with the Watson Institute of Genetics...or was, that is."

"American?"

Lou nodded. Then he saw that many of the people in the crowd had drinks and sandwiches in their hands. "Looks like lunch is being served someplace around here. Hungry?"

Kori shrugged. "Now that you mention it..."

They exchanged stories as they searched through the crowded rooms and finally found the luncheon buffet table.

"Nothing like this has happened in Czechoslovakia in thirty years," Kori said, reaching for a sandwich. "Arrested in the middle of the night and carried off by the police...it's like stories my grandfather used to tell us."

Suddenly, his face brightened. "Ah! There are two men I know!"

Lou followed him as he rushed over to a pair of older men standing by the French doors, eating and talking quietly. One of the men was chunky, bald, very fair-skinned, dressed in shorts and pullover. The other looked Indian: dark, slim, and intense, slightly Oriental-looking. The plain-gray business suit he wore simply accentuated his exotic looks.

"Clark! Janda!" Kori called out as he rushed up to them.

"Anton," said the chunky man. "What on earth are you doing here. Or for that matter, what are any of us doing here? Do you know?" His accent was unmistakably English.

Kori introduced Lou to Clark Frederick and Ramash Jandawarlu, rocket engineers.

"Rocket engineers?" Lou echoed.

They nodded.

"We were working together—by fax and phone, mostly," said Frederick, "on an improved fusion rocket."

"For interstellar ships," Kori said.

"Interstellar . . . oh, like the probes that were sent out around the turn of the century?" In the back of his mind he was trying to remember whether it was Clark Frederick or Frederick Clark.

"Yes, like the probes, only much better," said Jandawarlu in his reedy voice. "Rocket engines that could propel manned vessels, not merely small instrument probes."

"Manned ships, to the stars?"

"Yes. It would have been something magnificent."

Clark huffed at his co-worker, "You speak as if it's all over for us."

The Indian spread his hands. "We are here. We are not working. I don't think they will allow us to work."

"But who are *they*?" Kori demanded.

Lou said, "The world government. For some reason they've rounded up the world's top geneticists and biochemists . . . and apparently a few rocket people, too,"

"But why?"

As if in answer, a voice came from a hidden loud speaker:

"Ladies and gentlemen, if you will kindly assemble in the main salon, we can begin the meeting."

For a second or two the big room was completely silent, everyone stood frozen. There were no sounds from anywhere in the house, no sounds at all except the low grumble of far-off thunder. Then, everybody started talking and moving at once. The hubbub was terrific as more than a hundred men and women poured back into the hall and headed for the villa's largest room.

It wasn't difficult to find the main salon. It was at the end of the front hall, a huge room hung with blue and gold draperies. There were three ornate chandeliers and a half-dozen floor-to-ceiling mirrors set into the walls. The floor was polished wood, for dancing. But there were rows of folding chairs arranged across it now. The far end of the room was bare except for a blank viewscreen on the wall, big enough for a public theater.

Once everyone was inside the room, the doors swung shut and clicked softly. *Nobody in sight, but they're watching us just the same,* Lou thought. And a shiver went through him.

Lou sat with Kori, Frederick, and Janda in one of the rear rows of folding chairs. He saw Kaufman and Sutherland up in the front row, next to Professor DeVreis.

The big viewscreen began to brighten and glow softly. A voice said:

"Gentlemen, you will be addressed by the Honorable Vassily Kobryn, Minister of Security."

The image of Kobryn's heavy, serious face took shape on the screen.

"Russian," muttered Kori.

"Gentlemen," Kobryn said slowly, "it is my unhappy duty to explain to you why you have been taken away from your work and your homes to this place. Believe me, the Council of Ministers has thought long and hard before going ahead with this drastic action."

It's going to be bad, Lou realized. *He's preparing us for something even worse than what's happened so far.*

"As you know," Kobryn continued, his face utterly grave, "the government has worked for more than thirty years to make this planet a peaceful, habitable environment. Our efforts have been made extremely difficult by two factors: nationalism and population growth. We believe that we have been successful on both fronts. There are no more national armies and no possibility of a major war between nations. And world population growth has leveled off in the past ten years. Admittedly, twenty-some billions is a much higher figure than anyone would call optimum, but we are managing to provide a livable environment for this population."

"What about the cities?" someone called out.

"Quiet!"

"Let him get to the point."

Kobryn seemed almost glad of the interruption. He answered, "Yes, the cities. I admit that most of the larger cities of the world are completely savage...unlivable, by civilized standards. In plain terms, we lost the fight in the giant cities; actually, we started too late. But we have not given up. A considerable portion of our work is being devoted to long-range programs to gradually win the cities back to civilization."

"Why are we here?" a strong voice demanded.

Nodding, Kobryn said, "I am coming to that. You see, we live in a world that is dangerously crowded. There are many who feel that we have passed the point of no return, that our population is too large. They feel that the barbarians of the cities will engulf us all, sooner or later. Even the optimists among us agree that our present population is too large, and we are constantly on the verge of a disaster. If the crops fail anywhere in the world, if a major earthquake or storm escapes our control...the repercussions could be tragic for the whole world.

"We have eliminated wars and prevented large-scale starvation. But just barely. We can handle twenty billions of population—*but only if we keep the worldwide society absolutely stable.*"

Kobryn's voice took on a ring of steel at those words. "We must have stability. At any price. All our computer predictions and all our best social planners come to the same conclusion: unless we have stability, this crowded world of ours will crumble into chaos—starvation, disease, war, barbarism. Without stability, we will destroy ourselves and poison this planet completely."

There was a long, silent moment while Kobryn stared at them from the viewscreen, letting his words sink in. No one in the audience spoke. The quiet was broken only by somebody's cough and the nervous shuffling of feet.

"The price we must pay for stability is progress. You and your work are part of that price."

Now everyone stirred. A sort of collective sigh went through the big room, almost a gasp but not strong enough. More worried and afraid than shocked or angry.

Kobryn went on, "Most of you are geneticists and biochemists. You have proven in recent experiments that you can alter the genetic material in a fertilized ovum, so that you can control the physical and mental characteristics of the baby that is ultimately born. Professor DeVreis, you yourself told me that within a few years, you could produce a superman...."

"Yes," DeVreis agreed in his rickety, aged voice. "A superman... or a zombie, a slave with bulging muscles and just enough intelligence to follow orders."

"Just so," Kobryn said, his face expressionless. "In either case, the result would be a complete shattering of society's stability. We cannot allow this to happen."

"Can't allow..."

"What does he mean?"

"You can't stop science!"

"Gentlemen, please!" Kobryn raised his voice. "Think a moment! No matter how attractive the picture you have of raising a race of supermen, you must realize that it will never come to pass. Who will be the first superman? How will you select? Don't you understand that twenty billions of people will bury you in their stampede to have their children made into godlings? Or worse still, they might slaughter the first few supermen you produce in an insane fit of fear and jealousy."

"No, it wouldn't happen that way...."

"We wouldn't let..."

"No matter how you look at it, any large-scale tampering with mankind's genetic heritage will destroy society as we know it. Believe me! We have spent a year and more examining this question. The best computers and social engineers in the world have labored on the problem. Our world needs stability. Genetic engineering is a de-stabilizing element, a wild card that will destroy society. The government cannot permit this."

"But it will create a better society! A world of supermen!"

Kobryn shook his head. "No! It will create chaos. Look at what happened in the last century, when vast groups of peoples suddenly became aware that they could be free of the social systems that had enslaved them. When the last vestiges of the European empires were removed from Asia and Africa, when the American Negro and the world's youth realized that they had political power, what happened? Was there a peaceful march toward a happy society? No, nothing of the sort. There were wars and revolutions, riots and assassinations—it took nearly the entire twentieth century before an equilibrium was reached. And for most of that time the world population was below five billions!

"Now, we have in our grasp this possibility of genetic engineering, the possibility of making our children into godlings—or slaves. Do you think the people of the world will stand patiently in line, waiting for you to work your miracle on them? Don't you understand that many would-be tyrants would use your knowledge to produce the zombies Professor DeVreis spoke of? In a world of twenty billions, we would never recover from such a violent upset to the social order. There would be no new equilibrium, only chaos. Our world would come crashing down in anarchy and rioting. Your laboratories would be destroyed, and you yourselves would be torn to pieces by the mobs."

There were a few halfhearted protests from the audience.

Finally Kobryn said grimly, "The government has decided that all research in genetic engineering must be stopped. Therefore, we have brought the leaders in this work to this meeting. You and your colleagues—some two thousand scientists, in all—are to be exiled...."

"Exiled!"

"What?"

"But you can't..."

"Permanently exiled, together with your immediate families, aboard an orbital satellite that has been set aside especially for you."

Kaufman was on his feet. "You can't do that! We're citizens and we have constitutional rights!"

"The world constitution specifically gives the Legislative Assembly the power to suspend constitutional guarantees in cases of extreme emergency," Kobryn replied. "Last week, the Assembly voted and approved your exile. The World Court has reviewed the situation and found that we are acting in a perfectly legal manner."

Kaufman stood there for a moment, hand up as if there was another point he wanted to make. Then slowly, like an inflated doll collapsing from a leak, he crumpled back onto his chair.

"No one regrets this drastic action more that the Council of Ministers," Kobryn said to the silent audience. "You men and women represent the world's best scientists. But for the safety and stability of the world's billions, a few thousand must be sacrificed. Your living conditions aboard the satellite, though rather crowded, will be as pleasant and even luxurious as they can be made to be. We do not wish to harm you. We have tried to find an alternate solution to the problem. There is none. And it is absolutely imperative that your work in genetic engineering is not allowed to affect mankind. We are trying to avert disaster. I hope you understand."

"Filthy liar," Kori muttered.

Frederick stood up and called out, "My name is Clark Frederick. I'm neither a geneticist nor a biochemist, but a rocket engineer. A few of my colleagues are here too. Are we included in this exile? And if so, why?"

Kobryn glanced away, at something or somebody out of camera range. Then he looked down, as if quickly reading something.

"Ah. Dr. Frederick, yes. You and several other scientists and engineers who have been working on interstellar rockets are also included—I regret to say. It was decided that your work could also upset the stability of society, and . . ." Kobryn shrugged, as if to say, *You know the rest.*

Frederick's face turned red with anger. "How in blazes can rockets to Alpha Centauri or Barnard's Star upset the social equilibrium on Earth?"

"Let me explain," said Kobryn. "If the masses of people on Earth believed that starships could transport them to new worlds, new planets of other stars, there might be millions who would seek out this new frontier. As you know full well, only a pitiful handful could ever hope to travel in a starship. It's much too expensive for true colonization."

"Of course. Everyone knows that," Frederick replied.

"No, not everyone. The great masses of people would expect your starships to transport them to new worlds, where they could begin new lives, free of Earth. And when we would tell them that this is impossible, they would not believe us. The result would be protests, riots, uprisings." Kobryn shook his head. "We cannot permit it. I am truly sorry."

Frederick sat down.

"Besides," Kori said to him, "they get to spend the money we were using on themselves."

Professor DeVreis was up again. "Minister Kobryn, you have sentenced several thousand men, women and children to permanent exile. We naturally reject this decision in its entirety. It is completely antithetical to the spirit of the world government and the liberty of mankind. We demand a fair and open hearing before the Council of Ministers, the Assembly, and the World Court."

Kobryn's face hardened. His giant image loomed over the frail old man. "You do not understand. The decision has been made. It is final. There is no appeal. We will begin transporting you to the orbital station tomorrow."

The viewscreen went blank, leaving them all sitting there stunned into silence.

[10]

By mid-afternoon the next day, a dozen men and their families had been taken from the villa by silent men in unmarked uniforms. The Kaufmans and the Sutherlands were the first to go.

Take the leaders first and the rest are easy to handle, Lou said to himself.

He wandered through the villa aimlessly. Everybody seemed to be in shock. People huddled in small groups, family groups mostly, talking in low and frightened tones. Lou was alone, a complete outsider. No family, not even his girl.

Again and again a shining black minibus would pull up the driveway and two men would get out. Unsmilingly, they would go through the rambling old house until they found the person they were looking for. A few moments of conversation, and then a family would follow the men out to the driveway, wide-eyed and shaken, to be bundled into the minibus and whisked away.

Lou stood on the balcony above the main entrance and watched one of the buses grind up the driveway, swaying top-heavily, and then swing out onto the road kicking up a plume of dust. It had showered the evening before, but the land was bone dry again this afternoon. Lou looked up. The sky was bright, but off on the sea horizon there were black clouds building up again.

A sleek little turbocar was coming down the road toward the villa, top down, two men in the front seat. It swung into the driveway in a flurry of dust and skid-screeching wheels, and pulled up to the entrance. Sitting next to the driver was the Norseman. He glanced up at the balcony and grinned.

61

"Very cooperative of you to be waiting for us," he called to Lou. "Will you join us, please?"

Despite himself, Lou felt startled. *It's my turn already.*

"Mr. Christopher," the Norseman said, "you won't try anything foolish, I hope."

Lou glared at him. Without a word of answer he turned and went inside to find the stairs that led down to the front hall.

The sky was filling up with thunderheads and the late afternoon sunlight had that threatening, electrical yellow cast, with the damp sweet smell of an impending storm. It was cool and exhilarating in the back seat of the convertible, the wind clean and strong, tearing at your hair and clothes, making you squint your eyes and press your lips shut as the car roared along. They had come down the dusty coast road and turned onto a broad plastisteel throughway. For many miles the convertible was the only car on the road, but gradually the traffic built up. Now Lou could see the towers of a city off among the distant hills, and big trailer trucks were whizzing along beside them on air-cushion jets, streaking toward that city.

Lou knew better than to ask questions. Conversation from the back seat of the speeding car was next to impossible anyhow, even if they could or would answer. He simply sat there, enjoying the wind and watching the clouds blot out the sunshine and make the countryside look dark and gloomy.

Take a good look, he told himself. *It's probably the last time you'll ever see any of this.*

They barely beat the rain. The convertible, still top down, threaded through a maze of elevated highways at the city's outskirts and then dove into a tunnel as the first big drops splattered on Lou's bare legs. The tunnel must have had acoustic insulation of some sort, because even though the car didn't slow down, the roar of its turbine didn't echo and thunder the way it would have in a normal tunnel. They pulled into an underground garage and stopped in front of an unmarked doorway. The Norseman got out and held the door open for Lou. As soon as they were both out of the car, the driver revved the engine and drove off.

The Norseman led Lou into the building, down a hallway, and to an elevator that was waiting with its door open. He was watching Lou warily, and stayed slightly behind him, out of reach, as Lou stepped into the elevator cab. Then he walked in, flicked a finger at the topmost button on the control panel, and the doors swished shut.

As the elevator slid smoothly upward, the Norseman turned to Lou. "I understand that you people are being moved to a satellite."

"We're being exiled," Lou said, feeling his anger returning.

"Yes, so I heard."

"For life."

The Norseman nodded.

"Whole families. Several thousand people."

"I know . . . I'm sorry."

"Did you know it when you brought me here from the States?"

He shook his head.

"Would it have made any difference to you if you had known what they were going to do with us?"

The Norseman looked at Lou. "I was only doing my job. . . ."

"Would it have made any difference?" Lou insisted.

"Well . . . no, I don't suppose it would have."

"Then don't tell me you're sorry."

"But . . ."

"Stuff it."

The elevator stopped and the doors slid open. Lou had expected to see a hallway, a corridor. But instead he stepped directly into a huge, sumptuously furnished room. Thick red carpeting, a long conference table surrounded by tall comfortable chairs, all in the rich brown of real wood. Two of the walls were a smooth cream color, a third was splashed with an abstract mural. The far end of the room was plastiglass, but all Lou could see through the windows was mist and the streaks of raindrops. There was a massive desk near the windows, its black leather swivel chair unoccupied at the moment. The air felt cool and clean, the room even seemed to smell of authority and power.

"You will wait here," the Norseman said.

Lou turned back and realized that his escort hadn't gotten out of the elevator. The doors slid shut with a soft sigh.

Completely puzzled, Lou walked across the big room to the windows. His steps made no sound on the luxurious carpet. It was raining so hard now that the city was only a blurred gray outline. Then Lou heard a door open. He turned and saw a smiling middle-aged man enter. He was shorter than Lou, stocky but not yet turning soft. His hair was still thick and dark, although his forehead had started to recede. He wore a light business suit.

"Mr. Christopher, a pleasure to meet you," he said, gesturing toward one of the plush chairs by the desk.

He spoke with a European accent of some sort, Lou couldn't place it. And Lou had the feeling that he had seen this man before, on Tri-V newscasts, perhaps.

"My name is Rolf Bernard," he said, taking the chair behind the desk. "That probably means nothing to you. The Finance Ministry is often behind the news, but seldom in it."

"Of course," Lou said. "The Minister of Finance."

Bernard smiled. "You know my name? I am flattered."

"I...uh..."

"Yes. You are wondering why you are here. It is very simple. Not everyone in the Council of Ministers is a monster, Mr. Christopher. The decision to exile you and your colleagues was not a unanimous one, I assure you."

Lou felt more puzzled than ever.

"Mr. Christopher, I will come directly to the point. There is nothing I can do to save your friends from exile. Even as Minister of Finance, I am powerless to stop this cruel and degrading action." He hesitated a moment, then added, "At this time."

Lou felt his innards tighten. "What do you mean?"

"I am totally against this decision to exile the geneticists," Bernard said, his voice firm. "There are a few others on the Council of Ministers who agree with me. We do not have sufficient power to reverse the decision of the Council, but we will not sit by idly and watch this happen without taking steps to correct the situation."

"But, I don't see..."

"How can you see? No one is certain of anything at this point in time. Except for this: I am certain that a few of my fellow Ministers will work together to free your comrades and bring justice out of this exilement."

Lou nodded.

"Now then, as a more concrete action, I am prepared to offer you an escape from exile."

"Escape?"

"Reprieve, parole, whatever word you wish to use."

"What do you mean?"

Smiling broadly now, Bernard said, "There is no way for me to save any of the geneticists or biochemists. Not now, at any rate. But you are not a geneticist nor a biochemist. I can take...eh, certain action, that will remove your name from the list of those who are to be exiled."

"What? How..."

Bernard stopped him with an upthrust hand. "Never mind how. Believe me when I say that it can be done. You need not be exiled to the satellite station. There are a few others, also, who I can slip out of the lists and save."

"But the geneticists?"

Shaking his head sadly, "Nothing can be done to save them, at present. Rest assured, they will be comfortable enough in the satellite. Physically, at least. And also be assured that powerful men, myself included, will be working night and day to rescue them and return them to their rightful places here on Earth."

Lou sank back in his chair. His head was starting to spin. Everything was happening so fast.

"Now then," Bernard went on, "you realize of course that your Institute has been permanently closed, as have all the leading genetics laboratories around the world. There are still plenty of geneticists and biochemists, plenty of working laboratories, left on our planet. But the best people, the leaders, the *elite*—they have been exiled. In this manner, the government hopes to stifle the progress of your science."

"In the name of stability," Lou muttered.

"Yes. You understand, I trust, that the government will not allow you to begin work at any of the genetics laboratories that have been left open. If they learn that you are working in this field, they will take you again and exile you. Or perhaps kill you."

"But..."

The big smile returned, and somehow it began to look slightly wolfish to Lou. "Hear me out. I have taken the liberty of starting a small genetics laboratory of my own—safely tucked away from prying eyes. You and several others whom I am able to save from exile can work there. I will try to bring some of the best geneticists and biochemists available to work with you. They will not be the leaders of their fields, of course, but they will be the best of those who have escaped exilement. Your work can go on while we try to end the exile of your friends."

Lou could hardly believe what he was hearing. "After all that's happened over the past few days . . . it's . . . well, meeting a sane man in the government is a jolt."

Bernard laughed. "It is not so much that I am sane; I am unafraid. The others on the Council fear your science. They seek safety in stability and order. I welcome change. I welcome your science. Without progress, the world will sink into barbarism."

For the first time since the marshal had arrested him, Lou felt himself really relaxing. He grinned at the Minister of Finance. "You don't know how important those words are."

Nodding, Bernard added, "I have also taken the liberty of bringing some of the equipment and animal stock from various laboratories to my new location. I understand one of your animals is a gorilla that can talk! Absolutely marvelous!"

"Big George," Lou murmured. "He's okay."

"Yes, the gorilla is healthy." Bernard seemed amused, "Apparently he was asking for you."

Lou nodded.

"Now you must realize," Bernard went on, hunching forward at the desk, his face grown serious, "that my laboratory is a private, even a secret affair. None of the other Ministers know about this. It is located on an island, and once you are safely there, you will not be allowed to leave. Until, that is, the entire business of the exile is settled."

"But why secret?" Lou asked. "Why don't you tell the world about the exile? Why keep everything hushed up? That's just what the government wants."

"My dear young friend, this is a very complicated business, and the stakes we are playing for are extremely high. If we make the smallest mistake, we will lose everything. You must trust me to do what is best. At the proper time, the world will learn what has happened, I assure you."

"Well," Lou said. "Okay, I guess you know more about this than I do."

"Fine!" Bernard started beaming again. "Now, is there anything else you will need to continue your work? We have already dismantled your computer and are bringing it to the new laboratory."

Before he realized what he was saying, Lou blurted, "There's a computer programmer—her name's Bonnie Sterne. She..."

"You want her at the new laboratory?"

"Yes, but she's not one of the exiles. She's in Albuquerque. And she might not want to come...."

Bernard waved his objections away. "She will come. I know women a little better than you do. If we tell her that you are safe and want her to be with you, she will come."

Lou felt almost numb as he left Bernard's office. The Norseman met him at the elevator again and guided him back to the waiting car. Lou felt as if his mind was somehow stuck in neutral gear. So much had happened. So much to absorb.

As he sat in the back seat of the car, driving through the chilling late afternoon rain, he tried to tell himself that he should feel happy. At least Bernard was on his side, on the side of justice and reason. *Okay, so living on this island will ba an exile of sorts, too. But at least you'll be working, and Bonnie'll be there. What more do you want?*

But somehow it didn't work. Lou didn't feel happy at all, just vaguely uneasy, wary. And then he realized that he didn't have the faintest idea of where they were driving him.

[11]

The new laboratory was on an island, all right. A Pacific island, Lou guessed, from the number of Orientals around the place. Most of the office people were Chinese or Malay. Half the computer programmers were Japanese.

Lou had been flown in the same day he had talked to Minister Bernard. They wasted no time. Anton Kori was on the plane with him, the only other passenger. Most of the trip was made at night, so neither Kori nor Lou could tell where they were going, except that they had been heading roughly southeastward when the sun set. The crew—two Arabic-looking pilots and a black engineer—said nothing to them.

Lou and Kori were separated at landing. A Chinese, about Lou's own age, drove him in an open-topped turbowagon from the jet landing pad through a narrow dark road that seemed to be cut into a jungle. He pulled up at a plastic prefab dormitory building and showed Lou to a room on the ground floor. Not much furniture, but the bed was comfortable and Lou was asleep before he had even taken off his shoes.

The next morning, breakfast was brought to him by the same Chinese.

"The director of the laboratory asked me to convey his greetings to you," he said. "He requests that you enjoy yourself this morning in any way you desire. He will meet you here for lunch. At noon precisely."

Lou glanced at his wristwatch.

"I took the liberty of setting it correctly for you."

Looking up sharply at him, Lou asked, "While I was asleep?"

The Chinese nodded, with the faintest trace of a smile on his otherwise impassive face.

So Lou spent the morning walking around the island. It was small, no more than a half-dozen kilometers long, and half that wide. It was really nothing more than a pair of heavily-wooded hills poking out of the water. The trees were palms and other tropical species that Lou couldn't identify.

The sun was hot, but the ocean breeze was beautiful. The place really was a tropical island paradise.

There were lovely white sand beaches all the way around the island, and a coral reef further out where the surf broke, except for a small inlet at one end. Lou saw a fair-sized, air-cushion ship resting in the gentle swells of the inlet. There was a dock there and a few plain white buildings. Slightly away from the buildings was the jet landing pad, a square of well-kept grass. The plane was gone now. There was no runway for bigger jets anywhere on the island; the vertical landing type were the only planes that could come down.

The dormitory building was at the opposite end of the island, connected to the inlet by the single road out through the trees. In the middle of the island, set into the fairly flat area between the two hills, were the laboratory buildings.

The labs were tucked away in the shade of tall trees. There were six buildings in all, filled with the bustling, nearly frantic action of men unpacking huge crates of equipment and working hard to set them up as quickly as possible. Their shouting and hammering drove Lou away very quickly. He only stayed long enough to make certain that they weren't damaging the equipment that they were handling. They weren't. They knew what they were doing.

And then, as he passed between two of the labs, Lou heard a scratchy hoarse voice calling:

"Uncle Lou!"

He looked and saw Big George standing erect, his huge arms upraised so that his hands rested on the top of the nine-foot wire screen fence that stood between them. The fence bulged dangerously under his weight.

"Hey, Georgy!" Lou felt his face stretch into its biggest smile in days as he ran toward the fence.

The gorilla jumped up and down and slapped his sides with

excitement "Uncle Lou! Uncle Lou!"

"Georgy, you okay?" Lou asked as he reached the fence.

"Yes, yes. Strangers scared me at first, but they are very nice to me. It was lonesome, though, without you or any of my other friends."

"Well, I'm here now. Everything's going to be okay, Georgy. Come on down to that gate over there and I'll get you out of this compound."

Big George lumbered along the fence, knuckles on the ground. Lou saw that the gate had no lock on it, just a simple latch. With a shrug, he opened it.

George lurched out and grabbed Lou in his immense arms.

"Hey! Careful!" Lou laughed as George lifted him off his feet, strong enough to crush him, gentle enough to handle an equal amount of nitroglycerin without danger.

Lou pounded the gorilla's massive hairy shoulders happily. The warmth of his body, even his scent, carried the impression of huge jungle strength. And if the gorilla could have laughed or even smiled, he would have right then.

A pistol shot cracked nearby. Startled, George jerked and nearly let Lou fall. Lou saw sudden fear in the gorilla's eyes, then turned to see some sort of uniformed guard pointing a pistol at them.

"Stop! Put that man down!" the guard yelled—from a safe distance away. He was wearing a khaki-colored shirt and shorts, with a little cap on his head and that big gun in his wavering hand.

"Shut up," Lou snapped. "And put that stupid gun away. We're old friends. He's not hurting me."

The guard's mouth dropped open.

"Let me down," Lou said softly to George. The gorilla stood him carefully on his feet.

Walking to the wide-eyed guard, Lou said, "Put that gun away and don't let me catch you doing anything that hurts that gorilla or frightens him in any way. Do you understand?"

"I . . . I thought . . ."

"You thought wrong. Big George wouldn't hurt anybody— unless they scared him so badly that he lashed out in fright."

"I was only . . ."

"You were wrong. Now get out of here."

"Yessir." The guard turned and walked away, fumbling the gun back into the holster strapped to his hip.

Lou stayed with Big George until lunchtime—but inside the relative safety of the wire screen that marked off the gorilla's compound. *Too many people out there who've been frightened by bad movies. And too many guns.* The compound was wide and wild, Lou saw. George had plenty of room, big trees, a stream, even the slope of one of the hills to climb.

"You'd better stay inside," Lou said as he left the gorilla at the gate, "until the people around here get to know you better. I wouldn't want you to get into trouble."

"I know," George whispered. "I'll be good."

Lou smiled at him. "Sure you will. I'll see you soon."

Lou walked briskly back toward his quarters, knowing that George would spend the better part of the afternoon feeding himself. It took a huge supply of fruits and vegetables to keep a gorilla satisfied. By the time Lou approached the white prefab building, he felt sweaty and uncomfortable. It was beginning to get really hot, and the breeze had slackened.

The turbowagon was sitting in front of the dorm, with a driver wearing the same sort of khaki uniform that the gun-waving guard had worn. The driver also had a holster strapped on.

In the back seat an older man was reading some papers. His face was mild and milky white, with a high balding forehead and thin sandy hair that had started to turn gray. He looked slim to Lou, and was probably getting near-sighted, judging from the way he held the papers close to his nose. He wore a starched white shirt, short-sleeved, and full-length trousers.

He looked up as Lou's sandals crunched on the gravel of the driveway.

"Ah... Mr. Christopher."

Lou nodded and put on a smile as he walked up to the wagon.

"I'm Donald Marcus, the head of the laboratory," Marcus put his hand out and Lou shook it. The grip was limp, almost slippery.

"Get in and we'll go down to the lab area. I want you to see the computer set-up before we have lunch."

Lou climbed up into the wagon and sat beside his new boss.

"By the way," Marcus said as they drove off, "did you know that you're three minutes late?"

Without even blinking, Lou snapped back, "My guard must've set my watch wrong."

Marcus looked a little startled, but said nothing.

The computer was housed in a building of its own, off to one side of the lab complex and not far from Big George's compound.

Inside the one-story building was chaos. Workmen were uncrating bulky consoles, ripping off the protective plastic coverings, leaving huge gobs of spongy foam heaped all over the floor. Carpenters were putting up partitions with whirring drills and power saws. Someone was pounding on a wall someplace. Everyone was talking, calling back and forth, shouting orders or responses, mostly in sing-song Chinese. Lou was nearly run down by four men who, with backs bent and heads down, were wheeling in the massive main control desk at breakneck speed from the open double doors at one end of the building.

It was hot and sticky, and the room smelled of new plastic and machine oil. Lou felt perspiration trickling down his body.

"Most of these components," Marcus yelled over the din, "come from your computer system at the Genetics Institute."

Lou nodded but kept his eyes on the nearest workmen, who were busily laying a heavy cable across the floor.

"We brought the logic circuits and the whole memory bank."

"What about the voice circuits and input software?" Lou shouted.

Marcus lowered his voice a notch. "Um, we didn't bring the voice circuits or the vocal input units. You'll have to type your inputs to the computer and get the replies on the viewscreen or printer, just like any ordinary machine."

"What? How come?"

Marcus avoided Lou's eyes. "Well, we didn't have the time or the transportation capacity to take everything. Besides ..." his voice lower, so that Lou had to bend down a bit to hear him, "with all these Chinks around as workmen and technicians, if they heard a computer talk they'd probably get scared out of their skulls. They'd think it was devils or something supernatural."

Lou stared at him. "You're kidding. Nobody's..."

Marcus stopped him with an upraised hand. "No, I'm serious. Sure, we've got some good people on the technical staff, but the hired hands are straight from the hill country, believe me. My own driver—he's a great mechanic, don't get me wrong. But he keeps some powdered bones in a bag around his neck. Claims they keep evil spirits away."

When they went outside and climbed back into the car, Lou took a careful look. Sure enough, the driver had a thin leather thong tied around the brown skin of his neck, with a tiny bag at the end of it.

They had lunch on the veranda of Marcus' quarters, a house made of real stone and wood, with a red tile roof that overhung the walls by several feet and made welcome shade against the heat of the sun. The house was atop the hill that overlooked the little blue-water inlet, and the breeze from the ocean made it very pleasant on the veranda. Lou leaned back in a wicker chair, watching the moisture beading on the outside of his iced drink, listening to the songbirds in the flowering bushes that surrounded the house.

"A month ago," Marcus was saying, "this was the only house on the island. By the end of this week, we'll have more than a hundred people here—twenty of them scientists, like yourself."

"I'm not a scientist," Lou said automatically. "I'm a computer engineer."

Marcus smiled wanly. "Yes, I know. But anybody who understands this genetics business looks like a scientist to me. I'm a civil engineer, by training. Right now, I guess I'm just a straw boss."

The young Malay driver served them lunch on a round bamboo table, his little bag of magic dangling between Lou and Marcus whenever he bent over to put something on the table.

"Minister Bernard's plan," Marcus said as they ate, "is to carry on the work that was going on at the top genetics labs."

Lou shook his head. "Twenty men can't do the work of two thousand. Especially when those two thousand were the best men in their fields."

Marcus chewed thoughtfully on a mouthful of food. He swallowed and then said, "I know it won't be easy. We've brought some good people here, but you're perfectly right, they're not the best. And we couldn't bring too many of them either, without the government catching on to what we're trying to do."

"Just what is it that you *are* trying to do?"

"Exactly what I told you," Marcus said, concentrating his gaze on a leaf of salad that was eluding his fork. "We're going to continue the work you were doing at the Institute. We're going to complete it, and show the world that we can alter a human embryo deliberately, and safely. Once we've announced that news, and told the people that the government tried to prevent this work from being completed, the government will have to relent and allow your friends to return to their homes and their work."

Lou felt an old excitement tingling through his body. "The next step in evolution," he said so softly that it was almost a reverent whisper. "Man's conscious improvement of his own mind and body."

Marcus leaned back in his chair.

"It's criminal," Lou flared, "for the government to stop this work! In a generation or two we could be turning out people who are physically and mentally perfect!"

Smiling, Marcus said, "Yes, we can. And we will, if you can do your part in this job. You realize, don't you, that you're the most important human being on Earth?"

(12)

Lou felt physically staggered. He stared at Marcus, who was smiling easily at him.

"Me? What are you talking about?"

"It's very simple," Marcus explained. "All of the world's top geneticists and biochemists have been put into exile. They're being shipped up to their satellite prison right now. Of all the top men working on genetic engineering, you're the only one we've been able to save."

"But..."

"Oh, sure, we've rounded up a few of the second-string people, and we've brought in a couple of young pups, bright boys, but the ink is still wet on their diplomas. You're the only experienced top-flight man we have."

"But I'm only a computer engineer."

Nodding, "Maybe, but your work is the key to the whole project. You've got the computer coding system in your hands. Unless we can get the computer to handle all of the thousand of variables that are involved in any tinkering with the genes, we don't dare try to do anything. It would be too dangerous."

Lou agreed, "Yeah...you've got to have the computer plot out all the possible side effects of any change you make. Otherwise you'd never know if you were making the zygote better or worse."

"Right," Marcus said. "And you're the only man who was close enough to the geneticists to really understand what the computer coding system must be. We've checked all across the world, believe me. None of the other labs were as close to success as your Institute. And none of them had a computer system as sophisticated as yours. So that makes you the key man. The fate of your friends—the fate of the whole world—is in your hands."

Grinning foolishly, Lou said, "Well... it's really in Ramo's hands. Ramo's got the whole thing wrapped up in his memory banks."

Marcus tensed in his chair. "The whole thing?"

Lou nodded. "All I've got to do is run through the programs and de-bug them. Then we'll be ready for the first experiments. Take me a few weeks, at most."

"This is critically important to us," Marcus said. "I don't want you to rush it. I want it done right."

Feeling a little irritated, Lou said, "It's almost finished. In a few weeks, we'll be ready."

"You'll be able to scan the zygote's genetic structure, spot any defects, plot out the proper corrective steps, and predict the results?"

"To twenty decimal places," Lou insisted. "And it'll all be done in in less than a minute of computer time."

"If you can do that..."

"*When* we can do that," Lou corrected, "we'll be able to mend any genetic defects in the zygote and make each embryo genetically perfect. Ultimately, we'll be able to produce a race of people with no physical defects and an intelligence level way beyond the genius class."

"Yes," Marcus said. "Ultimately."

Lou sat back, Marcus smiled pleasantly and sipped his drink. Then Lou noticed, through the chirping of the songbirds, the drone of a jet high overhead. Marcus heard it too. He looked up at the silvery speck with its pencil-thin line of white contrail speeding along behind it.

Glancing down at his wristwatch, Marcus said, "That's our next supply shipment. Your programmer friend should be on that plane."

"Bonnie?"

Marcus nodded. "I understand she's quite a lovely girl." He grinned at Lou.

Pushing his chair from the table, Lou got up. "I'll go down to meet her at the landing pad."

"Sure, go right ahead. Her quarters are in the same building as yours. She's on the second floor."

"Okay. Fine." Lou started toward the front of the house. Suddenly, he didn't want to be bothered by Marcus or anyone else. He just wanted to see Bonnie.

"I'm afraid the car's already down there," Marcus said, trailing along behind Lou. "You'll have to walk it."

"That's okay. See you later."

He left Marcus standing in front of the house and started down the dirt road toward the harbor area. The jet sounded closer now, and Lou could see it circling, still pretty high out over the sea.

From behind him he heard the whine of another turbo-wagon. Turning, he saw Kori jouncing in the back seat as the wagon worked slowly down the rutted road toward the harbor. Lou waved and Kori yelled for the driver to stop. They lurched off together toward the landing pad.

"Going to meet the plane?" Lou asked.

"Yes. They're bringing some equipment in for me. And some data tapes from *Starfarer* that came in just before I was arrested."

"The interstellar probe?"

The road leveled out and they picked up speed. Light and shadows flickered across Kori's face as they drove past a stand of tall palms.

"Yes. If everything was working right, these tapes might have close-up pictures of Alpha Centauri on them."

"Really? But I didn't see anything in the newscasts about it. . . ."

The road wound along the edge of the harbor now, and the driver pushed the turbine to top speed. There was no other traffic. The wind tore at Kori and Lou in the back seat.

"The government kept it quiet," Kori hollered back. "Remember what Kobryn said, back in Sicily? Alpha Centauri is a threat to the stability of the world," Kori laughed bitterly.

The car screeched to a halt alongside the landing pad. Billowing dust enveloped them for a moment. Blinking and coughing, Lou jumped out of the car and walked clear of the slowly-settling dust cloud. Kori came up beside him, walking in a slow gangling gait.

"Are you going to be working on the probe data? Is that what Marcus wants you to do?"

Kori made a little shrug. "He said I can work on analyzing the data. But what he really wants me to do is to make some nuclear explosives for him."

"Explosives? You mean bombs?"

"No, no, nothing so big," Kori answered, grinning. "Just little things, toys, really. The kind that engineers use on construction jobs. Why, if you exploded one of them in a city, it would hardly take out a building."

The plane was circling low now, its jets roaring in their ears. Lou watched as its wings spread straight out for landing and the jet pods swiveled to the vertical position. Slowly the plane settled on its screaming exhaust of hot gases, flattening the grass beneath it. Through shimmering heat waves Lou saw the plane's wheels touch the ground and the weight of the jet settle on them. Then the turbine's bellowing whine died off, like some supernatural demon melting away.

Lou took his hands down from his ears; they were ringing slightly.

The hatch of the jet popped open, and a three-step metal ladder slid to the ground. A broad-shouldered young man stepped out first, then turned around and reached up to help the next passenger. It was Bonnie.

She was wearing shorts and a sleeveless blouse. Her hair was pinned up the way she usually wore it at work. Her face looked grave, utterly serious, perhaps a little scared.

Lou felt something jump inside of him, and then he was running toward her, calling to her.

"Bonnie! Bonnie!"

She looked up, saw him, and smiled. Lou ran up to her, past the guy who had helped her down the steps. He wrapped her in his arms and swung her around off her feet.

"Am I glad to see you! You came! You did come."

She looked surprised and happy and worried, all at the same time. "Lou...you're all right. They didn't hurt you or anything...."

"I'm fine, now that you're here."

Without ever letting go of her arm, Lou took Bonnie's one travel bag from the Chinese guard who was unloading the baggage and started walking her back toward the car. Kori was still standing beside the wagon, so Lou introduced them.

Kori said, "Why don't you two drive back to the dormitory?

I'm sure you'll want to get unpacked and settled in your room, Miss Sterne. It'll be some time before all my junk is unloaded from the plane. Lou, if you'll just send the car back here. . . ."

"Fine, fine, I'll do that." Lou was grinning broadly as he helped Bonnie into the back seat of the car and got in beside her.

She was very quiet as they drove away from the pad and the harbor. Lou chattered about what a beautiful island it was, and how good it was to see her again. All Bonnie did was to nod once in a while. By the time Lou had carried her travel bag up to the door of her room, his own joy at being with her had simmered down to the point where he could see that something was wrong.

There were no locks on the dormitory doors, only latches that could be pushed home from the inside. So Lou opened her door and gestured her into the room.

Bonnie walked in and looked around.

"This will be my room?"

"Right. It's not much, I know, but . . ."

She went to the window and looked out. Turning back to him, she asked, "And your room is in the same building?"

"Downstairs."

"How many other women are in this building?"

Lou shrugged. "This whole second floor is for women, I think. And there are a few married couples living on the island. They've got their own houses, though."

"I see."

"Look, Bonnie, you're not sore about what I said when those Federal marshals arrested me, are you? I was scared, and surprised. . . ."

Her face softened a little. "No, it's not that, Lou."

He walked over to her. "Then what's wrong? Why'd you come if you didn't . . ."

"Why'd I come?" She almost laughed at him. "I didn't get much choice. Two men picked me up at the office where I had just started working and packed me off. That was it. No questions, no explanations. Just enough time to pack one bag. That's all."

"They didn't tell you . . ."

"Nothing. In fact, I'm still not sure of what's going on."

Lou sank down into the nearest chair. "But Bernard must have . . ."

Bonnie knelt down beside him and put her hands in his.

"Lou, I'm sorry. When I saw you there by the plane, all of a sudden I thought it was *you* that had me kidnapped."

"You haven't been kidnapped!"

"I haven't been invited to the prince's ball."

He laughed at her.

"Lou, what's going on? Is everything going crazy?"

Shaking his head, he tried to explain it as carefully as he could. The exile. Minister Bernard's offer to help. The work that was going to be done on this island.

Finally, she understood. "You mean we're going to stay here . . . indefinitely? As long as they want us to? We can't get off?"

He looked into her pearl gray eyes and really didn't care about politics or exilements or science or anything else. But he forced himself to answer, "We stay until we've finished the work that was going on at the Institute. When we show the world that genetic engineering can be done, then there's no more point in keeping Kaufman and the others in exile."

"But that could take years," Bonnie said.

"It won't take that long."

She looked away from him, off toward the window, like a prisoner who's suddenly realized that the outside world is forever barred away.

"I shouldn't have asked them to bring you here," Lou said.

She didn't answer.

"Bonnie . . . if you had known . . . if they told you that you'd have to live on this island until the project is finished . . . with me . . . would you have come?"

She turned back to look at him, and there were tears in her eyes. "I don't know, Lou. I just don't know."

(13)

There are more than three hundred trillion cells in the human body. Counting ten cells per second, it would take more than a million years to count them all. In each cell there are forty-six chromosomes; under the microscope they look long and threadlike, and they've often been described as "strings of beads." Each "bead" is an individual gene, and altogether there are some forty thousand genes in any human cell.

The zygote—the fertilized egg cell that develops into an embryo and within nine months into a baby—contains about forty thousand genes, just like any human cell. Half of this number come from each parent. Each individual gene is a complex molecular factory built of deoxyribonucleic acids (DNA), ribonucleic acids (RNA), and proteins. All the physical characteristics of the resulting baby are determined by the genes. Eye color, tooth structure, basic metabolic rate, chemical balance, size of brain, shape of nose—everything is controlled by the genes in the zygote.

Lou's work seemed simple and straightforward to him. He was training Ramo, the computer, to look over the detailed structure of each gene in a zygote and compare it to the structure of a healthy, undamaged gene.

Ramo, being a computer, knew only what his human co-workers told him. But he had two advantages that no human possessed. First, he had absolutely perfect memory. Once the "map" of a healthy gene was stored in the microcosmic magnetic patterns of his memory bank, he would never forget it, never blur or warp it, never let any emotional conditions prevent him from seeing it exactly as it was given to him. Second, Ramo could work at the speed of light, rather than the tediously slower pace of the human nervous system. Ramo could scan dozens of genes and spot the imperfections in their molecular structure in the time it took Lou to count to ten.

Lou often thought of himself as a teacher. His job was to teach an extremely clever youngster—Ramo—how to do a very complicated job. A job that no human could do because it would take him too long, and his memory wasn't good enough. Just before the Institute had been closed, Lou had taught Ramo all the patterns of healthy gene structures. Ramo knew what healthy genes looked like on a molecular level. Now Lou had to teach him how to compare a real set of genes with the healthy structures he already knew, how to spot the things that might be wrong with real genes, and how to show these imperfections in his viewscreens. Once this was done, Lou would begin to teach Ramo the biochemists' remedies for fixing faulty genes. And once *that* was done, the immense task was finished. The work of genetic engineering could begin.

But, sitting at the master control desk of the computer, Lou was much less than happy. The desk was a huge collection of control panels and viewscreens that reached around his padded chair in a semicircle. Within the reach of his fingers were controls that touched every part of Ramo's enormous electronic mind.

Lou was frowning as he slouched in the chair. He could see his own reflection in one of the dead viewscreens. He looked the way he felt. It was mid-morning, according to the clock, but here inside the computer building it was hard to tell. There were no windows. The building was frigidly air conditioned and heavily soundproofed. Time meant very little to the computer.

Two weeks had gone by since Lou had come to the island. Two weeks, and Bonnie was still as cold and distant as she had been that first day. She worked for Lou, she did her job well. She had lunch with him most days and dinner a few times, in the tiny overcrowded cafeteria that Marcus had put up near the lab complex. She even mended a hole in his pants pocket. But she still acted more like a wary employee than a friend.

I should have never made them bring her here, Lou told himself for the millionth time that morning. *She'll never forgive me for it.*

The phone beside him buzzed. He punched the ANSWER button. Marcus' untanned, bland-looking face appeared on the main viewscreen.

"You wanted to see me?" he asked.

Nodding, Lou said, "Some of the biochemists have been asking me to help them program Ramo to handle their work. I don't mind helping them, but it's going to take time, and I thought you wanted me to plug ahead on the basic genetic mapping as fast as I can."

"The biochemists?" Marcus put on a worried frown. "Why do they need special computer programming?"

"They're working on something to do with drugs that affect the chemistry in the chromosomes, or something like . . ."

Marcus' eyes widened for a flash second. Then, he quickly regained his self-control. "No, you're quite right. You shouldn't be pulled off what you're doing to help with that. Let some of the other programmers help them."

Lou said, "Okay, fine . . . I'd be glad to help them if they need it."

"No," Marcus snapped. "Um, that is, they shouldn't interfere with your work in any way. I'll take care of it. If they come to you again, tell them to see me."

"Okay. thanks." Thanks."

Marcus nodded and cut off the connection. The viewscreen went blank, leaving Lou to look at his own frowning reflection again.

He worked at the control desk the rest of the morning, then around noontime phoned Bonnie. She was working with a trio of Chinese girls on the other side of the building.

"I'm afraid I can't go to lunch with you, Lou," she said without smiling. "The girls and I are eating right here at our desks; we've got mountains of work to do."

Lou punched the OFF button, and this time turned his gaze away from the viewscreen.

It was well past six o'clock when the phone buzzed again. It pulled Lou out of his total immersion in the work of teaching genetics to Ramo. He suddenly realized that he was bone tired: his back ached, his head was throbbing, his eyes burned. But on the main viewscreen Ramo was displaying a detailed enlarged map of the molecular structure of a single gene. And part of the map—the area of the gene that was flawed—was outlined in red.

Lou typed on the master input keyboard, GOOD WORK RAMO. PERFECT. He muttered the words to himself as the phone kept buzzing.

THANK YOU, Ramo flashed on the viewscreen.

Lou reached out and touched the phone button. Ramo's words disappeared from the screen and Anton Kori's lean angular face took form on it. He was grinning hugely, showing big white teeth with spaces between them that made them look like a cemetery to Lou.

"Can you have dinner with me?" Kori asked. "I have a lot to talk about, a lot to show you."

"Well, I don't know," Lou said. "I'm kind of beat...."

"Oh." Kori's smile faded, but only a little. "Maybe Bonnie can... you have no objection? I've got to show these pictures to someone!"

"Bonnie?" Lou felt his nerves flash a warning. "Um... look, Anton—I'll give Bonnie a call and we'll both drop over to your place. Okay?"

Kori bobbed his head up and down. "Wonderful. Come to my lab. Next to the instrument repair shop. Bonnie knows where it is."

I've got no right to be sore at her, Lou told himslf as he angrily punched out Bonnie's phone number. She wasn't in her room. Glancing at the clock, Lou tried her office phone.

Her face filled the screen and his anger melted.

"Oh, hello, Lou. I was just leaving for dinner."

Keeping his voice flat calm, "Kori just called. He's very excited about something, wants us to eat with him. Can you make it?"

"Sure." Without a moment's hesitation.

Lou asked, "Would you have been so free if I had asked you to have dinner with me? Alone?"

For an instant a frightened look flickered in her green eyes. "What do you mean, Lou?"

"You've been seeing a lot of Kori, haven't you?"

"Lou, I'm a tax-paying citizen... or at least I was until I got hijacked here...."

"So you *are* sore about my having you brought here!"

"Of course I'm sore!" she flashed back. "Weren't you sore

when they dragged you away? Do you enjoy being an exile? Is this island any better than the satellite or wherever it is that the rest of the Institute people were sent?"

Lou heard himself mumble, "You don't want to be around me, is that it?"

"Don't be sullen," she said, smiling for the first time. "Lou... whatever we had going between us back at the Institute, it can't be the same here. It just can't be."

"That's the way you want it?"

She looked sad and lonely now. "That's the way it's got to be, Lou."

"Yeah." He took a deep breath. "Well, how about dinner? I told Kori we'd both be over...."

"All right," she said softly. "As long as we understand each other."

He nodded, his face frozen into a bitter mask. "I understand."

He left his office, walked around the computer building, and picked up Bonnie. They walked across the lab complex in silence. Overhead the trees filtered an unbelievable sunset sky of pink and saffron and soft violet. Through the boles of the trees, off at the edge of the reddened sea, the sun was huge and distended as it touched the horizon.

If Bonnie and Lou had little to say to each other, Anton Kori more than filled their silence. The moment they stepped through the door into his cluttered laboratory/workroom, he started chattering.

"It's fantastic, you'll never believe it, it's like something out of the cinema...."

He bustled around the big room, dragging a table loaded with complex electronic gear across the floor and positioning it near the door.

"Lou, would you turn on the switch for the laser?"

Kori pointed to the wall over his workbench. "No, not that one! The next one, on your left. Yes."

Lou flicked the switch. He saw nothing in the room that looked like a laser, but there was a hum of electrical power coming from someplace.

"Wait 'til you see this... Bonnie, the lights, please. Behind you."

With a slightly amused smile, Bonnie turned off the overhead lights. In the darkened room, Kori's bony face was eerily lit by the glow of the equipment on his table.

"Now just a minute while I use this old slide for focusing. . . ." he muttered.

Lou found a rolling chair and pushed it over toward Bonnie. She sat, and he stood beside her, facing the slightly luminescent viewscreen at the far end of the room. A slide came on, some sort of graph, with many colored curves weaving across it.

"Now the focus," Kori mumbled. The graph suddenly became three-dimensional. The curves seemed to stand in the middle of the room. Lou felt he could walk around them and look at them from the other side.

"Okay, good." Kori said, so excited that his English had a decided Slavic edge to it. "Now we see what no man has ever seen before—except me."

The room went totally dark for an instant, and then it was filled with stars. Lou heard Bonnie gasp. It was like being out in space, stars as far as the eye could see: white, yellow, orange, red, blue—unblinking points of fire in the black depths of space. In the distance, the nebulous haze of the Milky Way glowed softly.

"Wide angle view, looking aft," Kori explained matter-of-factly. "That bright yellow star in the center is—the sun."

"These are the tapes from the *Starfarer?*" Lou asked, and immediately felt sheepish because it was such a needless question.

He sensed Kori nodding in the darkness. "It took the ship more than thirty years to reach the vicinity of Alpha Centauri. And it took more than four years just for the laser beam to carry this information back to us."

Another moment of darkness and then another picture of stars.

"Wide view forward," Kori said.

There was still a bright yellow star in the center of the field of view. Kori flicked through several more holograms. The yellow star grew brighter, closer. Soon, Lou could see that it was two stars.

"Alpha Centauri," Kori said in an awed voice, as if anything louder might shatter the pictures. "Proxima is so distant and faint from its two big brothers that I haven't been able to pinpoint it yet. It's out among those background stars someplace. We need an astronomer here!"

Lou shared Kori's awe. "Alpha Centauri," he echoed.

"You were right, Anton," said Bonnie. "This is fantastic...so beautiful."

"Wait," Kori answered. "You haven't seen the best yet."

He flicked through another dozen holograms. The double star grew larger. Lou could see that one of the stars was smaller and redder than the big yellow sun.

"What are those two flecks, near the yellow star?" Lou asked.

Kori giggled excitedly. "Flecks? Flecks indeed! Those are planets! Two planets orbiting around Alpha Centauri!"

Lou had no words. He simply stared at the screen as Kori flicked on several more holograms, closer and closer, of the two worlds. On the very last slide only the second-most planet was in view. It looked like a fat round ball, yellowish-green, streaked with white clouds.

"I haven't had a chance to analyze the spectroscopic data," Kori said, "but those clouds look like water vapor to me. It's a bigger planet than Earth, probably a heavier gravity. But if there's water, there could be life!"

It was very late when Bonnie and Lou walked with Kori back to the dormitory. None of them had eaten dinner. In their excitement over the star pictures they had simply forgotten all about it.

Kori stopped in the middle of the road, at a spot where the trees didn't overhang, and threw his head back.

"Look at them!" he shouted. "Millions and billions of stars. And millions and billions of planets. Some of them must be just like this Earth, waiting for us to reach them. And we can! We can reach them, and we will!" He laughed loudly, and then gave a shattering shrill whistle as he swung his long arms up toward the sky.

"Hey, easy...you sound like you're high," Lou said.

"I *am* high," Kori answered happily. "I'm drunk with joy and knowledge and power. We can reach out to new Earths. That's enough to make any man drunk."

Lou shook his head in the moonless dark. "Maybe we'll need new Earths. We've certainly fouled up this one."

Kori laughed. He wasn't in the mood for seriousness. "Wait

until the people of the world see these pictures. Wait until they realize what it means...."

"I thought the government wasn't going to let the news out," Bonnie said.

Lou answered, "Marcus and Minister Bernard will get the pictures out to the newsmen somehow, I'll bet."

Her voice was quiet but firm. "Will they? Do you really think that they intend to let the world know about this? Or about genetic engineering, when we get it to work right?"

Lou stopped and looked at her. In the darkness, he couldn't see the expression on her face.

"What are you saying?" he asked.

For a moment Bonnie didn't reply. Then, "I'm not sure... I could be wrong. There's nothing definite, but I've just got a... well, a feeling, sort of..."

"Go on."

"Well... why do they have Anton working on nuclear explosives? What guarantees do we have that our work will be made public? Why are the biochemists working on cortical suppressors...?"

"Suppressors?"

"Uh-huh. I just found out this afternoon," Bonnie said. "That's what they need the computer time for: to select the chemical suppressor that does the best job of degrading cortical activity—permanently."

"But that would destroy a person's intelligence," Lou said.

"I know," Bonnie answered. "And I think they're planning to use Big George as a guinea pig."

Lou felt a hot bomb go off in his guts. "No, they wouldn't... if this is true, then..."

"Then we've been tricked into working for a group of people who're planning to overthrow the government and turn half the world's people into mindless zombies," Bonnie said.

There was a long, long silence, broken only by the night sounds of insects from the trees and brush, and the distant sound of the surf. Finally, Kori's voice floated ruefully through the darkness:

"Well, at least I don't feel drunk anymore."

(14)

It took Lou nearly a week to convince himself that Bonnie was right.

He used Ramo as his source of information and his teacher. He didn't know very much about the work the biochemists were doing. So he followed their progress by checking Ramo's programs and memory bank every evening, after his own work was finished. Within his vast memory Ramo stored most of the world's knowledge of biochemistry. So the computer became Lou's teacher, and explained patiently and with machinelike thoroughness exactly what Marcus' biochemists were trying to do.

By the end of the week Lou knew enough.

He sat on the warm beach sand, Bonnie on one side of him and Kori on the other. About two dozen people, most of them men and women from the technical staff, were on the beach or swimming in the gentle surf that rolled in from the reef. Far off on the horizon, huge towering cumulus clouds paraded like happy children across the sky.

The three of them sat a little bit away from all the rest of the bathers. Bonnie was still wet from a brief swim. Her skin was glistening with droplets of water, and prickled from chill. Or was it fear, in this warm afternoon? In the back of his mind, Lou noted with appreciation that there was plenty of her skin to be seen with the brief swimsuit she was wearing.

But he kept his face serious and his voice low enough so that it could just be heard by the two of them over the shouting and laughter of the others on the beach.

"You were entirely right, Bonnie," Lou said. "The biochemists are working on suppressors. They've already produced test samples of a drug and they've injected it into mice. Ramo showed me the test results. Six mice starved to death in mazes because they couldn't find their way to the food at the end of the maze. Before they had been injected, the same mice had made it through the same mazes in less than a minute."

"Oh my God," Kori said. Bonnie shivered.

Lou went on grimly. "And today they asked Ramo for the complete cortical layout on Big George. There's no doubt about it...they're going to try the drug on him."

"And then on a human being," Bonnie said.

Lou glanced up at her face. Then he nodded. "Yeah, you're right. That would be the next step."

"What do we do?" Kori wondered aloud.

Lou shrugged. "There are only two things I can think of. First, we can stop the work we're doing...just refuse to do any more. That would slow them down on their genetic engineering and their nuclear bombs...."

"But it wouldn't stop this suppressor business at all," Bonnie pointed out.

"And they already have enough bombs to destroy Messina, if they want to," Kori said.

Lou nodded and traced a square in the sand with his finger. "Okay...then the only other thing we can do is wipe out Ramo."

"Blow up the computer?" Kori asked.

"No...I can just erase all his programs and memory banks. Take a little time and some tinkering, but I could do it."

"It would take more than a little time," Bonnie said. "Ramo's banks..."

"I know a few tricks I haven't shown you," Lou said grinning. "I could wipe Ramo clean in a night."

"Really? That would stop everything they're doing," Kori said.

"They'd still have the bombs," Lou countered.

Shrugging, Kori said, "Yes, but without the biological weapons they're trying to get, the bombs by themselves wouldn't be enough for them."

Bonnie shook her head. "You're forgetting something else that they'd still have."

"What?"

"Us . . . or really you, Lou. If Ramo is wiped clean, don't you think Marcus is smart enough to figure out who did it?"

"Okay," Lou said evenly. "So he'll know I did it. What good does that do him? Ramo will still be blanked out. Marcus will be stopped dead."

"And so will you be," Bonnie said. "He'll kill you."

"That wouldn't do him any good."

"It wouldn't do *you* any good, either," said Kori.

"Don't you see?" Bonnie said. "Killing you doesn't help him, I admit. But the threat of killing you will stop you from erasing Ramo."

Lou nodded. "It does take a lot of the fun out of the idea."

Kori said, "Wait . . . we've left something out of the equation. We're all assuming that we must stay on this island. . . ."

"You know a way off?" Lou asked.

"Well, there are boats every few days. . . ."

"Can you sail one? Can the three of us take over one of the boats? Can you navigate? Do any of us even know where on Earth this island is?"

Dismal silence.

Then Kori brightened again. "If we can't get off the island, maybe we can signal someone to bring government troops here to rescue us!"

In spite of himself, Lou laughed out loud. "Okay, great idea. How are you going to signal? And who do you signal?"

Frowning in puzzlement, Kori mumbled, "Well . . . there's a radio station down by the harbor."

"Yeah, and three armed guards at the door all the time. And even if we could get in and operate the radio, and make contact with somebody, we'd be dead before any government people got to this island."

Kori clasped his hands behind his head and stretched out on the sand. "Louis, my friend, I am a physicist, I have come up with a great basic idea. I admit that there are a few details to be ironed out. That's the work of engineers, not physicists." He closed his eyes and pretended to go to sleep.

Without a word, Bonnie picked up a fistful of sand and dumped it on Kori's face. He sputtered and sat up. They all laughed together.

Bonnie stood up. "Come on, let's take a dip before dinner. We're not going to solve the problem right now."

Lou got up beside her. "Maybe not. But we'd better solve it pretty fast. We don't have much time left."

Lou couldn't sleep that night. He lay in his narrow bed, peering into the darkness, listening to the night sounds outside. The room's only window was open to the sea breeze. A million thoughts kept crowding in on him. No matter how he turned or punched the pillow or forced his eyes shut or tried to relax, he still found himself lying in the rumpled bed, sticky with perspiration, his eyes open and jaw clenched achingly tight with tension.

Finally he admitted defeat, got up and dressed. He walked out into the darkness, down the road toward the laboratory buildings. And the computer.

He turned around the corner of the first lab building and went toward the fence of Big George's compound. Down the way he could see a guard sitting by the gate, drowsing. The moon was riding in and out of scudding silvery clouds, but inside the compound the shadows cast by the trees made everything dark. Straining his eyes, Lou thought he saw the bulky shape of the gorilla sleeping on a man-made pallet of wood, straw, and palm fronds. Then he heard a snuffle and the big dark shape moved sluggishly.

"It's okay," Lou called softly. "It's me, Georgy."

The gorilla sat up and Lou could see a glint of moonlight reflected off his eyes. Big George pulled himself off the pallet and shuffled over to the fence.

"Uncle Lou," he whispered.

"How are you, Georgy?"

"Good. I been very good."

Lou wanted to reach out and pat him, but the wire fence was too fine a mesh to allow his hand through.

"I know you've been good, Georgy. Do you like it here? Has everybody been nice to you?"

"I have lots of room to play and they feed me good. But nobody comes to play with me. I'm all alone."

"I'm sorry . . . I haven't been to see you as much as I should," Lou replied guiltily.

"But the doctor said he'd come and play with me," George whispered.

"The doctor? What doctor?"

"The doctor," George answered. "He was here today...or was it yesterday? Do you call it today if it was the day before tonight?"

"Never mind," Lou said impatiently. "What doctor? Who was he?"

"He's a new friend. He said he's going to play with me when he comes back again. And I didn't move or yell or do anything, even when it hurt."

"What did he do to you?"

The gorilla touched the back of his head with a huge clumsy hand. "He made a funny noise back here, and it hurt a little. But just a little. It feels all better now."

Spinal tap, Lou thought, his innards sinking.

"I promised I wouldn't move even if it hurt," George said.

"Georgy, listen. The doctor...he said he'd be back. When? When's he coming back?"

"Tomorrow."

Tomorrow. This morning, most likely. "Okay, Georgy, you get back to sleep now. I'll come and see you tomorrow."

"All right, Uncle Lou. Good night."

"Good night."

As the gorilla shambled back toward his pallet, Lou began to know what real responsibility felt like. *Big George trusts me,* he told himself. *He needs me to keep them from hurting him.*

And then with a shock Lou realized that the only way he could save Big George would be to destroy Ramo. He almost laughed as he stood by the wire fence in the moonlight.

Some family I've got, he thought bitterly. *A gorilla and a computer. One of them is going to die. And it's up to me to choose which one.*

He hesitated only for a moment. Then he turned and headed for the computer building.

(15)

The door to the computer building was locked. Not by a voice-code lock, but an old-fashioned mechanical type, the kind that has a set of nine buttons that must be pushed in the right combination.

Lou didn't know the combination. *And I'll bet Marcus has the building wired with alarms. There'd be guards swarming in here before I sat down in the control slot.*

He stood there for a moment, uncertain. *No sense getting shot if you can't do the job you set out to do,* he told himself. And then he smiled. *On the other hand, if you're smart enough, and quick enough, there might be a way to get the job done without killing anybody.*

Grinning with his new idea, Lou walked back to the dormitory, undressed quickly, and got into bed. He set his wristwatch alarm to buzz at six, then closed his eyes. In five minutes he was sound asleep.

He had less than three hours of sleep, but Lou felt bright and ready as he stood by the fence of George's compound again.

"Here's some fruit I saved from breakfast," he said to the gorilla. "Catch!"

He tossed a banana and two oranges over the fence. George backpedaled clumsily and managed to grab the banana in one huge hand. The oranges fell to the ground.

He stooped to pick them up, then jammed all three into his mouth.

"Thank you, Uncle Lou," Big George said juicily.

Lou laughed. "You're welcome, Georgy."

Out of the corner of his eye, Lou saw a guard walking past the lab buildings, stopping at each door briefly to touch out a combination on the lock. He talked with the gorilla for a few minutes more, then, when he was sure that the guard was out of sight, Lou walked briskly to the computer building.

The rest of the technical staff was probably just getting up, Lou thought as he glanced at the control panel clock. Sliding into the seat, he immediately started typing out instructions to Ramo.

It was mid-morning before he found out if his scheme had worked. Despite the computer room's nearly arctic air conditioning, Lou was sweating as he sat at the control desk. He was trying to do his own work, but it was going very slowly. His mind certainly wasn't on it.

The phone buzzed. Lou was expecting it, but it still made him jump. He touched the ANSWER button. The round Oriental face of the chief biochemist appeared on the screen. He looked unhappy.

"We seem to have a problem this morning," he said without preamble.

"Really?" Lou said as innocently as he could.

Still frowning, the biochemist said, "Yes. We went to run a routine check of yesterday's work and found that the data we recorded yesterday is missing from the computer's memory bank."

"Missing?" Lou shook his head. "Impossible. You're probably just searching the wrong bank."

They talked it over for nearly half an hour. The results of yesterday's spinal tap on the gorilla, the cortical map, even some of the chemical formulas that had been stored in the computer weeks earlier—were gone from Ramo's memory banks.

Lou forced himself to look serious. "I'll do a complete check to find the missing data," he said, "but it sounds to me like some of your people have goofed up. Running this computer isn't as simple as operating a typewriter, you know. You should have let me record your data ... or at least you ought to have a trained computer programmer or technician doing the job."

"They are trained technicians!" the biochemist snapped.

Lou shrugged. "Then they haven't been trained well enough.... Okay, I'll look for the data for you. But I'm willing to bet it was never stored properly in the first place, and it's simply not in the memory banks."

The biochemist was starting to look furious. "Two months of work lost!" He lapsed into Chinese.

It took them a week to figure out what was going on. Lou would spend his days at his own work, and then at the end of the day he'd have Ramo review the biochemists' work for him. It took him only a few minutes to erase some of their material from Ramo's memory banks. Lou never washed out very much material, just enough to slow them down.

The biochemists became a very unhappy group of people. Their chief went around screaming and purple-faced. The computer technicians who worked for them looked scared. By the end of the week, Lou was spending most of his day with the technicians, trying to find out why they couldn't do their jobs properly.

Lou told nobody what he was doing. But Bonnie and Kori guessed it. By the end of the week, at dinner with them in the noisy cafeteria, Lou said to Kori:

"You've got to figure out some way to get us off this island. It's only a matter of time until the biochemists figure out what's wrong with the computer programs, and then..."

"I know," Kori answered, hunching over the table and speaking as low as possible. "I've been trying to work out a navigational fix, so that we can at least find out where we are. But I'm afraid I'm not much of a navigator. And the sextant I've built isn't very accurate."

"But how do we get off the island?" Bonnie asked.

Kori shrugged. "Maybe we could build a raft...."

"Or a flying carpet," Lou replied acidly.

That ended their discussion.

It happened the next day. Lou wasn't really surprised when an armed guard showed up at the computer control room. It had been exactly a week since he had first started tinkering with Ramo's biochemistry banks.

"What is it?" Lou asked, tensing.

The guard said, with a Malay lilt to this voice, "Mr. Marcus wishes to see you."

"I'm busy at the moment. Tell him..."

"Now," the guard said. And he hitched a thumb on the holster at his hip.

Lou nodded. "Okay, just let me . . ."

"Do not touch the computer controls," the guard said softly, even gently. But his hand curled around the butt of his gun.

Lou found that his own hands were suddenly trembling, and well away from the controls. "Okay, okay, but the computer's in the middle of a run."

"Some other technicians are being brought in to take care of it. You will come with me, please."

Marcus' car was waiting outside, with another guard at the wheel. Lou climbed in and the first guard sat beside him. In a few minutes, Lou was ushered into the air-conditioned study of Marcus' house. It was a small room, lined with books and a single large window that overlooked the sea.

Marcus was sitting at a desk in front of the window. There were a few straight-backed chairs in the room, and a comfortable-looking sofa. Marcus was talking into the viewphone on his desk when Lou entered. Without looking up, he gestured Lou to a chair next to the desk.

If he was angry, he wasn't showing it. His face had it's normal calm expression as he said quietly to the phone screen, "We've tracked down the source of the trouble and we'll get things back under control and on schedule."

Lou couldn't see the screen, but heard the voice reply, "Very well. See that you do. The timing is very critical."

"I understand. Good-by."

"Good-by."

Marcus pressed the OFF button, stared into the screen for a few moments longer, then turned to face Lou.

"You surprise me," he said.

"I do?"

Marcus almost smiled. "Let's not play games, Christopher. You've been sabotaging our computer programs, slowing down our biochemistry project. Why?"

"How do you know it's me?" Lou stalled.

"It's fairly obvious," Marcus leaned forward in his chair slightly. "Now listen, Christopher. You're not in the States any more. You're playing in a different league, with different rules. I don't have to prove it's you who's screwing up the computer. I think it's you, and I'm going ahead on that assumption. I called you here to find out why you're doing it, and to tell you what's going to happen if you don't stop."

Lou felt anger rising up inside him. "Just like that, huh? Somebody's messing up the computer and I get blamed. What happens now, do you shoot me?"

"No, nothing so dramatic," Marcus answered. In a voice that sounded genuinely concerned, he said, "You know, I really think you're more worried about that gorilla than about your own skin."

"Yeah. I'm a gorilla freak."

Shaking his head like a patient father, Marcus said, "All right, play it tough if you want. But listen to this, and get it straight. We're going to overthrow the world government. Never mind who 'we' consists of. There are some very important people in our group. We're playing for the highest stakes there are, and we don't intend to let you or anyone else stand in our way."

"Is that why you've got Kori making bombs?"

"Of course. Did you ever hear of a government that allowed itself to be pushed out of power without a fight? We're developing three weapons here on this island: nuclear bombs, the cortical suppressor, and genetic engineering."

Lou said, "So you can blow up your enemies, turn the survivors into morons, and then—after you've taken over—you can control everyone's children."

"That's not one hundred percent right, but it's pretty close."

"It doesn't sound like a very happy world that you're aiming to set up."

"Oh no? And what kind of a world do we have now? The government's letting the cities fester worse and worse, more and more barbarians being born and pushing out into the civilized parts of the world. How long do you think it'll be before we see something like a plague of rats sweeping across the whole world? Two-legged rats, from New York and Rio and Tokyo and Calcutta and Rome . . . every big city in the world!"

"And your answer is to bomb them out or turn them into zombies."

"If we have to," Marcus said, in the same tone he would use to offer a drink. "The bombs are really for fighting the government troops. Once we've taken over, we'll have other means of handling the barbarians—including the suppressors."

Lou shook his head.

"I wish I could get through to you," Marcus insisted. "What's this government done for you? Put you in exile, you and all your friends. When we take over, you can go back to living normal, useful lives."

"Useful to whom?"

With great earnestness, Marcus said, "Listen to reason, will you? You and the other scientists will be among the top people in the new society. Your children will get the best genetic care that you yourselves can provide."

"Until somebody decides he doesn't like what we're doing, or what we're thinking," Lou answered. "This government's slapped us in exile—*your* friends might not be so lenient."

Marcus sank back in his chair, as if baffled. "I don't have the time to argue with you. We're going ahead, and there's nothing you can do to stop us. If you don't stop tinkering with our biochemistry project, you're going to get hurt."

"No I'm not," Lou flashed back. "You need me to make the genetic engineering a success, remember? And that's where the real jackpot is. Because you might be able to surprise the government and knock it off, you might be able to take over the whole world . . . but without genetic engineering, you'll never be able to *control* the world. I'm beginning to see how your minds work, and I know why genetic engineering is so important to you. You want to control everybody, don't you? Make your own children supermen, and everybody else's their slaves. Right?"

Marcus shook his head. "Not exactly. You make it sound . . ."

"Rotten. Filthy and rotten. And that's what it is. But you need it, and that means you need me. I'm the key man, you told me so yourself."

"There are others. . . ."

"Then why'd you yank me out of exile? Because it'd take anybody else at least a year to catch up to where I am. I understand the whole genetic engineering problem, and there's plenty of it tucked away in my head, not in any computer banks or notebooks. So don't try to threaten me, unless you want to wait a year or more for the ability to control the next generation of children."

Marcus leaned back in his chair with a more-in-sorrow-than-anger look on his bland face. Shaking his head wearily, he said, "You still don't realize what you're up against, do you? Why do you think we went to the trouble of finding that blonde girl friend of yours and bringing her here? We don't have to threaten you. If you're worried about what we're going to do to your precious gorilla, try to imagine what could happen to the girl. Things could get very unpleasant for her. Very unpleasant."

Lou gripped the arms of his chair hard enough to make his hands hurt. He was fighting an instinct to spring at Marcus and smash his bland, evil face.

"Just try to control yourself and do as you're told," Marcus went on. "If you can behave, everything will be fine for you. But if you keep working against me . . . the girl will suffer for it."

"If you hurt her I'll kill you." Lou was almost surprised to hear himself say it, to hear the cold flat metallic ring of his own voice.

Marcus' expression didn't change. "Christopher, we shouldn't be threatening each other. Just do your work and neither you nor anyone else will get hurt. That's all we're asking from you. As for the gorilla, it'll probably be happier at its natural intelligence level that it is now."

The greatest excuse in the world, Lou thought. *They'll be happier doing what I want them to do instead of what they themselves want to do.*

Without saying another word, Lou got up and started for the door.

"Wait a minute," Marcus called. "You haven't said . . ."

Lou turned. "You've got all the answers you need. There's no way for me to stop you."

Trembling with rage, he left the office, walked past the guard lounging outside the door, went out of the house, ignored the car still parked in front with its driver, and walked back toward the dormitory.

As he passed the lab complex, Kori came running up to him.

"Lou, I've been looking for you everywhere!"

Lou didn't answer.

"I've figured it out!" Kori whispered excitedly as he pulled up beside Lou. "How to get the government troops here. And quickly! Inside a few days!"

Lou shook his head. "It'll be too late."

(16)

Kori grabbed his arm and stopped him. "No, I'm serious. We can do it!"

Lou said, "In a few days they'll have ruined Big George, maybe killed him. And if we try to stop them, they'll take it out on Bonnie."

"What?"

"That's what Marcus just told me. If he doesn't like the way we behave, Bonnie'll suffer for it."

"But he can't..."

"Yes he can. And he will. I bet he'd even enjoy it."

Kori's face turned as red as the setting sun. "That pudding-faced pipsqueak. I'll..."

Now Lou took Kori's arm. "Hold on. There's nothing we can do about it."

He felt Kori's surge of anger fade away, saw his face return to normal, except for a sullen smoldering in his eyes.

"What do we do now?" Kori asked.

"I don't know," said Lou. "What was your scheme all about? How can you signal for government troops?"

"Oh that.... With the navigation satellites."

"Navigation satellites? How..."

"They have sensors on them to detect nuclear explosions."

"They what?"

Kori started walking toward the dorm again, and Lou trudged along beside him. "It's a holdover from the old days, before the world government disarmed all the nations," Kori explained. "All the navigation satellites have a special array of sensors to watch out for nuclear explosions. If anybody sets off a bomb on the Earth's surface, in the atmosphere, or even in space, the government is alerted instantly. Inside of a few hours, there's an inspection team at the site of the explosion to find out what's going on. An *armed* inspection team. With troops ready to follow at an instant's notice."

"But nobody's set off a bomb for..."

"I know, but the government still has the teams, and they even hold practice drills. I was an advisor to a group of new recruits two years ago."

Lou chuckled. "I guess once a government agency gets a job to do, they keep on doing it, whether it's needed or not."

"Don't complain," Kori said. "Now then, the bombs I've been making are stored in caves at the far end of the island. If one of them went off, and a satellite spotted the blast, there would be an inspection team here in a matter of hours."

"Can you set them off?"

"Them?" Kori laughed. "One will be enough. If they all go off, they'll wipe out this entire island. Do you know how much destructive force even a single kiloton contains?"

When they got to the dormitory, Lou sent Kori up to get Bonnie. He didn't want to talk inside of any building. Too easy to plant electronic bugs indoors. As he stood by the dormitory entrance, Lou got the feeling he was being watched. *Nerves,* he told himself. But he knew that if he were in Marcus' place, he'd have guards out watching the troublemakers. *And we're going to make enough trouble to slide this island into the sea, if we have to,* Lou thought unsmilingly.

They ate a quick dinner in the cafeteria and then walked out to the beach. Walking ankle-deep through the warm-lapping waves, with the surf booming on the reef a kilometer out, they talked over their plans as the dying red sun stretched their shadows fantastically before them.

"I'll need at least two days to round up the proper equipment," Kori was saying.

"Make it one day," Lou answered over the roar of the surf. "Big George doesn't have two days to spare."

Kori glanced at Bonnie, then looked at Lou. "We want to do this right. If we rush, something might..."

"One day," Lou said flatly.

Shrugging, Kori agreed. "All right. One day."

"Where can we plant the bomb without setting off all the others?" Bonnie asked.

"That's why I wanted the extra day," Kori said, "to find the best location. Probably the best thing to do is to bury it in the beach sand across the island from the storage caves. That ought to be safe enough."

"Will it make a big enough explosion for a satellite to see if you bury it?" Lou asked.

Kori laughed. "Have no fear. A few feet of sand isn't going to smother one of my toys."

"Okay."

"I'll need two things," Kori said, more seriously. "A car to carry equipment and everything, and a diversion so I can get into the storage caves and do what I must do without being stopped by the guards."

"What about the guards at the caves?" Lou asked.

"There's usually only one. I think I can handle him easily enough."

"You're sure?"

Kori drew himself up to full height. He towered several inches over Lou, but he still looked spindly. "My friend, I was a national fencing champion five years ago. I still keep in good shape. Besides that, I'm sneaky. I'll ask the guard to help me carry some equipment and then hit him when his hands are full and his back turned."

Laughing, Bonnie said, "My hero."

"Never mind," Lou said. "Heroics are exactly what we don't need. We need good, sneaky, practical action that works. I don't want to win any moral victory; we'll all end up dead that way."

Kori nodded.

"Okay," Lou continued, "so you need a car and a diversion. We'll figure that out, shouldn't be too tough a problem. But the big question is, how do we protect Bonnie?"

"She's got to disappear," Kori said.

"Great. How do we do it?"

Silence.

They walked slowly under the purpling sky. A surge of sea curled around their ankles, then ebbed away. A lone gull glided low over the waves, calling sadly as if looking for long-vanished friends.

•

Finally Bonnie said, "Big George! I could stay in his compound for a day or so. There are plenty of trees and bushes to hide in and the guards never go in there."

"With the gorilla?" It was too dark to see Kori's face, but his voice sounded aghast.

"We're friends," Bonnie said. "We've known each other since George was born."

"He wouldn't hurt her," Lou agreed. "Or anybody else, for that matter. Trouble is, he'd want you to play with him. You wouldn't be able to stay hidden. He'd give you away."

"No, not if I explained it to him."

Kori shook his head. "I know you think a lot of that animal, and his intelligence has been boosted. But I wouldn't plan to stay inside that fence with him for ten minutes, let alone twelve hours or more."

"Oh, you've seen too many movies," Bonnie said. "George wouldn't hurt anybody."

They went on talking, planning, arguing until it was completely dark. The stars filled the night and the shimmering band of the Milky Way arched across the sky, bright and beckoning.

"Look up there!" Kori said.

In the darkness they could see his shadowy outline pointing skyward. Looking up, Lou saw one star moving silently, purposefully through the heavens, as if it had detached itself from its normal position to carry out some mission.

"Is that one of the satellites?" Bonnie's voice floated through the dark against the *basso* background of the surf.

Kori glanced at his luminescent wristwatch. "Yes. And right on schedule."

"Thank God," said Lou.

Lou didn't sleep much that night, and the next day at the computer building he hardly paid any attention to his work. He went through the motions, but his mind was racing, thinking about all that had to be done that night. Get the car for Kori, get Bonnie into hiding, create a diversion that will draw off the guards long enough for Kori to work unnoticed.

Toward the end of the afternoon, Lou couldn't stay cooped

up in the control room any longer. He stepped outside and took a deep breath of warm, salt-smelling air.

Then the quiet afternoon was shattered by the tortured scream of an animal. A scream of rage and pain and fear.

"George!"

[17]

Lou ran to the gorilla's compound. He got there in time to see two of the biochemists carrying a third through the gate. Big George was nowhere in sight. A half-dozen guards were clustered around the gate and more were arriving on the run, guns drawn.

"What happened?" Lou shouted.

They ignored him. A pair of guards took the unconscious biochemist from his co-workers. His face was bloody and one arm was hanging at a weird angle.

Lou grabbed one of the sweating biochemists.

"What happened? What did you do?"

The little Oriental looked up at Lou with fear and anger in his eyes. In a nasal, heavily-accented English he said, "Ape got frightened by injections. Anesthetic wore off. Restraints not strong enough. Ape broke loose, knocked down Dr. Kusawa, ran back into trees."

"Injections?" Lou demanded. "The suppressors?"

The biochemist nodded, pulled his arm out of Lou's grasp, and tottered away, following the guards who were carrying his boss.

Lou went to the gate.

One of the guards started shaking his head and motioning Lou away. "No. Danger. Keep away."

"Let me in there. He won't hurt me. He's scared and hurt."

The guards were clustered around the gate, which was now firmly locked. Most of them were peering into the trees and brush. Big George was not in sight. The other guards were watching Lou.

"Danger," said the one guard to Lou. "Go away."

Slowly, reluctantly, Lou walked away.

At dinner that night, Kori shook his head. "That makes everything different. Bonnie can't stay in there with him now."

"Sure I can," Bonnie said. "George will be all right by now, and the guards will never dream of searching his compound. It's a better hiding place than ever, now."

"No," said Lou. "There's no way of telling what those injections did to him. It's too risky."

They sat at their table in the cafeteria, leaning forward in a tight little huddle, ignoring their cooling dinner trays, oblivious of the fact that many eyes were watching them in the busy, noisy cafeteria.

Bonnie insisted that George was all right. "Let's go down to his compound and talk to him. Then we'll see for sure," she suggested.

Lou nodded agreement. Kori simply looked worried.

They walked down to the gorilla's compound, but stayed away from the gate where the guards stood watch. They moved up onto the slope of the hill to a spot close to the trees inside the compound.

"Georgy," Lou called out softly. "Georgy, it's me, Uncle Lou."

A snuffling grunt, and from the shadows in among the trees a pair of baleful eyes suddenly gleamed out at them. Despite himself, Lou shuddered. Those eyes were glaring like a jungle beast's.

He forced his voice to stay calm. "Georgy, it's all right. It's me, Uncle Lou. And Bonnie is here, too. And another friend...."

A growl.

Lou turned to Kori. "Maybe it's a good idea for you to go away, Anton. George must be scared out of his wits of strangers right now."

"He doesn't sound scared."

"He is."

Stubbornly, Kori said, "But I want to see the gorilla's reactions for myself. I don't want you two make any mistakes about this...."

"Shove it!" Lou snapped, keeping his voice down to avoid

frightening Big George. "You think you're the only one with brains? I'm not going to let Bonnie take any chances."

"Stop arguing," Bonnie said. To Kori she added, "He won't come out as long as you're here."

Kori left, muttering to himself. After another ten minutes of coaxing and soothing, Big George lumbered out of the trees and up to the fence.

"George," Lou said, gripping the fine wire mesh of the fence. "Are you okay?"

"Head . . . head hurts."

"It's all right, Georgy," Bonnie said. "The hurt will go away soon."

"Hurts . . . bad men . . . hurt . . ."

Is it just me or does his voice sound strange? Like it's hard for him to put words together. Lou felt his eyes stinging and realized there were tears in them. "Georgy, don't be afraid. It's going to be all right. The bad men have gone away. They won't come back."

The gorilla merely blinked.

Bonnie said softly. "Georgy, in a little while I'm going to come and stay with you. I'll bring you lots of food, and some medicine to stop the hurt.

"Hurt . . . scared . . . bad men . . ."

"I'll stay with you," Bonnie repeated. "And the medicine will stop the hurting. Don't be afraid."

"And I'll make sure that the bad men don't ever come back," Lou said, feeling anger welling up within him. "Not ever."

"Uncle Lou . . ." Big George started, but his voice trailed off and he never finished the thought.

Lou said as gently as he could. "It's all right, Georgy. No one's ever going to hurt you again."

As they walked away from the compound, Bonnie put a hand on Lou's arm.

"You're shaking," she said.

Nodding, Lou answered, "You know . . . last night I couldn't sleep. I was scared. Still am, I guess. We could all get killed tonight. But I think what was really scaring me the most was the thought that I might have to kill somebody myself. Or at least try to. But now . . . seeing what they've done to Georgy . . . to a harmless animal like that . . . I'm not shaking from fear anymore. That's anger."

"It's all right," Bonnie said. "Everything's going to be fine."

"Do you really think you'll be okay in there with George?"

"Yes, of course. I'll bring him some candy and sedatives. He'll sleep like a baby."

Lou nodded.

"You'll see," Bonnie said. "It's all going to go like clockwork."

"Yeah." Lou glanced at his wristwatch. *X minus four hours and counting.*

Exactly at eleven o'clock the three of them met at the doorway to the dormitory building. They had spent the intervening hours checking final details and then pretending to go to their separate rooms for the night. Now they met in the darkness and started wordlessly for the lab complex. They had found identical black stretch pullovers and slacks among the disposable clothing supply in the dorm. *Identical, but Bonnie's sure looks better than ours,* Lou thought.

There were two cars on the island, turbowagons, both of them. One was usually parked for the night at the lab complex. The other stayed at Marcus' house.

"Do you think anybody's watching us?" Bonnie asked in a whisper as they walked along the side of the road toward the lab area, sticking to the shadows of the trees and shrubs.

Kori whispered back, "They've got guards posted at the lab complex, the gorilla's compound, the bomb storage caves, and Marcus' house. Why should they watch us? We can't do any harm unless we get to one or more of those spots."

"Well, if they are watching us we'll find out about it soon enough," Lou said, pointing to the glow up the road that marked the lights of the lab complex.

They skirted the lighted area by detouring through the trees, making a wide circle, and doubling back to the far side of Big George's compound. While Kori stayed well away, Lou and Bonnie walked up to the fence and softly called the gorilla.

Big George lumbered up to the fence. "Hello, Georgy," said Lou. "How do you feel?"

"Head . . . hurts . . ."

"I've brought some medicine to make it feel all better," Bonnie said. "And some candy for you."

They talked for a few moments more with the gorilla, then Lou boosted Bonnie up to the top of the wire fence. George reached up and grasped her around the waist, his huge hands circling her completely. He put her down inside the fence as gently as a ballet dancer handles his ballerina.

Lou watched them, his innards suddenly knotting as he realized how easily Big George could kill Bonnie. But she reached up and patted his massive head. They turned and went toward the trees together as Bonnie reached into the bag at her waist for some candy.

Despite his fears, Lou grinned at the slim blonde girl and the hulking gorilla. *If only Edgar Rice Burroughs could see this!*

He looked down at his watch. *Eleven-thirty already.* Hurrying back to Kori, Lou mentally went over their plan for the thousandth time. Next step: Get Kori his car.

He met Kori, assured him that Bonnie was safe. They started back to the lab buildings. From the back of Kori's lab, out on the fringe of the lighted area, they could see a lone guard patrolling slowly between the buildings. He looked bored and sleepy. But on his hip was a big pistol.

Kori looked at Lou and nodded. Then he stepped out and walked straight up toward the guard.

"Say there," he called out, "can you help me? I'm trying to get into my lab here ... there's some work I have to do...."

The guard was instantly alert. "All buildings locked. No one can enter until morning."

"Yes, I know but..." That's all Lou heard. He ducked around the back of the building and circled it, coming up behind the guard. He could see Kori talking intently to the guard, and the youngster resting his right hand lightly on the butt of the pistol. They were standing about ten meters from the corner of the building where Lou crouched, with the guard's back to him. Across the lighted space between the buildings, Lou could see the car they wanted.

Ten meters. Quickly and quietly, Lou slipped of his sandals, then tried to tiptoe and hurry at the same time. The sound of his bare feet on the gravel seemed deafening. The guard started to turn around.

Lou covered the last few meters with a flying leap and pinned the guard's arms to his sides while Kori clouted him across the windpipe. He gagged and went down, thrashing, with Lou on top of him. Kori calmly leaned over, pushed Lou's face out of the way, and chopped hard at the back of the guard's neck. He went limp.

Lou got to his feet, sweating, panting. "Is he dead?"

"I doubt it," Kori said. He went to the lab door and punched the buttons of the combination lock. The door opened and the lights went on automatically.

"See?" said Kori smiling, "No alarms. I rigged them this afternoon, at the same time that I changed the lock's combination. There's some benefit to being a physicist after all."

Lou dragged the guard inside and stuffed him in a cabinet, then locked it. Meanwhile, Kori filled a tool kit with the equipment he wanted.

Wordlessly, they left the lab and re-locked the door. Then they went to the car.

"Are you sure you can handle everything by yourself?" Lou asked as Kori slid the tool kit onto the back seat.

"If you can keep them busy on the other end of the island," Kori said. He pulled the guard's pistol out of his belt. "Here. I'll get another one from the guard at the storage caves. Do you know how to use it?"

"I think so...."

"It's simple. Just release this catch here and it's ready to fire. Pull the trigger and it goes off. It should have at least a couple dozen charges in it. Laser pulse does as much damage as an explosive bullet...like hitting something with an ultrasonic hammer."

Lou nodded and took the gun. It felt heavy in his hand.

"Very good," Kori said. "I'll wait here until you start making noise down by the harbor."

"Right." Lou tucked the gun into his waistband, then saw Kori extend his hand. He took it and said, "Good luck."

Kori grinned. "See you tomorrow."

"Yeah." *If we're both alive tomorrow.*

Lou hurried through the star-lit night down toward the harbor. The road passed Marcus' house, where the only other car on the island was parked. Lou looked around, saw no one, and then slid in behind the wheel and released the brake. The car started to roll down the slight incline and into the worn gulley of the road.

Suddenly there were footsteps behind him and a man calling, "*Wei! Li tsai tso sheng mo?*"

Lou let the car glide to a stop, slid out, and crouched down behind the car. A light came on at the front of the house. Two guards were standing in front of the place, staring at the car. Lou pulled the gun out and set the safety release.

The guards didn't seem to know he was there. They were walking slowly toward the car. Lou stood straight up and fired over the car. The gun went *crack! crack!* as hundreds of joules of electrical energy were suddenly charged to invisible pulses of infrared laser light. The first guard was bowled over backward, as if hit in the chest by a giant's fist. The second spun and sprawled on his face. Neither of them moved once they hit the ground.

His hands shaking, Lou set the safety again and tucked the gun back into his waistband. Then he forced himself to go over to the bodies and take their guns. *They're still breathing.* He felt a little better as he went back to the car and tossed their guns onto the front seat.

Five past midnight. Running late. He got in behind the wheel again. He turned on the car's headlights and saw the road running down toward the harbor. *Time for Kori's diversion.* With a deep breath, Lou turned the starter key. The turbine whined to life. Lou pressed the throttle pedal firmly down to the floor. The engine coughed, then roared. Lights went on inside the house.

He raced the engine once again, then put the car in gear and roared off down the road. The shrubs and trees by the roadside blurred by; the wind tore at his face as he plunged down the twisting road toward the harbor. Lights were going on down there, too, where the guards' living quarters were.

He came screeching out on the flat, tore into the harbor area, and pulled the car to a screaming, tire-burning, skidding stop at the foot of the lone dock. There was a small boat tied up at the end of it. The game was going to be to make it look as if he wanted to get off the island on that boat.

Men were piling out of several buildings in the darkness,

shouting in languages Lou didn't understand. He went to the back of the car, lifted the engine hood and groped for the fuel feed line. He ripped it out and felt a spurt of fuel slick his fingers. Then he went back to the front seat, grabbed the two extra guns, and fired several shots into the engine compartment, backpedaling onto the dock as he did so. The third shot did it; the car erupted in flames.

Lou raced down the dock, the burning car between him and anyone who wanted to come and get him. There were a few crates piled on one side of the wooden dock, and Lou ducked behind them. In front of him was the flaming turbowagon; through the blurring heat waves of its fire he could see men running around the dockside area, some of them brandishing guns, all looking red and lurid in the light of the fire. Behind him was the open harbor, and the small boat tied up at the end of the dock.

But somebody had already thought about the boat. Lou heard a funny crunching sound, and then the crash of breaking glass. Looking over his shoulder, he saw a chunk of the boat's gunwale poof into splinters and vapor. *Laser rifle! They're breaking up the boat to keep me from using it. Maybe they think I'm on board it already.*

Then another thought: *When they find out I'm where I really am, they'll start blasting those rifles at me!*

Lou froze into a motionless, thoroughly frightened little knot of humanity, crouched behind the packing crates, trying to look totally invisible or at least as small and unnoticeable as possible. Long minutes ticked by. The fire in the car died down, the boat slid over on its side, gurgling obscenely.

Things up on dockside had quieted down. It was harder to see now, but there must have been dozens of guards milling around during the height of the blaze. Lou knew he was trapped and he was going to die. But not just yet. He realized that he had picked up a splinter in his left foot and it hurt. And his jaws ached from being clenched. He wondered how Kori was doing.

Maybe I ought to make some more noise or something, he thought. On the other hand, maybe the guards thought he had been aboard the boat and was now drowned. *If I let them know I'm here, I'm just inviting them to shoot me.*

He shook his head. *They're going to find you sooner or later, hero. Right now your job is to make enough noise to distract them from Kori.*

Squinting out into the darkness, he could barely make out a row of what looked like fuel drums lined up neatly on the shore, near the foot of the dock. A dozen drums. Maybe fifty meters away. An easy target.

It took him five shots before one of the drums burst into flame. In an instant they all went up.

Now the shouting and running began all over again. Nobody was shooting at him, either. They were all running toward the fire or away from it. Lou watched the guards. They were good, no question of it. After the first momentary shock and surprise, they fought the raging fire with hand extinguishers, blankets, anything they could find. Finally, somebody trundled up with a portable foam generator and they started smothering the blaze with billowing white foam. But it took time, lots of time.

The fire was smoldering and smoking when Lou heard:

"Christopher! I know you're out there on the dock. Give yourself up, you can't get away." Marcus' voice.

Lou almost laughed. Marcus didn't sound angry or frightened or even very upset. He was talking as calmly as the first day they'd met. That meant that he didn't realize what Kori was up to, or that Bonnie was hidden.

Or, Lou heard himself counter, *it could mean that he's got Kori and Bonnie and the whole game's lost.*

"Christopher, I don't want to have you killed. Come out now and stop this nonsense."

Like a schoolteacher scolding a kid, Lou thought.

"You can't get away, Christopher. We know you're sitting behind those packing crates. We . . ." Suddenly his voice cut off.

Lou peeked out from behind the crates. Marcus was listening to a guard who was gesturing and pointing up the road, toward the other end of the island.

"So the three of you are in on this together!" Marcus' voice sounded a little edgier now. "All right, we'll just find the other two and bring them out here. You can watch and see what happens to them."

"Marcus!" Lou called out.

Everyone at dockside froze. In the back of his mind, Lou

realized that it was nearly dawn. There was enough gray light to see the whole dockside area now.

"Marcus, did you ever stop to think of what a good target you make?"

Marcus jerked a step backward.

"No, don't move!" Lou yelled. "Don't any of you move. If anybody twitches, you'll get it, Marcus. I mean it!"

Marcus stood frozen at dockside. He was out in the open, the nearest guard a meter or so away, the nearest cover the burned-out hulk of the car, at least ten meters away. Lou prayed that none of them knew how many shots it would take him to hit anything at this distance.

"Christopher, you can't get away with this."

Lou grinned. "Can't I?"

As if in answer, the packing crate in front of him exploded in a deafening blast and a shower of splinters. Lou felt himself soaring, slow motion, tumbling off the dock, seeing the green land swing wildly and the greener water rushing up toward him. As he hit the water and lost consciousness, his last thought was that some rifleman had missed his head by just about a centimeter.

(18)

The pain woke him up. It would have been pleasant to stay asleep, unconscious, oblivious to everything. But he hurt everywhere, like knives were being twisted under his skin.

His eyes were gummy when he tried to open them. Everything was blurred, out of focus. There was a gray expanse of ceiling over his head. And faces. He tried to raise his head, but somebody's hand pushed him back onto the pillow.

Turning his head slightly, he could make out a window off to his right. It was bright, bright enough to make him shut his eyes.

What time is it? flashed through his mind. He started to speak, but all he heard was a thick, scratchy-throated groan.

"He's conscious," said a voice.

Marcus' face slid into view. Still calm. But was that perspiration beading his brow?

"That was a foolish bit of nonsense," Marcus said without rancor "What have you done with the girl? And where's Dr. Kori?"

Lou found the strength to shake his head.

"It's a small island, Christopher. We'll find them sooner or later."

"Not before...," he croaked.

"Before what?" Marcus asked.

"Nothing."

Marcus leaned closer. "We can find out. You can't keep any secrets from us."

"Go ahead and torture me...it won't..."

"Don't be an ass," Marcus said. "There are drugs that will make you do anything."

"No..."

Somewhere beyond Lou's vision a door opened and footsteps clicked quickly toward his bed. A voice muttered something, too low for Lou to hear.

"What?" Marcus snapped. "Why wasn't I told sooner? When did..."

Marcus' face slid into view again. It was red now. With anger. Or fear? Lou smiled.

"Where's Dr. Kori? What's he doing with a bomb?"

"Planting it in your lunch."

Lou saw Marcus' hand blurring toward him but couldn't move out of the way. It stung and snapped his head to one side. He tasted blood in his mouth.

"Get him talking. And quickly," Marcus ordered.

Someone grabbed at his arm. It flamed agony. Lou saw it was red and sore with thousands of splinters from the packing case that had exploded in front of him. An expressionless Chinese doctor took his arm from the guard, held it gently, swabbed a relatively undamaged spot on the underside of the arm, and then pressed a pneumatic syringe into the area. He put Lou's arm back down on the bed carefully, then looked at his wristwatch.

"The reaction should take a few minutes," the doctor said to Marcus.

Marcus paced the room nervously. The doctor stood by the bed, patiently watching Lou. *What time is it?* Lou wondered. *How much time does Kori need?*

Somebody giggled. Lou was startled to realize it was he himself.

The doctor turned toward Marcus. "He should be ready now."

Marcus came to the bed and leaned over Lou. "All right now, Christopher. Where is Dr. Kori, and what's he doing with the bomb he stole?"

"Playing in the sand," Lou said, laughing. It was funny, everything was so funny. Marcus' face, the thought of Kori digging sand castles with a nuclear bomb tucked under his arm. The whole thing was uproariously funny.

"Listen to me!" Marcus shouted, his face red and sweaty. "Quickly, before..."

The flash of light was bright enough to feel on your skin. For an instant everything stopped, etched in the pitiless white light. No sound, no voices, no movement. Then the bed lifted, the window blew in with a shower of glass, a woman screamed, and a roar of ten thousand demons overpowered every other sensation.

Somebody fell across Lou's bed. The roar died away, leaving his ears aching. People started to move again through a dusty plaster haze, crunching glass underfoot. Marcus staggered up from the bed.

Lou heard somebody say in an awed voice, "Look at that...a real mushroom cloud, just like in the history books."

Then Lou heard his own laughter. He couldn't see Marcus, but he knew he was still there.

"You've lost, Marcus. You might as well admit it. There'll be a government inspection team here in a matter of hours. Followed by troops, if you want to fight. It's all over. You've lost."

"I can still kill you! And the girl!"

Lou was laughing uncontrollably now. *The drug,* he knew in the back of his mind. But there was nothing he could do to stop himself. "Sure, kill me. Kill everybody. That's going to help you a lot. An enormous lot."

He laughed until he passed out again.

It was pleasant to be unconscious. *Or am I dead?* But the thought brought no fear. He was floating in darkness, without pain, without anxiety, just floating in soft warm darkness. Then, after a long, long while, the darkness began to turn a little gray. It brightened slowly, like a midnight reluctantly giving way to dawn.

Bonnie's face appeared in the grayness. There were tears in her eyes, on her cheeks. "Oh, Lou..."

He wanted to say something, to touch her, to make her stop crying. But he couldn't move. It was as if he had no body. Then her face faded away and the darkness returned.

He heard other voices in the grayness, and once in a while the black turned gray again and he could see strange faces peering at him. He would try to talk, try to signal to them, but always the darkness closed in again.

Then, abruptly, he opened his eyes and everything was in

sharp focus. He was lying in a hospital bed. The walls of his room were a pastel blue, the ceiling clean white. There were viewscreens and camera eyes in the ceiling. Lou found that he could turn his head. It hurt, but he could do it. There was a window at his left. He couldn't see out of it at this angle, but sunshine was pouring in. A night table was next to his bed, a rolling tray crammed with plastic pill bottles and syringes and other medical whatnots. A door, closed. A single plastic sling chair standing beside it.

He tried sitting up, and the bed followed his motion with an almost inaudible hum from an electric motor. Leaning back in a half-sitting position, he suddenly felt woozy.

At least I'm not dead, Lou told himself.

His body felt stiff. Looking down, he saw that his hands and arms were wrapped in bandages. So was his chest; white plastic spray from windpipe to navel. His face felt raw. as if he'd shaved with an old-fashioned razor.

The door suddenly opened and a nurse appeared. "Good day," she said with professional cheeriness.

"H . . . hello." Lou's voice was terribly hoarse; his throat felt rough.

She must be pushing forty, Lou thought. *She still looks pretty good, though.*

"How do you feel?" the nurse asked.

He considered the question for a moment. "Hungry."

She smiled. "Good! That's one condition that the automatic monitors can't record yet."

She was gone before Lou could say anything or ask any questions.

Within minutes a food tray slid out of the wall and swung over to the bed. It was clumsy, eating with bandaged hands. By the time Lou was finished, there was a knock on the door and it opened wide enough for Kori to stick his head through.

"Hi. They told me you were finally awake."

Lou's voice felt and sounded better. "Come on in. How are you? Where are we? What happened? Where's Bonnie?"

Kori grinned and pulled the chair up next to the bed. As he sat on it, he answered. "Bonnie's fine. She's here in the hospital, too, getting treated for radiation dosage. There was a considerable amount of fallout from my little toy, you know. I stayed inside a cave until the government troops arrived, but I got a touch of it, too."

"Marcus and the others?"

"They gave up without much of a fight," Kori said. "A government inspection team 'coptered to the island in four hours and eleven minutes after the blast. Inside of another two hours they had a little army of government troops covering every square centimeter of the island."

"And what happened to me?" Lou asked. "I remember trying to hold them down at the dock. Then somebody shot me and I fell into the water. Then..."

Kori was trying not to laugh, without being very successful at it.

"What's so funny?"

"Well, forgive me, but you are. Do you know how they found you?"

Lou shook his head.

"You were lying flat on your back in one of the bedrooms of Marcus' house. Stark naked. Sixty million splinters all over your face and body and arms and legs. And you were laughing! Laughing your head off!"

"Very funny," Lou said. "Marcus had me shot full of happy-juice, so I'd tell him where you were. So he could find you and kill you."

"I know," Kori said, still giggling. "Forgive me. It just presents an odd picture."

"Is Bonnie going to be all right?" Lou asked.

"Oh yes, certainly. She'll be visiting you herself in a day or so."

"And Marcus and his crew?"

Kori shrugged. "In jail, I suppose. The troops took them away."

Lou felt himself relax against the supporting bed. "That takes care of everybody, I guess. Oh! What about Big George? Who's taking care of him?"

Kori's face suddenly went somber. "That... that's the one bad part of it, Lou.... He's dead."

"What?"

"Somebody shot him," Kori said, his voice low. "We don't

know who did it. It might have been Marcus' guards or the government troops. Bonnie was right there, and she couldn't tell who fired the shot."

"Killed him? But why?"

Shaking his head, Kori answered, "We'll never know. There was a little fighting when the troops landed. Maybe it was just a stray shot. Or perhaps someone got frightened at the sight of the gorilla. At least he didn't suffer at all. One shot...he died instantly."

"Poor Georgy," Lou said.

For a moment neither of them said anything. Then Lou asked, "Where are we, anyway?"

Kori's face didn't cheer up at all. "Back where we started. In Messina. It looks to me like we're going to be shipped up to the satellite as soon as you and Bonnie are well enough to travel. To begin our exile."

(19)

The doctors made Lou stay in bed for a week, while his torn skin healed and he got his strength back. He saw Bonnie and Kori almost every day. But most of the time he lay in bed, thinking. So much had happened in so short a time. Now he could think about it, look back on it and try to fit all the fragments together, to form a coherent picture of what had suddenly happened to him and his life.

Why? he tought bitterly. *Why Big George? The main reason we tried to go against Marcus was to save George, and he was the only one that didn't get through it all right.* Lou thought of the bomb explosion and how it must have terrified the gorilla. The last few hours of his life must have been hell for such a peaceful, gentle animal. *We didn't do right by you, Georgy,* Lou said silently. *I'm sorry.*

Looking toward the future, Lou was just as bleak. They were going to exile him, of that he was sure. Kori was more optimistic, though.

"After all we've done for the government?" Kori said one afternoon, at Lou's bedside. "Risking our lives to stop Bernard's attempt at a coup? They won't exile us, they'll give us medals. You should get an award anyway; you've set a new international record for splinters."

Lou grinned with the young physicist. But inwardly, he knew the government couldn't let them go free. They would tell the world about the exile, and the government would never be allow that.

There was something different about Bonnie. She was up tight, holding back something that she didn't want Lou to know.

One afternoon, as they strolled together through the busy hospital corridors, he asked her.

"What's bothering you?"

She didn't seem surprised by the question. "Does it show?"

He nodded.

"I've got to make a decision," Bonnie said. Her gray eyes looked troubled, sad.

"About Kori and me?"

"In a way. You see, Lou, I'm not officially on the list of exiled persons. I can go back to Albuquerque, if I want to. Or I can go with the rest of you to the satellite."

"And stay for the rest of your life."

"Yes."

He took a deep breath.

If you married me, he said to her in his mind, *you'd have to share my exile. So I can't ask you for that. I can't even mention it.*

She was staring at him, trying to read his face, looking for something and not finding it.

Aloud, he said, "Bonnie, you might never allowed to make that decision. You're in pretty deep with us now. The government might decide to exile you along with Kori and me."

Bonnie stopped, right there in the corridor. "They can't do that...they wouldn't."

"They might," Lou said. "And if they do, it'll be my fault."

"There you are! I've been looking all over for you two!" Kori ran down the corridor, dodging between frowning nurses and muttering patients. Breathlessly, he told Lou and Bonnie, "The General Chairman...he's asked to see us. To talk to us. Tomorrow morning. The General Chairman!"

Lou turned to Bonnie. For the first time, he felt hope. If not for himself, then at least for her.

Despite his anger, despite his hatred of what had been done to his life, Lou felt as awed as a peasant in a palace when the three of them were ushered into the General Chairman's office. Bonnie and Kori, he saw, were also wide-eyed and silent.

The office was impressive. It covered the entire top floor of the tallest tower in Messina, stretching from the elevator doors where they stood to the sun-bright window-wall where the

Chairman's old fashioned ornate desk stood.

"Come in, come," said the little man behind that desk, in a voice cracked with age.

They walked silently across the thick carpeting, past a ten-foot globe showing the world in color and relief, complete with networks of tiny satellites orbiting around it. The whole globe hung in mid-air, suspended magnetically. The entire office was decorated in shades of green, dark jungle greens for the most part. The furniture was all richly polished natural wood. There was a scent of orchids and other lush tropical aromas in the air. And the climate control for the big room was warm, moist, almost sticky.

"Forgive me for not rising," the Chairman said. "I suffered a slight stroke recently, and the doctors want me to exert myself as little as possible." His voice was soft, gentle, and friendly, with an undisguised Brazilian accent. He was small, slight, his bony face high-domed and haloed with wisps of white hair, his hands fragile. He was very old. His skin was white and powdery-looking, laced with networks of fine etched wrinkles.

"However," the Chairman went on, "I did very much want to meet the three of you. Please . . . sit, make yourselves comfortable. Would you like anything to drink? To eat?"

Lou shook his head as he pulled up a leather-cushioned chair. He sat between Bonnie and Kori, and the three of them faced the Chairman.

Before the silence could become awkward, the Chairman said, "I want to express my personal thanks for your courageous actions on the island. You prevented an uprising that might have taken many lives."

"We did what we had to," Lou said.

The Chairman nodded. "It must have been quite a temptation, though, to put in with Bernard's people and avoid going to exile."

Shrugging, Lou answered, "As far as I'm concerned, we *were* in exile on that island. There was no difference between the way the government has treated us and the way Bernard's people were treating us. The government was a little more polite, maybe. That's all."

"Besides," Kori added, "I think we all felt that the people running the island would be worse than the people running this government, if they got the chance."

With a smile, the Chairman said, "Thank you. It's good to know that we are not completely at the bottom of the list."

Kori grinned back at the old man.

Somehow their smiles irritated Lou. "From what you've said, it sounds like the exile is still in effect, and we're going to be shipped out to the satellite."

The Chairman's face grew somber. "Yes, I am sorry to say. If anything, this attempt by Minister Bernard to seize power proves the wisdom of the exile. Your work on genetic engineering is simply too powerful to be used politically."

"So we spend the rest of our lives in a beryllium jail!"

"What else can we do?" The Chairman waved his frail hands helplessly. "We are not monsters. We have no desire to make you suffer. We will supply you with everything you desire aboard the satellite. Anything..."

"Except freedom," Lou snapped.

"Regretfully true," said the Chairman. But now there was a hint of steel behind the softness of his voice. "If I must choose between the welfare of twenty billions and two thousand or so, I will choose the twenty billions. The mere knowledge that you might soon be able to control human genetics has already triggered one attempt at revolution. I will not see the world destroyed. We have worked long and hard to avert destruction from war and from famine. I am not going to permit destruction to come from a test tube or a computer. Not if I can help it."

"But what about Kori? The work of the rocket scientists doesn't really threaten the world."

"Perhaps not," the Chairman admitted. "I must confess that I didn't realize anyone except those working on genetic engineering had been sentenced to exile. Someone in the bureaucracy considers the starship scientists a threat to world stability. I must find out why. If they cannot convince me that you are a threat, Dr. Kori, then you will be released from exile and free to resume your normal life. You, and any of your colleagues who have been placed in exile."

Before Kori could say anything, Lou went on, "And Bonnie, here... what about her?"

She murmured, "Lou, you shouldn't..."

"No, I want to find out about this. Bonnie wasn't sentenced to exile. She was picked up like the rest of us, and then released. She came to the island and found out what's going on. Now where does she stand? Is she going to be shipped off with the rest of us or not?"

If the Chairman was angered by Lou's insistent questions, he didn't show it. "Miss Sterne is not a scientist nor an engineer. There is absolutely no reason for her to be exiled. Unless she wishes to accompany you, for her own personal reasons."

"You can really say that with a straight face!" Lou raged. "You can sit there and promise her freedom when you know you don't mean it!"

"Lou, what are you saying?" Bonnie reached out for his arm.

The Chairman's eyes narrowed. "Explain yourself, Mr. Christopher. Why do you call me a liar?"

Almost trembling, Lou said, "If you let Bonnie go, if you let Kori go, what's to stop them from telling the newsmen about this exile business? What's to stop them from telling the whole world? Will you want them to sign a pledge of silence, or will you do surgery on their brains? Because we both know you can't risk having them tell the world about what you've done to the scientists...."

"Why not?" the Chairman asked gently.

"Why ... why? Because the people of the world will demand that you release us. They'll want genetic engineering ... they'll want us free. You can't throw two thousand of the world's top scientists into prison and ..."

The Chairman silenced Lou with an upraised hand. "My brave, impetuous young man, you are completely wrong about so many things. Firstly, I do not lie. When I offer Miss Sterne her freedom, and raise the possibility of freedom for Dr. Kori, I am not lying. Why should I? Please do me the honor of granting me honest motives.

"Secondly, the people of the world already know about your exile. We have not kept it secret. There would be no way to do so, even if we desired to. You cannot whisk away so many prominent men without anyone knowing it."

"They ... they know?"

"Of course they know. And they do not care. Do you think that the teeming billions on Earth care about a handful of scientists and engineers?" The Chairman shook his head. "No, they care about food, about jobs, about living space, about recreation and procreation."

"But genetic engineering. I thought . . ." Lou felt as if he were in a glider that was spinning out of control.

"Ah yes, your work," The Chairman said. "I admit that if you were on Earth and *showing* the world, step by step, that it could be done—then there would soon be an enormous demand for it. Catastrophic reaction. Everyone would want his next child made perfect.

"But today, you are only talking about the possibility of doing this sometime in the future. You might be successful next week, or next year, or next century. I confess that our public information experts have tried to make it sound more like next century than next week. And having you all out of the way has made the job that much easier."

"And . . . nobody cares?"

The Chairman looked truly sad. "The people are quite accustomed to talk of scientific miracles. Rarely do they see such miracles come true."

"But the food they eat, weather control, medicines, space expeditions . . ."

"All part of the normal, everyday background," said the Chairman. "Once a miracle comes true, it quickly becomes a commonplace. And the people hardly ever connect today's commonplaces with your talk of tomorrow's miracles. So your promises of genetic engineering do not excite most people. Grasping politicians, yes; hungry workers and farmers, no."

"So it's over . . . completely finished. No way around it." Lou sank back in his seat numbly.

"I am afraid so. I have lived with this problem for more than a year now, trying to find some alternative to exile. There is none. I am sorry. Somewhere, we have failed. We build gleaming technologies to turn ourselves into devils." The Chairman shook his head. "I am ashamed of myself, of the government, of the entire society. We are doing you a dreadful injustice."

"But you're going ahead and doing it," Lou muttered.

"Yes," the Chairman shot back. "That is the most terrible part of it. I hate this. But I will do it. I know you can never accept it, never agree to it, never understand why it must be done. I am sorry."

The four of them lapsed into a dismal silence.

Finally, the Chairman said, "As I told you, I will personally examine the matter of the rocket scientists. Dr. Kori, I cannot promise you your freedom, but I do promise to try."

Kori nodded and tried to look grateful but not too happy, glancing sidelong at Lou.

"And Miss Sterne," the Chairman went on, "you are free to go whenever you wish. The government will furnish you with transportation back to Albuquerque, or any place else you may desire to go. And you will be reimbursed for the troubles that you've been put to, of course."

Bonnie said, "Sir? Would it be possible for me to go to the satellite? On a temporary basis?"

Lou stared at her.

"Most of my friends are there," Bonnie said, looking straight at the Chairman and avoiding Lou's eyes. "Maybe I'd rather live there than anywhere else. But I can't tell unless I've tried it for a while."

The Chairman folded his hands on his thin chest and gazed thoughtfully at Bonnie. He looked as if he knew there was a lot more to Bonnie's request than she had stated.

"How do you think the others will feel, knowing that you can return to Earth anytime you wish to?"

Bonnie's face reddened slightly. "I . . . I would only stay a few weeks. I'd be willing to make a final decision then."

"A few weeks," the Chairman echoed. "And then you would make a decision that would be irrevocable . . . for the rest of your life?"

She nodded slowly.

A little smile worked its way across the Chairman's wrinkled face. "I can picture Kobryn's reaction. Highly irregular. But—very well, you may have a few weeks aboard the satellite. But no more."

"Thank you!" Bonnie said. And then she turned, smiling, to Lou.

(20)

It was literally another world.

Lou never saw the satellite from the outside. He, Bonnie, and Kori were tucked into a shuttle rocket that had no viewports in the cargo/passenger module. They sat in padded plastic contour chairs amidst cylinders of gas, packing crates of foodstuffs, motors, pumps, furniture. Lou swore he could hear, through the airlock that connected to a second cargo module, the bleating of a goat or sheep.

The satellite was huge, of course; a small town in orbit. From the inside it was a strange, different kind of environment. For one thing, you always walked uphill. The corridors all curved uphill, in both directions, because the satellite was built in a series of giant wheels, one within another. Most of the living quarters were in the largest, outermost wheel, where the spin force almost equaled the full gravity of Earth's surface. It took no extra physical effort to walk along the constantly uphill corridors because you didn't have to work against the spin-induced gravity.

His compartment—you couldn't call it a room—was a marvel of compactness, plastic-trimmed with aluminum spray paint. Lou thought of it as a cell. An astronaut would feel comfortable in it; a scientist on duty in a satellite for a month would put up with it; Lou realized he'd be living in it for the rest of his life.

Edmond Dantes had a bigger cell than this.

Life had already settled into something of a dull routine in the plastic little world. Lou, Kori, and Bonnie were met by a greeting committee when they stepped through the airlock from the shuttle rocket. They were shown to their quarters. After he had unpacked his lone travel bag, Lou received a phone call from Mrs. Kaufman, who was acting as her husband's secretary now, asking him to meet with the Director's Council right after breakfast the following "morning."

Time, of course, was completely arbitrary aboard the satellite. So everyone ran on the same clock, set on Universal Time. When it was midnight in Greenwich, England, it was midnight aboard the satellite.

Lou spent his first "evening" prowling through the uphill corridors. He couldn't find Bonnie, didn't know where her quarters were or what her phone number was. Same thing for Kori. He could have asked someone, but instead he started walking along the main corridor. It was completely featureless, bare plastic walls broken only by bare plastic doors. All alike, except for tiny room numbers on them.

There were other people drifting through the corridors, most of them strangers, but a few men and women that he had worked with at the Institute. They nodded recognition or mumbled a hello. If they were surprised to see him, or wondered why they hadn't seen him before this, they didn't show it in any way. All Lou could see in their faces was a vague guilt, a shame at being locked up here.

Like the living dead, Lou thought of them.

The only change in the long, sloping, featureless corridor was that every ten minutes or so there was a spiral ladderway that led up toward the next wheel, in closer to the hub of the slowly spinning satellite. After passing several of them, Lou decided to go upstairs and see what was there.

The ladderway ended in another curving corridor, much like the first one, but smaller, narrower, with doors on one side only. *This left side must be an outside bulkhead.* Lou expected the gravity to be lighter in this second level, but if it was he could detect no difference. Which meant that the satellite must be much larger than he had envisioned it. He began to realize how big the satellite would have to be to hold two thousand scientists and their immediate families.

As he walked aimlessly along the corridor, he came to a section that was dimly lit. Only a few dull red light panels overhead broke the darkness; it was barely light enough to see your way along. Ahead of him, Lou saw a motionless figure. As he got closer, he recognized him.

"Greg! Hey, Greg!"

Greg Belsen jerked as if startled, then turned to see who had called him.

"Greg!" Lou said, smiling and reaching out to grab his friend's shoulder. "Boy am I glad to see you!"

"Hello, Lou," Greg said quietly. "I heard they finally got you here."

Lou's smile vanished. This wasn't the same Greg he had known at the Institute. The nerve had been taken out of him. Then he saw why Greg had been standing at this spot. There was a viewport in the wall: a small circle of heavily-tinted plastiglass. And outside that viewport hung the Earth. Rich, blue, laced with dazzling white clouds, beckoningly close, alive. It was swinging around in a slow circle, the reflex of the satellite's spinning motion.

"She's only a few hundred kilometers away," Greg said in a soft flat voice that Lou had never heard from him before. "Less than the distance between Albuquerque and Los Angeles. You could go to one of the airlocks and practically jump back home."

Lou's blood ran cold.

Lou finally met Bonnie and Kori again the following morning, after a fitful, tossing few hours of dream-filled sleep. They all arrived at the autocafeteria at about the same time, and found each other at the "menu"—actually a wall panel studded with selector buttons. Only the breakfast buttons were lit. The cafeteria could seat perhaps fifty people, at long narrow tables. It was nearly empty.

"No morning rush to work, at least," Kori said, trying to sound cheerful.

When neither Bonnie nor Lou answered him, he shrugged his bony shoulders and turned to the selector panel to study the available choices for breakfast.

"Are you supposed to meet with Kaufman and the Council this morning?" Lou asked Bonnie.

Kori answered, "Yes, at nine-thirty," while Bonnie shook her head *no*.

Surprised, Lou said to Kori, "You are? But you're not from

the Institute. Why would Kaufman want you to report to him?"

"Your Dr. Kaufman has been elected head of this colony," Kori answered. "Didn't you know?"

"No, I didn't. I thought it would be Professor DeVreis...."

With a shake of his head, Kori said, "DeVreis died of a heart attack his first day here."

"Ohh." Somehow, Lou felt as if someone close to him had died. He hardly knew DeVreis, but it seemed so unfair for a man who had lived such a rich and useful life to be tossed into exile, to die here, in this place.

Kori turned back to the selector panel and tapped buttons for orange juice, eggs, muffins, sausage, and coffee. Almost immediately a part of the panel slid back to reveal a steaming tray bearing his order.

"Well," he said, "at least the food looks good."

Sure it looks good, Lou found himself thinking. *You've got a chance of getting off this jail.*

Turning to Bonnie, he asked, "Kaufman hasn't sent word to you?"

She shook her head. "No, nobody's said anything to me about meeting with the Council. I guess they're going to ignore me unless I decide to stay permanently."

Lou agreed. "Well, I'm supposed to see them at nine."

He was a few minutes late. It took him longer than he had expected to find Dr. Kaufman's office, which was in the second wheel.

It was a long and narrow room, just long enough to have a slight curve to the floor. Kaufman's desk was at one end, a long conference table at the other. All the furniture was made of plastic and light metals; it all looked temporary and cheap.

Kaufman sat at the head of the table. He had lost weight, Lou saw. There were new lines in his still-proudly handsome face. His thick hair seemed a shade whiter than it had been at the Institute. Greg Belsen, Kurtz, Sutherland, and two strangers filled all but one of the remaining chairs. Lou took the last chair, at the end of the table.

After introducing the two new faces—representatives from labs in Europe—Dr. Kaufman said, "We're all trying to accustom ourselves to our new environment. The reason for meeting with you this morning is to ask you to select some sort of project for your working hours."

"Project?" Lou asked.

"Yes," said Dr. Kaufman. "I don't believe that we should sit around and do nothing. The government won't let us have the major types of facilites that we need for our old work...."

"There's no computer aboard?"

Greg almost laughed. "No computer, Lou. No big toys for any of us. No electron microscopes, no ultracentrifuges, no microsurgery equipment—nothing but early twentieth-century stuff: optical microscopes and Bunsen burners, the kinds of things you buy kids for Christmas."

Lou felt his lips press into a grim tight line.

Dr. Sutherland explained, "The government doesn't want us to do anything more on genetic engineering. Even here. They're afraid that if we start making progress again, we'll smuggle the information back to Earth. And that's exactly what they don't .want."

It all made horrible sense to Lou. "But...what are we supposed to do up here? Turn to rust?"

"Nothing of the sort," Kaufman said, waving his hand in a negative gesture. "We may not have modern equipment but we can still do good science. We'll simply have to be more ingenious, more inventive, and make do with the simple equipment that we're allowed to have."

Allowed to have, echoed in Lou's mind. This was a jail, no two ways about it.

"For instance," Ron Kurtz said, leaning forward on the fragile-looking table, "I've never had the time to really write up all the work I've done over the last three or four years. I've published a few little notes in the journals, but now I can sit back and write up everything carefully, the way it ought to be done."

To be published where? Lou asked silently. *In the chronicles of wasted time?*

"It's quite clear that we won't be able to make any further progress in genetic engineering," Kaufman said, taking charge of the discussion once again. "At least we won't be able to follow our previous route, which required large-scale equipment. So we're all trying to evolve ideas for useful research that can be accomplished with the laboratory equipment that we now have.

We'd like you to think about what you can do, and how you can do it."

A computer engineer without a computer. Then Lou thought of Greg's elaborate lab back at the Institute, millions of dollars worth of automated chemical analysis equipment. *No wonder he's ready to jump ship.*

Aloud, he said, "Okay ... I'll try to think up something."

He started to get up from the table.

"Oh yes," Kaufman added. "You must have some very interesting tales to tell about your adventures over the past several weeks. Maybe you'd be good enough to tell the whole population, tonight, over our closed circuit Tri-V system."

That caught Lou by surprise. "Well, I don't know ..."

"Of course you will," Kaufman said. The discussion was ended.

Lou stood there awkwardly for a moment. Then the others started to get up. He turned and headed for the door. As he stepped out into the corridor, Greg said from just behind him:

"Don't get up tight about being a Tri-V performer, buddy."

Lou turned to him. "Easy for you to say."

Greg put an arm around Lou's shoulder and they started up the corridor together. "Don't worry pal. All you'll have to do is sit down with me and one or two other guys and we'll talk. That's all. You won't even know the camera's on you. It's simple."

"My big chance in show business."

Greg smiled, but there was sadness in it. "Listen ... we're all going a little crazy for something to do, something to talk about. It hasn't been easy, suddenly finding yourself cooped up in this squirrel cage...."

They were heading toward the dimly-lit section of the corridor, where the outside viewport was.

Lou asked, "And what's your scientific research project for the next fifty years?"

"You don't want to see a grown man cry, do you? Weren't those guys pathetic in there? They're talking about re-doing Calvin's work on photosynthesis or writing their memoirs. Lord, they're just going to fill in some time before they curl up their toes and die."

"That would be very patriotic of them," Lou said. "The government would be awfully pleased if we all just passed away, nice and neat, without a fuss. It's exactly what they want down there."

"Hmp."

They were in the darkened part of the corridor now. Greg stopped in front of the viewport. There was Earth, swinging slowly, majestically, in rhythm to the satellite's spin.

"That's what makes it hard," Greg said, staring. "Seeing her out there. Knowing she's only a few hundred kilometers away...."

Lou grabbed his arm. "Come on, snap out of it. Let's get some coffee. You going back in to talk with Kori? He's due to see the Council at nine-thirty."

Pulling himself away from the viewport, Greg said, "I know... but I'm not going back in there. Those guys are looking more like a morticians' convention every day. I think I'm going to go crazy... and soon, too."

Lou tried to laugh at him. It sounded hollow.

It was an empty day. Lou spent it prowling through the satellite's different levels, the wheels within the wheels. He found a fairly decent library, a tiny auditorium, some small telescopes and other astronomical gear scattered here and there. And there was an extensive hydoponic garden running all the way along one of the smaller, innermost rings. The big event of the day was watching a shuttle rocket link up to the satellite's main airlock, at the zero-gravity hub, and unload fresh food and medical supplies.

He called Bonnie for dinner, and they went together to the cafeteria.

"Do you know where Kori is?" Bonnie asked as they put their trays down on a table.

Lou shook his head. "And I'm not going to look for him. I'd like to have you to myself for once."

She smiled at him.

They ate with very little conversation. Finally, as he toyed with a gelatin dessert, Lou burst out:

"God, this is awful! Depressing! It's just terrible.... How in the name of sanity are we supposed to stand it! To spend the rest of our lives like this!"

She reached out and touched his hand. "Lou... people are staring at you."

"Bonnie, get out of here. Tell them you want to get off on the next rocket. Don't stay. Get out while you can."

"It does look bad, Lou," she said quietly, trying to tone him down. "But it'll get better. I know it will. Right now, everybody's still sort of in shock. Nobody's used to this yet. It'll get better...."

"No. It's going to get worse. I can feel it. Everybody's so hopeless! There's no purpose to their lives, there's nothing to live for!"

"They'll adjust," Bonnie said. "So will we."

"We?"

Just then, Kori came striding into the cafeteria, long-legged, loose-jointed, and spotted them. He ambled over to their table, smiling broadly. "I've been looking every place for you."

Looking up at him, Lou snapped, "How can you be so blazing cheerful?"

Kori shrugged, "Well, I had good news for you. Greg Belsen said you'd be glad to hear it. But if you don't want me to tell you..."

"All right...all right. Sit down, wise guy." Despite himself, Lou was grinning back at Kori. "Now tell me the good news. I could use some."

"Well...on the shuttle rocket today they brought my holograms. The ones from *Starfarer*. Dr. Kaufman said I could show them tonight, and you won't have to talk about your glorious adventures after all."

"Great," Lou said. "Best news I've heard all day."

"Greg said you'd be pleased."

Lou walked Bonnie back to her quarters, while Kori went to find the special compartment that had been set up as a Tri-V studio.

"You can't stay here in jail." Lou told her as they walked down the corridor, "I won't let you."

"But I can't go back to Earth and know that you and Kori and the others are trapped here. I just can't, Lou."

"Do you think it'll make me feel any better knowing that you're staying here because you feel sorry for me?"

They were at her door now. "I don't know," Bonnie said. "It's lousy no matter which way you look at it."

Lou nodded agreement.

"Would you like to come in and watch Kori's show?"

"Sure . . . I tried watching Tri-V shows beamed up from Earth for a while this afternoon. It kind of hurts; comedies and love stories and newscasts . . . all of it happening where there are cities and trees and mountains and wind and . . ."

"Stop it!" Bonnie snapped.

He looked at her. "It hurts," he said.

She put her arms around him and rested her head against his shoulder. "I know it hurts, Lou. I know."

A loudspeaker set into the ceiling broke in: "Tonight's special showing of photographs from the *Starfarer* mission will begin in five minutes."

Bonnie straightened up, looked briefly into Lou's eyes, and then turned to open the door.

They sat side by side on the sofabed, the only sittable piece of furniture in the cramped compartment, and watched the viewscreen set into the wall next to the door. The listened to Kori's voice explaining what the pictures showed, watched the stars, the myriad stars. They saw Alpha Centauri again, and focused on the fat yellow-green planet with its ice-white clouds.

Then suddenly Lou was on his feet, shouting:

"The stars! That's the way out! The stars!"

He felt as if someone had just lifted a heavy mask from his eyes.

Bonnie was standing beside him, her eyes wide with bewilderment. "Lou, what is it? What's wrong?"

He grabbed her and lifted her off her feet and kissed her.

"The stars, Bonnie! That's our escape, that's our purpose. Instead of staying here in exile, we can leave! Head for the stars! We can turn this prison into mankind's first starship!"

(21)

"Flatly impossible," snapped Dr. Kaufman.

Lou was standing at the end of the conference table in Kaufman's office. Kori was sitting at his side. The members of the Council showed a full spectrum of emotions: from thoughtful skepticism to outright scorn.

"It's absolutely impossible, the most ridiculous suggestion I've ever heard," Kaufman continued.

Lou held on to his steaming temper. "Why do you say that? The scheme is physically possible."

"To turn this entire satellite into a starship? Accelerate it to the kind of velocity that *Starfarer* reached, or even more? Nonsense!"

Kori said, "With the kind of fusion engines we now know how to build, we could accelerate this pinwheel to reach Alpha Centauri in less time than it took *Starfarer*. After all, the *Starfarer* was launched nearly two generations ago, it's a primitive ship, compared to what we can do now."

"But your own pictures showed that Alpha Centauri's planets are not enough like Earth to serve as a new home for us," said Mettler, one of the Europeans on Kaufman's Council.

"You're missing the point," Lou countered. "The important thing is that Alpha Centauri has planets. Barnard's Star has planets, they've been detected from Earth. Seven of the nearest ten stars are known to have planets; one of them is bound to be enough like Earth to suit us."

"Yes, I know. But it might take you a century or two to find a fully Earth-like planet."

"Let me ask something else," Charles Sutherland said in his

nasal whine. "Have you thought about the structural stresses on this satellite when you hook a fusion drive engine to it?"

Kori answered, "I've done some rough calculations. It doesn't look too bad. I'd need a computer to do the job properly, of course."

"And there's no computer here," Sutherland said, grinning sardonically. "And the government won't give us one. Neither will they give us fusion engines. So the whole scheme is meaningless."

"I think they *would* give us anything we asked for," Lou said, "if they knew they'd be getting rid of us. Permanently."

"Oh, it'll be permanent, all right. One way or the other," Sutherland said.

Kaufman frowned. "By even asking for permission to try such a stunt, we'd be telling the government that we've given up all hope of ever being reinstated on Earth. We'd be admitting that we expect to be exiled for the rest of our lives."

"Don't you expect to be here for the rest of your life?" Kurtz asked.

"No!" Kaufman slapped the table with the flat of his hand. "I have friends who are working right now to end this nonsense. I'm sure they are. And I'm sure that they must be making some headway. And so do the other leaders from the other laboratories around the world. The government can't keep this farce going forever."

Lou shook his head. "I've talked with the General Chairman himself. There's no doubt in his mind that we're here to stay."

"He's a feeble old man. He'll be replaced soon."

"By Kobryn," said Mettler. "Who is not going to hand out any pardons."

Greg Belsen turned to Kori, sitting beside him. "You really think you can do it? Get us out to the stars?"

"Of course. It's only a question of getting the right equipment and support from Earth."

"And finding the right planet," Lou added.

"The planet needn't be exactly like Earth," Greg mused. "We could modify our children genetically, so they're physically adapted to the conditions on their new world."

"But the rest of us could never live on that world," Kaufman said.

"Mmm...well," Greg said, "it's just a thought; we'd still be able to make a homeworld for the children, even if we couldn't find one exactly suited for us. I think it's worth the gamble. Let's try it. If nothing else, it'll give us something substantial to work on."

"Until the government refuses to give you what you need," Kaufman muttered.

"Let's vote on it," Greg suggested.

"Now wait," said Kaufman. "Before there's any voting..."

But there were already three hands in the air: Greg's, Ron Kurtz's, and Mettler's. With a shrug, Tracy, the other European on the Council, added his hand. Only Kaufman and Sutherland were opposed.

Kaufman snorted. "All right. We'll look into it. Dr. Kori, you can ask your colleagues to help you with the rocketry and astronautics work." From the tone of his voice, it was clear that Kaufman expected the older rocket scientists to regard Kori as a madman.

Some of them did just that. They shook their heads and walked away from Kori, unbelieving. But a few accepted the idea. More as an amusement, perhaps, than a real possibliity. But they toyed with the notion, they started jotting down notes, equations. Within a week the handful of rocket scientists and engineers aboard the satellite were all hard at work, no matter how implausible some of them thought the scheme to be. They soon took over all the desk top calculators in the satellite, watching the numbers flickering fluorescently in the viewscreens, getting more enthusiastic each day.

Greg Belsen was eager from the beginning. He started looking into the possibilities of deep-freezing people, putting them into suspended animation in cryogenic sleeping units. It was done on Earth, in rare medical emergencies, for a few days at a time. Greg wanted to put most of the satellite's seven thousand people into cryogenic sleep for decades.

"Either most of the people are going to sleep most of the time," he told Lou, "or we have to rebuild this ship into a gingerbread house. Do you have any idea of how many megatons of food seven thousand people can eat in a century or so?"

Gradually, some of the other biochemists started working

with Greg. Even a few of the geneticists let themselves be dragged into the problem, although it was well out of their field.

Within a month, Lou was asking a very suspicious government computer expert for time on high-speed computers. After a week of checking with Earth-bound scientists and government officials, the computer man allowed Lou to establish direct radio and Tri-V contact with a huge government computer in Australia.

"They're double-checking everything we do," Lou told Bonnie, "to make sure we're not slipping in any work on genetic engineering. Slows us down, but we're getting there just the same. Kori says he can't see anything to stop us. If we can get the engines built and the radiation screens, and the other equipment, that is."

Bonnie nodded at him. She had begged the authorities for more time to stay on the satellite, to help with the work Lou and the others were doing. The General Chairman himself signed the papers that let her stay indefinitely. But if Lou had really looked closely at her, he would have seen that she never smiled anymore, even though she tried to.

It took six months before they were certain. Six months of hectic work, calculations, conferences that lasted all hours, arguments, cajolings. Six months in which Lou saw Bonnie maybe twice or three times a week, sometimes not that often. And always he talked of the work, the plans, the hopes. And she said nothing.

Then, abruptly, Lou was telling Kaufman, "There's no doubt about it. We can turn this jail into a starship. We can freeze most of the people. We can reach the stars. Now we have to get the government to give us the equipment we need."

Kaufman said reluctantly, "I'll ask for a conference with the proper authorities."

Shaking his head, Lou countered, "The General Chairman once told me that if we needed anything, we could ask him. I'm going to call him. Directly."

It was one of those moments when time seems to have snapped, and you're back in a spot where you had been months or years ago. Exactly the same place.

Lou stood in the General Chairman's office again, Bonnie

and Kori beside him, as the elevator doors sighed shut. The room was unchanged. The Chairman called to them from his desk. The past six months aboard the satellite suddenly seemed like a remote and unpleasant dream. *Did I actually live aboard that plastic prison? In that artificial little world?* After a drive from the rocket field, through the green farmlands and bone-white villages, through the scented winds and steady call of the surf, through the noisy, crowded, living city—the satellite seemed totally unreal.

The Chairman listened patiently to their story, nodding and rocking in his big leather chair, steepling his fingers from time to time, even smiling once or twice. Then Lou finished talking.

For a long moment, the Chairman said nothing. Finally, "Your ingenuity amazes me, in a way. And yet, somehow, I am not truly surprised that you have come up with an amazing idea." He looked at the three of them, his dark eyes clear despite his many other signs of age.

"I will not presume to comment on why you want to leave our world entirely," the Chairman said. "I suppose that even death among the stars is preferable to you than a long life of exile." He laughed, softly, to himself. "I never expected to be faced with such a decision. I never expected man's first attempt to reach the stars would be made under conditions such as we find ourselves in."

"Then you'll allow us to go?" Lou asked eagerly. "You'll help us, you'll give us the engines and . . ."

The Chairman silenced him with a spindly upraised finger. "You say that there are many among you who are opposed to this idea . . . many who do not wish to fly toward the stars."

"Yes," Lou admitted. "Our work to date has simply shown that it's physically possible for us to make the journey. Dr. Kaufman and many of the others—especially the older people—don't want any part of it."

The chairman sighed. "You realize, of course, that it all comes down to a question of money. Everything does, it seems. Sooner or later."

"Money?"

Nodding, the Chairman explained, "It will take billions to outfit your satellite for a journey to the stars. . . ."

"We've figured that out," Lou said. "It's expensive, but still cheaper than keeping us in orbit indefinitely. This way, you pay one big bill and we're gone. If you keep us, you'll have to feed us, doctor us, everything...."

"I feel like Pharaoh arguing against Moses," the Chairman complained. "I would be perfectly willing to spend what must be spent and help you on your way, if that is what you wish. But—what of those who don't wish it? I cannot keep some of you in orbit and still spend the money necessary to send the rest of you out to the stars. It must be one or the other. It cannot be both."

"Then we'll have to vote on it," Lou said.

"Yes," said the Chairman. "I suppose you will."

So they left the Chairman's office, went back down the whispering elevator and into the car that took them back through the semitropical seaside farms of Sicily, toward the rocket field. But now the grass and sunshine and cottages were cruelties, sadistic reminders that the satellite was real and permanent and they were only visitors in this beautiful world; their prison awaited them.

They rode in the back of the open turbocar in silence, eyes wide and all senses alert to drink in every sight and sound and fragrance that had been commonplace all their lives but now were small miracles that they could never expect to experience again.

A second car followed a discreet distance behind them, and somewhere overhead a helicopter droned lazily. They were prisoners, no doubt of it.

As they got close enough to the rocket field to see the stubby shuttles standing in a row, Bonnie turned to Lou.

"You shouldn't have brought me with you today, Lou. You shouldn't have."

Surprised, "What? Why not?"

"Because I'm not as strong as you are," she said, shouting over the wind and turbine whine. "I . . . Lou, I can't leave all this, not permanently. It's bad enough in the satellite, when you can see the Earth outside the viewports. But to leave forever . . . to go out into that blackness . . . Lou, I can't do it. If they vote for going to the stars, I'll come back to Earth."

"But I thought..."

Even Kori, sitting on the other side of Bonnie, looked shocked.

"I'm sorry, Lou... I can't help it. I checked this morning. The government will still let me return, if I want to. I can't leave Earth forever, Lou. I just can't!"

"But... I love you, Bonnie. I can't leave without you."

She put her head down and cried.

(22)

Lou sat tensely in front of the Tri-V cameras. Next to him sat Dr. Kaufman, in an identical sling chair that creaked under his weight.

They were in the special compartment that had been turned into a Tri-V studio. Everyone in the satellite was watching them as they explained their positions on Lou's starship proposal.

As Dr. Kaufman spoke in his vigorous, emphatic manner, driving points home with the accusatory thrusts of a stubby forefinger, Lou's mind was far away.

He kept seeing Bonnie's stricken face when she admitted that she would never go with him to the stars. Kept seeing the green countryside, the lemon orchards and vineyards, the safe blue sky and friendly sea that he would never visit again.

"I can't leave Earth forever, Lou. I just can't!"

Can I! he wondered. *Can any of us? Turn our backs on the whole world, on a billion years of evolution? Is that what I want them to do? Is it what I want to do?*

Dr. Kaufman was saying, "It is desperately important that we all realize exactly what is involved here. No one has ever built a manned starship. No one has even attempted to. You all know that we get supplies from Earth, every week. Even though we have closed-cycle air and water systems, we still need replenishments of air and water at least once a month.

"As long as we remain in orbit around the Earth we can get those supplies and replenishments whenever we need them. But if we leave Earth, if we try this foolhardy scheme for going to the stars, we must have air and water and food systems that are absolutely foolproof. Now, I realize that manned missions to

145

Jupiter and Saturn have used closed-cycle systems, and they've worked quite well for periods of up to six years.

"But this star-roving we're talking about will take decades! Perhaps a century or even more! Why, none of us are even sure that a truly Earth-like planet exists out among the stars."

Kaufman shook his head, making a lock of his gray mane tumble over his forehead. "No, this star-roving idea is too risky, even on purely technical grounds. We just don't know how to build a starship. And even if the best engineers on Earth were assigned by the government to help us, we wouldn't be able to keep the ship in working order, once we left Earth. We wouldn't be able to repair it and maintain it. How many engineers are there among us? A handful. We're research scientists, not grease monkeys!"

Lou was listening with only half his mind. The other half was remorselessly reminding him: *Life is ruled by the laws of thermodynamics, just as all physical processes are. You can't get anything without paying the price. Not anything. If you want the stars, you must leave Bonnie behind. If you want Bonnie, the price is perpetual imprisonment.*

What's the difference? he asked himself. *Would it be so different, pushing this beryllium nuthouse toward the stars? We're all going to spend our lives inside this shell, wherever it's going.*

He answered himself, *Don't try to cop out. Heading for the stars gives everybody an aim, a purpose. Staying here is riding an orbital merry-go-round for the rest of your life, without hope, without anything but that big blue world hanging in front of your eyes, reminding you every minute of what's been taken away.*

"And remember," Kaufman was saying, "that as long as we stay in orbit here, there's always the chance that the government will have a change of heart, that we'll be freed. Once we break away, once we start out for the stars, there can be no turning back. It's an irrevocable step. None of us will live to see us reach our destination. Our children will age and die aboard this vehicle. Perhaps our grandchildren may find a world they can live on. Perhaps. That's a very thin hope on which to hang the lives of every man, woman, and child among us."

Kaufman stopped talking and leaned back, making the chair

creak again. He turned expectantly toward Lou.

Suddenly Lou's mouth felt dry and sticky, his palms moist with perspiration. The cameras were on him now, it was his turn to speak. Should he try to convince them, or should he toss the whole idea away?

He looked past Kaufman's handsome features to the big electronic board that had been jury-rigged along the far wall of the studio. There was a light for every person aboard the satellite aged fifteen or older. When Lou finished speaking, they would all vote. A green light would show for each yes vote; a red one for each vote against the starship idea.

"You can't miss," Kori had told him before the Tri-V broadcast had started. "Most of the no votes will come from the older people, the over-thirties. But we outnumber them. I just checked the population figures."

Greg had added, "We fought like kamikazes to get them to drop the age limit down to fifteen. After all, those kids are going to spend more of their lives in this pickle jar than any of us will."

"All you need to do," Kori had said, gripping Lou's arm earnestly, "is to make a strong speech. Put it on the line for everybody. The kids will vote for going to the stars. I know they will!"

Now Lou sat there looking into the cold eyes of the cameras, but seeing Bonnie's face, hearing her voice, watching her tears.

He heard himself clear his throat. He shifted uneasily in the chair. Then he said:

"Dr. Kaufman has pointed out some of the technical risks in trying to reach the stars. He's perfectly right. It is dangerous. Nobody's done it before. I don't know—nobody knows—if we can make the engines and air pumps and water recyclers work for a century or more without fail."

Lou hesitated a moment. "Dr. Kaufman also told you that if we stay here in orbit around Earth, there's always the chance that we might win a reprieve. We might regain our freedom and be allowed to return to Earth and take up normal lives again. That's also true. It could happen."

Again he stopped, but only for the span of a heartbeat. Only long enough to call silently, agonizingly, *Bonnie . . . Bonnie . . .*

Then, "When I first came aboard this satellite, Dr. Kaufman asked me to go on Tri-V and tell you something about what had happened to me. I'm going to do that now."

And he told them. He told them about the Federal marshal and his ride to New York. Told them about the man's unhappiness at missing his family picnic. Told them of his night in New York, the gangs, the knives, the running, the terror. Told them how the Institute looked, emptied of everyone but Big George. Of his arrest, his arrival in Messina, his audience with Minister Bernard. Told them of the island, of Marcus, of what they planned to do, how they wanted to use genetic engineering and the offshoots of their biochemistry as weapons alongside an arsenal of nuclear bombs. Told them of what they did to Big George, and what they wanted to do to all mankind.

And finally he told them of the gently implacable General Chairman, of how he admitted that their exile was a horrible injustice, but could see no other course of action. And the people, the great masses of people, the twenty billions of people for whom they were being sacrificed, the people who knew of their exile but didn't care.

"This is the world we've been exiled from. A world where a few people can destroy the lives of the best scientists on the planet, along with the lives of their families. A world where savages rule the cities and civilized monsters battle to control the government."

He turned toward Kaufman. "This is the world you want to go back to! So let's assume that we're allowed to go back; let's assume that the government changes its mind and frees us. What will they do with our work? Can we trust them to use our knowledge? Can we trust them in any way? What's to stop them from exiling us again? Or quietly having us killed? Nobody cares about us. All they want is the power that our knowledge can give them. The *kindest* thing they were able to to was to exile us!"

Looking directly into the cameras, Lou said, "We have no one to turn to but ourselves. The choice is ours. We can orbit this planet, slowly dying, and hope that someday the government will allow us to return. *But do we really want to return?* I don't. I've seen that world down there, and despite all its beauty I don't want to return to it. In this universe, with all its stars and space, there's got to be some place where we can make a better world for ourselves and our children. I say we should go to the stars."

Lou collapsed back in the chair, feeling weak and trembling

inside. Then the lights caught his eye. The vote shocked him: the green lights overwhelmed the few red ones.

Somewhere behind the cameras, people were laughing and clapping their hands. Somebody whistled shrilly. A door opened and Lou saw Kori and Greg heading toward him, grinning.

Lou knew that Bonnie was in her compartment. Packed and ready to leave. She was probably past tears now. Crying wouldn't help anymore. The pain won't be eased by tears, or words, or regrets.

"You're making a terrible mistake," Kaufman said, shaking his head. "Everything we need and desire is here, and you're going to force us to turn our backs on it all. You're making us leave our homes and head out into emptiness. There's nothing out there for us, Christopher. Nothing!"

Nothing, Lou thought. *Except the universe.*

FLIGHT OF EXILES

To the Pratt family,
with thanks for fine times.

[1]

"Fire . . . it's on *fire!*"

"EMERGENCY, EMERGENCY, EMERGENCY."

"Attention everyone. Emergency in cryonics area six. Damage Control and Life Support groups to cryonics area six immediately. Emergency."

"The whole area's a mass of flames! The standby equipment is out! Get more men up here, quick!"

The starship had no name. The people aboard merely called it "the ship." It had originally been a huge artificial satellite orbiting around Earth, a minor city in space, hugging close to the Mother World. Then it was made into a prison for thousands of the world's best scientists and their families. Now it was a starship, coasting silently from the solar system toward the triple star system, Alpha Centauri.

Inside the main control center, things were anything but quiet.

"There are fifty men and women in cryosleepers in number six area. If you can't get that fire under control they'll die."

Larry Belsen was standing up on the ship's bridge. It was actually a long curving row of desk consoles, where seated technicians worked the controls that watched and directed every section of the mammoth ship. Larry's job was as close to a ship's captain as any job on the ship; he was in charge of this Command and Control center, he had a finger on every pulsebeat in the ship.

The technicians were hunched over the keyboards, fingers flying over the buttons that electronically linked all of the great ship's machinery and people. In front of each of their desks were

viewscreens that showed them pictures, graphs, charts, every
kind of information from each compartment and piece of
equipment aboard: engines, computers, life support, living
quarters, work areas, cryonics units, power systems...all on
view in the hundreds of screens.

Normally, Larry thought of the curving ring of screens as the
eye of a giant electronic insect, multifaceted to see into all the
areas of the ship. He had studied about Earth's insects briefly in
a biology course, on the learning tapes. But now his attention
was riveted to one particular screen, where the fire was raging in
cryonics area six. There wasn't much he could see: smoke
obscured almost everything.

He put a hand on the shoulder of the girl working that
console.

"Can't you get the emergency equipment functioning?"

She was a thin, dark-skinned girl, with close-cropped hair.
Glancing up at Larry, "It should've gone on automatically. But
it won't respond at all. I've tried...." Her eyes were wide with
fear, anxiety.

"It's not your fault," Larry said calmly. "Don't blame
yourself."

"But there are fifty sleepers in there!"

Larry shook his head. Without bothering to go across to the
life support displays, he said, "They must be dead by now,
Tania. No sense tearing yourself up over it."

He took a step to the guy sitting at the next desk console.
"You in touch with the Damage Control group?"

"Yes...they've plugged into a wall phone out in the main
corridor, just outside area six."

"Who's in charge?"

"It's Mort Campbell's unit, but he's not the one on the
phone."

"Let me talk..."

"Is it cryonics six?"

Larry turned to see Dan Christopher at the door down at the
far end of the bridge. For an instant, everything seemed to stand
still: people frozen at the console desks, communications
speakers quiet, viewscreens stilled.

The two of them looked almost like brothers, at first glance.
Larry was tall and slim with dark hair that he kept clipped fairly

short. His eyes, though, were a cold gray, like a granite rock floating in space far from the warmth of a star. Dan was the same height and also youthfully slim. His hair was a lighter shade, and almost shoulder length. It curled slightly. His eyes were fiercely black, deep and flashing. Both of them were wearing workshift coveralls; Larry's the blue-gray shade of the ship's Command and Control personnel, Dan's the howling orange of the Propulsion and Power section.

"Is it six?" Dan demanded, his voice rising.

Larry didn't answer; he merely nodded slowly.

"My father's in there!"

By now Larry had crossed the plastic tiled floor of the bridge and was within arm's reach of Dan. He took him by the arm.

"So is mine! There's nothing you can do, Dan. The Damage Control group's already there, but..."

"My father!"

Dan pulled loose and yanked the door open. Larry stood there and watched him disappear down the corridor, running, until the door automatically slid shut again.

With a sad shake of his head, Larry went back to the control desks and viewscreens.

"You still in contact with the Damage Control party?"

The fellow nodded and pointed to the main screen over his desk, in the center of a group of seven screens. A scared-looking teenager was in view. He was looking somewhere off camera, coughing in the smoke that was drifting past him.

"What's going on up there?" Larry asked sharply.

The kid in the screen seemed to jerk with surprise. Then, turning full face toward the screen, he said:

"Mr. Campbell and the crew are in there.... I saw flames coming through the main hatch a few minutes ago, but there's only smoke now."

"Is anybody hurt?"

"I don't know. They're all inside there...nobody's come out."

"Did they have smoke masks?"

"Yeah..."

"Where's yours?" Larry asked.

The kid looked startled again. "I...uh...yeah, it's right here.... I got it...."

More gently, Larry said, "Don't you think it might be a good idea to put it on? It can't protect you while it's zipped to your belt."

Larry found that he was bending over the shoulder of the seated technician. He straightened up and glanced at the life support screens on the next console. They were blank, dead.

Fifty people in there. Dan's father . . . and my own.

"Larry . . . look."

He turned his attention back to the viewscreen. The Damage Control group was trudging wearily back into the corridor. Their faces were smudged, their coveralls blackened. The foamers and other fire-fighting equipment they dragged seemed to weigh tons.

There was hardly any smoke coming from the hatch now. The last man to step out into the corridor slowly unclipped his smoke mask. Larry recognized him as Mort Campbell stocky, slow-moving but always sure of himself, one of the oldest men working on this shift—nearly thirty.

Then Dan Christopher came dashing into view. He pushed wordlessly past the first few men of the Damage Control group, his eyes wild, his mouth open in silent frenzy.

Campbell stopped him at the hatch. Dan tried to dodge around him, but Campbell grabbed Dan by his slim shoulders and held him firmly.

"Don't go in there. It's not pretty."

"My father . . ."

"They're all dead."

Watching them in the viewscreen, Larry felt his insides sink. *You knew he was dead,* he told himself. *But knowing it in your head and feeling it in your guts are two entirely different things.*

He knew all the technicians, all up and down the long row of consoles, were staring at him now. He stood unmoved, his face frozen into a mask of concentration, and kept his eyes on the viewscreen. Inside his head, he was telling himself over and over, *You never knew him. He was frozen before you were old enough to remember him. There's no reason for you to break up.*

Dan's reaction was very different.

"NO!" he screamed, and he twisted out of Campbell's grasp and darted into the still smoky cryonics area. The older man slipped his face mask back on and went in after him.

"The cameras inside the cryonics area aren't working now," the girl tech said quietly, her fingers still tapping on her keyboard, trying to coax life back into the dead machines.

"Never mind," Larry said woodenly. "There's nothing in there that we should see."

(2)

Larry sat in his living quarters, in the dark. It was a single compartment, barely big enough for a bunk, a desk, and a chair. The bunk and desk were molded into the curving walls of the compartment. Drawers and sliding partitions to the closet and sanitary blended almost invisibly with the silvery metal of the walls.

In the darkness, as he sat in the only chair and stared at nothing, there was only the residual glow of the viewscreen at the foot of the bed and the faint fluorescence of the wall painting that Valery had done for him years ago, when he had first been assigned a compartment of his own.

So you've lost a father you've never known, Larry still argued with himself. *You're not the only one. Every one of those fifty frozen people was a father or mother to somebody aboard the ship. Look at Dan; it's hit him a lot harder.*

But as he thought about it, slowly Larry began to realize that something else was bothering him. It wasn't the deaths. Not really. That left nothing but a cold emptiness inside him. It was something else....

What caused the fire?

According to the ship's computer records, they had been crawling through the huge gulf of space for nearly fifty years. Twenty-some thousand human beings, exiles from Earth, on their way to Alpha Centauri in a giant pinwheel of a ship. Nearly fifty years. Almost there.

But the ship was starting to die.

The men and women who had started on this long, long voyage were exiles. They had been scientists—molecular geneticists, most of them. The world government had rounded them up and placed them in a prison, this ship, which was then only a mammoth satellite orbiting Earth. Earth was over-crowded, it needed peace and above all it needed stability. The scientists represented the forces of change, not stability. The geneticists and their colleagues offered the ability to alter the human race, to make every baby into a superman or a slave, into a genius or a moron. On demand. Pay your money and take your choice.

The world government was humane. And very human. Its leaders decided such power would be too tempting, too easy to corrupt. So, as humanely as possible—but with thorough swiftness—they arrested all the scientists who were involved in genetic engineering and exiled them to the satellite. Their knowledge was never to be used to alter the precious, hard-won peace and stability of Earth.

It had been Dan Christopher's father—with the help of Larry's father—who worked out the idea of turning their satellite prison into a starship. The Earth's government agreed, reluctantly at first, but then with growing enthusiasm. Better to get rid of the troublesome scientists completely. Let them go toward Alpha Centauri. Whether they make it or not, they will no longer bother the teeming, overcrowded Earth.

But the ship itself was overcrowded. Twenty thousand people can't be kept alive for year after year, decade after decade, for half a century or more. Not on a spacecraft. Not on the ship. So most of the people were frozen in cryogenic deepsleep, suspended animation, to be reawakened when they reached Alpha Centauri, or when they were needed for some special reason. The ship was run by a handful of people—no more than a thousand were allowed to be awake and active at one time.

All this Larry knew from the history tapes. Much of it he had learned side by side with Dan, his best friend, when they were kids studying together. Both their mothers had died of a virus infection that killed hundreds of people before the medics figured out a way to stop it. Their fathers had handed the infant sons over to friends to be raised, and went into cryogenic sleep, to be awakened when they reached their destination.

If they made it.

The people who had built this ship were engineers of Earth.

The people who lived in it, riding out to the stars, were mostly scientists and their children. The ship had to operate for more than fifty years, if they were all to stay alive. The time was almost over, and the ship's vast intricate systems were starting to break down, to fail. Youngsters trained as engineers and technicians had all the learning that the tapes could provide. But could they keep the ship going indefinitely?

A month ago it was the main power generator that failed, and they began to ration electrical power. Last week it was a pump in the hydroponics section; if they hadn't been able to repair the pump they would have lost a quarter of their food production, plus the even more important oxygen-recycling ability of the green plants that grew in the long troughs of chemical nutrients. And now the fire. Fifty people dead.

Will any of us make it?

A soft tapping at his door. Fingernails on plastic. Valery.

"Come in," Larry said, getting up from his chair.

The door slid open and she stood there framed in the light from the corridor.

Valery looked small, but she was actually almost Larry's height, and he had known since their childhood together that she was as tough and supple as plastisteel. Her face was broad, with high Nordic cheekbones and wide, always-surprised-looking eyes. Changeable eyes; sometimes blue, sometimes green, sometimes something else altogether. Very fair skin with a scattering of freckles. Very, very pretty.

She was wearing a simple white jumpskirt and blouse. Like most of the girls aboard the ship, Valery made her own clothes.

"I heard about your father," she said, her voice low.

Without waiting for him to say anything, she stepped into the compartment. Automatically, the door slid shut behind her. The room was suddenly plunged into darkness again. In the faint glow from the fluorescent painting, he started to reach for the light switch.

"No...." she said. "It's all right like this. We don't need lights."

"Val—"

She was standing very close to him. He could smell the fragrance of her hair.

"I saw Dan. They took him to the infirmary. He collapsed."

"I know," Larry said.

He wanted to touch her, to put his arms around her and let her warmth engulf him. But he knew he couldn't.

"You'd better...sit down," he said.

Valery went to the plastic chair in front of the desk. She sat on it and tucked her feet up under her, as simple and feminine as a cat. Larry could see her in the darkness as a gleam of white, like a pale nebula set against the depths outside. He sat on the edge of the bunk.

"I wish there was something I could say," Valery began. "I just feel so helpless."

Larry found himself gripping the edge of the bunk hard with both hands. "Uh...how's Dan?"

"Asleep. The medics have sedated him. He's...he's not strong, like you."

"He does his thing, I do mine," Larry said. "He shows his grief on the outside."

"And you keep yours locked up inside you, so nobody can see."

He didn't answer.

"I can see it," Valery said, her voice soft as a star-cloud. "I came over to tell you. I know what's going on inside you, Larry. I..."

"Stop it!" he snapped. "You're going to marry Dan in two more months. Leave me alone."

Even in the darkness, he could sense her body stiffen. Then she said, "But I don't love Dan. I love you."

"That doesn't make any difference and you know it."

"You love me, Larry. I know that too."

He shook his head. "No...I don't. Not anymore."

Her face was lost in shadow, but her voice smiled. "Larry—remember when we were just six or seven and we snuck into the free-fall playroom...you and Dan and me? And we were playing tag, and you got racing so fast that you flew smack into a wall...."

"It was the ceiling," he said.

"You hurt your shoulder, but you kept telling us it wasn't hurt. But I could see your pain, Larry. I could see it."

"Okay, so I broke my shoulder."

Suddenly she was beside him, kneeling alongside the bunk. "So don't say you don't love me, Larry Belsen. I know you do."

"It's no use," he said, his voice as cracked and miserable as he felt inside. "The computer selection was final. Not even the Council can revoke it. You can't have people just flying off and marrying anybody they feel like marrying! That's what happened to old Earth. The genetics went from bad to worse. We've got to live by the rules, Val... there's no other way."

"And the rules say I have to marry Dan."

"He loves you, Val."

"And you don't?"

He couldn't answer. Instead, he stared down at her for an infinite moment, then pulled her up to him and kissed her. She felt soft and good and loving. She clung to him hard, warmly. Everything else left his mind and he thought of nothing but her.

When he finally surfaced for air, she asked sleepily, "You don't have a duty shift, do you?"

Shaking his head, "No. Excused from duty until after the funeral services."

"Oh."

He sat there on the bunk, loving her and hating himself. *This is all wrong. What I'm doing...*

"Larry?"

"What is it?"

"If the Council would allow it, would you want to marry me?"

"Don't make it worse than it is, Valery."

"But would you?"

"Sure."

She sat up beside him. "We can do it, you know. If you really want to."

"You must be..."

"No, we can," she insisted. "The Council's due to vote on the new Chairman in two days, right? The Chairman and the permanent Council members are Class A, aren't they? Their genetic options are much wider than B's, aren't they?"

"Yes, but..."

"I checked it all out. The computer selection rated you and Dan so close together that it wasn't until the third-order effects were taken into account that it rated Dan ahead of you. And then it was only a shade. But if you're elected Chairman, then..."

Larry shook his head. "It's Dan's turn to be Chairman. He's a year older than I am. Besides, he wanted to revive his father when we got to Centauri and turn the Chairmanship over to him."

"But that's all changed now."

Larry frowned. "No... Dan and I talked it over a long time ago. He's a year older than I am, so he'll get a chance to be Chairman first...."

Very softly, Valery said, "That means in two months I'll be Mrs. Christopher. Unless you do something about it *now*."

"I can't...."

"Dan's in no condition to run the Council," she said. "When they vote, two days from now, he'll still be in the infirmary. And a lot of the older Council members have always thought he's much too emotional to be Chairman, even if it's only for a couple of months. Especially now, when we're about to make landfall ... they'd rather have a stronger, cooler Chairman. You can ask my father; that's what they're saying."

Larry knew. He knew all of it. *To be Chairman when we reach the new world.* Every eligible young man and woman aboard wanted that honor.

"Do you think Dan could handle that responsibility?" Valery asked, sliding a hand around the back of Larry's neck.

Not as well as I can, he answered silently.

"As Chairman, you can marry me," she said.

"Val..."

"Don't send me to Dan. Please. It's you I want."

I CAN do a better job than he would. And marry Val.

"Larry, do I have to beg you?" She leaned her cheek against his. It felt wet. Tears.

"But it's wrong," he muttered. "It's like kicking my best friend when he's down."

"It's the only chance you've got, Larry. We all need you, everybody aboard the ship. You're the best one to be Chairman, everybody knows that. And I need you! I can't live without you!"

He closed his eyes and heard himself saying, "All right. I'll do it. I'll do it."

[3]

The ship was built on the principle of wheels within wheels. It consisted of seven ring structures, starting from a central bulbous hub. Going outward, each ring was bigger and held more room for equipment and living space. The entire ship was turning, revolving slowly, to provide an artifical gravity. The outermost wheel, level one, was at one full Earth *g*, and everyone felt his normal Earth weight there. Going "upward," toward the hub, weight and gravity fell off consistently, until at the hub itself, there was effectively no gravity, weightlessness.

The thousand or so people who were awake and active had their living quarters in level one. All the levels were linked by tubes.

The infirmary was on the second level, where the spin-induced gravity was slightly less than 1 *g*. It made for an unconscious buoyant feeling, a sense of well-being and optimism, that the medics claimed helped to get patients recovered from their ailments.

The infirmary stretched over a long section of the second level. Instead of viewports looking outside, the main wall of the infirmary was made up of viewscreens that showed constantly changing pictures of Earth; old Earth, before the bursting population had torn down most of her forests, ripped open her mineral-rich lands, covered vast stretches of ground with festering cities.

Dan Christopher was sitting up in his infirmary bed, floating lightly on the liquid-filled mattress. He had drifted in and out of sleep several times this morning. When he had first been awakened for his morning check by the automated sensor system at his bedside, the scene on the wall screens outside his plastiglass-walled cubicle had shown an impossible blue sky and a vista of rugged white mountains dotted by patches of green, under a gleaming sun.

Dan knew that the sun was a star, but it didn't look like any star he had ever seen. Now, later in the morning, the scene was a deep green forest, where the sunlight filtered down in dusty shafts and strange four-legged animals tip-toed warily through the underbrush.

Wasting electrical power to show these scenes, he told himself. Dan still felt woozy, as much from the medicines they had been filling him with as from the dreams that haunted his sleep. The medics had pumped him full of tranquilizers, he guessed. But underneath their flat calming effect he knew there was a core of terror and rage inside him.

He's dead. The man who gave us this ship, the man who started this mission, the man who gave me life. The most important man aboard. Dead. A couple of months before we're due to reach our destination. A couple of months before he'd be reawakened and I'd get to really know him. Now he's dead.

Two nurses walked briskly past his cubicle, chatting together. Dan paid no attention to them. The chief medic would be here soon. Dan wanted to get out of the infirmary.

A tapping on his door snapped him fully awake. Through the plastiglass he saw Joe Haller: solid, dependable Joe. A good engineer and a good friend. Joe's long hair and beard turned off many of the older people, but he was one of the most reliable and brightest men aboard. Next to Larry, Joe was Dan's best and longest friend.

Dan waved him in, and Joe opened the plastiglass door and stepped into the cramped cubicle. There was no room for a chair, so he simply stood next to Dan's bed.

"How're you feeling?" he asked.

Dan said, "Good enough. I've got to get out of here today. How long have I been here?"

"This is the third day."

Dan could feel a shock race through him. "Three days? Then the Council meeting..."

"It's over. They picked Larry as Chairman."

"Larry!"

Joe shrugged and evaded looking straight into Dan's eyes. "Larry was there, you weren't. I don't know what went on before the meeting, what Larry did to convince them. The rumble is that Larry let them know he wanted to be Chairman, and as long as you were too sick to depend on, he ought to have the job."

Dan sagged back in the bed.

Looking worried, Joe added "They . . . uh, they held services for the people who died in the fire—yesterday."

"Yesterday."

"Yeah."

"My father too? They didn't wait . . ."

"Everybody. One single service. Their remains went into the hydroponics tank."

"They couldn't wait for me?"

Joe shrugged and looked away.

Dan reached up and grabbed his wrist. "They couldn't wait a day or two for me to be there?" he shouted. "For my own father!"

"Larry decided . . ."

"Larry!"

"Listen," Joe said, his voice suddenly low and urgent. "I know you and Larry have been friends since you were kids. But he sure isn't acting like a friend of yours right now."

Dan let himself sink slowly back into the yielding warmth of the bed again. He could feel his heart racing. Deliberately, he took a deep, calming breath.

"I've got to be calm," he said, his voice steady now. "If I get excited, the medics will trank me again. If I show them I'm calm and relaxed, then they'll let me out."

Joe looked at him for a moment. "What're you going to do when you get out?"

"I don't know," Dan said. "Something . . . but I don't know what."

Joe left shortly afterward. Dan held himself rigidly under control, not speaking, not moving, trying to not even think. He concentrated on the sensor screens next to his bed. Keep those luminous traces as calm and steady as you can. Watch them wiggle across the screens; heartbeat, blood pressure, alpha wave, respiration, basal metabolism. Calm and steady. Calm and steady. Stare at them, let them hypnotize you. *Feel* your heart muscle working inside you. Slower. Slower. Calm. Steady.

He fell asleep watching the screens. And he dreamed. Dreamed of the luminous lines worming across the screens; they were ropes, they were snakes, twining around him, choking him, crushing him. But then he was watching from somewhere far off as the glowing snakes squeezed the life out of someone else. His father! Himself!

He woke screaming.

"The more I think about it, the more glad I am that we voted you Chairman," said Dr. Loring.

Larry Belsen was sitting in the main room of the Lorings' quarters. Valery sat next to him on the foldout couch. Her father was comfortably sunk in the depths of a webchair. Every time he moved, the plastic webbing creaked; Larry was afraid it would give way under his weight.

Dr. Loring was one of the twelve oldest men awake, and thus was a permanent member of the Council. He had been a child when the ship had left Earth, and had never undergone deepsleep. "I want to see it all, from beginning to end," he often said. The Council balanced age, tradition and stability against youth, vigor and change. The twelve oldest people awake were permanent members. The remaining Council seats were filled by younger men and women, and the Chairman was always elected from the younger generation, for a one-year term.

"Yes, you'll be a good Chairman, Lawrence, my boy," Dr. Loring went one. "Frankly, I always had my doubts about Dan..." he glanced at his daughter, "...as far as being Chairman is concerned. Too emotional. That's not bad in some aspects of life, of course, but as Chairman..."

Valery smiled at the old man. "Dad, you've told us the same thing three times now."

"Oh? Really? Well..." He shook his head, looking slightly embarrassed. Dr. Loring was a heavy man, big-boned and round with paunch. He was nearly bald, nothing but scraggly white tufts of hair sticking out around his ears. His eyes were big and moist and always blinking. Larry thought of him sometimes as a frog who'd been turned into a prince...fifty years ago.

Dr. Loring turned in his webchair, producing a chorus of groans from the plastic, and called to his wife: "What about dinner?"

She was standing in the kitchen alcove, thoughtfully

watching the bank of dials set alongside the eye-level oven.

"I'm trying to time everything so that it's all done together, and everything will be hot when we sit down. . . . Valery, you can fold out the table and set places."

As Val got up, Dr. Loring complained, "It was a lot easier when the microwave ovens were working. This business of using heat for cooking . . . it's barbaric."

Larry said, "We just can't afford the electrical power for microwave cooking until the main generator's back on the line."

"Hmmph. There's another thing about Dan. How long has that generator been out? It's his responsibility. . . ."

"Now don't go blaming him," Larry said strongly. "It's not his fault. Nobody aboard ship knows much about the generator. . . . Dan's had to train himself and a special crew just to get ready to tackle the job."

Dr. Loring mumbled, "Well it's been a long-enough time, certainly."

"They've got to be very careful," Larry insisted. "Joe Haller's going through the computer core for instructions about the generator. If they goof, you know, we'll be in real trouble."

"Don't get so upset, dear," Mrs. Loring said. "Dinner's ready at last . . . I think," she added.

The meal was fine. The vegetables and fruits came from the ship's hydroponics gardens; the synthetic meat came from the biochemists' "ranch," where nutrients and enzymes and other special chemicals were put together to form a constantly-growing blob that had all the nourishment of real organic protein. No one awake had ever tased actual meat from a real animal, except in dimly remembered childhood, but the biochemists insisted that their synthetics tased "just like steak . . . even better."

Larry found that he was getting more and more nervous as the meal went on. *Got to tell them about us sooner or late,* he kept saying to himself. But the dinner-table conversation kept rolling along, and he couldn't find an excuse to bring the subject around to himself and Valery.

He kept glancing at Valery, waiting for her to say something, to help him get started. But she looked more amused at his consternation than anything else.

As usual, Dr. Loring was doing most of the talking. Ordinarily, Larry could let the old man's rambling speeches go in one ear and out the other; but tonight he was getting edgy. *Damn, I wish he'd shut up for a minute!*

It was Mrs. Loring who finally came to his rescue. She was the model from which Valery got her looks. Even at her age, she still looked lovely, strong, vital. Her hair was still the same sun-gold as Valery's; her eyes sparkled the same way.

She laid a hand on her husband's arm and said, interrupting him, "Dear, why don't we have some wine with our dessert? Is there still some left in that bottle you made?"

He looked at her, puzzled, for a moment. "H'mm? Uh, why yes... but..."

"I know we save it for special occasions," Mrs. Loring said, "but this is a special occasion, isn't it? After all, it's not every day that we elect a new Chairman."

As Dr. Loring pushed his chair back from the table, Larry took the opportunity:

"It's a double occasion.... Valery and I want to get married." He said it as quickly as he could.

"What? Married..." Dr. Loring blinked at him.

Mrs. Loring didn't seem surprised at all. "Why, that's marvelous. And now that you're Chairman, you don't have to be hemmed in by all those silly computer rules, do you?"

Dr. Loring broke into a huge grin and grabbed Larry's hand. Pumping it hard enough to shake the table, he said heartily, "Congratulations. I'm very glad... *very* glad!"

Larry felt a thousand kilos lighter. He looked at Valery. Her mother kissed her cheek. They were both beaming.

"The wine," Dr. Loring said, finally letting go of Larry's hand. "Yes, by heaven, this *is* a special occasion." He got up from the table and waddled back toward the kitchen alcove. Opening a closet door, he muttered, "It's in here someplace."

"I'm very happy for the two of you," Mrs. Loring said quietly. "I know that Valery thinks the world of Dan—but you were her first choice."

Larry grinned foolishly, but inwardly he was thinking about Dan. *First the Chairmanship, now Valery. He's going to hate me. And I don't blame him.*

Valery said, "I've been thinking... maybe it would be best if we didn't tell Dan about... us. Not yet. He's upset enough right now."

Mrs. Loring nodded. "Yes, you're right."

"I don't know..." Larry started to object.

Valery turned to him and smiled her prettiest. "Please, Larry. It wouldn't be fair to Dan to hit him with this. Not just now."

"But it's not fair to let him think..."

"Let me handle it," she said.

"Well..."

"Please?"

He melted. "All right. But don't let him think the wrong thing for too long. It'll just get worse, the longer we wait."

"I know how to handle him," Valery said.

Dr. Loring pulled a green bottle from the bottom of the closet. "Ahah!" He held the bottle up by the neck. "Not much left, but enough to toast the happy couple."

Larry smiled, even though he didn't feel particularly happy at that moment.

(4)

Dan Christopher floated in nearly perfect weightlessness in the bulbous plastiglass observation blister at the ship's hub.

There was no up and down; or rather, any direction could be up or down, depending on your own point of view. At the moment, Dan was gazing out at a particularly bright star. It stood out among the millions of stars that were sprinkled like gleaming powder across the infinite black of space. Looking closely at it, Dan could see that it was actually two stars: the two main members of the triple star system, Alpha Centauri. Their destination.

Far, far behind the ship—nearly forty trillion kilometers, if you were silly enough to express interstellar distance that way—lay the sun, and Earth.

It was cold in the observation blister. The death-cold of emptiness seeped through the plastiglass. Dan pulled his electrically heated robe tighter around him.

"The dreams," he muttered to himself. "If only I could stop the dreams."

He had told no one about them. The medics hadn't wanted to release him from the infirmary, but he had argued them into it. He was perfectly healthy, except for the dreams. And in the week since his father's death, he had steeled himself to dream without screaming, without even tossing in his sleep. *Your mind controls your body,* he told himself. *Your mind can make your body do anything.*

All the anger and terror was buried inside him now, seething inside. But no one could tell it was there, not even the medics, although they hadn't been happy about releasing him.

Dan heard a hatch sigh open behind him. He turned, and in the dimness of the blister's anti-reflection lights, made out the sturdy form of Joe Haller. He was upside-down as he came through the hatch. He drifted that way in midair as he floated toward Dan, slowly righting himself in the last few meters as he approached.

"So this is where you are," Joe said.

"This is where I am."

"I went to see you at the infirmary, but they told me you'd been released. I've been searching the ship for an hour...."

"I came up here to think," Dan said quietly.

"Geez, it's cold in here...wish we could get the main generator back on the line. We're going to need it when we get to Alpha C."

"Will the work be done by then?"

"Think so...if we don't run into any major snags."

Dan nodded. Then, "What caused the generator's failure? Have you found that out yet?"

"Old age, more'n anything else. You just don't run a machine for fifty years without wearing it out. Even if it doesn't have any moving parts."

"Wasn't it overhauled regularly?"

"Sure...but still, some of the electrical connections and the insulation hasn't been changed since day one."

Dan thought for a moment, then asked, "Is there any evidence of...tampering?"

"Tampering?"

"Deliberate damage. Sabotage."

Even in the dim lighting, he could see Joe's mouth hang open. "Sabotage? Who in hell would do a thing like that?"

"You found no evidence."

"Nobody looked for any. We're just in there to get the damned thing fixed, not play detective."

"Then the generator could have been deliberately knocked out."

Joe shook his head, a motion that made his body drift away slightly in the zero gravity. "Who'd want to do that? It's like slitting your own throat. We all need that electrical power...."

Dan turned away from him and looked back at the stars. At the double star, close, beckoning.

"One thing leads to another," he said. "The generator blows out. This puts an extra load on the auxiliary power units. The circuits in the cryonics section overheat. A fire starts. My father dies. I get hospitalized. The Council elects a new Chairman...."

"Do you realize what you're saying?" Joe's voice was barely audible, shocked.

Dan nodded grimly. "That's why I'm speaking softly, and saying it here, and only to you. If I had anything more than a few bad dreams, a few ugly thoughts—I'd be screaming it over the intercom system and going after the murderers with any weapon I could lay my hands on."

"Murderers? Dan—that's crazy!"

"Is it? Is it really?"

Joe didn't answer, merely shook his head.

"In another two months we'll be in orbit around the major planet of Alpha Centauri," Dan said. "Key people among the cryosleepers will be awakened. My father—who was in charge of this when the voyage started—would have naturally resumed command..."

"No, the Chairman elected by the Council would be in charge."

"I would have been that Chairman! But Larry's taken it over. He took it while I was locked in the infirmary. And after my father died."

Joe actually backed away from him now. "Dan...you're accusing Larry...my god, he lost his father in the fire, too."

"I'm not accusing anyone," Dan replied, barely controlling the heat he felt within himself. "Not yet. There's no proof of anything. But it looks rotten to me, Joe, and I'm going to find out if I'm right or wrong."

"How?"

"I don't know.... I'll need help. Your help."

"Doing what?"

Dan grimaced. "Watching. Looking for evidence. I ... could be all wrong, I know that. But—Joe, I can't sleep, not until I'm certain that this is all a nightmare, or..." his voice hardened, "... or, I find the proof and punish the murderer."

"Murder," Joe whispered back to him. "Do you really think somebody aboard the ship could...murder?"

"I don't know. I wish I did."

* * *

Larry sat nervously at the head of the long Council table.

The Council members were filing into the narrow room, in twos and threes. Dr. Loring took his seat close to Larry, smiling at him. *Trying to make me feel at ease.* The permanent members were seated in the even-numbered chairs. The younger temporary members sat between them, heads of thick dark hair, or blond, or red, alternating with the grays, whites, and bald heads of the older generation. Of the twenty-four Council members, nine were women.

The table was almost filled when Dan Christopher and Joe Haller came in together.

Larry felt a flash of surprise go through him. Then he rose from his chair and went down along the table to Dan.

"Hey, it's good to see you back on your feet again," he said, putting out his hand. "How do you feel?"

Dan shook Larry's hand without enthusiasm. "I'm all right," he answered.

"I didn't know you'd be out of the infirmary today," Larry apologized. "I was going to visit you. I did drop in once, but they told me you were sleeping."

"I'm fine now," Dan said.

And sore as hell, Larry realized. "Look . . . uh, why don't we get together after this meeting and talk. There's a lot we ought to hash over."

Dan nodded. "Okay."

Feeling even shakier than before, Larry went back to the Chairman's seat and opened the meeting. He let the automatic procedures of every meeting smooth over his nervousness, and sat there listening to his pulse beating in his eardrums as the minutes of the previous meeting flashed on the wall screen at the far end of the long, narrow room.

They rumbled through old business, and listened to Joe Haller's report on progress with the generator. Adrienne Kaufman, head of the Genetics Section, recommended that the Council offer its official expression of sympathy for those who lost family members in the recent fire. Larry glanced at Dan while the unanimous vote was made; Dan was staring at him, his eyes ablaze.

Then came new business, and Larry heard himself saying:

"As you know, we'll be in the Alpha Centauri system in about two months. Our trajectory will bring us to a point where we fly-by the major planet. At some point before our closest approach, we must decide if we want to decelerate and take up orbit around the planet, or continue onward and out of the Centauri system. So it's time for us to begin a serious review of what's known about the planets and to consider launching our remote probes, to gather more data on them."

Pressing a stud set into the tabletop before him, Larry said, "Here's the best holo of the major planet that we have, taken by the original probe from Earth, nearly a century ago."

The wall screen seemed to dissolve. In its place, deep space itself took form, with stars hanging everywhere, and a fat, yellowish ball of a planet sitting in the middle of the emptiness.

"Dr. Loring, could you review what's known about the major planet?" Larry asked.

"Not terribly much, I'm afraid," Loring began in his most pedantic style. "That primitive probe was woefully small, and a horrendous communications problem—transmitting holographic data over more than four light-years is no simple problem, believe me! And, of course, the men who launched the probe weren't considering settling down on the Centaurian planets to live. In fact, they didn't even know there were any planets in the Alpha Centauri system when the probe was launched."

"All right," said one of the other elder Councilmen. "Now how about telling us what we *do* know?"

"Certainly, certainly," Dr. Loring replied. "I won't even discuss the minor planet...it's airless, bare rock, baked by the big star, Alpha Centauri A...which, as you know is almost exactly like the sun. I don't foresee any radiation problems for us from A...and star B is small and cool, no problems there either. No worries about high fluxes of ultraviolet or x-rays and such. Now Proxima—the third star of the system—is so dim and so far away that it will look like an ordinary star up in the sky. No influence on the planet at all."

"What about the planet itself?" Adrienne Kaufman asked sharply.

"Oh, yes...Frankly, it's not going to be paradise. The white clouds you see flecking the surface are water vapor, all right, and the temperature range of the planet should permit liquid water on its surface. But, as you can see, that surface is mostly yellow-green. Watery planets, such as Earth, tend to look blue."

"What is the yellow-green stuff?"

Loring shrugged elaborately. "I wish I could tell you. The spectroscopic data returned by the original probe was very scant. I've been doing additional work with our equipment in the hub, but it's still very skimpy data. There's no evidence yet of liquid water on the surface. The planet's density appears to be rather high, judging from the orbits of its little moonlets. Its surface gravity might be as high as $1\frac{1}{2}\,g$ ... certainly no lower than 1.2. Anyone standing on that planet is going to feel heavier than he does now by 20 to 50 percent."

"That could make life unpleasant."

The chief medic said, "It could make life impossible for us on the surface. Human beings can't live normal, active lives under a continuous 1.5-g load. It would ruin your back, your abdominal wall, your feet and legs."

"But the data's so sketchy...."

Larry took over. "It's very sketchy, and it could be wrong, too. I think we ought to launch our own probes as soon as possible, and start to get more detailed and reliable information."

There was a general murmur of agreement.

Dan Christopher spoke up. "What happens if we find that the planet is as bad as we fear?"

Silence. Everyone turned to look at Dan, sitting down at the far end of the table, then one by one they turned back to look at Larry for an answer.

Larry hiked his eyebrows. "We'd have two possible alternatives. Either stay in orbit and live in the ship until we can raise a generation of children who are genetically altered so that they're suited for life on the planet's surface ... or keep going and look for another star with a more Earthlike planet."

"Which would you recommend, in such a case?" Dan asked.

Larry sensed danger, a trap. "It's much too early to try to answer that question," he said slowly. "There are too many variables, too many unknowns."

Joe Haller said, "Truthfully, I wouldn't want to bet on this bucket of transistors making it much farther than Alpha Centauri."

"And we know nothing at all about possible Earthlike planets around other stars," Dr. Loring pointed out.

"Then we've got to stay at Alpha Centauri and modify our children to live on the major planet," Dan said.

Larry found himself shaking his head. "We don't know yet. There's a chance that we won't be able to do that, even if we want to. And to expect the rest of us to live out our lives here in the ship while we're raising children who'll leave us and go live on the surface . . . well, I think we might run into some psychological problems there."

"Wouldn't there be psychological problems connected with sailing off for some unknown destination?" Dan asked.

"Yes, sure, but . . ." Larry stopped himself. *Why does he want to start an argument?* "Look, there's no sense talking about this until we have some data back from the close-up probes."

Emile Polanyi, chief of the engineering department, said in a deep voice that still carried traces of old Europe, "We can launch the probes after a few days' checkout. They are capable of high acceleration, and could be in orbit around the major planet in a few weeks."

"What about landing on the planet itself?" Dan asked.

"The probes are equipped with instrument packages that can be soft-landed on the surface."

"Good. We ought to begin the checkout at once," said Dan.

Only then did Larry realize what was happening. *He's trying to take the meeting away from me. He's trying to show everyone that he's in charge, no matter who they elected Chairman.*

(5)

The meeting ended.

Much more swiftly than they had drifted into the meeting room, the Council members cleared out. Larry watched them leave, all of them except Dan. Finally he was alone in the room except for Dan. They sat at opposite ends of the table staring at each other.

I've known him all my life, Larry thought, *and now he's a stranger.*

He got up from his seat and forced himself to walk down along the table to where Dan was sitting.

"I guess you *do* feel okay," Larry said, putting on a smile. He sat on the edge of the table, next to Dan's chair. "You sure made yourself heard."

Dan was slouched back in his seat. He looked up at Larry and asked, "Why'd you get yourself elected Chairman? We agreed that I'd take it this year."

"I know," Larry said, feeling rotten. "You ... well, you were laid up in the infirmary, no telling how long you'd be there. The medics kept saying you were okay physically, but emotionally ..."

"So you stepped in."

"Yes."

"And being Chairman gives you the right to marry Valery, too, doesn't it?"

God, he can see right through me!

"Don't tell me that never entered your head," Dan insisted.

Keeping his voice steady, Larry answered, "You know we've both been in love with Val since we were kids...."

"The Lorings raised all three of us. But we're not playing brothers and sister anymore. Are you going to marry Val?"

"That's . . . up to her," Larry said.

"She's promised to me!"

"Computer selection. That's not final."

Dan's eyes flared, but he said only, "You're willing to let her make the decision between us?"

"Yes."

"All right."

Larry felt the breath sag out of him in relief.

But Dan went on, "Have you appointed a board of inquiry to investigate the fire?"

"Board of . . . no, we have the report of Mort Campbell's Damage Control group. That's enough. What good would a board of inquiry do?"

Straightening up in his chair, Dan said, "The cause of the fire should be investigated. Fifty people died, and we should know why. Somebody's responsible; accidents have causes."

Feeling bewildered, Larry said, "We know why. The circuits were overloaded, the insulation gave. . . ."

Dan banged a hand on the tabletop. "I want a full investigation! With a formal board of inquiry. And I want to head that board. If you won't set it up, I'll call for it at the next Council meeting."

"But that would be like slapping Mort Campbell in the face. After all, he's in charge of Life Support. . . ."

"I don't give a damn about Campbell!" Dan shouted. "Will you appoint a board or do I have to get the Council to do it?"

Larry felt ice-chilled inside. *Another try to get the Council under his own control.* "All right," he said slowly. "I'll appoint a board. You can even be its head. But you won't find anything that hasn't already been found."

"Maybe." Dan pulled himself out of the chair and strode to the door without another word or a backward glance. The door slid shut behind him with a click.

Larry sat there alone in the Council room for several minutes. Then he went back to his own seat and punched out a phone number on the tabletop keyboard.

"Infirmary," said a pretty nurse. Her face was ballooned many times larger than life on the wall screen.

"Give me the chief psychotech, please."

"Dr. Hsai? I'm afraid he's busy at the moment. . . ."

"See if you can interrupt him, will you? This is the Chairman; I must speak to him right away."

"Oh . . . yessir, I'll try."

The screen went blank for a moment while a part of Larry's mind smiled a little. *Rank hath its privileges.* The features of a thin-faced oriental in his thirties appeared on the screen.

"Mr. Belsen, what can I do for you?"

"I'm sorry to bother you, Doctor, but this is important. I'm worried about Dan Christopher . . . he's acting . . . well, strange."

Hsai made an understanding face. "Yes, that is to be expected. He feels the loss of his father very deeply, you know."

"Too deeply, do you think?"

The doctor smiled. "To paraphrase a venerable adage; How deep is too deep?"

Larry hesitated for a moment, then decided to say it. "Deep enough to unbalance him."

"Ahhh . . . I see. You feel he is unstable?"

"He's acting strangely, Doctor. Making veiled accusations. He wants to investigate the accident in which his father died. He talks as if he thinks somebody caused the fire deliberately."

"Really?"

"Really."

Hsai thought for a moment. "Well, I had planned to check on him within a few days. Perhaps I had better make it sooner. And deeper."

"I'd appreciate knowing what the results are."

"Eh, the doctor-patient relationship . . ."

"Yes, I know. But Dan can be a very influential member of the Council. It's important that I know whether or not we can trust his judgment."

"I see. Well, I suppose I can give you some feeling in that regard without violating any sacred oaths."

"I'd appreciate it."

"Very well, Mr. Chairman. I shall see him tomorrow."

"Thank you, Doctor."

Larry's office, as chief of the Command and Control section, was actually a cubbyhole set between the ship's bridge and the computer center. Barely big enough for a desk and a small wall-screen viewer, the office was well suited for someone who was frightened of crowds and open spaces—or for someone who hated to spend much time at a desk and preferred to be moving around the ship.

Larry went into his office and sat at the desk. Suddenly he was very tired. He ran a weary hand over his brow.

A tap at the door.

"Come in."

It was Dr. Loring. "I am interrupting something?"

"No, not at all," Larry said. "Sit down." He gestured to the only other chair in the room.

Loring's bulk seemed to make the walls bulge outward. He squeezed around the plastic chair and then plopped down on it. Larry winched as the metal legs seemed to sag.

"I wanted to congratulate you . . . you ran a good meeting, despite certain, ah—interferences."

Larry nodded absently. "You know," he mused, "I hadn't really understood until today how likely it is that the planet we're heading for *won't* be suitable to live on."

"Yes. That would be a disappointment."

"Disappointment?" Larry swiveled his chair around to face Dr. Loring directly. "It'll be a catastrophe. It'll mean rethinking the whole purpose of this voyage. Do we really want to stay at a world that's not like Earth, and change our children into . . . into something different from us?"

"Frankly, I don't see any alternative," Loring confessed. "We don't know of any better planets elsewhere."

"Well, we'd better start looking," Larry said firmly. "I don't like being put in a corner. I want to have some choice as to whether we stay at Alpha Centauri or not."

Loring looked mildly shocked. "You're serious? You would actually consider going farther?"

Larry nodded.

"But . . . everyone on the ship thinks that our voyage is almost over."

"I know," Larry said. "It might be just beginning."

Dr. Loring shook his head, making his heavy jowls quiver. "The people won't like it. They are not emotionally prepared for going farther. The ship isn't built to . . ."

"The ship can be repaired, overhauled. The people—well, the people will make the final decision, I guess. But I'd like them to understand the alternatives. Or at least to *have* an alternative to Alpha Centauri."

"We don't have the equipment on board to study planets of other stars from the ship. We can barely make out details of the major Centaurian planet, as it is."

"Then you'll have to build the equipment," Larry said.

"In two months? I'm . . ."

"You've got less time than that," Larry said, his voice hard and cold as plastisteel. "I want to be getting some data before we're forced to settle into an orbit around the major planet."

For once, Loring was speechless. He sat there open-mouthed, blinking wetly.

"You'll get all the help you need," Larry said. "I'll see to that. But I want evidence of other Earthlike planets. They've got to be out there somewhere."

"Why? Because you want them to exist?"

Larry could feel his teeth clenching. He forced himself to stay as calm as possible while answering, "No . . . it's not just that. I don't want to see my children altered to live on an inhuman world. Val's children. Your grandchildren."

Dr. Loring was silent for a long moment. Then, "He's called her, you know."

"Dan?"

"Yes. He wants to have dinner with her tonight."

"She agreed?"

"Yes. I expect she'll tell him about her decision to marry you."

With a shake of his head, Larry replied, "No, I don't think so. He's been through enough recently; I don't think Val will want to add that to his troubles."

"But she's got to!" Dr. Loring's face started to redden. "Otherwise . . . she can't let him think . . ."

"I know," Larry said. "I know. But I'm afraid that Dan's right on the edge of a real mental crackup. He's like a man who's gone outside and tethered himself to the level one wheel. He's spinning around and around . . . and the more he spins, the wilder he feels."

It had been a quiet, tense dinner. Valery and Dan had eaten in the ship's main autocafeteria, in one of the shadowy little booths far away from the main dining area and the pickup lines with their crowds and noise.

They had said very little. Val looked beautiful but very serious in a red jumpsuit. Dan was dark and silent in a black coverall.

Now they were walking down a quiet corridor, back toward Dan's quarters, a one-room compartment exactly like Larry's. It even had one of Val's paintings on its wall.

"You've decided on Larry, haven't you?" Dan asked abruptly.

She stopped walking, right there in the middle of the nearly deserted corridor. "I think so. I told him yes."

He took her arm and resumed walking; she had to quicken her former pace to keep up with him. Without looking down at her, he asked, "You love him?"

"I love you both. You know that."

"But you want to marry him."

"He...he's asked me to."

"And you want your children to be the Chairman's son and daughter."

"No, it's not that!"

"And if I were Chairman?"

Valery shook her head. "You're not."

"I could be."

"No...not now. Larry has it and they'll re-elect him. You won't get another chance."

Still looking straight ahead, he asked, "Suppose he's voted out? Even before his first year's over?"

"What?" She stopped again and pulled her arm free. "What are you saying, Dan?"

With a shrug, he answered, "Chairmen have been voted out before their terms were up. When the Council decides that the Chairman can't handle the job. Or when they think there's a better man available."

"Don't try it," Valery said earnestly. "You'll be hurting Larry and you'll be hurting yourself even more."

"I deserve to be Chairman," Dan insisted. "But more than that—much more!—I want you. I love you, Val. I've always loved you. I'd tear this ship apart to get you, if I had to."

"Oh, Dan...don't...please..."

He reached out and took her into his arms. "You're not going to marry Larry or anybody else. Only me. You think you've made up your mind, but just wait. By the time we go into orbit around the planet out there, you'll see everything differently. You'll see."

Something in her head was telling Valery to push free of him, but something even stronger made her stay in his arms. Looking up into his intent, deadly serious face, she said, "Dan . . . don't make me come between you and Larry. You've been friends. . . ." It sounded pathetically weak, even while she was saying it.

"Larry might have murdered my father."

"*What?*" In sudden amazement, she did push out of his grasp.

"I don't think that fire was an accident. Somebody caused it. Larry benefited from it."

"Dan, that's insane! Larry's own father . . ."

"What'll you think when I prove it?" Dan said, his voice rising to nearly a shout. "Would you like to be married to a murderer?"

"Dan, stop it!"

"Well, would you?"

Valery turned suddenly and began running back down the corridor, the way they had just come.

"Val . . . wait . . ." He raced after her, caught her arm.

"I'm going home!" She pulled her arm free. "If you have any sense of decency at all you'll never mention such a crazy thing again. Do you understand? Not to me or anyone else!"

She left him standing there, looking suddenly alone and helpless—and yet, as Valery glanced back toward him, Dan also seemed darkly resolved, strong and purposeful. She shuddered. Larry, a murderer? It was insane. But . . . that meant that Dan was—insane!

Which was it?

And with a final helping of horror, Valery realized, *Whichever it is, I've helped to cause it!*

Dan watched her hurry down the corridor, knowing that he had driven her away.

Maybe I am crazy, he said to himself. *How could Larry . . . he couldn't, not Larry!*

But another part of his mind droned with remorseless logic:

*Someone caused the fire. Someone killed fifty people and kept
you from your rightful position as Chairman. Someone wants to
change everything, have everything his own way.*

Feeling sick and confused and more angry with himself than
anyone else, Dan made his way back to his own quarters.

It wasn't until he had dropped onto his bunk that he noticed
his viewscreen had MESSAGE WAITING written in glowing yellow
letters across it.

He sat up on the bunk and punched the yellow button among
the cluster on the keyboard beside the screen. The face of a
young man appeared on the screen. Dan couldn't quite place
him; he knew he had seen him before, but didn't know him
personally.

"I'm Ross Cranston, from the computer section. I have a
private message for Dan Christopher. I'll be in my quarters until
first shift starts tomorrow morning."

The taped message faded from the screen. Puzzled, Dan
touched the green button and said, "Get me Ross Cranston,
please."

The computer-directed phone circuits answered with nothing
but a faint hum. Then the same face appeared on the screen.

He looked just a little startled. "Oh...you're Dan Christopher, aren't you?"

"That's right," Dan said. "You wanted to speak to me."

Cranston said, "Yes. But not on the phone. Are you busy?
Can I come to your quarters...or you can come to mine."

"What's this all about?" Dan asked.

Nervously, Cranston answered, "I'd rather...it'd be better
to talk in private."

"About what?" Dan insisted.

"Your father."

Dan was instantly taut with tension. "I'll come to your place.
What's the number?"

Ten minutes later Dan was tapping on Cranston's door.
Politeness dictated a light tap with the fingernails; the
compartments were all small enough for that sort of noise to be
heard instantly, and it didn't disturb the next compartment, just
a few steps away. But something in Dan wanted to pound on the
door with both fists.

Cranston slid the door open. He was much shorter than Dan:

sandy hair, worn long; roundish face, too puffy for a young man but not yet really fat. Nervous, light brown eyes darting everywhere.

"What's this all about?" Dan said as he stepped into the compartment. It was like all the other living quarters, except that Cranston had covered its walls with graphs and odd-looking sketches that appeared to be printouts of computer-directed drawings.

Cranston gestured Dan to a chair. He himself pulled a large pillow off his bunk, let it drop to the floor, and then sat on it cross-legged.

"I'm with the computer section," he began.

"You said that on the phone."

"Yes. Well, earlier today we were running routine statistical checks, inputting those fifty deaths so the computer could keep its memory banks up to date..."

Dan felt his insides churning. "And?"

"Well... when we input your father's name, a special subroutine must've been triggered. We got a message."

"A message?"

Cranston nodded. "It's kind of strange.... I'm not even sure what it means. But I thought you ought to know about it."

"What did it say?" Every nerve in Dan's body was tightening.

Cranston reached lazily up to his desk, beside him. "Here, I had a paper copy made."

Dan snatched the flimsy paper scrap from his hand. He looked at it, shook his head, and looked at it again. It said:

PRTY SBRTN 7, PRM MMRY 2337-99-1

"It's gibberish."

"No," Cranston said. "It's just a shorthand that computer programmers used around the time when the ship began the voyage. I checked that much."

"Then what's it mean?"

"If I'm right—and I think I am—it means that there's a priority subroutine number seven, in one of the prime memory banks. Those prime banks date back to the beginning of the voyage."

"What do the numbers mean?"

"It's some sort of code index, to tell us where the subroutine's located."

Suddenly Dan's temper exploded. "Subroutine, code index, memory banks... what the hell are you talking about? Speak English!"

Cranston actually backed away from him. "Okay... okay, it's simple enough. It looks to me like somebody put a special priority message of some sort into one of the earliest memory banks in the computer. The message was to be read out only in the event of your father's death, because the computer didn't tell us the message existed until we told the computer he had died."

"A message from my father?" Dan's pulse was going wild now. "Could he have suspected... did he *know*...?"

Cranston was staring at him quizzically.

Dan grabbed the computer tech by his coverall shirtfront. "You find that message, do you hear? Find it as quickly as you can! But don't tell anyone else about it. Not a soul!"

"O... okay... whatever you say...."

"How quickly can you get it for me?"

Pulling free of Dan's grip, Cranston said, "I dunno... hard to say. A day or two... if I have to keep it a secret from everybody else, maybe a few days."

"Get it as fast as you can," Dan repeated. "And not a word to *anybody*. Understand?"

"Yeah... sure..."

"All right then." Dan got up and strode out of the compartment, leaving the computer tech squatting there on the floor, looking dazed and more than a little frightened, slowly smoothing his rumpled shirtfront.

A message from my father, Dan told himself. *He must have known what was going to happen to him!*

(6)

The bridge crackled with excitement.

Larry stood at his usual post, behind the curving bank of desk consoles and the seated technicians who operated them. Viewscreens flickered, showing every part of the ship, the pulsebeat of every system.

For an instant the whole bridge was silent, the silence of tense expectation. Everyone was holding his or her breath; the only sounds were the faint whispering of the air fans and the slight electrical murmur of the consoles.

Larry stood rooted behind one of the techs, watching a viewscreen on her console that showed the long glistening cylinders of four automated rocket probes. A red numeral 10 glowed on the screen, down on its lower right corner.

"Still holding at minus ten seconds," the tech muttered.

Another tech, at the next desk, added, "All systems still in the green."

On the desk just to the left of where Larry stood was a viewscreen display of a computer-drawn star map. Dozens of pinpoints of light were scattered across it. Off to one side of the screen, one of the pinpoints was blinking. This represented their target, the major planet of Alpha Centauri. It was moving across the screen, heading for a dotted circle drawn in the middle of the map.

Larry watched the map. The blinking dot reached the circle and stopped there.

"Acquisition," said the tech at that console. "We're in the launch window."

The numerals on the picture of the probes began to tick downward: nine, eight, seven . . .

"Launchers primed and ready." A light on a console went from amber to green.

"...six, five..."

"Probes on internal power."

"...four, three, two..."

"Hatch open."

Larry could see that the metal hatch in front of the probes had slid away, revealing the stars outside.

"...one, zero."

"Launch!"

The four cylinders slid smoothly away and disappeared in an eyeblink into the darkness of space.

"Radar plot," a voice said crisply. "On course. Ignition on schedule.... All four of 'em are on their way."

Larry didn't realize he had been holding his breath until he let it out in a long, relieved sigh. The technicians whooped triumphantly, turned to each other with grins and handshakes and backpoundings. The girls got kissed.

"They're off and running," one of the techs said to Larry. Neither of them knew where the phrase had come from, but it sounded right for the occasion.

He stood in the center of the celebrating crew, smiling happily. *In another month we'll have close-up data on the planet. Then we can decide to go into orbit or fly past and head out-system.*

They were all standing around him now, clapping him on the back and laughing with him.

Larry threw up his hands. "Hey, I didn't have anything to do with it. You guys launched the probes. I just stood back and watched you. You deserve all the congratulations, not me."

They milled around for a few minutes more, before Larry finally said, "Okay, okay, you got off a good launch. Now how about the regular duty crew getting back to their stations. Don't want to give the computer the impression it can run the ship by itself, do you?"

They grumbled light-heartedly, but most of the techs returned to their desks. The few extra people who had been present for the launch drifted away from the bridge, out the two hatches at either end of the curving row of consoles.

Satisfied that everything was going smoothly, Larry went

over to his own seat along the back wall of the bridge and relaxed in it. But not for long.

Dr. Loring pushed his way past the last of the departing launch techs and entered the bridge. Larry suppressed a frown as the old man stood there momentarily, fat and wheezy and blinking, peering at the console screens.

He knows no one's allowed up here without permission unless he's a member of the working crew!

Loring turned his frogeyed face toward Larry. "Ah, there you are," he said, and lumbered over to Larry's seat. "Congratulations. I was watching on the intercom. The launch seemed to go quite smoothly."

Larry got up slowly from his chair. "Thanks. But...you know that the bridge is off limits for non-crew personnel."

Loring waved a chubby hand in the air. "Oh, yes, of course. I apologize. But I, ah...I have other reasons for looking you up." He glanced around at the techs, who were all busily at work with their backs to him. "Ahh...could we step into your office for a moment? This is rather delicate."

There were times when Dr. Loring amused Larry, and other times when the old man exasperated him. This was one of the latter times. *Stay cool*, he told himself. *After all, he is practically a father to you. He thinks he's got a right to butt in.*

Nodding, Larry led Dr. Loring through the door in the middle of the bridge's back wall. It opened onto a short corridor that linked the bridge with the computer center. Off to one side of this hallway was Larry's office. They stepped inside and Larry passed his hand over the light switch. The infrared sensor in the switch detected his body warmth and turned on the overhead light panels.

Larry gestured to the webchair and sat himself behind his desk. Loring sat down with great caution, lowering his weight onto the fragile-looking chair very slowly. The plastic squeaked.

"What's the matter?" Larry asked.

"It's about Dan Christopher," Dr. Loring said, looking troubled.

Larry waited for the old man to add something else. When he didn't, but merely sat there looking unhappy, Larry urged, "Well? What about Dan?"

"And Valery."

Larry automatically tried to hide the jolting shock that went through him. *Idiot! What are you afraid of? She loves you.*

Patiently, he asked Dr. Loring, "Okay, what about Dan and Valery?"

Shaking his head, Dr. Loring said, "She's seen him a couple of times since the fire. Had dinner with him . . . alone."

"I know that."

"I told her that I didn't think it was right; nothing can come of it but trouble."

"Is that what you came here to tell me? Val's told me about it already. We're not keeping secrets from each other. There's nothing wrong with her having dinner with old friends. . . ."

"He still wants her, you know."

"I know." *I remember how I felt when she was promised to him.*

"He's asked her not to marry you until after we've decided about the Centaurian planet."

Larry nodded again.

"He's going to cause trouble."

Larry's patience was starting to wear thin. "Look, Dr. Loring, I know how Dan feels. I know he's trying to gain control of the Council and have me pushed out. But you've got to remember that he and I were friends for a long time and . . ."

"He believes," Dr. Loring said, his voice rising to interrupt Larry, "that the fire in the cryosleepers was no accident. He thinks his father was deliberately killed. Murdered."

"Murdered?"

"That's right."

"By whom? Who'd do such a thing? Why?"

Dr. Loring almost smiled. "You see, there are some things that you don't know. Valery's been afraid to tell you everything, for fear that it would cause more trouble between you and Dan. But I wormed it out of her. She can't keep secrets from her father!"

"Why in hell would Dan think his father was murdered? What possible reason could there be?"

Shrugging, Loring replied, "I happen to know that he has a computer technician digging through the oldest memory cores on the ship for some special instructions that his father fed into the computer—apparently when the voyage first began. Perhaps even before the voyage started, when the ship was still in orbit around Earth."

Larry sank back in his chair.

"Take my word for it," Loring insisted, shaking a stubby finger in the air, "Dan is dangerous. I think he's unbalanced . . . insane. And he's determined to get his own way—with the ship, with Valery, with everything. That means he's got to get rid of you, one way or another."

Dan Christopher's job aboard the ship was in Propulsion and Power.

Trained from childhood in physics and electrical engineering, Dan watched over the ship's all-important hydrogen fusion reactors, the thermonuclear power plants that provided the ship's rocket thrust and electrical power. Using the same energy reactions as the stars, the fusion reactors were small enough to fit into a pair of shielded blisters up on level seven—the innermost ring of the ship, closest to the hub. Small, yet these reactors had enough power in them to drive the ship across the light-years between the stars and to provide all the electrical power needed by the ship and its people for year after year after year.

The fusion reactors were like miniature suns. Inside each heavy egg-shaped radiation shield of lead and steel was a tiny, man-made star: a ball of glowing plasma, a hundred million degrees hot, held suspended in vacuum by enormously powerful magnetic fields. Deuterium—a heavy isotope of hydrogen—was fed into the fusion plasma almost one atom at a time. Energy came out, as the deuterium atoms were fused into helium. The same process that powers the sun, the stars—and hydrogen bombs.

There was enough energy in the fusion reactors to turn the entire ship into a tiny, glowing star—for an explosive flash of a second.

In theory, the reactors were expected to be quiet, almost silent. And the energy converters that changed the heat of the fusion plasma into electricity were supposed to be virtually silent too.

Yet as Dan prowled down along the metal catwalk that hung over one of the reactors, he could *feel* through the soles of his slippered feet the low-frequency growl of a star chained to a man's command. The metal floor plates vibrated, the air itself seemed to be heavy with the barely audible rumbling of some unseen giant's breathing.

Dan leaned over the catwalk's flimsy railing and peered down at the work crew on the floor below. The railing could be flimsy because the gravity factor at level seven was only one-tenth of Earth-normal *g*. The ship's designers had put the heaviest equipment in the areas where weight was almost negligible. People had to live at full Earth *g*, so that the living quarters were down in the outermost wheel, level one. But the big equipment was up here, where a man could haul a five-hundred kilo generator by himself, if he had to.

Dan could feel the frail railing tremble in his hands from the reactors' deep-pitched subsonic song. The reactors themselves were little to look at, just a pair of dull metal domes some twenty meters across: like a brace of eggs lain by a giant robot bird. Off on the other side of level seven was another pair of reactors, and the smaller auxiliary electrical power generators. Between the two blisters housing the big equipment was nestled the control instrumentation and offices for the Propulsion and Power group.

The work crew on the main floor below the catwalk was still trying to get the main generator going. All the repairs had been made, and the generator had been reassembled in its place between the two reactors. But it would still not light off.

As Joe Haller had put it after an exasperating week of working on the generator: "It's an engineer's hell. Everything checks but nothing works."

Dan knew they'd get it going sooner or later. But he couldn't help wondering why the generator wasn't working, when all the calculations and tests showed that it should.

Is there a saboteur in Joe's team? he wondered, watching them work. *And if so—why? Who's behind all this?*

"MR. CHRISTOPHER, MESSAGE FOR YOU," said the computer's flatly calm voice over the intercom loudspeakers.

Dan reluctantly turned away from the sweating crew beneath him and strode back toward the control area. The magnetized metal foil strips in his slippers clung slightly to the floor plates of the catwalk.

Shutting the door behind him, Dan felt the bone-quivering rumble of the reactors disappear, to be replaced by the higher-pitched hum of electrical equipment: monitors, computer terminals, viewscreens. A half-dozen people were seated at monitoring desks, watching the performance of the reactors and generators.

Dan spotted an empty desk, slid into its chair, and touched the phone button. "Dan Christopher here," he said.

The little desktop viewscreen glowed briefly, then Dr. Hsai's features took shape. The psychotech smiled a polite oriental smile.

"Kind of you to answer my call so quickly," Dr. Hsai said softly. "I know you must be very busy."

Dan smiled back. "You're a busy man, too. What can I do for you?"

Looking slightly more serious, the psychotech replied, "I am concerned that you haven't kept in touch with us, Mr. Christopher. We have set up three appointments for your examination, and you haven't shown up for any of them."

Dan shrugged. "As you said, I'm very busy."

"Yes, of course. But your health is of primary importance. You cannot perform your exacting tasks if you are in poor health."

"I feel fine."

Dr. Hsai closed his eyes when he nodded. "Perhaps so. But your condition may not reflect itself in physical symptoms that are obvious to you. You were discharged from the infirmary with the understanding that you would return for periodic examinations. . . ."

Dan could feel the heat rising within him. "Now listen. I *am* busy. And all you want to do is ask me more stupid questions and probe my mind. I don't have to allow that. I'm performing my job and I feel fine. There's no way you can force me to submit to your brain-tinkering!"

"Mr. Christopher!" Dr. Hsai looked shocked.

"Let me remind you of something, Doctor," Dan went on. "We're right now decelerating toward Alpha Centauri. Our reactors are feeding the ship's main engines on a very, *very* carefully programmed schedule. This ship can't take more than a tiny thrust loading—we're simply not built to stand high thrust, it'd tear us apart...."

"Everyone knows this."

"Do they? This is a very delicate part of the flight. A slight miscalculation or a tiny flaw in the reactors could rip open the ship and kill everybody. I'd suggest that you stop bothering me and let me concentrate on my job. Save your brain-picking for after we're safely in orbit and the rocket engines are shut down."

"I am only..."

Dan could sense that the others in the control room had turned to stare at him. But he concentrated on the phone screen. "I don't care what you are only," he snapped. "And I don't care who's trying to find reason to slap me back in the infirmary...even if it's the Chairman himself! I'm going to stay on this job and get it done right. Understand?"

Dr. Hsai nodded, his smile gone. "I am sorry to have interrupted your very important work," he said.

The psychotech gently touched his phone's switch, and Dan Christopher's image faded from the screen. Dr. Hsai sat in his desk chair for a long moment, eyes closed, mouth pursed meditatively.

(7)

It was late at night. Dr. Loring padded slowly up the long, winding metal stairs toward the observatory section in the ship's hub. The tubes that connected the lowermost rings of the huge ship had power ladders, and a man could ride comfortably at the touch of a button. Most people climbed the stairs anyway, because of the shortage of electricity while the main generator was down. But Dr. Loring felt it was his privilege to ride the power ladders.

Up here, though, above the fourth level, it was all muscle work. No power ladders, just endless winding metal steps. Not easy for a heavy old man. Even though the gravity fell off rapidly at these higher levels, Loring sweated and muttered to himself as he climbed. It was dark in the tunnels. The regular lights had been shut off, and only the widely spaced dim little emergency lights broke the darkness.

He stopped at the seventh level to catch his breath. Halfway up the next tube, he knew, he could just about float with hardly touching the steps at all. Time for a rest.

The hatch just to his left opened onto the Propulsion and Power offices, he knew. The hatch to his right led to the reactors. Loring wanted no part of them. With an effort he began climbing the next set of steps, leaving level seven below him.

"Insomnia," he muttered to himself. "The curse of an old man. Bumbling about in the dark, ruining my heart and my stomach, when I ought to be sound asleep in my own bed."

The weightlessness was getting to him now. No matter how many times he came to the observatory, the first few minutes of nearly O g always turned his stomach over. It felt like falling, endlessly falling. Something primitive inside his brain wanted to scream, and his stomach definitely wanted something more solid to work with.

If only it wasn't so dark, Loring thought. He held tightly to the stair railing as his feet floated free of the steps. At least he could keep some sense of up and down; that would help. Like a swimmer guiding himself along a rope, he pulled himself along the railing until his balding head bumped gently on a hatch.

Dr. Loring swore to himself softly, opened the hatch manually—the automatic controls were shut down—and floated through into the observatory.

For a terrified moment he thought he was outside in space itself.

The observatory was almost entirely plastiglass, a big dome of transparent plastic that made it look as if there was absolutely nothing between him and the stars. In an instant his fright passed, and then he smiled and floated like a child on a cloud, turning slowly around in midair to see his oldest friends:

Alpha Centauri, and 'way out there, I see you, Proxima. The Cross and Achernar. He turned again. *How dim and far away you are, my Sun. And Cassiopeia, and bright Polaris . . . yes, still there. Eternally, eh? Eternally. Or close enough to it.*

Gradually, he became aware of dark shapes around him, blotting out parts of the sky. He knew what they were. Telescopes, recording equipment, video screens and cameras, computer terminals. The tools of the astronomer's trade.

He "swam" down to the desk that was shoehorned into the midst of all the equipment, and touched a button on its surface. The viewscreen on the desktop lit up, showing an intensified view of what the main telescope was looking at: the two main stars of the Alpha Centauri system, and between them, two specks of light that were planets.

Dr. Loring swiveled his chair around and activated the computer terminal. Its smaller screen stayed dark, but the READY light beside it glowed green.

Checking the time on his wristwatch, Dr. Loring stated the date, his name, and the code words for the computer memory section that his work was being filed under. Then:

"Re-position the main telescope for observation of Epsilon Indi."

The hum of electrical motors, and the bulky shape of the main telescope began to swing across the background of stars over the old man's head. Loring watched the viewscreen, and saw a bright orange star center itself in the picture.

"Analysis of last week's observations have shown," he recited for the computer's memory bank, "that both Epsilon Eridani and Epsilon Indi have planetary companions. Both stars are K-sequence, brighter and hotter than the red dwarfs observed earlier. The mass of Epsilon Eridani's companion is about one-hundredth of Jupiter's or roughly three times Earth's. This is a preliminary figure, and may apply to the total masses of several planets, although only one has been observed so far. The purpose of tonight's observation is to gain mass data on the companion or companions of Epsilon Indi. Spectroscopic measurements can be . . ."

He stopped. There was something moving among the shadows. The only light in the huge sepulcher-like observatory came from the dimly glowing viewscreen and the stars themselves. But something had definitely moved out near the main telescope.

"Who's there?" Dr. Loring called out.

No answer.

Annoyed, he raised his voice. "I know I saw someone moving out there. Now, I don't want to ruin my night sight by turning on the lights, but if you don't come out and . . ."

A hand on his shoulder made him jump.

"Wha . . . who . . ."

"You weren't supposed to be here," a voice whispered. "Old fool, you should have been safely in bed."

"Who is it? What . . ."

Loring caught just the swiftest impression of a hand swinging toward him, then his skull seemed to explode and everything went completely blank.

As the old man slumped in his seat, the lean figure standing over him bent down and felt for a pulse. Then he pushed Loring out of the seat. The astronomer drifted weightlessly off, bumped against the computer terminal desk, and slid gently to the deck.

The lithe dark figure touched buttons on the computer terminal. Dr. Loring's series of observations played out on the screen: all the astronomer's words, the notes he made, the figures he had the computer draw up, the tapes of the telescope pictures.

The finger touched one more button: ERASE.

The computer thought it over for a microsecond, then flashed a question onto its screen: PLS CONFIRM ERASE COMMAND.

"You don't want to be blanked out either, do you?" The figure smiled, and touched the ERASE button again.

WORKING, the computer flashed. ERASURE COMPLETED.

The dark figure nodded solemnly, then turned and picked up Dr. Loring by the collar of his coverall and dragged him lightly to the hatch. Opening it, he pushed the astronomer's portly body through. It floated down the tube, slowly at first, but as the gravity force steepened, it began to fall faster and faster. The dark figure watched as Loring's body flicked past the dim emergency lights.

"Dropping like a bomb," he murmured without humor, without hatred, without any emotion at all. "They'll find him three or four levels below... what's left of him."

Larry strode stiffly down the corridor, which was still shadowy in the dim night lighting. It seemed like an endless treadmill, featureless except for the doors on each side. The soothing pastel colors of the walls were faded to an undistinguished gray in the poor light. The tiled floor curved up and away in both directions, following the huge smooth circle of the ship's largest ring; it was uphill no matter which way you looked, although there was never any sensation of climbing at all.

But it looked uphill, and Larry felt as if he was straining up a sheer cliff wall. He didn't even bother to glance at the nameplates on the doors: he knew exactly which door he wanted.

He got there and stopped. With a deep breath, he tapped lightly on the door.

Valery opened it immediately.

"Larry, what is it?" she whispered urgently. "What's wrong? On the phone you looked..."

He still looked haggard, worried, deeply troubled.

"Is your mother awake?" he asked as he stepped into the Loring's quarters.

"No, I didn't wake her. I think Dad's up at the observatory.... I heard him go out a couple of hours ago. He was trying to be quiet, but he can never..."

She saw the expression on his face and stopped talking. Now Valery looked alarmed.

"There's been an accident," Larry said.

Her mouth opened but no sound came out.

"Your father...he must've slipped off and fell...down three levels of tube..."

"Oh no!" Val covered her face with her hands.

Larry went on in an emotionless monotone. "One of the camera monitors spotted him. We've got him in the infirmary—the medics don't think he'll make it. He's pretty badly mangled."

She collapsed into his arms. Larry held her and fought down every impulse to relax his inner self-control. *Somebody's got to be strong. Somebody's got to keep his head clear. Can't give in to emotions. Can't relax. Not now. Not yet.*

So he was strong and calm, any sense of fear or sadness or guilt bottled deep inside him. He helped Val to calm down. Then they woke Mrs. Loring and broke the news to her. It took the better part of an hour before she was dressed, trembling and with tear-streaked face. The three of them went wordlessly to the infirmary.

Dr. Loring was in the same cubicle that Dan had been in. His body made a puffy mound on the liquid-filled mattress. His face was unrecognizable: half hidden in plastic spray bandages, half battered and discolored. Arms and legs were covered by plastic casts. Tubes ran from a battery of machines alongside the bed into his body, his nostrils, his head.

Larry glanced at the life indications panel above the bed: heart rate, respiration, alpha rhythm, metabolic level, blood pressure—all low, feeble.

Mrs. Loring collapsed. She simply fainted, and Larry had to grab her before she slumped to the floor. A pair of nurses appeared out of nowhere and took her off, muttering, "Shock...hypertensive..."

A medic came in a few moments later.

"I think it would be best for us to keep Mrs. Loring here, at least for the rest of the night."

Larry nodded.

"How's..." Val's voice was shaky. "Wh...what are the chances for my father...?"

The medic tried to smile but couldn't quite force it through. "We're doing everything we can. I think he's stabilizing—that is, his life signs aren't growing any worse, at least not over the past half-hour or so. But he's in very poor shape...he needs extensive surgery. It's probably beyond our limited capabilities...."

Larry said, "There are expert surgeons in cryosleep, aren't there?"

"A few." The medic nodded. "I don't know the details of their backgrounds...."

"I'll have them checked out. Maybe we can revive them."

"Revive them? That takes special permission...."

"I know," Larry said.

"And the revival procedure itself takes weeks," the medic went on. "We'd have to suspend Dr. Loring in cryosleep until the surgical team could be made ready for him. I'm not certain he'd survive freezing, in the condition he's in."

Larry could feel Val's weight leaning against his arm. Without looking down at her, he told the medic, "Dr. Loring is a very important member of the Council, and as close to me as my own father. Closer, in fact. I want every resource at our disposal brought to bear to save him. I've already lost one father...I don't want to lose another. Do you understand?"

"Certainly, Mr. Chairman." The medic almost bowed. "Everything that can be done, will be, I assure you."

Turning to Val, Larry said, "All right. Come on, let's get out of here. There's nothing we can do except wait."

Slowly, he led her out of the infirmary.

As they walked along the curving corridor to nowhere in particular, Larry said, "I want you to call a friend, somebody who can stay with you. I don't want you to stay alone."

"All right," she said quietly.

He glanced at his wristwatch: almost time for the morning shift to start.

"Larry..."

"What?"

Valery's face was pale, her eyes frightened. "It's like a sickness is sweeping through the ship, isn't it? The fire, and Dan's accusations, and now Dad...everything's going crazy."

For a few moments Larry didn't answer. The only sounds

were the padding of their slippered feet on the floor tiles, their own breathing, and the vaster breathing of the ship's air circulation fans.

"Maybe," he said at last, "it *is* a sickness. Maybe there's a madman among us."

She should have looked surprised. But she didn't. "You mean Dan." It wasn't a question.

Larry shook his head. "I don't want to make accusations. Dan's been acting peculiarly since his father died, but that doesn't mean..."

"It's all my fault!" Val suddenly burst out, her eyes filling with tears.

"Your fault?"

"I've come between you. Dan hates me because I picked you, not him. He wants to get rid of you...destroy you! He thinks you killed his father, deliberately. And now...and now..." She couldn't speak anymore. She was crying.

And now he's tried to kill Dr. Loring, my foster father. Is that what she's saying?

The Council members were already in their seats, looking deathly grim, when Larry entered the Council room. The only empty chair was Dr. Loring's.

Taking his own seat, Larry said as unemotionally as he could, "I'm sorry to be late. I was in the infirmary. Dr. Loring is still alive, but just barely. The medics have decided to place him in cryosleep until a surgical team is revived for an attempt to save his life."

"If there is such a team among us," said one of the older Council members. "I don't seem to recall too many surgeons among our original number. Biochemists and geneticists, yes, plenty of those. But surgeons...?"

Larry nodded curtly. "The computer is searching the personnel files for the right people. If they're found, I assume the Council is willing to waive the usual rules about retiring one person for each person revived? This is an emergency situation, after all."

They muttered and nodded assent.

"And if there is no surgical team capable of helping him?" Adrienne Kaufman asked.

"We'll just have to keep Dr. Loring in cryosleep until some of our younger members can be trained sufficiently well to operate on him."

"That could take a generation!"

"Once he's in cryosleep safely, it doesn't matter."

"The old man shouldn't have been wandering around the tubes by himself," said a young Councilman. "Accidents can happen to the best of us...."

"Was it an accident?" Dan Christopher asked, from his seat at the far end of the table. "Seems to me we've been having far too many *accidents* lately."

"What do you mean by that?"

Larry wanted to say something, to take command of the discussion, but he didn't know how to do it without stirring Dan's antagonism even further.

"What was Dr. Loring doing up there," Dan asked, "at that time of night? What was he working on? His daughter tells me he's been spending lots of his time in the observatory on some special task...."

A couple of the Council members turned to glance at Larry. *He would mention Valery,* Larry said to himself, trying to keep cold hatred from numbing his whole body.

"It's no secret," Adrienne Kaufman said haughtily. "Everyone knew that Dr. Loring was looking for other Earthlike planets, around other stars. At least, *almost* everyone knew." She stared icily at Dan.

"But there's no record of his work in the computer memory," Dr. Polanyi said. "I ran a check yesterday, when I first heard about the accident."

"It was no accident," Dan said firmly. "And his work was erased from the computer."

"What?"

"How can you say that?"

"It's ridiculous."

Dan leaped to his feet. "Ridiculous, is it? How'd you like to see *proof* that there's a murderer among us?"

Everyone started talking, arguing, shouting at once.

"*Quiet!*" Larry roared.

They all froze in mid-word. Arms stopped waving, voices hushed, and everyone turned to look at the Chairman.

Quietly, calmly, coldly, Larry said to Dan, "What's this all about?"

"I've been checking into the computer, too," Dan said, his dark eyes flashing. "And I've found something that shows there's an organized plot to undermine our whole flight . . . a madman's running loose, trying to kill us all!"

They all started jabbering again.

"Wait," Larry said, silencing them with a raised hand. "Dan, if you have such proof, by all means, let's see it. Right now."

Dan jabbed at a button on the small tabletop keyboard at his place. "You'll see it all right."

The wall screen at the far end of the room lit up and showed a human face. Louis Christopher, Dan's father, the driving force that made the ship, the voyage, their lives possible.

As Louis Christopher began to speak, Larry could think of nothing except the enormous likeness between father and son. The same long, lean, dark face. The same handsome features. The same intense, burning eyes.

"None of you will see this tape until I'm dead," Louis Christopher was saying. "The fact that you are viewing it now means that I have died. I hope that my death was a solitary affair, and hasn't affected the performance of our ship or the success of our voyage."

Christopher seemed to be staring straight at the camera, trying almost to hypnotize it, Larry thought. The effect was as if he was staring straight at the viewer, face to face.

"As I speak to you, our journey has just begun. Earth still looms large behind us. The stars are very far away. There are many among us who oppose this voyage, who think it's madness. Many among us were satisfied to remain aboard this ship in orbit around the Earth forever, prisoners, exiles for life.

"We voted to aim for the stars, though, and that's where we're going. Still, many are grumbling. They fear the unknowns of deep space. They're afraid of leaving Earth behind permanently.

"They may try to subvert our voyage. They may decide that they'd rather be exiles near Earth than free men among the stars. They may try to get us to return to Earth.

"That's why I'm making this tape. Since I must now be dead, it makes no further difference to me what you do. But it does make a difference to the future generations, to our children and their children. Continue the voyage! Don't let this magnificent ship, and our wonderfully brave people, be taken over by the fearful and timid. The stars are ours! We have the opportunity to reach Alpha Centauri and begin a new life there, on a literally new world. *Reject anyone who would do otherwise!*"

Several of the Council members shifted in their chairs. A few turned to glance at Larry.

"Our people have worked hard and struggled against titanic odds and risked everything they have," Louis Christopher continued, "to get to Alpha Centauri. We've pledged ourselves and mortgaged future generations yet unborn to make a new world for ourselves, far from Earth's decay and madness. You must continue until you reach that goal.

"Now let me point out another danger. It seems unlikely that the planets of Alpha Centauri will be exactly like Earth. We have, though, the means to adapt our children genetically to live on a different world. Don't be tempted to go further than Alpha Centauri. I know the construction of this ship, its limits and capabilities. It won't last long enough to reach another star. Settle on Alpha Centauri; to do otherwise will be to destroy the ship, the voyage, and every one of you.

"It won't be easy to change your children physically so that they can live on a strange world. But it must be done. It is the only way. Be strong. Be brave. Good luck. And good-bye."

The screen went dead.

For a long half-minute no one moved or spoke. Then one of the Councilmen coughed nervously, and they all turned in their seats, murmuring to each other. Dan remained standing by his chair, visibly trembling with emotion.

Larry said as gently as he could, "Is that what you call proof of murder?"

"What more proof do you need?" Dan blazed back. "*He* knew this would happen! He knew someone would try to subvert the whole voyage, push on to another star, get us all killed. He warned us."

"But how does that prove he was murdered?" one of the women asked.

"Or that Dr. Loring's accident wasn't accidental?"

Glowering at them, Dan replied, "We all know that if my father were alive now, he'd be revived and we'd vote him Chairman."

Larry said nothing.

"And we also know that Dr. Loring was looking for another planet around some other star. If he had found such a planet he'd be blathering it all over the ship. He said nothing, because he couldn't find another Earthlike world. In fact, he must have found evidence for no planets, or hostile planets...because whoever tried to kill him erased his work from the computer memory so that we'd never know what he'd found."

Larry pointed toward Dan and shouted out, "Or he might have found a new Earth somewhere, much better for us than the Centaurian planet, and his would-be murderer tried to keep us from finding *that* out!"

They glared at each other from opposite ends of the table, wordless for a moment.

"This is getting us nowhere," Adrienne Kaufman said.

Larry took a deep, calming breath. "The truth of the matter is that there's no evidence of murder, not of anyone at any time. All the deaths and near-deaths that we've had can be attributed to accidental causes. And anyone," he stared right at Dan, "who insists on finding foul play behind every accident on this ship is running the risk of being thought insane."

Dan stood there, shaking with rage, face flaming. Then he spun around and stamped out of the Council room.

Larry turned to the chief meditech, who was sitting halfway down the table.

"I want him in the infirmary immediately. And I want him checked out even if you have to strap him down. We can't have a madman running loose aboard this ship!"

Because if he is insane, Larry said to himself, *maybe he is a murderer!*

[8]

The cryonics room felt like gray November to Larry.

He had never known Earthly seasons, except through poetry and the videotapes he had watched during his school years. But here in the stark, cold, silent area where the frozen members of the ship's people slept away the years, he shivered with the incipient chill of winter.

The cryonics sections took up two full levels of the ship. The big compartments, called bays, were filled with row after row of massive covered couches, like the granite sarcophagi of ancient Egyptian pharaohs. But these coffins were for the living, not the dead; and they were made of stainless steel and plastic and honeycombed with tubes that carried liquid helium at 4.2 degrees above absolute zero. Instead of elaborate carved heiroglyphics, the cryogenic couches bore dials and gauges, automatic read-out viewers that showed the condition of the sleeper inside. Alive. Frozen, unmoving, unbreathing, silent and still for year after year. But alive.

Larry had never been frozen. The prospect bothered him somehow. It was too much like death.

The entire cryonics bay was like death, like winter; cold, lonely, silent. His breath hung in misty clouds before his face, and he felt chilled to the marrow despite the electric jacket he wore over his coveralls. The glareless lights overhead made everything look even flatter, grayer. The softly padded flooring muffled even the sounds of his footsteps.

Dr. Hsai was already there, Larry saw. The oriental psychotech was waiting for him, several rows up ahead. Larry quickened his pace.

"This is a strange place for a meeting," Dr. Hsai said as Larry came up to him. He seemed more curious than upset.

"I wanted to talk with you privately," Larry explained. "This is one of the few places aboard ship where we can be sure of no interruptions or eavesdroppers."

The psychotech's thin eyebrows arched upward, "Ahh...just what was it that you wanted to discuss?" If he felt cold, Hsai wasn't showing it.

"I understand that you want to release Dan Christopher."

Hsai bobbed his head once. "There is no excuse for keeping him in the infirmary. He has been there for almost a month now. I have seen him every day. There is no evidence of mental abnormality—nor should we expect to find any, under these circumstances."

"What do you mean?"

"Mr. Christopher is not suffering from a physically caused abnormality. He is not schizoid, which is the result of molecular imbalances in the nervous system. Nor does he have any brain lesions, nor any other physically connected disease."

"But..."

Dr. Hsai raised a slim, long-fingered hand. "Please. Allow me to continue. His problems are strictly emotional. Under the controlled conditions of the infirmary, this type of problem doesn't come to the surface."

Larry felt himself frowning. "But you can probe his mind...analyze what he's saying and thinking...his dreams and tests..."

"Alas," said Dr. Hsai, "I am only a psychotechnician, not a psychiatrist. Our only psychiatrist died in the epidemic a few years ago, you recall; the other two are here, in cryosleep."

"But can't you tell..."

"I can tell you that there is no physical reason for abnormal behavior in Mr. Christopher's case. His behavior in the infirmary was, at first, very hostile and suspicious. He was angry at being...as he put it, 'arrested and jailed.' But he adjusted to the situation within a week or so, and has been behaving very calmly ever since."

Larry muttered, "And there haven't been any accidents during the past month, either."

Dr. Hsai shrugged. "Either there is nothing wrong with him at all, or..."

"Or?"

"Or he is clever enough to hide his emotions from me, and he's waiting until he's released to work out his hostilities."

"Can someone be . . . well, can he act normal and still be . . ."

"Neurotic? Psychotic? Insane?" Dr. Hsai smiled sadly. "Oh, yes. The paranoids, in particular, can behave very normally . . . until they're placed in a certain stress situation. Then their psychosis shows up."

Larry shuddered, only partly from the cold. "What can we do?"

"It's doing no good to keep him in the infirmary. Frankly, he has every right to be released and resume his duties."

"But if we do, we run the risk of his going amok . . . causing more 'accidents.'"

Softly, Dr. Hsai said, "My own opinion is that there's nothing wrong with the young man, except anger and frustration. He feels the loss of his father very deeply; but even more deeply, he feels the loss of his expected position as Chairman and the loss of his chosen girl."

"In other words, he's sore as hell at me."

"Exactly."

"And he'll do whatever he can to get Valery back, and get himself elected Chairman."

"Yes."

Larry took a deep, cold breath. Looking straight into the psychotech's dark, calm eyes, he asked, "Do you think he's capable of committing violent acts? Like murder?"

Hsai shook his head. "Under the proper circumstances, anyone is capable of murder. Even you and I."

That's a big help, Larry complained to himself.

"He should be released," Dr. Hsai repeated. "You can have him watched as carefully as you wish, but there is no good to be accomplished by keeping him in the infirmary."

"All right," Larry agreed unhappily. "Let him go."

Hsai nodded and started walking away, toward the nearest hatch leading back to the warmth of life. He glanced over his shoulder once, looking slightly puzzled that Larry wasn't coming with him, or at least following him.

But Larry stood rooted to the spot, beside one of the bulky cryosleep couches.

Dan wants Valery, and he wants to be Chairman.

"You knew that," he said softly to himself. "That's nothing new."

Yes, his mind echoed back. *But if he is insane, if he has done all these crazy things—including murder—then it's because of me. The blame is partly mine. Maybe almost entirely mine. Especially if he's insane. Then he's not responsible for his actions. But I am. I am!*

"All right, so it's at least partially your own fault. What can you do about it now?"

He wanted to answer, *Nothing.* But instead he knew. *You can give him what he wants. Let him have the Chairmanship. Let him have Valery.*

"You know you can't do that. Not if you want to stay sane. Not if you want to go on living."

You can sleep. Right here. Sleep for as long as you want to. Sleep until they're both dead. Then start a new life.

"Sure. Or maybe never wake up."

It's your choice.

With a sudden shock, Larry realized he was standing in front of Dr. Loring's cryosleep unit. The graphs showed that the old man was still alive, waiting in frozen limbo for a surgical team to be organized for the attempt to save his life.

Give up the Chairmanship? Give up Valery?

"No."

Then you'll be pushing Dan even further. He might do something even worse.

Larry was sweating now. Despite the cold, beads of sweat were trickling down his face. "I can't do it!" he whispered fiercely. "I won't let him have his way! I won't!"

It was always noisy in the main cafeteria. Big enough to handle three hundred people at a sitting, the cafeteria doubled as an eating place, an entertainment center, and an auditorium. It was brightly lit, gaily decorated, and bustling with crowds nearly all the time. One entire wall was a long viewscreen that showed constantly changing scenes from Earth, from outside in starry space, or from inside the ship itself.

At the moment Dan entered the cafeteria's big double doors and stood blinking in the entryway, the long wall screen was showing an ocean beach on Earth: surging powerful breakers rolling up to smash against grim rocks in spectacular sheets of spray. The sky was blue, the sun a golden ball starting to turn red as it neared the horizon. People dotted the tiny slice of beach that lay between the rocks. Farther back, atop the higher rocky cliffs, there were houses.

Dan stood at the entryway and took it all in: the videotaped scene, the noise and brightness of the cafeteria. After a month in the quiet confinement of the infirmary, it was like coming to life again after being in cryosleep.

People jostled through the entryway past him. Several of them smiled at him, or said some brief words of greeting:

"Good to see you back, Dan."

"Hi, Dan."

"Hey, pal, how're ya doin'?"

"Can't keep a good man down, huh, Dan?"

He grinned at them, nodded, even shook a few hands.

Then he saw her far across the room, sitting by herself, looking tense. She had a tray of food before her, but she wasn't touching it; Valery was merely looking off into space, waiting.

Dan quickly made his way to the selector wall, punched buttons for the food he wanted, and went to the receiving slot. All the while he kept one eye on Valery's golden hair. He took his steaming tray straight to her table.

"I hope I haven't kept you waiting," he said.

She looked up, wide-eyed, almost startled. "Oh—no, I just got here a few minutes ago."

He sat down on the other side of the little table. "It was good of you to agree to meet me."

She seemed wary, almost afraid. "This is a funny place to meet . . . I mean, it's so noisy."

A group of half a dozen teenagers appeared on the stage at the other end of the room and started setting up electronic musical instruments.

Dan grinned. "It's alive. I like it. Kind of hard on the ears, but it's fun."

"You . . . you look very good," Valery said.

"You're scared of me," he realized. "Why? Do you think I'm crazy, too?"

"Who . . ."

He took her hand in his. "Come on, Val. I know what Larry

thinks. I know he's the one who kept me locked up for the past month."

Pulling slowly away from his grip, she answered, "Dan, I don't want you and Larry to be enemies. You ought to be friends again...."

"I wish we could. I really do. I think I'd even let him keep the Chairmanship, if only I could be sure..."

He shook his head. "It'd never work. You're the one I want, Val. If I had you, I'd almost be willing to let the rest of it go."

"The rest of it?"

"Yep... I had a lot of time to think, you know, sitting there in the infirmary. A lot of time. I understand there haven't been any accidents since I went in."

She hesitated, then admitted, "That's right."

"You see? He's been damned smart about it... damned smart."

"What do you mean?"

"He's trying to make it look like it's all my fault. Larry's got half the people on this ship believing that I'm crazy, that I've been causing the accidents, that I tried to kill your father."

She stared at him. "Did you?"

He looked back into her Arctic-blue eyes, sensing all the turmoil, the fear, the pain that lay behind them.

"Have you asked Larry that question?"

"What do you mean?"

"You know what I mean, Valery."

"But why?" she asked, so softly that he could barely hear her voice over the cafeteria din. "Why would Larry do it?"

"Have you ever thought," Dan asked slowly, "that if there really is a madman aboard this ship, it's got to be Larry?"

"No! It couldn't be!"

"Couldn't it?"

"Dan—you're wrong. The accidents... they could be just that: accidents."

"Then why is Larry trying to prove that I'm insane?"

"He's afraid..."

"Afraid of me."

The words were gushing out of her now. "Larry's afraid that if you are sick, you'll hurt more people, hurt the ship, kill us all."

"That's just what *he's* doing."

"No..."

Dan could feel his temper rising, his face getting hot and red. "He's afraid of me because he knows that I know I didn't cause any of those accidents. He knows that I can't rest until I show everyone who did cause the accidents—that killed my father and nearly killed yours. *That's* what he's afraid of!"

Valery's voice was pleading, "Dan, listen to me. Believe in me. If you keep going this way, one of you—or both of you—are going to be killed! Stop it now. Let it stop."

He shook his head solemnly. "I can't, Val."

"Even if it means my sanity? My life? I can't stand by and see the two of you tear each other apart."

"There's nothing else . . ."

"Suppose," she said shakily, tears in her voice, "suppose I tell Larry that I've changed my mind . . . that I want to marry you. Will you stop then?"

He felt suddenly as if he were in the zero gravity hub of the ship, in free fall, dropping, dropping endlessly, spinning over and over again, dizzyingly. . . . He squeezed his eyes shut. *Stop it! Stop it stop it stop it.*

Looking at her again, so intent, so beautiful, so afraid and lonely, he said, "Val . . . I don't want you as a bribe. It wouldn't work that way. We'd end up hating each other. I . . . no, it's got to be Larry or me. We've got to settle this between ourselves."

"You'll kill each other," she said, all the energy drained from her voice.

"Maybe."

"You'll destroy the ship."

"That's what I want to prevent."

"You—the two of you—you're going to destroy me."

And she abruptly got up from the table and ran out of the cafeteria, leaving him sitting there alone.

[9]

For more than a month, the four gleaming torpedo shapes of the ship's automated probes had coasted silently through space, toward the major planet of the Alpha Centauri system. The only link between the probes and the ship was a continuous radio signal, of the lowest possible power, in order to conserve the energy of their batteries.

Then, as they neared the two main stars of Alpha Centauri, the solar cells along their outer skins began to convert sunlight into electricity. The radio signals gained in strength. Like sleeping servants, one by one the instruments aboard the probes awakened with the new flow of electrical power and began reporting back to the ship. But now the reports—full and complex—were carried by laser beams.

Some of the instruments took precise measurements of the probes' positions in space, and their courses as they approached the major planet. This information was studied by men and computer aboard the ship, and minor course corrections were transmitted back to the probes. The probes responded with the correct changes in course, and the men and women aboard the ship congratulated themselves. The computer accepted no congratulations, but took in all data impassively.

The probes successfully skirted past the steep gravity pull of Alpha Centauri B, the smaller orange member of the two main stars, and let the pull of Alpha Centauri A—the yellow, sunlike star—bring them close to the major planet. Then, more course corrections, more microscopic puffs of gas from the tiny attitude jets aboard the probes' bodies, and they fell into orbit around the planet.

Back on the ship, people celebrated.

Now streams of data began pouring across the near-emptiness of space between the probes and the approaching ship. The data were coded, of course, in the languages that the engineers and computers could translate into meaningful information. Pictures were sent, too, directly over the laser beams that linked the probes with the ship.

Two of the probes released landing capsules. One never made it to the surface, or at least never sent any information back after entering the planet's high atmosphere. The other touched down on solid ground and began sending pictures and data from the surface of the new world.

Larry was hurrying down a corridor on level two, where most of the labs and workshops were. Dr. Polanyi had been excited when he called: the first pictures from the planet were ready to view.

He saw someone heading toward him, from the opposite direction. The door to the data lab was halfway between them. Larry recognized the blazing orange coverall before he could make out Dan's face.

They had kept apart since Dan's release from the infirmary. Now they met at Polanyi's door.

"Hello Dan," Larry said automatically, as soon as they got close enough so that he didn't have to shout.

Dan nodded, his face serious. "Hello."

Larry reached for the finger grip on the lab door, but found Dan's hand was already there and sliding the door back.

"Polanyi called you, too?" Larry asked.

"He called all the Council members," Dan replied. "Any objections?"

Larry knew he was glaring at Dan. "No objections—as long as you can spare the time from your regular job."

Dan gestured for Larry to go through the doorway first. He followed, saying, "The job's getting done. We finally got all the bugs out of the rebuilt main generator. It'll go back into service today."

"That's fine. Glad to hear it." But Larry wasn't smiling.

"Ah, the first two here," Dr. Polanyi called to them.

He was sitting at a workbench halfway across the big,

cluttered room. The data lab was really a makeshift collection of instruments, viewscreens, workbenches, desk, computer terminals, and odd sorts of equipment that Larry couldn't begin to identify. Half a dozen white-coated technicians were tinkering around one of the bulky, refigerator-sized computer consoles. A wall-sized viewscreen was set up next to it, on legs that looked much too fragile to support it.

Polanyi fussed around the viewscreen and verbally prodded the technicians. Larry saw that there were a few chairs set up, so he sat on one. Dan joined the technicians, watching what they were doing from over their shoulders. In about ten minutes, most of the other Council members showed up. The older men and women among them took the available chairs. Larry got up and joined the loose semicircle of younger men that formed behind the seats.

The technicians finally scattered to various control desks around the big room, and Polanyi turned to face his audience.

"You recognize, of course, that what we're going to see will not be holograms," he said. "There is holographic information in the transmitted data, but we have not deciphered it completely as yet. I thought it would be much more desirable to see what there is to see as quickly as possible, even if it is only a flat, two-dimensional picture."

Larry nodded and asked, "Are any of the views we're going to see from the surface?"

"Only the last three," Polanyi answered. "Data transmission from the surface has been very difficult, for reasons that we have not yet determined. The orbital data is quite good, however."

Larry suddenly realized that he had lost track of Dan. Turning and looking through the crowd, he spotted him, standing off to one side of the group.

The overhead lights dimmed out, and Larry turned his attention back to the screen. It began to glow. Colors appeared, forms took shape.

It was a still photo, taken from far enough away from the planet to show its entire sphere.

"This is the first photo the probes took," Polanyi's voice floated through the darkness. "Probe number one took this one, as you can tell from the numerals down in the lower right-hand corner of the picture."

The planet was yellowish. Broad expanses of golden yellow, dappled here and there by greenish stretches. Larry found that he couldn't tell which was land and which was sea. The entire planet was streaked with white clouds, which obscured much of the underlying terrain. But there seemed to be no major cloud formations, such as the huge storm systems he had seen on tapes of Earth.

"Next," Polanyi's voice called.

This view was much closer. Mountains showed as wrinkles, like a bedsheet that had been rumpled. The land was yellow, Larry saw. The green stretches weren't vegetation, they were water.

For more than an hour they studied the orbital photos. The planet had no major oceans, only a scattering of large seas. There were no ice caps at the poles.

Polanyi kept up a running commentary, explaining what they were seeing, filling in information from the other instruments aboard the probes. It all added up to a disappointing picture.

The planet was actually slightly smaller than Earth, but about the same density. Surface gravity was apparently one third higher than Earth's.

Somebody said in the darkness, "1.3 g. That means a ninety-kilo man will feel like he's carrying thirty extra kilos around with him all the time."

"Like hauling an eight-year-old kid on your back."

"It certainly will strain the heart," Larry recognized the last voice as belonging to the chief meditech.

The air had slightly more oxygen in it than Earth normal, but also had dangerously high levels of nitric oxides and sulfur oxides.

"Volcanism," Polanyi explained, pointing to a photo of the planet's night side, where a series of brilliant red lights gleamed. "Active volcanoes . . . many of them. The infrared scans confirm it. The volcanoes are spewing out sulfur oxides and other harmful gases."

Larry grimaced.

The vegetation was a yellowish green. Chlorophyll was there, identified by the spectral readings from the orbiting probes. But the plant life obviously wasn't the same as Earth's greenery.

"What about data from the surface lander?" someone asked.

"Yes, it is coming up next."

The picture on the viewscreen suddenly changed to show a startling landscape. It was golden: yellowish plants everywhere, some of them thick and tall as trees, with ropy vines hanging from their arms. Yellowish sky, even the clouds had a golden tint to them.

"This photo was taken near local sunset," Polanyi explained. "I believe that accounts for the peculiar color effect . . . some of it, at least."

It was beautiful. Larry gazed at a golden world, with hills and clouds and soft beckoning grass of gold. Something deep inside him, something he had never dreamed was in him, was stirred by this vision. A world, a real world where you could walk out in the open air and look up into a sky that had sunrises and sunsets, climb hills and feel breezes and swim in rivers. . . .

He shuddered suddenly. It was like self-hypnosis. This golden world was a trap. It was deadly. A man couldn't last five minutes on it, not unless he wore as much protection as he needed to go outside the ship and into space.

The picture changed. Now they were looking off in a different direction. The yellow grass and trees sloped down into a gentle valley. In the distance there were rugged mountains of bare rock, their tops shrouded in clouds.

"There are at least two active volcanoes among those distant mountains," Dr. Polanyi said. "The clouds themselves are mainly steam from the volcanoes."

It still looked so beautiful.

The picture changed again. It showed the view from the opposite side of the lander. The hillside swept upward, still covered with golden grass and shrubs. Up near the top of the hill, silhouetted against the bright sky, were four dark shapes.

"They appear to be animals," Polanyi's voice said. "From their distance, we have judged their size to be roughly comparable with that of an Earthly sheep."

It was hard to tell their shape. There seemed to be a head, the suggestion of rounded haunches. No tail was visible. You couldn't tell how many legs, because their lower halves were hidden in deep grass.

The overhead lights suddenly went on, and the picture on the viewscreen faded.

"That's everything we have so far," Dr. Polanyi said.

Larry squinted against the sudden glare. And found himself frowning. Looking around, he realized that he had spent his life in a prison. A jail. A metal and plastic confinement, breathing the same recycled air over and over again, knowing every face, every compartment, every square millimeter of space. Out there was a *world*. A whole broad, beautiful golden world that no one had set foot on, waiting to be explored, to be lived on.

Waiting to kill us, he reminded himself.

They were all murmuring, muttering, a dozen different conversations buzzing at once.

Then Dan's voice cut through it all. "So we have our first view of the promised land."

Larry stepped toward him. "It doesn't look very promising to me. A man can't live there."

"We can't," Dan shot back, "but our children could."

"If you make them capable of breathing sulfur and strong as a man-and-a-third."

"The geneticists can do whatever needs to be done."

Larry was about to reply, but caught himself. Instead, he said, "This isn't the place to debate such an important issue. I'd like to have a formal meeting of the Council tomorrow morning. We'll have to decide if we want to make this planet our home, or look further."

Dan said nothing. He merely watched Larry, with a quizzical little smile, playing on his lips.

It was late evening. The corridor lights were dimmed. Larry and Valery had eaten dinner in the Lorings' quarters, with Val's mother. Now, after a long walk around level one, they were approaching her quarters again, strolling along the empty corridor, hand in hand.

They came to an observation port and stopped. The port was an oblong of thick plastiglass. A padded bench ran along the bulkhead alongside it. They sat and for a long, wordless while gazed out at the sky.

The stars were thick as dust. One yellow star stood out

brighter than all the rest. Nearby it, almost lost in its glare, peeped a dimmer orange star.

"Tomorrow the Council meets to decide," Larry said wearily.

"Do you think this is the end of the voyage?" Val asked.

He shook his head. "It can't be. We can't live on that planet . . . even though . . ."

"Even though?"

"It's so beautiful!" he said. "I saw the pictures from the surface today. It's so beautiful. If only we *could* survive there."

She asked, "Can't the geneticists . . ."

"Sure, they can alter the next generation of children so that they'll be able to live on the planet. But—the kids would have to be brought up in a separate section of the ship. They'd have to be put under a higher gravity, different atmosphere. The parents would have to wear pressure suits just to visit their own children."

"Ohhhh . . ."

"And what about the parents? Do you think people can stay aboard this ship, in this cocoon, this prison, and let their kids go down there to live? It won't work; the planet's beautiful, but too different from us. If we try to make it work, it'll tear everybody apart."

"Then we have to move on," Val said.

"Right. But Dan won't see it that way. He'll put up a fight."

"You'll win."

He looked at her. "Maybe. I wish I didn't have to fight him."

"He thinks the ship won't be able to go much farther," Valery said. "He's afraid we'll all get killed if we try to find another star, another planet."

In the dim light, Larry could see that Val wasn't looking at him, but gazing out at the stars. He reached for her chin and turned her face toward him.

"You've seen him several times since he got out of the infirmary, haven't you?"

"Yes," she said softly.

He let his hand drop away. "I don't think I like that. In fact, I know I don't."

"Larry," she said gently, "I'm a free human being. I can do what I want."

"I know, but—well, I don't want you to see him."

"Don't you trust me?"

He felt miserable, tangled up inside himself. "Of course I trust you, Val, but..."

"No buts, Larry. Either you trust me or you don't."

"I trust you." Sullenly.

"Well you shouldn't," she snapped.

"Wha...?"

"Oh Larry—it's all so mixed up! I don't want Dan to hurt you. He...he said he'd almost be willing to let you stay Chairman if I'd marry him."

Larry felt his insides going numb. "And you said?"

"I...I let him think I'd do it, if he'd forget about trying to hurt you."

He knew how it felt to have liquid helium poured over you; scalding cold. "You let him think that."

"I did it for you!"

"Thanks. That's an enormous favor. Now he knows that anytime he crooks his finger, you'll come running to him. All he has to do is start an argument with me, and he's got you."

"No...that isn't..."

Larry's hands were clenching into fists. "I must have been out of my mind to believe that you'd prefer me over him. You've always wanted him. Now you've got the perfect excuse to get him."

He heard her gasp. "Larry...no...please..." Her voice sounded weak, far away.

"All this time you've been letting me think that you loved me...it was only because Dan seemed out of it. But whenever he's around, you end up going for him."

"You've got it all wrong!"

He stood up. For an instant, staring out at the stars, he felt as if he could fall right through the metal and plastic wall and tumble endlessly into the cold of eternity.

"Wrong?" he asked in a near-whisper. "Do I have it wrong?"

And then she was standing up in front of him, her face suddenly blazing with anger.

"You two are exactly alike!" Val snapped. She didn't raise her voice, but now there was steel in it, hot steel that threw off sparks. "You think that you can own me. Both of you. Well, I'm not a possession. I'm *me*, and I'm not going to sit around here like some silly Earth flower while you two big strong men fight over me. From now on, you and Dan both can do without me. I don't want to see either of you! Do you understand?"

Larry staggered a step backward. "Val..."

"If you and your ex-friend want to battle it out, it will have to be over some other reasons than me. I'm not a prize to be handed over to the winner. You two can knock your heads together... I don't care anymore! I tried to save you, both of you. I love you both! Can't you understand that? I love you both, but I've always loved you best, Larry. *I'm* the one who made you go after the Chairmanship... because *I'm* the one who wanted you. But you're so intent on flexing your muscles and being jealous.... You're scared of Dan! And you'll never be able to be happy or free or yourself until you stop being scared of him. And the only way *that's* going to happen is for you to kill him... or him to kill you. That's what you're both heading for. But I won't have any part of it! Go ahead and kill yourselves! See if I care!"

And she turned away and ran down the corridor.

Larry was too thunderstruck to go after her. Besides, he knew she was right.

(10)

The conference room filled slowly with Council members. At the head of the table, standing there and watching them drift in, Larry thought they looked almost reluctant to get the meeting started.

They know that a battle's coming; they've got a hard choice to make, and they don't want to face it.

His own thoughts kept slipping back to Valery, to the angry, sad, scared look in her eyes the night before. *She can't stay away from us both,* he knew. The ship's laws were lenient in some ways, but inexorable in others. Valery was at the age for marriage. She must marry. The computer's genetics program had listed the men who were genetically suited for marriage with her. There was no way for her to avoid it; she had to marry someone on that list.

Either Dan or me, Larry thought. Then, *Or somebody else? No, she couldn't marry somebody else. She wouldn't.*

But now there was another part to the problem. *If the Council decides to stay at Alpha Centauri, then we'll have to genetically alter this next generation of children. Val's children—whoever she marries—will be sulfur-breathing, high-gravity monsters. She won't be able to live with them; they couldn't stay in the same sections of the ship, except for brief visits. They couldn't breathe the same air.*

Someone coughed, and Larry snapped his attention back to the conference room, the Council meeting, the men and women who were now in their seats and looking up at him.

Only three seats were still vacant: Dr. Loring's, Joe Haller's,

223

and Dan's. Before Larry could say anything, the door at the far end of the room slid open and Haller and Dan stepped in. Dan was smiling.

They took their seats at that end of the table, and Larry sat in his chair.

"I assume you've all reviewed the minutes of our last meeting, and know the agenda for today."

A general mumble and nodding of heads.

"We've all seen Dr. Polanyi's data tapes from the probes."

Assent again.

The nervousness that Larry had expected to feel just wasn't there. He hunched forward in his chair, feeling . . . detached, remote from all this, as if he himself, the *real* Larry Belsen was somewhere lightyears away, looking back and watching the meeting, watching the person in his skin the way a scientist watches an experimental animal.

Leaning his forearms on the table, Larry said, "All right, we can get right down to it. The basic question is simply this: do we end our voyage at Alpha Centauri, or do we go on to try to find a better, more Earthlike planet at another star?"

For a moment none of the Council members said anything; they looked at each other, none of them apparently willing to start the debate.

Then Mort Campbell cleared his throat. His voice was deep, his usual speech pattern was slow and methodical. Put together with his solid frame and beefy face, he gave the impression of being a stolid, slow muscleman. But Campbell was the ship's champion chess player, as well as its top wrestler. His scientific skills, as chief of the Life Support group, spanned medicine, cryogenics, electronics, and most of the engineering disciplines. When he talked, no matter how slowly, people listened.

"I can't really say much about the choice we have," he rumbled. "But I do know something about the life support equipment on board this ship. We're in no condition to go farther. The air regenerators, the waste cyclers, the cryonics units, the rest of it—everything's being held together with that leftover gunk from the cafeteria that the cooks call coffee, plus what little hair I have left."

Several people chuckled. Campbell grinned lazily.

"Seriously," he continued, "I think it's foolish to talk about going farther." He turned toward Dan's end of the table. "How about you lads in Propulsion and Power? Is your equipment in as bad a shape as mine?"

Dan gestured with one hand. "We haven't started pulling out our hair yet, but the reactors and generators aren't going to last another five-six decades. Not even five or six more years."

"And what choice do we have?" Joe Haller asked. "There's no evidence of a better planet anywhere."

"Dr. Loring was searching for such evidence when his accident occurred," Dr. Polanyi said. "Unfortunately, there was no record of his work in the computer memory core."

Larry started to reply, but Polanyi went on, "However, I received a call last night from Dr. Loring's daughter. She believes she has found some of her father's handwritten notes, and she would like to tell the Council about them."

"What?" *Val's got evidence of her father's work?*

Suddenly Larry was totally alert, every nerve tight, every muscle tense.

He forced his voice to stay calm as he asked, "What do you mean, Dr. Polanyi?"

The old engineer shrugged. "Exactly what I said. Miss Loring apparently has uncovered some of her father's notes, and she feels she can tell us something, at least, about the progress of his work."

Larry glanced down the table at Dan. He seemed just as surprised as Larry himself felt.

"Then we ought to hear what she has to tell us," Larry said.

Nodding vigorously, Polanyi answered, "Precisely. I took the liberty of asking her to wait in the outer room. Shall I call her in?"

Larry looked around the table. No dissenting voices. "Yes," he said. "Ask her to come in."

Polanyi got up from his seat and went to the door nearest Larry's end of the table. He slid it open and gestured; Valery stepped into the conference room. She was wearing a dress instead of her usual slacks or coveralls; she looked very serious. And tired.

She must have stayed up all night.

"Why don't you take your father's seat," Larry suggested to her.

She nodded to him and went to the empty chair. Polanyi held it for her.

Dan called, "You have some evidence about your father's attempts to find other Earthlike planets?"

Valery's voice was low, weary. "Well, I don't know if you can call it evidence, exactly. It's just some scribbled notes that he left in our quarters, in his desk. I found them accidentally last night.... I was going to write a letter...." She glanced up at Larry, then turned and looked straight across the table at Polanyi.

"The notes don't make much sense by themselves, but they reminded me of some of the conversations wc had at home.... Father liked to talk about his work, you know."

She hesitated a moment. Larry could see that she was fighting to keep her self-control, struggling to keep her mind away from her father's accident—and who caused it.

"He was trying to determine what kinds of planets are associated with two particular stars: Epsilon Indi and Epsilon Eridani. Both are orange, K-sequence stars, somewhat cooler than the sun. Both definitely have planets orbiting around them. That much he was sure of."

"There are lots of other stars that are just as close as those two, or closer, aren't there?" Adrienne Kaufman asked.

Valery nodded. "Yes, but they're almost all red dwarfstars—so dim and cool that the chance for finding a planet with Earthlike temperatures, liquid water, and livable conditions—well, the chances are almost nil."

"I see."

Someone asked, "These planets your father was studying, are they like Earth?"

"That's what he was trying to determine," Val answered, "when ... when he was injured."

Larry could feel the electric tension around the table.

"As nearly as I could make out from his notes, and from the few conversations we had on the subject," Val went on, "he had determined that Epsilon Indi—the nearer of the two stars—had more than one planet. Its major planet is a gas giant, like Jupiter, completely unfit for us."

"And the others?"

She shook her head. "He never found out. He had been talking about building better electronic boosters for the main telescope. I guess he needed better magnification and resolution to study the smaller planets."

"We could build such equipment," Dr. Polanyi said. "But who would use it? Dr. Loring was our only qualified astronomer."

"Perhaps we could revive an astronomer who's now in cryosleep."

"Are there any?"

Valery raised her voice a notch. "If the Council will allow it, I would like to handle the astronomical work myself."

"You?"

"I realize that my place is in Computing. But I've always followed my father's work very closely, and I think that I'm the best qualified person here for continuing his studies. . . . Unless, of course, you want to go to the trouble to revive a sleeping astronomer."

"But can you make the necessary observations in less than a month? Otherwise we must go into orbit around the Centaurian planet."

"I haven't the faintest idea," Valery replied.

"We're going to have to take up a parking orbit around the planet anyway," Dan said firmly.

Everyone turned to him.

"I've been checking with all the different groups on board. Mr. Campbell's little speech earlier was the last stroke. Just about every group says their equipment needs to be overhauled, repaired, rebuilt. . . . We can't keep expecting the ship to function indefinitely without major repairs."

He pushed his chair back and stood up. "We can't make major repairs while we're running all the equipment full blast. But if we go into orbit around the planet, we can afford to shut down some sections of the ship for weeks or even months at a time."

"And once we're in orbit around the planet," Larry countered, "the temptation to stay and make it our new home might just become overpowering. Right?"

Dan shrugged. "Could be. All I know is that the reactors need deuterium. Our supplies are too low to last much longer—a few years, at most. That planet has water on it, so there must be deuterium there, too. It's that simple."

"So we must stop. Whether we want to or not," Larry said.

Dan nodded, smiling.

Everyone else around the table was nodding, too. Larry saw that there was nothing he could do about it. He was outmaneuvered, outvoted, outsmarted. The whole business of trying to decide what to do was a complete shambles. They were going to fall into orbit around the Centaurian planet, no matter what.

"I believe," Dr. Polanyi said, "that orbiting the planet may have some definite advantages. We will be able to study it close-up, even go down onto the surface with exploration teams. Miss Loring can use the time to make further astronomical observations. And we can repair and refurbish the ship at our leisure. After all, even if we decide to stay at Alpha Centauri, those of us who are alive now will still have to spend the rest of their existence aboard ship. We will not be able to live on the surface."

Dan said, "But our children will."

Val's children, Larry thought bitterly.

"All right," he said aloud. "It seems there's no way around it, and therefore we don't need to decide about heading elsewhere. Not right now, at least." He turned to the chief medic. "Will you please start the procedure for reviving an astronaut team? It looks like we're going to be sending groups of people down to the planet's surface."

The meditech nodded.

The meeting broke up soon afterward. As people got up from their seats and headed for the doors, Larry went straight to Val.

"You didn't tell me about your father's notes," he said.

She was standing by the table, looking very serious and even more beautiful than he had ever known before.

"It happened just as I said." Her voice was strained, as if she was trying to keep any emotion out of it. "I went to the desk to write a letter to Dan, to tell him what I'd told you, and found father's handwritten notes in the drawer."

"You haven't changed your mind...about last night."

She looked away from him. "No. I'm not going to be the

reason for you and Dan to hurt each other. I simply refuse."

"But what's this about you doing astronomical work? I didn't know..."

"There are lots of things about me that you don't know," Val said. "But I know all about you and Dan. Both of you think the other one deliberately tried to kill Father. Well, if someone else started to work in the observatory, what's to stop the would-be killer—if there is one—from attacking him?"

Realization dawned on Larry, together with a sinking feeling in the pit of his stomach. "You mean that if you're the one working in the observatory..."

"Neither you nor Dan will hurt me. There. It sounds silly and terrible at the same time, doesn't it? But if you're both convinced that one of you is a murderer, then the only person who *can* continue the astronomical work has to be me."

"But...suppose there is a murderer, and it's neither one of us? Suppose it's somebody else?"

Valery didn't hesitate an instant. "If that happens, then maybe you two idiots can work together to find out who the real madman is!"

She turned and headed for the door. From the set of her slim shoulders, the stubborn toss of her golden hair, Larry could see quite clearly that she didn't want him to try walking with her.

He sagged back against the table, feeling utterly drained. *The whole world is falling apart...everything's breaking up and there's nothing I can do....*

Then a thought struck him. Dan had said that they'd have to get fresh deuterium for the reactors from the water on the planet. That meant sending a complex load of equipment down to the surface, together with people trained to run it. *It means Dan will have to go down to the surface of the planet.* The dangerous, maybe deadly surface.

Larry almost smiled.

[11]

Guido Estelella was an astronaut, the only man on ship—asleep or awake—who had experience in piloting rocket craft from orbit down to the surface of a planet and back up again. He hadn't been one of the political prisoners, back when the ship had been an orbital jail, a place of exile for Earth's scientists. He had been a free man, an astronaut by training. It was his joy.

But the same Earth government that made prisoners of thousands of scientists and sent them into orbital exile with their families had also cut space flight down to almost nothing. Orbital flights, mostly to repair communications and weather satellites; a few flights to the Moon each year, bringing workers to the factories there. That was all. No more Mars flights. No further exploration of the solar system. Earth could not afford it.

So when the prisoners coaxed Earth's government into letting them drive their orbiting prison out toward the stars, Estelella volunteered to join them.

"After all," he said, "it's my namesake, isn't it?"

So he went to the stars, frozen in cryosleep for nearly fifty years, to be awakened when he was needed. Now he was awake and working.

And most unhappy.

Guido Estelella stood in an insulated pressure suit on the surface of the new world. Everyone else called it Major, a contraction from "Alpha Centauri's major Planet." But in his own mind, Estelella called it Femina: a woman, a certain kind of woman—beautiful, selfish, treacherous, hot-tempered, dangerous.

He always felt tired here. Maybe it was the high gravity, putting an extra load on his muscles. Maybe it was just the constant fear.

For six weeks now, Guido had been flying a small landing craft down to the ground from the main ship, which was now orbiting five hundred kilometers above the planet's equator. At least twice each week he carried men and equipment down to the small base camp they had made by the shore of one of Femina's landlocked seas. The rest of the time he trained youngsters to fly the landing craft. There had been one wreck, killing two men and a girl. There had been several very close calls. Guido had aged more in the past six weeks than he did in his fifty years of cryosleep. Far more.

At the moment he was standing halfway between the stubby, winged landing rocket and the sprawl of equipment and plastic bubble tents that made up the base camp. A strong wind was whipping the green water of the sea into whitecaps, but inside his pressure suit, Guido felt the wind only as a faint screeching sound, muffled by his earphones. What was bothering him wasn't the wind, but the ugly brownish-yellow cloud that it was carrying toward them from the sea horizon.

"Ship to camp," a girl's voice crackled in his earphones. "We've confirmed that there's a new volcano active on the far coast of your sea, and the prevailing wind is bringing the fallout in your direction."

Guido nodded unhappily inside his helmet. He clicked a button on his waistband panel.

"I think we'd better get the shuttle up and out of here before that cloud arrives."

"Take off early? But we're not ready." It was Dan Christopher's voice, coming from the camp, much stronger than the ship's transmission.

Guido began to head toward the shuttle craft. "The last time I saw a cloud like that, it brought with it a lightning storm that kept us grounded for two days. And the rain had such a high sulfur content and so many stones in it that we had to resurface the entire top of the shuttle. The heat shield, even the pilot's bubble were pitted and etched. I don't want to get caught on the ground like that again."

"But you can't take all of us with you. Some of us will have to stay here during the storm. And the equipment..."

"My first responsibility is for the shuttle. Your equipment is protected, and you can sit out the storm in the underground shelter." He reached the shuttle's hatch, popped open the access panel, and pressed the stud inside. The hatch cracked open and the ladder unfolded at his feet.

"Wait," Dan's voice responded. "I'll send out as many people as we can. How many do you have room for?"

"Four. Unless you want to remove some of the cargo we packed aboard this morning."

"The deuterium? No chance. It's worth a helluva lot more than any of us."

Guido looked at the sea. It was frothing heavily now, steep breakers building up and dumping their energy on the sandy shore. The grass and trees were swaying in the mounting wind. The cloud was closer, spreading, blotting out the sunshine and the golden sky.

"I can wait about ten minutes," he said.

Inside the main bubble tent of the camp, Dan frowned and glared at the radio set. The main tent was a hodgepodge of radio equipment, viewscreens, cooking units, tables, crated supplies, folding tables and chairs, and five busy people.

Dan could hear the wind's growing anger outside. One of the girls seated at an analysis workbench glanced up at the roof of their transparent bubble: the plastic was rippling in the wind, making an odd kind of crinkling noise that they'd never heard before. It had taken them days to get accustomed to things like wind, and the noises that an open world makes. Now it was starting to sound frightening.

"Nancy, Tania, Vic ... you three get into suits right away and get to the ship. Ross, you and I are going to stay. Vic, bring the latest tank of deuterium with you."

"But it's less than half full," Vic argued.

Dan waved him down. "I know, but we'd better get it shipboard. No telling how bad this storm can get; might damage the equipment. The deuterium's far too valuable to risk."

Vic nodded.

"Get into a suit," Dan said. "Ross and I will hang on here."

Ross Cranston glanced sharply at Dan, but said nothing. He didn't like being second-best to a meter-tall tank of stainless steel, even though he knew that the deuterium gas inside it *was* more important to the ship than any computer operator.

The two girls and Vic were suited up in a few minutes, moving slowly in the heavy gravity. Vic hefted the tank by its handles, his knees giving slightly under its weight.

"Can you manage it?" Dan asked anxiously.

"Yeah." Vic's voice was muffled by his helmet.

The three of them cycled through the airlock and started trudging heavily through the wind-blown sand and grit toward the sleek little shuttle rocket. Dan watched them through the tent's transparent plastic. The two girls each grabbed a handle of the tank and helped Vic to carry it.

Turning, Dan saw that Ross was already at the hatch to the underground shelter.

"I'm going to suit up and make a last check of the refining equipment," Dan told him. He had to raise his voice to make himself heard over the wind, even though Ross was only a few meters away.

Ross nodded, visibly unhappy.

"Stay by the radio while I'm outside," Dan said as he reached for one of the two remaining pressure suits hanging stiffly by the airlock.

Ross frowned, but nodded again.

He's scared, Dan said to himself. *Scared of the storm, and scared that I might get hurt and need him to come out and help me.*

Neither of them had been on the ground when the first storm had struck, several weeks ago. Two people had been badly hurt when the wind toppled their communications antenna squarely onto the main tent. After that, the underground shelter was dug and the antenna was moved away from the rest of the camp.

By the time Dan had his suit zipped up, the shuttle's rocket engines had roared to life, out-howling even the mounting fury of the storm. Dan reached for his helmet and held it in both hands as he watched the shuttle trundle forward on its landing wheels, then gather speed and scream past the tent toward the beach. Its image shimmered and grew hazy in the heat from its own exhaust, but, squinting, Dan made out the delta-shaped craft as its nose lifted from the ground. It rolled along on its rear wheels for a moment longer, then it seemed to shoot almost straight upward, angling into the sky like a white arrowhead against the gathering darkness of the clouds.

In less than a minute the rolling thunder of the rocket's takeoff had rumbled away, leaving only the keening of the wind and the flapping of the tent's supposedly tearproof plastic.

As he put the helmet on, Dan thought, *There's a big difference between seeing storms on videotapes and really being in one.*

He checked the suit radio. "I'm going out now, Ross."

"Okay."

Dan turned to see Ross through the helmet's faceplate. The computerman looked scared and sullen.

"If you go down into the shelter, tell me before you leave the radio. I don't want to be stuck alone out there."

"I will."

Dan nodded and opened the inner airlock hatch. While the airlock was busy sealing itself and pumping out the good breathable air, Dan was trying to calm himself.

He wasn't frightened, he was excited; happy, really. He knew that was dangerous. *If you're scared, like Ross, you don't take chances.* But Dan was soaring high, spaced out on the excitement of being on the surface of a planet, *the* planet, the new world, facing its dangers unafraid. The storm, the wind, the crashing of the sea, the tossing golden trees, the dust and sand that was blowing through the air in ever-thickening clouds—it was wild and free. Not like the ship. Not like the quiet, orderly world where everything went according to schedule and there was absolutely no difference between one day and the next. This was *life*!

The airlock lights turned green. Dan clumped heavily to the outer hatch and turned its control wheel. It moved slowly, slowly, then the hatch popped open and a gust of grit-filled air puffed into the airlock.

Dan had to lean hard against the hatch to get it to swing open wide enough for him to go outside. Already his muscles felt strained. The high gravity made everything feel heavier than it should: the suit weighed down on him, the hatch opened grudgingly. It was an effort to lift one booted foot off the floor of the airlock and place it on the sandy soil outside.

The wind caught Dan by surprise. He had heard it long

enough, but now he felt it as physical force. Even inside the suit he could feel the wind buffeting him, trying to push him down.

He grinned.

Turning his back to the wind, he began trudging along the edge of the circular tent, heading for the once-gleaming jumble of metal shapes that was the refinery.

It gleamed no longer. Many weeks of being exposed to this corrosive atmosphere had dulled its exterior finish, and the storms and rains had etched and pitted the metal. *But the insides still work,* Dan told himself as he looked along the length of pipes that led down to the sea. Take in sea water, extract the deuterium, then return what's left—about 99.97 percent of it. *We don't want much from you,* Dan said silently to the sea. *Just three hundredths of a percent. Enough to live on.*

A shriek of metal against metal made him jump in sudden fear. From inside the helmet, he couldn't see what was happening. He had to turn around and lean his whole body backward to look up.

One of the solar battery panels—the collection of silicon-based cells that converted sunlight into electricity—had ripped loose from the roof of the refinery's storage tower. Now it was sliding along the bulbous metal domes of the separation equipment, banging, screeching . . . It blew free and sailed like a jagged enormous leaf into the wind, pinwheeling as it disappeared into the dust clouds that were blowing everywhere.

"Never worked right anyway!" Dan yelled. The solar batteries had been badly eroded by the sulfur-rich air. Dan had been forced to fly a small generator down from the ship to provide electricity for the base camp.

Everything else on this side of the equipment complex looked tight and safe. *Even if the other solar panels rip off, that's no problem. Unless they tear into the tent.*

Dan's legs were starting to tremble with exertion. He forced himself to plod around the side of the big refinery. As he turned the corner, the wind caught him head-on and nearly toppled him backward. Leaning heavily into the wind, he trudged on.

It was getting very dark now. And the wind was screaming insanely. Dust clouds made it hard to see any distance at all.

Lightning flashed. Dan heard it crackle in his earphones as it flickered out over the sea, brightening the whole scene for an eyeblink's time. It sent a jolt of irrational fear through him.

Then came the boom of the thunder, distant but menacing. Dan moved on.

He couldn't see the radio antenna in the darkness and dust. Then another flash of lightning and there it was, swaying like a gigantic, leafless, branchless tree. But it held firm. The new anchor pins were doing their job.

A sudden gust of wind actually lifted one of Dan's boots off the ground. He swayed for a moment, fought hard for balance, then planted the foot back on the ground.

"Ross?" he called into his helmet microphone.

No answer.

"Ross! Are you there? I'm coming in . . . be back in a minute."

Silence. Only the crackling of lightning static in his earphones. *He's gone back into the shelter,* Dan realized.

Bending into the wind, Dan clumped forward slowly. It was painful, each step. Another horrible tearing sound, and he saw out of the corner of his eye another of the solar panels flipping off madly, hitting the ground with one corner and bouncing along like a child's runaway toy.

Then a more ominous sound. A groaning, gut-wrenching sound, like the earth itself being pulled apart. Dan looked up at the metal domes and towers alongside him, but couldn't see any cause for the . . .

It moaned again. And fainter, the sound of—flapping. Something soft, something plastic . . . *the tent*!

Dan pushed himself madly along the side of the refinery, trying to get to the side where the tent stood. If it still stood. He stumbled and fell face forward, but hardly stopped at all. He crawled on all fours for a few paces, then painfully pushed himself to his feet again. The wind was getting intolerable.

Grabbing hold of a projecting ladder-rung from the metal tower he stood next to, swaying in the howling insanity of the wind, Dan rested for a moment, then pushed on. He rounded the corner and saw what the groaning noise was.

The tent was collapsed and flapping on the ground like some monstrous dying pterodactyl. Dan couldn't see the airlock, couldn't tell if Ross had made it to the underground shelter before the collapse. If he hadn'd he was dead inside there.

Only one thing was certain. There was no way for Dan to get inside to safety.

The storm howled triumphantly.

In the ship's observation center, at the zero-gravity hub, the only sound was the faintest whispering of the air-circulating fans.

Larry hovered weightlessly at the transparent wall of the big plastiglass blister, staring out at the massive curving bulk of the golden planet below. A huge yellow-brown smear was staining one section of the planet's surface: the storm.

He touched the plastiglass wall with his fingertips, anchoring himself lightly in place. There was a wall phone within arm's reach, but he didn't want to use it, didn't want to hear what was happening.

"Dan's still down there."

Before he turned, he knew it was Valery's voice. In the golden light coming up from the planet, she looked like an ancient goddess, shining against the darkness of the observation center's dim lighting. Her face, though, was very human: worried, almost frightened.

Larry said, "The shuttle came back about fifteen minutes ago. Estelella brought the two girls and Vic O'Malley with him. Dan and Cranston stayed. Dan made certain that he sent every gram of deuterium they had processed."

"And now he's in the middle of the storm." Her voice was calm, but just barely. Larry could hear the beginnings of a tremble in it.

"They've got the underground shelter. He'll be all right."

"Has he sent word? Do you know for sure...?"

Larry jerked a thumb toward the storm cloud. "Can't get radio transmission through that stuff. We've tried every frequency. Too much electrical interference."

"He could be dead."

"No. He's tough and smart. He'll get through it all right."

She stared out at the swirling muddy-colored storm cloud. "It looks alive...like some monster eating...." Val reached out for Larry. "Can't you do *anything*? Send the shuttle down for him? Something!"

He took her in his arms and rocked her gently. "There's not a thing we can do but wait. The shuttle would be wrecked trying to fly through that. All we can do is wait." And his mind was asking him, *If it were you down there and Dan safely up here, would she be this upset?*

"It makes you feel so helpless," Val whimpered.

"I know. I know."

"How long will the storm last?"

Larry shrugged. "Nobody knows. Not enough data on the weather patterns of this planet. The last one took two days to blow past the camp. But we don't know if it was an unusually big one, or . . ." He let his voice trail off.

"Or an unusually small one," Valery finished for him. "This one looks bigger, doesn't it?"

Larry didn't answer.

She kept staring out at the planet, at the storm. "Oh, Larry, if he dies there . . ."

"It'll be my fault."

Val turned sharply enough to bounce slightly away from the plastiglass. "Your fault? Why should it be your fault?"

"I sent him down there, didn't I?"

"It's part of his job. He wanted to go."

Larry said, "I could have stopped him. I could have ordered somebody else to go down instead. I knew it was dangerous down there."

Val was drifting freely in a small semicircle around Larry. He had to turn his back to the plastiglass to keep his eyes on her. She floated in midair, a golden goddess shining against the night.

"Did you *want* him to be exposed to danger?" she asked.

"You mean, did I want him to risk getting killed?" Larry closed his eyes and found the answer in his mind. "No, I didn't."

"Not consciously," Val murmured.

"What?"

"You knew he'd be running into danger."

Nodding, Larry admitted, "Sure. I even thought about going down there with him . . . but I'm not qualified for any of the jobs that need doing down there. I couldn't justify taking up space on the shuttle and in the camp, just to show everybody I'm as brave as Dan is."

"But in the back of your mind you knew he might be killed."

"Of course. But that doesn't mean . . ." He began to see what she was driving at. "Val, you don't think that I . . . you *can't* believe that!"

"I don't," she said. But it sounded weak, unconvincing.

Larry thought, *It would certainly settle all the problems if he got killed down there.* Then another part of his mind screamed, *And that would make you a murderer, whether you planned it beforehand or not!*

Valery seemed to sense the turmoil in his mind. She took him by the hand and pushed against the plastiglass wall, driving the two of them into a slow drift across the big, darkened, empty-looking chamber.

"I guess you're right," she said over her shoulder to him. "There's not much we can to except watch and wait."

"Val . . . I didn't want it this way, honestly. I didn't . . ."

"I know," she said soothingly. "I know."

They touched down on the floor easily, their velcroed slippers catching and holding gently against the carpeting there.

"As long as we're here," Valery said, leting his hand go and walking carefully, in a slow zero-*g* glide, toward the desk and instruments in the middle of the room, "I might as well show you what I've found out about the other stars."

She's changing the subject, Larry realized, *trying to get both our minds off Dan.*

Val sat at the desk while Larry stood beside her. She touched buttons on the desktop keyboard and pictures appeared on the viewscreen.

To Larry, they all looked like tiny white dots. The stars were bigger and brighter; in some pictures they were glaringly bright. But the planets around the stars were all featureless blobs of light.

Valery shook her head after showing about twenty of the pictures. "Those are the best we have so far. And it's all pretty depressing. Nothing even close to being Earthlike."

Larry blinked at her. "None of those planets . . ."

"They're mostly gas giants, like Jupiter. Or little balls of rock, like Earth's Moon."

"Can you be sure?"

She ran a hand through her hair. "Oh, I'm still working on it, trying to get better data, more precision in the spectrograms and visuals . . . but it looks very bad."

Larry sagged into a half-sitting, half-leaning position against the desk's edge. "And this goes for both Epsilon Indi and Epsilon Eridani."

"Yes, both stars. I'm afraid the planet here is the only choice we're going to have, Larry."

He sat there a moment longer, his mind turning slowly, wearily. "When...when will you report this to the Council?"

"I want to make the data much more precise," she answered. "I haven't shown this to anyone yet...you're the only one. In a week or two, I'll report it to the Council."

He nodded dumbly.

Valery went to turn off the last picture from the viewscreen. "Oops!" She pulled her hand away from the keyboard as if it were burning hot. "I almost hit the ERASE button. That would've been stupid."

"Huh?"

"All this data—weeks and weeks of work—would be erased from the computer's memory bank if I had touched that button just now." She pressed the proper button and the viewscreen went blank. Looking up at Larry, she added, "The only two places where the data's stored are in the computer's memory bank...and my own head."

Larry nodded at her, but said nothing.

(12)

The wind was getting even worse.

Dan tried to flatten himself into a niche between two of the big water-treatment tanks, but he felt the wind tearing at him, trying to pry him loose and bowl him along like the solar panels had been blown away. It was getting hard to stay on his feet. The noise was overpowering, and he could barely see a dozen meters ahead because of the dust and flying sand. He could hear the gritty stuff grinding against his suit; a yellowish film was building up on his helmet faceplate. He wiped at it awkwardly with a gloved hand, smearing it even worse than before.

Can't stay here, he knew. *Got to get into the shelter.*

He edged away from the metal tanks far enough to poke his head around their curving flanks and look at the tent. A sudden gust of wind nearly knocked him over. The tent was flapping wildly in the roaring wind, snapping and tearing like a huge blanket. It cracked against one of the slim metal pipes leading from the squat round dome of the centrifuge and the pipe went *clang!* and snapped in half. Dan suddenly got a picture of what would happen if that tent-whip hit him.

It was getting difficult to move the arms of his suit. *Muscles tired...or are the joints getting jammed with grit? Probably both.*

Then he started wondering what would happen if his suit sprung a leak, if the sulfurous air ate through his plastic oxygen tubing, if the grit made the suit completely immovable, if...

Stop it! he commanded himself. *Try to think. Think calmly. Are you safer here or should you try to get into the shelter?*

The question was answered for him. A half-dozen spears of

lightning flickered off in the distance, far enough to be still out over the sea, close enough so that the thunder exploded almost immediately with shattering noise.

Lightning! Dan remembered what he'd been told about the last storm. The lightning bolts loved the big high-standing metal equipment that stood there. Dozens of bolts had hit the refinery.

If I'm out here when the lightning starts striking . . .

He knew he had to get to the shelter.

Slowly, carefully, Dan hunkered down onto his knees and then flattened out on his belly. The wind-blown dust was even worse down at ground level; he could barely see an arm's length before him. The wind tried to lift him up off the ground, sail him like a glider. He pressed himself into the ground as hard as he could.

He crawled. Centimeter by agonized centimeter, he crawled on all fours toward the tent. He was guided more by the flapping, whip-cracking sounds of the tent's loose fabric than by vision. All he could see was flying sand and wind-flattened yellow grass.

It seemed to take hours. Dan knew it was only a few meters from where he had been standing to the edge of the tent, but it seemed more like lightyears now. A new blast of lightning turned everything glare-white for an instant, and the thunder seemed to be trying to crack him open like an eggshell. Every muscle in his body ached and burned, and he was drenched with sweat.

Got to stop . . . rest . . . But something inside him said fiercely, *Stop now and you're dead. Keep going, dammit! Keep going!*

He inched along. A lightning bolt struck metal somewhere close beside him with an unbelievable burst of light and a deafening explosion. Something hit Dan's right leg and the suit seemed to go completely stiff there. He couldn't move the leg at all.

Or is my own leg hurt? He didn't feel any extra pain there, but he knew that shock sometimes cut off pain. And besides, every part of him already hurt so much. . . .

His outstretched hand bumped into something. The flat, circular plastisteel foundation of the tent.

Dan raised his head and saw the tent's fabric looming up, flapping wildly, right in front of him. Like a nightmare monster.

Rising up, up, filling all his visions with its rippling, snapping immensity. Then with a whip-crack it flattened out again, only to begin rising once more immediately.

Can't go through that, Dan realized.

He fumbled at his belt for the suit's tool kit. It was almost impossible to feel shapes with the gloves on, but at last he pulled out the little pistol-shaped laser that they used for cutting and welding.

Hope it's charged up. Dan pressed the snub nose of the laser against the edge of the tent's foundation and pulled on the trigger. The pistol didn't make a sound or vibration, but after a moment or two Dan could see the plastic fabric of the tent glowing, tearing, separating from the foundation.

With an agonized screeching sound, the plastic ripped free of the foundation and went billowing into the wind, disappearing into the howling storm like a giant bird suddenly let loose.

Dan clung to the foundation's edge for a long, weary moment, then pulled himself slowly over the lip. He dragged himself, using his arms and his one movable leg, groping for the hatch to the underground shelter. Desks, chairs, viewscreens, even the heavy computer consoles had been blown over by the wind, bowled away like so much dust. Another bolt of lightning struck with shattering force, blinding and deafening Dan for several moments.

Then his hands found the hatch. He pulled himself up onto his elbows, nearly unconscious with pain and exhaustion. Eyes stinging and nearly blinded with sweat, he groped for the control switch. He found it and leaned on it heavily. It wouldn't move. He forced his weight on the tiny switch as hard as he could. Nothing.

Jammed by the grit.

He raised a fist, taking all the strength he had, and pounded on the hatch itself. *If Cranston's down there . . . if he's not dead . . .* Even his thoughts were getting fuzzy now. Pound. Raise the fist and let it drop. Raise the . . . fist and . . . let it *drop.*

The hatch moved! It pushed against his inert arm. A straining, rasping sound and Dan could see the hatch lifting slowly. A gloved hand was pushing it open from the inside.

Everything seemed to go hazy, foggy, blood-red and then dead-black. Dan could feel his body moving—being moved?—

and the noise of the wind's evil howling dimmed, muffled. Somebody was talking to him, urgent words crackling in his earphones. Then the blackness swam up and surrounded him and pulled him downward into oblivion.

When he awoke, his helmet was off. Cranston was completely out of his suit, dressed only in blue coveralls. The little underground shelter seemed cool and snug and safe. The wind was a distant mumble somewhere outside. The shelter was bright and quiet. Its curving walls and ceiling seemed to gather around him protectively. Its bunk felt soft and comfortable.

Cranston was standing by the cooking unit.

"Do you think you could eat something?" he asked, looking worriedly at Dan.

Dan realized he was sitting on one of the bunks, slouched against the curving wall of the shelter.

"Yeh...sure." Every muscle ached. His head throbbed horribly. His mouth felt dry and caked with dust.

Glancing down at his legs, he saw that Cranston had taken off the bottom half of his suit, as well as his helmet.

"There was a bad dent on the left leg of the suit," the computerman said. "I was worried that your own leg might've been hurt. It's bruised pretty bad, but I don't think it's anything worse than that."

"When..." Dan tried to lick his lips, but his tongue was dry. He croaked, "When did you...come into the shelter?"

Cranston flashed him a guilty glance, then turned his attention to the cooker. "Uh...I tried calling you on the radio...no answer. I didn't know what was happening. Then...uh, the tent...it looked like it was going to collapse...."

"It did," Dan said wearily. "You did the best thing."

"Oh...okay..." He smiled, still looking slightly guilty.

Dr. Hsai's quarters looked like pictures of Japanese homes that Valery had seen on the education tapes.

The compartment was no bigger than any other single man's quarters. But it looked different. There were living green vines climbing along one wall, reaching upward to the ceiling light panels. A painting filled part of the same wall, showing soft green hills and a river with a delicate bridge arching over it. The vines seemed to blend into the picture, the two merged and became a single experience. The bunk was austere, hard-looking, but a beautiful red drape hung beside it. There was no other furniture visible, except two little pillows on the floor and a low-slung black lacquered table.

Dr. Hsai himself was dressed in a loose-fitting robe of black and white, with just a hint of gold thread at the collar.

"What a beautiful robe!" Valery said, despite herself, as Dr. Hsai ushered her into his quarters.

"Thank you very much." The psychotech smiled pleasantly. "It belonged to my great-grandfather and has been handed down through four generations."

"It's very lovely."

He smiled again and bowed ever so slightly. "I am afraid," he said, "that I have no western furniture for you to sit upon. I usually receive visitors in the office of the infirmary. But you seemed so insistent...."

"I can sit on the floor," Val said. She curled up next to the bunk.

Dr. Hsai offered her one of the pillows, and Val put it behind the small of her back, then leaned against the edge of the bunk.

"You wish to ask me a medical question?" Dr. Hsai inquired, sitting in the middle of the tiny room.

"A psychological question," Val replied.

He nodded. "I might have guessed. Unfortunately, my knowledge of psychiatry is far from expert, although I have been studying the available tapes on the subject very carefully these past few weeks."

"Why?" Val asked. "Do you think there's a killer aboard the ship, too?"

Hsai smiled patiently. "Not at all. At least, I hope not. But certain individuals believe that there might be a killer among us, and I am trying to pin down the origins of these fears."

"There have been these ... accidents."

"Yes."

"Including my father."

"Yes."

Valery was starting to feel uncomfortable. What she wanted to ask suddenly began to sound silly in her own mind. Worse still, she felt that Dr. Hsai knew what she wanted, but was being too polite to bring up the subject himself.

"Dan Christopher has been under great emotional stress," the psychotech said, mainly to keep the conversation from faltering. "He is a very troubled young man. Perhaps it would have been wise to revive one or more of our sleeping psychiatrists, to examine him thoroughly."

"Yes, I was wondering why you didn't do that," Val said.

"Larry Belsen said it wouldn't be necessary. As Chairman, he has the responsibility to pass on all requests for revival."

"Larry disapproved?"

"Yes. I asked him specificially if he wanted us to revive a psychiatrist.... It was when Dan Christopher was in the infirmary for observation, and I could find nothing psychologically wrong with him."

"And Larry said he didn't want a psychiatrist revived?"

Dr. Hsai almost frowned. "Not in those words, but he told me he thought it would be unnecessary. You know, of course, the difficulties involved in reviving a person, and the limited resources we have. It cannot be done lightly. And we cannot ask the person, once revived, to return to sleep a few days or weeks later. It is not medically wise, for one thing."

"I know." Valery suddenly realized that she was gnawing on her lip. A nervous habit. She looked back at Dr. Hsai. "About the question I wanted to ask you..."

"So?"

Somehow it didn't feel so silly now. "Could ... could a person do things—violent things—and not know it?"

Hsai looked puzzled.

"I mean, could somebody commit a murder and then not remember he did it? You know, his conscious mind doesn't even know what he's really doing."

Hsai gave the faintest of shrugs. "I have heard of such cases in my education, of course, but... of course, I have never dealt with such a situation myself."

Before she could think about it, Valery spilled out, "Do you think that the reason Larry didn't want a psychiatrist revived is that he was afraid the psychiatrist might find out something about him—about Larry himself?"

For an instant, Hsai looked shocked. Then he dropped a

mask of oriental and professional calm over his face. "You believe that Larry Belsen might be unbalanced?"

"My father's injury was no accident," Val said, feeling miserable. "Somebody did it. Either Dan or Larry...or somebody else."

For several moments Dr. Hsai sat there silently, his eyes closed. Then he looked up and said, "I will immediately take steps to revive the ship's best psychiatrists. If your suspicions are even remotely close to the truth, this is an emergency situation. There is no need to wait for the Chairman's approval under these circumstances."

"The only trouble is," Val said, "that Dan might already be dead."

(13)

Dan knew it was a nightmare, yet it still had him terrified.

He was running, or trying to. He seemed to be caught in some thick syrupy liquid that made all his motions languidly slow. Something was roaring behind him, getting louder, catching up to him. When he tried to look over his shoulder, all he could see was a giant pair of hands reaching for him.

He tried to run faster, but couldn't. The roaring became ear-shattering. Lightning crashed and the hands grabbed at him, caught him, bore him down, pushed him under, beat at him, pummeled him. He couldn't breathe, couldn't even scream....

He woke up, wide-eyed and drenched with sweat, trembling. Half a meter above his face was the curving ceiling of the underground shelter. In the bunk below him he could hear Cranston snoring lightly. The hum of electrical machinery was the only other sound, beside his own throbbing pulsebeat.

The wind had died!

Dan pushed himself up to a sitting position, and his back muscles screamed agony. For a moment he was dizzy. Forcing both the pain and faintness down, he swung his legs slowly over the edge of the bunk and slid down to the plastic flooring. The jolt when his feet hit the floor sent a fresh spark of pain shooting through him.

He shook Cranston awake.

"Huh . . . whuzzit . . ."

"I think the storm's over," Dan said. "You try the radio while I get suited up."

Cranston swung out of the bunk slowly. For a long moment he sat on its edge, head drooping tiredly.

"What . . . how . . . what time's it?"

Dan glanced at his wristwatch. It was set on ship time. "We must've slept more than twelve hours. Come on, try the radio."

"How d'you feel?" Cranston asked as he pulled himself to his feet.

"Black and blue all over. Otherwise okay."

"It's this damned gravity."

Cranston shuffled over to the little desk that bore the communications transceiver, minus viewscreen. As he flicked it on and started talking into the speaker, Dan pulled on the one usable pressure suit they had left.

By the time Dan was checking the seal of his helmet, he could hear Cranston saying, "No use. Can't get through to them. No answer."

"Interference from the storm?"

The computerman shook his head. "Not much static. Just silence. I don't think this set has enough muscle to reach the ship without the main antenna and the amplifier up in the tent."

Dan said nothing. He clumped to the airlock, stepped through it, and shut the inner hatch. The airlock cycled through, pumping all its air into storage tanks, then flashed the green "all clear" light.

Dan reached up and unsealed the outer hatch. He pushed it upward, and a fine powder of yellowish sand and ash trickled down onto his faceplate.

Stepping up the rungs of the metal ladder set into the airlock's wall, Dan pushed the outside hatch all the way open and stuck his head up above the opening.

The camp looked as if it had been bombed. The tent was completely gone, not a shred of it left. The desks and consoles and other gear from inside the tent were nowhere in sight, either. Nothing there but the plastisteel foundation, and even that was buried under several centimeters of powdery sand and ash.

The sky overhead was gray now, sullen-looking. The clouds were high, but moving with great speed. Dan turned stiffly with the suit and tried to look in all directions. No break in the clouds anywhere: gray from horizon to horizon.

The refinery was a complete shambles. The big cylinders and spheres were cracked open, blackened and burned. *Not much to salvage from it,* Dan realized. He knew he should have been glad just to be alive, but somehow he felt terribly dejected, defeated, let down.

The communications mast was gone, of course. So were most of the trees. The grass was still there, though, poking through the sand and ash, its cheerful yellow strangely incongruous in the somber scene of destruction.

Dan stepped down the ladder again, lowering the hatch after him. He sealed it, set the airlock to recycling again; the native sulfurous air was pumped outside, the breathable air that had been stored away hissed out of the tanks and filled the tiny airlock once again. When the light flashed green, Dan opened the inner hatch and stepped back into the main area of the shelter.

He took off his helmet. It felt as if it weighed a ton.

Cranston was still seated in front of the radio. "No response. We can't reach them."

"They can't see us, either," Dan said grimly. "Cloud deck's still covering us."

"Isn't there any way we can tell them we're here? Can't they spot us with radar or infrared or something?"

Dan plopped on the lower bunk and reached for the zips on his suit legs. "Radar won't tell them if we're alive or not. But if we could make a big enough hot spot, IR might pick it up...."

"A hot spot. With what?"

Dan shrugged. "I don't think we've got anything bigger than the suit lasers. That won't do."

"Uhmm..." Cranston started to look concerned. "How much air and water do we have?"

"We pull our oxygen out of the planet's air," Dan answered. "Clean out the sulfur and other gunk so we can breathe it. That's not problem. Water, though... our water purification gear was all topside. It's gone.... There's probably not more than a couple days' worth in here."

"And how long will the clouds cover us?"

Dan shrugged. "Maybe we ought to try to figure out how to make a big hot spot."

Larry was pacing back and forth along the bridge, followed by Joe Haller and Guido Estelella. The technicians working the various consoles kept their faces turned very carefully to their work.

"But you can't let them sit down there without even trying to pick them up!" Haller was shouting.

Larry whirled and pointed to one of the viewscreens. It showed nothing but gray cloud scudding across the planet's face.

"There's absolutely no evidence that they're still alive," he snapped back, lower-keyed but still with an edge of anger to his voice. "You want me to risk our only qualified pilot and our only landing shuttle on the chance that they might have survived the storm?"

"Hell yes!"

"I'm willing to try it," Estelella said.

Larry shook his head. "We have no idea of what conditions are like under those clouds. The whole surface could be buried under tons of volcanic ash."

"We have other landing shuttles," Haller insisted. "You can order them taken out of the storage depot and reassembled."

"Can I replace our one qualified astronaut?" Larry demanded.

"But he's volunteered to go!"

"No." Larry pushed past Haller and started pacing the bridge again.

Haller followed doggedly. "You're killing two men!"

"They're already dead," Larry said. "We'd have heard from them by now if they were still alive. The storm's been over nearly two days."

"Their communications gear might've been damaged. They could be hurt, trapped in wreckage . . . anything."

Larry countered, "Nothing survived that storm. You saw the electrical signals we were getting from the lightning. Like a continuous sheet of flame. The wind speeds were right off the scale of our meteorological instruments. Those clouds are still moving at fifty kilometers an hour. How do we know what the wind and weather conditions are like under the clouds?"

Haller's shoulders slumped. "How much longer are the clouds supposed to last?"

"Nobody knows," Larry said. "They're coming from the chain of volcanoes on the other side of the sea. It might end in a few hours or a few weeks. Nobody knows."

"So we're just going to sit here and wait."

"That's all we can do."

Haller looked as if he wanted to say something more, but

instead he turned abruptly away from Larry and marched off the bridge. Estelella stood there for a puzzled moment, then, with a shrug, he walked off too.

Larry turned to the viewscreens showing the planet's surface. Gray clouds covered almost everything. He shook his head. *They're dead,* he told himself. *They must be dead.*

But if they're not, he knew, *you're killing them.*

Abruptly, he went over to one of the technicians and said, "I'm leaving the bridge. Take over for me."

The girl looked up at him, surprised, "Where will you be?"

"You can reach me on the intercom. Page me, if you need me."

Larry ducked through the doorway into the corridor that connected to his office. He hesitated for just a moment, then entered the compartment. Without bothering to slide the door shut, he went to the phone and punched it on savagely.

"Get Valery Loring here, right away."

The computer's voice said calmly, "Working."

Valery appeared at his door ten agonized minutes later.

Larry was still fidgeting beside his desk when she arrived.

"You sent for me?"

He wanted to reach out and hold her. Instead, he said flatly, "They think I want to kill Dan."

"Who does?"

Larry saw his hands flutter angrily. "Haller, Estelella, the whole damned crew on the bridge, for all I know."

Standing uncertainly by the door, Valery said, "Do you want to kill him?"

"No! Of course not! What kind of a question is that?"

"Then why are you afraid of what they think?"

"You don't understand," he said quietly. "None of you understands at all."

"Understands what, Larry?"

"I'm the Chairman. Can't you see what that means? I have to decide. Me. My decision. Life or death. I have to decide on sending Estelella down there ... maybe getting him killed. Or forcing him to stay aboard the ship while we can't tell for certain what the surface conditions are. And that'll probably kill Dan, if he isn't dead already."

"There's still no word from him?"

"Nothing. We've been scanning the area with every instrument we've got. No indication that they survived. Nothing at all."

"They could be in the shelter."

"I know." He pulled out the desk chair and sank into it.

Valery remained standing by the door.

"I have to decide," Larry repeated.

"Does Estelella want to try a landing?" she asked.

"Yes. But it's my decision to make, not his."

"I know. I wish there was some way I could help you."

"Nobody can help."

She took an uncertain step into the tiny office. "Larry ... what do you *want* to do?"

He stared at her. The answer was obvious to him. "I want to send Estelella down there and see if they're still alive. Do you think I want to kill Dan?"

She said, "I think you want to do what's right, but you're letting your responsibilities as Chairman get in the way of your best judgment."

"But suppose he wrecks the shuttle? Suppose he's killed trying to land? We don't know very much about the conditions down there. . . ."

"He volunteered to try," Val answered. "You want to try it. Even if he's killed, at least you'll both have tried. It's better than sitting around and doing nothing, isn't it? If you don't try, we know Dan will die. But if you do try . . ."

He nodded unhappily. "You're right . . . they all know . . ."

"There's something that *I* know," Valery said.

"What is it?"

"I know that no matter what's happened . . . or what's going to happen . . . you'd never willingly hurt anyone. Not even Dan."

"He . . . he was my best friend. We were all friends, once."

"A million years ago." Val's voice was faint and distant.

Larry took a deep breath. Standing, he said, "All right, we'll try it. But I'm riding down with Estelella myself."

Valery didn't seem surprised. "There's no need for that. You don't have to prove anything. Not to me or anyone else."

"No, I want to do it."

"But you can't. You're the Chairman. And besides, you'd only be wasting valuable mass and space aboard the shuttle.

There's nothing you can do to help . . . except to make the right decision."

Dan was standing out on the surface in the protective suit. His face was haggard, with several days' worth of dark scrubby beard mottling his chin. His mouth was caked and dry.

He was staring at the sea, only a few hundred meters from the wrecked base, where he stood. The waves were lapping up softly, sliding up onto the sandy beach. He could walk out there and be waist-deep in the water . . .

Can't drink it, he was telling himself. *It's got to be purified. The contaminants in it will kill you.*

"Another few hours," he mumbled, his voice thick and raspy, "and it won't make any difference what's in the water. We'll have to try it."

Cranston was back in the shelter, in his bunk, paralyzed by the fear of dying. Dan found that he couldn't stand being in the cramped little shelter with him. It was better up here on the surface, even though he had to stay inside the suit. His own body smell was getting overpowering, though.

He almost smiled. *Larry's going to get his way, after all. I can just see him. Death-planet, he'll call it. Too dangerous. Got to move on.* The smile faded. *He's going to make sure we die.*

A distant crack of thunder and its following rumble made him look up. Another storm? No, the sky looked the same as it had for the past three days: gray, completely overcast, but not stormy. The wind was so light that he couldn't notice it except as a gentle swaying of the grass.

Dan looked up again. And blinked. There was a white streak etching across the clouded sky. A thin white line. A *contrail!*

If he could have jumped inside the heavy suit, he would have. He wanted to leap up and down, to dance, to shout.

Instead he stood rooted to the spot, watching as the streak swung around overhead. He could make out the tiny arrowhead form of the shuttle rocket now. It grew, took on solidity. The sweetly beautiful roar of the craft's auxiliary turbo engines came to him, even through the helmet and earphones. The ship banked smoothly, raced low across the water and came up toward him, landing wheels out. It touched down with a puff of dust, rolled past the ruined base.

Dan stood there motionless as the shuttle craft taxied

around, nosed back toward the base and edged slowly toward him, engines screeching and blowing up a miniature sandstorm of dust and ash behind it.

Then the roar died away. The bubble canopy popped open and a pressure-suited figure stood up.

In sudden realization, Dan reached for the radio switch on his belt.

"...just stand there, will you? Say something, wave, *do something*! What's the matter, are you frozen?"

"I'm okay," Dan croaked, his voice sounding strange and harsh, even to himself. "Just...thirsty."

"You're alive!" It was Estelella's voice, and there was no missing the elation in it. "Don't move... I've got plenty of water with me. Be right there."

If Dan had still had enough moisture in his body, he would have cried for joy.

They celebrated that night.

Nearly everyone on the ship, all those who weren't absolutely needed on duty, gathered in the cafeteria and ate and drank and sang together. Dan had to fight off the determined medical insistence of the whole infirmary staff, but he made the scene too. In a wheelchair.

"It's my party, dammit!" he shouted at them.

For the first time in months, Dan, Valery, and Larry found themselves at the same place, even at the same table. And for a few hours, it was almost like old times. No one mentioned Larry's reluctance to send a ship down to the surface. Old tensions, old fears were forgotten. For a while.

They laughed together, remembered happier times. They sang far into the early hours of the morning.

But then, as the party was finally winding down and people were tiptoeing or staggering or lurching homeward, somebody said loudly enough for everyone to hear:

"I guess this proves that we can't stay on the surface. Too dangerous. We were lucky to get you guys back alive."

Dan's face went deathly grim. "It proves that we need much better equipment and precautions to work on the surface. But if we lived through that storm, we can live through whatever else the planet throws at us."

"I don't know..." Larry began.

Valery said, "We still need more deuterium, don't we? Someone will have to go back to the surface, with more equipment."

"That'll be a long, tough job."

"But it's got to be done."

Dan pushed himself out of the wheelchair and got to his feet. He still looked gaunt, eyes dark and haggard. "We can do what needs to be done. And our children, when they've been specially adapted for life on the surface, will make that planet their playground."

Larry glanced at Val. She was looking up at Dan. And the only thing he felt in his heart was hatred.

(14)

It was the next morning when Dan tracked down Valery in the ship's library.

She was sitting in one of the small tape-reading booths. There were two viewscreens mounted side by side on the booth wall, and Val was comparing some of the spectrograms she had made with the big telescope against the special analysis charts in the library's files.

Dan tapped on the glass door of the booth. She turned, smiled, and waved him in.

He slid the door open and squeezed into the booth. There was only one chair, and hardly enough room for him to stand beside her. The door slid shut automatically as soon as he let go of it.

"Cozy in here," he said, grinning.

"It's not built for comfort," Valery agreed, shifting her weight slightly on the stiff metal chair.

"I wanted to know if you're free for dinner tonight?" His voice rose enough to make it a question.

Val shook her head.

"Lunch?"

"Dan," she said sadly. "I told you and Larry the same thing. Until the two of you stop fighting each other, I'm not going to have much to do with either of you. I won't be the bait in a battle between you.

"But you said . . ."

"I've said a lot of things. Now I'm saying that the answer to both of you is *no* . . . as long as you're fighting each other."

"But Larry is . . ."

"I don't want to hear it."

Dan could feel hot anger rising inside him.

She almost smiled at him. "You don't have to look so grim."

"Don't I?"

"No. . . . Look, here are some of the results of the spectra I've taken with the main telescope. I haven't shown them to anybody else, but I'll show them to you."

He shrugged. "Big thrill."

"Don't be fresh. And you've got to promise not to tell anyone until I make my report to the Council next week. I don't want these data leaking out before I've had a chance to check everything through thoroughly."

"I can keep a secret," Dan said tightly.

"Well . . ." Val lowered her voice to almost a whisper. "Both stars seem to have Earthlike planets."

"What?"

Nodding, Val went on, her voice rising with excitement. "Epsilon Indi is the closer of the two stars, so I can resolve its planets more easily. Not that I've been able to see anything except a pinpoint of light, even with the best image intensification. But the gravimetric measurements look good, and the spectral data . . ."

She turned to the twin viewscreens. "Look . . . here's a spectrum I made twenty-four hours ago of the innermost planet of Epsilon Indi—the one that's about Earth's size and mass. And here, on the other screen, is a spectrum I made of Earth with the same telescope, a few days earlier. We're just about the same distance from both planets—about four lightyears."

Dan squinted at the two viewscreens. Each showed a smear of colors, crisscrossed by hundreds of dark lines. The Earth spectrum seemed to be dominated by shades of yellow, while the Epsilon Indi spectrum seemed more orange.

"The background continuum isn't what's important," Valery explained. "Look at the absorption lines. . . ." She pointed from one viewscreen to the other. "Oxygen here. And here. Nitrogen, on both. Water vapor . . . carbon dioxide," her slim hand kept shifting back and forth, "and all at just about the same concentration. It's fantastic!"

"You mean this planet's just like Earth?"

"So close to each other that it's hard to tell where they're different, from this distance, at least."

"But . . ." Dan's insides were churning now. "But, the Epsilon Indi planet is just as far from us now as Earth and the solar system."

"Yes, that's true," Val admitted.

"We could never make it there."

Instead of answering, Valery turned back to the keyboard in front of the viewscreens. One of the pictures disappeared, to be replaced by another spectrogram.

"This is the spectrum of Femina . . . it's much more intense than the Epsilon Indi planet's, because we're right next to it."

"And the other spectrogram is still Earth's?"

"Yes," Val said. "And look at the differences in the atmospheric constituents. Sulfur oxides, big gobs of carbon dioxide and monoxide, other things I haven't even identified yet."

Even Dan's unpracticed eye could see that the two spectrograms were very different from each other.

"Considering what you went through down there on the surface," Valery said, "I should think you'd want to repair the ship and then push on for Epsilon Indi."

Dan said nothing. He leaned against the acoustically insulated wall of the tiny booth; his face was pale, his eyes troubled.

"Thanks for showing me," he said quietly. "I . . . won't tell anybody until you give your report at the Council meeting."

And then he pulled the door open and stepped out of the booth, leaving Valery there alone to watch him walking quickly, through the tape shelves of the library.

Now I've told each of them, the exact opposite of what he wants to hear, she thought. *Which one will come after me and try to silence me before the Council meeting?*

Four days passed.

Larry sat in the main conference room, at his usual chair at the head of the table. But the table was mostly empty. Only Dan, Dr. Polanyi, Mort Campbell, and Guido Estelella were there, all clustered up close to Larry's seat.

"From everything you've been telling me," Larry was saying, looking at the chart on the viewscreen at the far end of the long, narrow room, "we have no choice but to go down to the surface again and try to repair the refining equipment."

Polanyi folded his hands over his paunchy middle and agreed. "Whether we eventually decide to stay here or to move on, we still must have enough deuterium for many more years of living aboard the ship."

"And we've got to overhaul just about everything on board," Campbell added. "Doesn't make a bit of difference if we're going to live here or find another planet. The ship's starting to fall apart. We've got to patch her up."

Larry turned to Estelella. "What about rebuilding the refining equipment? That'll take a lot of shuttling back and forth to the surface."

The astronaut tilted his head slightly to one side. "That's what I'm here for. . . . I'm no use to anyone just sitting around."

"No, I suppose not," Larry said seriously. "How many flights will be necessary? Will you have to do all the flying yourself or will some of the other kids you've been training be able to help?"

"There are at least three or four who can fly the shuttle almost as well as I can," Estelella said. It could have sounded like a boast, but he said it as a simple statement of fact. "And we can take the back-up shuttles out of storage and use them, too."

Larry nodded thoughtfully.

"I think," Dan said, "it'd be a good idea to have a spare shuttle on the ground next to the camp at all times. That way we'll always have an escape route, in an emergency."

"Good idea," Larry said.

"The only real danger on the surface that we've run into are the storms," Estelella muttered.

Polanyi said, "They appear to be tied in with the volcanic disturbances. If we could revive our full meteorological and geological teams, perhaps we could get accurate predictions of when to expect storms . . ."

Larry cut him off. "We can't revive large numbers of people until we've made a firm decision to stay here. And that decision won't be made until we get a full report on the other available planets."

"We're still going to be orbiting *this* planet," Dan argued, "for a long time. Years, maybe."

The others nodded agreement.

Dan went on, "I'm going down there with the first

crew . . . got to see how bad the damage to the refinery really is."

"You just got back," Larry said. "And the medics are still . . ."

"I'm responsible for the equipment," Dan snapped, his voice rising a notch louder than Larry's. "It's my job. I'm going down."

Larry forced down an urge to shout back at him. "All right," he said coldly, "then the only question is, when do we start?"

"Sooner the better," Dan said.

"The campsite is in darkness now," Estelella said, with a glance at his wristwatch. "It'll be daylight there again in about . . . eight hours."

"That puts it close to midnight, ship time."

"Right."

Dan said, "Let's get a landing group together and get down there as soon as there's enough light to see."

"We can take off at midnight," Estelella said.

"Good. You, me, and enough equipment to get the camp started again. Who else will we need?"

Larry was getting that helpless feeling again. Dan was running things his own way.

"You'd both better get some sleep," he said. "And I'll get the maintenance crew to crack the back-up shuttles out of storage, so you can get them into action as soon as possible."

"Right."

They got up from their chairs and headed for the door. Larry was the last to reach the doorway. Dan was still there, lingering, waiting for him.

"You're not fooling me," Dan said.

Larry frowned at him. "What do you mean?"

"You don't have any intention of staying here. I know that. You're going to get the ship overhauled and patched up, and then try to convince everybody we ought to push on."

To where? Larry almost said. But he wouldn't give Dan the satisfaction. Instead, he asked, "You enjoyed your trip to the surface so much? You think it's a fun place to be?"

"It's better than this ship."

Larry snorted. "That's like saying that death is better than life."

"Wrong!" Dan snapped. "Can't you see it's wrong? This is where we have to stay. Trying to push farther is just going to kill everybody. Is that what you want?"

"We've had this argument before, Dan."

"You're still not convinced?"

"This planet is a killer," Larry said. "We can alter the next generation or two or even three . . . but I still don't think they'll be able to survive on Femina. The Planet's deadly: Guido picked a good name for it."

Dan started to answer, but Larry went on, "It's a huge universe out there. It would be criminal of us to settle for this planet when there've got to be better worlds for us. Somewhere. There's got to be."

"We'll see," Dan said, his voice shaking. "We'll see. And soon."

Midnight.

There was no way to distinguish time on the bridge. Along the ship's corridors and tubes, in the rec areas and cafeteria, the overhead lighting was dimmed during the night shifts. But in the working spaces, such as the bridge, everything looked the same whether it was midnight or noon. Only the people working changed. And the twenty-four hour clocks.

Larry stood behind the launch monitor, watching over his shoulders the viewscreens that showed the planet below them and the shuttle rocket sitting on the ship's launching platform, up near the hub.

The campsite was in daylight now; under the highest magnification of the observation scopes, Larry could see a blackened smudge where the camp had been.

He turned to the screen that showed the shuttle craft. He could make out the two pressure-suited men sitting side by side in the pilot's bubble. Estelella's voice was checking off the countdown routine:

"Internal power on."

". . . nine, eight, seven . . ."

"Rockets armed and ready for ignition."

". . . five, four . . ."

"Tracking and telemetry on," said a technician.

". . . two, one, *zero*."

The electric catapult slid the shuttle craft out past the open airlock hatch. Larry watched the viewscreen. It showed the shuttle dwindling, dwindling, becoming one more speck among the endless stars.

"Rocket ignition," came Estelella's voice.

The speck blossomed briefly into a glow of light. Then even that disappeared.

"Tracking on the observation telescope," said a tech.

Larry turned toward the sound of her voice. The main screen on her console showed the shuttle craft, a tiny red-glowing meteor streaking across the broad golden landscape of the planet.

"Telemetry and voice communications strong and clear."

Larry pressed the shoulder of the tech he was standing behind. "I'm going to my quarters to grab some sleep. Call me when they've landed."

He stepped out of the glare and bustle of the bridge, into the soft shadowy nighttime lighting of the corridors. His own room was dark. He didn't bother turning on a light, just slouched onto the bunk and waited.

The phone chimed. He touched the VOICE ONLY button. "Yes?"

"They've landed. Estelella reports all okay, they're getting out of the shuttle and starting to look around."

"Thank you."

Larry sat on the bunk, motionless for a long while. Then he turned to the phone again. "Valery Loring, please."

A pause. *Of course. She's asleep by now.*

Mrs. Loring's face appeared on the viewscreen. "Larry, is that you? I can hardly see you. Don't you have any lights on?"

"I'm sorry to wake you," he said. "Is Val there?"

"I wasn't asleep," she said. "Haven't been sleeping well lately..." Her voice trailed off. Then, "Valery's up in the observatory. She's been keeping very odd hours lately."

"Oh, All right. Thank you. I'll call her there."

But he knew he wasn't going to call her on the phone. He had to go up there and see her, face to face.

Two more nights, Valery was thinking. *Two more nights, and then on the third morning the Council meets. Then I'll have to tell them all the truth.*

Each night for the past week she had been staying up in the

observatory, sitting at the desk her father had used. The myriads of stars sprinkled across the blackness outside seemed to make the place feel colder, lonelier. Their light brought no warmth. The huge bulk of the planet was out of sight, down below the floor of the observatory, on the other side of the ship.

The big spidery telescope bulked blackly against the stars, and the smaller pieces of equipment made a hodgepodge of shadows. Black on black. Dark and darker. Only the little glowlights from the computer terminal and the viewscreens lit Val's post.

She tried to stay awake through each night, of course. She actually got quite a bit of work done. But for long stretches of the night the telescopes and cameras and other instruments were doing their tasks and there was almost nothing for her to do. Except think. And—too often—drift into sleep, lulled by the weightlessness of the observatory and the silence.

Click!

She tensed instantly.

The sound of a hatch opening. Val strained her eyes, but could see nothing in the darkness. There were several hatches leading into the observatory, and with the tubes on nighttime lights, there wouldn't be much of a glow to see when one of them was opened.

Padding footsteps. Slippered feet walking softly across the observatory floor.

"Who's there?" she called.

No answer.

Dan went out on the shuttle, she knew.

"Larry, it's you, isn't it?"

His lean dark form seemed to coalesce out of the shadows. "Yes," he said quietly, not five meters away from her. "It's me."

Her pulse was racing. "Oh . . . you scared me . . . a little."

"I didn't mean to."

He was close enough now for her to see his face in the glow of the desk lights. He looked infinitely weary. He pulled up a chair and floated softly onto it. Valery noticed that he didn't snap on the zero-*g* restraining belt. As calmly and unhurriedly as she could, she unclipped her own lap belt. It clicked loudly and snapped back into its resting sockets.

"Why...what brings you up here?" she asked.

For a moment he didn't answer, merely stared at her. "I just had to talk to somebody," he said at last. "I...lately, I've had the feeling that I'm completely alone. Totally cut off from everybody. No friends, nobody."

"I'm still your friend, Larry," she said softly.

"It's hard for us to be friends, Val. After everything that's happened...we can't be friends. Not really."

"I don't understand."

He seemed miserable. "Can't you see? When you tell the Council that you haven't been able to find an Earthlike planet, they're going to vote to stay here. They'll elect Dan Chairman and the geneticists will be put to work preparing the next generation of children for that deathworld down there. *Your* children, Val! Yours and Dan's. They'll be monsters. Sulfur-breathing, gorilla-sized monsters."

She had to struggle to keep her voice from shaking. "But what else can we do?"

"We've got to keep on going. Got to find an Earthlike planet somewhere. In this whole universe..."

"There might not be any," Valery said. "Maybe Earth is a unique place. Why should we expect anything closer to Earth conditions than the planet down below us?"

Larry didn't answer. He just sat there and lifted his head back, gazing up at the stars that crowded all around.

"I can see why you like it up here," he said. "It's peaceful here. Like being alone in the universe...floating free among the stars. It wouldn't be a bad way to die, just floating out there. No cares, no weight, just out there in the universe, without the ship to hem you in."

"Wh...what do you mean?"

He snapped his attention back to her. Valery felt a chill as his ice-blue eyes focused on her.

"You got Dr. Hsai to start revival procedures on a team of psychiatrists," Larry said flatly.

"I...we talked about it, yes..."

"Why?" Larry asked, rising up from his chair like a ghost. "I told Hsai it wasn't necessary. Why did you get him to countermand my decision?"

"He thought it would be best," Valery said, her voice going high, the words coming out fast. "I didn't tell him to do it; he decided for himself."

"He didn't decide until after you talked to him." He was standing over her now, feet barely touching the floor, looming over her.

Valery got up from her chair, bumping Larry slightly so that he bobbed away gently.

"Larry...you and Dan are both certain that there's a madman aboard this ship. A killer. You think it's Dan and he thinks it's you."

"So?"

Carefully, Val edged over in front of the desk and sat on it. Her feet no longer touched the floor. She gripped the edge of the desk with both hands.

"So shouldn't we have a psychiatrist on hand to examine him? And—and you?"

"Me? Why me? I'm not the killer."

Suddenly Val didn't know how to say what she knew had to be said. She plunged ahead anyway.

"Larry—have you ever thought that maybe, if Dan is the killer, he doesn't know it?"

"Huh?"

"He might be doing things that his conscious mind isn't aware of. And, besides, he hasn't killed anybody. Not really."

"He tried to kill your father. And the fire in the cryonics unit might have been deliberately set. That's still a possibility."

"All right," Valery said, inching the top desk drawer open with her right hand. "Even if he did . . . maybe he doesn't know about it. He might be sick, insane."

"That doesn't mean he's not dangerous."

"I know," Val agreed. "But—you can understand that he might be doing all these things without being consciously aware of it."

Looking puzzled now, Larry said, "Yes . . . I guess that's possible."

Val held her breath for an instant, then blurted, "Then you can see that it might be *you* who's doing it! You could be the sick one and not even know it!"

"Whhaaat?"

Larry's eyes went wide with shock. He seemed to stagger back.

"No!" he roared. "That can't be."

Tears were springing up in Val's eyes, and her vision was getting blurry. "Larry, it could be. It could be!"

"You're wrong. That's crazy...it's not me...."

Her hand closed on the cold hard metal she was seeking.

"Why did you come up here tonight?" Val asked. "Why did you come up here the night my father was nearly killed?"

"No!" he shouted again, and started for her.

Valery pulled the sonic stunner out of the desk drawer and fired point-blank. The gun made a barely-audible popping sound. But Larry's body stiffened, his eyes glazed, his arms froze outstretched barely a few centimeters from her. He didn't fall, he couldn't in zero-gravity. He merely hung there, unconscious.

Val found that her hands were shaking wildly now, and she was sobbing.

Then:

"Very neat work. The two of you are being very cooperative."

Dan Christopher stepped out of the shadows from beyond the desk, grinning.

(15)

Valery blinked back her tears.

"Dan! But I thought you..."

He was still some distance away from the desk, just close enough to be seen as a tall, lithe shadow. "That was Joe Haller on the shuttle. I asked him to take my place at the last minute."

"What... what are you doing here?"

"The same thing I tried to do when your father first started this nonsense of looking for another planet."

Val felt completely confused. "But... I thought..."

Dan laughed. "You made just about every mistake you could make, Val. You thought it was Larry, when all along it's been me."

"You're the madman?" The question popped out of her involuntarily.

Still hovering off near the shadows, Dan said grimly, "Wrong again. I'm not insane. It's not insanity when you fight to protect yourself from your so-called friends. Not when they're laughing at you behind your back. Plotting against you. Taking everything away from you."

"I... never laughed at you, Dan."

"Not much." His voice was getting hard, steel-edged. "You talked Larry into the Chairmanship. You probably got him to kill my father. Don't tell me the two of you weren't laughing at me."

"Dan, you're wrong... can't you see?"

"I see perfectly. I've seen it all along. You kill my father. While I'm mourning him, Larry take over the Chairmanship and you takes over Larry. Then the two of you scheme to move the ship on to another planet, another star. Not where we're *supposed* to go, where we're *destined* to go. Oh no! You've got to have your way in everything, don't you?"

Valery realized she still held the stunner in her hand. "Dan, it isn't like that at all."

"You even got your father to help you, didn't you?" he went on. "Searching for other planets. I fixed him. But you wouldn't let it rest there. Now I've got to take care of you, too. . . ." His voice seemed to break.

"Dan? Dan, please."

"No," he said, almost sobbing. "Val, I loved you. I would have given my life for you. But you've always been against me. You've always loved Larry better than me. You've all been against me, all along."

"Dan, you're wrong. Come here," she gripped the stunner firmly, "and let me prove how wrong you are."

"Sure, I'll come to you." His voice grew stronger. "As soon as you toss that popgun away."

Valery brought it up to fire, but Dan melted into the shadows before she could pull the trigger.

"It's a very short-range weapon," she heard his voice call to her, echoing mockingly. "And very directional. Now this laser I borrowed from the pressure suit is only a working tool . . . but at this distance it can burn your arm off the shoulder."

A blood-red pencil-beam of energy shot past Valery's ear.

She screamed and jumped, hitting the edge of the desk with her legs.

"The next one won't miss, Val. Throw your gun away."

She tossed it from her. The gun went spinning weightlessly into the darkness.

Dan stepped closer, close enough for her to see his face in the faint glow of the desk lights. He didn't look wild-eyed or twisted at all. He seemed perfectly at ease, calmer than usual. Serene.

"What are you going to do?" she asked.

"What can I do?" he shot back. "You've left me no alternative. For a while, I tried to figure out some way of getting you to agree to cryosleep, so I wouldn't have to kill you. But that's not possible. Not now."

"Dan, you've got to stop. You can't kill everyone that . . ."

"Everyone that gets in my way? Everyone who takes what's

rightfully mine? Yes, I can kill them all. You just watch me do it."

"You're sick!"

"Sick of being cheated by those who claim they love me." He gestured with the laser pistol. "Erase all your data tapes."

"I..." Val's mind was racing. "If I do, will you let me live?"

"That's impossible."

"I'll go into cryosleep. You can take me down there yourself. Right away."

He hesitated a moment. "Erase the tapes."

She turned and flicked her fingers over the keyboard. Lights on the computer terminal's face flickered on and off.

Turning back to Dan she said, "Well? You don't have to kill anyone."

Dan glanced at Larry's inert form. "You want me to let him be frozen, too?"

"Yes."

"So the two of you can awake together? Never," Dan said firmly. "He killed my father."

"No one killed your father," Valery said, her voice rising. "It was an accident."

"Don't argue with me!" he shouted. "He killed my father and I'm going to kill him. He's always been after everything that's mine. Now he's going to pay for it."

"Then you'll have to kill me too!" Val shouted back.

He pointed the gun at her. Val slid sideways, away from the computer terminal. "Look!" she yelled. "It's not on erase, it's on *record*! And I put the intercom on, too. Everything you've said for the past minute or two is being broadcast all over the ship. There must be an emergency crew heading up here right now!"

"You..." Now Dan's eyes glittered dangerously, and his breath became ragged, gulping.

"It won't do you any good to kill us, Dan," Val said as calmly as she could manage. "Everyone knows now. Just give up and let the medics take care of you."

With a bellowing roar, Dan fired the laser into the computer terminal. It exploded in a shower of sparks. Valery leaped upward as the desk lights blanked out, then angled to one side and desperately tried to put as much distance between herself and Dan as she could.

"I'll get you!" He was screaming. "Both of you! All of you!"

Larry! Somewhere in the vast, completely darkened chamber, Larry's unconscious body floated. If Dan found him first... Valery saw a gaunt framework of shadows moving up toward her. The main telescope. She put out both hands and grabbed at one of the girders, slowing her impact.

Hanging there weightlessly, she peered into the darkness, letting her eyes adjust to the dim starlight. *There.* A body floating silently off in the darkness. *Is it Larry, or a trick of Dan's?*

The click and creak of a hatch opening made her turn her attention toward the sound. A shaft of light flickered through the observatory, and Valery caught the shadow of Dan's form squeezing down through the hatch, then slamming it shut behind him.

She launched herself across the room toward Larry. Another hatch opened, off to the other side of the observatory, and a man's voice called out:

"Miss Loring, are you all right?"

"I'm here! Get some lights and help me. Larry Belsen's unconscious."

Talk about irony, Larry thought.

He was sitting in Dan's desk chair in the Propulsion and Power control center, one level below the observatory. The gravity was still low enough for his arms to tend to float up off the chair arms. Someone was holding a vibrator to the back of his neck, soothing away the roaring headache that the stunner had given him.

Valery was standing in front of him, looking very pale and frightened.

Half a dozen engineers and technicians were at their stations. All of them wore stunners on their belts.

"How does your head feel now?" a girl's voice came from behind him.

Too stiff and aching to turn toward her, he replied. "Like somebody's running a rocket engine inside it."

The girl moved in front of him, where he could see that she was wearing a white nurse's coverall. "I'll get you a pain-killer." She opened a kit on the desk.

Larry looked up at Valery. "So you thought it was me."

Her eyes were red from crying, he noticed.

"I was *afraid* it was you," she answered quietly.

"Do you feel any better," he asked bitterly, "knowing that it's Dan?"

"Not much," she confessed. Then she added, "But...I'm glad it wasn't you. Even if you'd been doing it unconsciously."

The nurse turned back to him and handed him an immense blue pill.

"I'll get some water," Valery said.

"Make it a bucketful," Larry called to her. To the nurse, he asked, "Will this make me sleep?"

She shook her head. "No, it's a selective depressant. If you want to sleep..."

"No, I've got to stay awake."

Val came back with a plastic cup of water. Larry swallowed hard on the pill, nearly choked, but finally forced it down.

"Any idea of where Dan is?" he asked.

Val said, "No. Mort Campbell is heading up the emergency squad. They're searching the ship for him."

"Could you get Mort on the phone for me, please?"

She handled the desk phone, while Larry rubbed the back of his still stiff neck.

Campbell's heavy-featured face showed up on the screen.

"Where are you?" Larry asked.

"Storage area seventeen. One of the maintenance men working on the extra shuttles said he heard some strange noises down here."

"Anything?"

Campbell's beefy face settled into a scowl. "Who knows? This area's big enough to hide the whole ship's crew. We've got kilometers of corridors and tubes to search, thousands of sections and compartments...a few dozen men can't hack it. Not even a few hundred."

"He's got to be someplace. I'll make sure that all the working and living areas are guarded. He'll have to show up sooner or later...even if it's just to get some food."

"I know. But I wouldn't count on that. Anyway, there are video monitors on all the important areas of the ship. I've got a special squad of people monitoring the viewscreens on the bridge."

"Good."

Campbell said, "I understand he's armed."

"He was. But I want him brought in alive. No rough stuff. If you have to fight, use the stunners."

"He must really be sick."

"And scared. Be careful with him. But don't take unnecessary chances; he's perfectly willing to kill."

Campbell's eyes flickered with just the barest hint of surprise. "Yeah, I guess you're right," he said.

The picture on the viewscreen faded.

Larry got to his feet. For a moment he felt a surge of dizziness. Val was beside him and he rested a hand on her shoulder.

"Come on," he said. "We can be in better touch with the whole ship down on the bridge."

"Wait a minute?" she asked. "I had an idea, while you were talking with Mr. Campbell."

"What?"

"Dr. Hsai. He's spent a lot of time examining Dan, talking with him..."

"And finding zero," Larry grumbled.

"Yes, but he might be able to find something in his records...or maybe something he'll remember...some clue to where Dan might be hiding, what he's doing."

Larry thought it over for half a moment. "It's worth a try." He turned to the nearest technician, who was seated at a monitoring console, watching the computer-produced graphs that gave second-by-second reports on the performance of the reactors and generators. "Your name's Peterson, isn't it?"

The blond youth smiled, obviously flattered that the Chairman knew his name. "Yessir, that's right."

"Would you please call Dr. Hsai and ask him to meet me on the bridge as soon as he can possibly get there?"

"Yessir. Right away."

The oriental psychotech was already on the bridge, waiting patiently, when Larry and Val got there. All the way down the now fully lit connector tubes, padding down those spiraling metal steps, Larry had half-expected Dan to leap out at them. No sign of him. Nor of Campbell's search parties and emergency squad.

It's a big ship, Larry reminded himself. *You could roam around for weeks without seeing another person, if you really wanted to.*

All the technicians on the bridge were wearing sidearms as they sat at their consoles. And there were two grim-faced guards scowling at the door Larry and Val stepped through.

Dr. Hsai was unarmed, of course. Larry quickly explained what he was after.

The psychotech pursed his lips thoughtfully. "I must admit that nothing comes to mind right now. But I will review all my records. Perhaps there *is* something he inadvertently revealed that will help you."

There'd better be, Larry thought. To Val, he muttered, "Dan could do a lot of damage to the ship, if he wants to."

"But all the vital areas are protected now, aren't they?"

He scanned the viewscreens and nodded. "They seem to be . . . but the ship's too big. Too many soft spots. He could cut electrical connections, air lines, water pipes . . . anything."

"Why would he do something like that?" she asked.

"How should I know?" Larry snapped. "Why would he do any of the things he's doing? He's crazy!"

She didn't respond, but her chin dropped slightly.

"I'm sorry," Larry said immediately. "I didn't mean it that way. Guess I'm getting edgy."

"I know," Valery said.

The hours wore on. Larry finally had to sleep; he couldn't stay on his feet any longer. He woke up two hours later and groggily made his way back to the bridge.

Mort Campbell was there, unshaven, bleary-eyed, sipping coffee from a steaming mug.

"Anything?" Larry asked.

"Nine dozen false alarms, that's all." Campbell sipped, then winced. "Cheez, that's hot! No . . . everybody and his brother thinks they've seen him. But none of it checks out. Wherever he's hiding, it's a good place."

Larry stood through two full shifts. Most of the time he remained on the bridge, although he put in a swing with one of Campbell's search squads, spending several hours going through corridors and unused work and storage areas. All of them were sealed tight and lay under half a century's worth of dust.

He had dinner with Val in the cafeteria.

"I'm going to assign a couple of men to guard you."

"Me?"

"He was after you, wasn't he?"

"That's only because I showed him that Epsilon Indi's closest planet is almost exactly like Earth. He wanted to destroy that evidence, to make sure we stayed here."

"Oh . . . Now he knows you were lying to him."

She grinned, a bit sheepishly. "No, I was telling him the truth. It was you that I lied to."

"What? But you said . . ."

"It was a lie," she replied. "To see if . . . well, if you were the one who'd try to . . . stop me from reporting to the Council."

Larry stared at her. "You mean there really is a planet like Earth at Epsilon Indi?"

She nodded, grinning again.

"That's fantastic! Fabulous!" Larry felt like jumping up on the cafeteria table. Then he remembered about Dan. "But I still want you guarded. He's dangerous, and he might come after you. I don't want you to be bait anymore."

"I'll be all right in my own quarters. Mother's there, and we have a phone. . . ."

"And there will be two guards with you at all times," Larry said firmly.

"At *all* times?" Her eyebrows arched coyly.

Larry put on a sour face. "They'll stay outside your door when you go home."

"But . . ."

"No arguments, or I'll make it four guards."

She put her hands up in mock surrender. "Yessir, Mr. Chairman. To hear is to obey."

"Stuff it." Now he was grinning. "Uh . . . this might not be the right time, but—well, I still love you."

"I know," she said, much more softly. "I never stopped loving you."

He leaned across the table and kissed her. Seven dozen people in the cafeteria stopped their meals to watch, but Larry couldn't have cared less. Even if he had noticed them.

*   *   *

"He's got to be *someplace*," Larry fumed.

He was on the bridge again, talking to Mort Campbell, who was slumped tiredly on the chair of an unoccupied console.

"A man just can't disappear for three days," Larry insisted. "It's a big ship, but you should have been able to flush him out by now."

"I know, I feel the same way," Campbell said, nodding his heavy head. "Either he's damned clever or . . ."

"Or what?"

"Or he's got friends helping him."

Larry made a chopping motion with his hand. "No. That I can't believe. A madman aboard the ship is one thing, but other madmen to help him? No."

"He got Joe Haller to take his place on the shuttle, didn't he?"

"We've gone through all that with Joe. He had no idea of what Dan was up to. Dan asked him to fill in for him, and he did. That's all."

Campbell threw his hands up in disgust. "Then where the hell is he? Why can't we find him?"

"If I knew, Mort, I'd . . ."

"Emergency signal!" sang out one of the techs.

Larry went over to her like a shot. "What is it?"

The girl pointed to a flashing red light on the console in front of her, between two viewscreens. Her hands flew over the keyboard. One of the viewscreens brightened and showed a guard, bleeding from a gushing cut on his scalp. The blood was pouring down into his eyes.

"He . . . he's here . . ."

"What's the location?" Larry yelled at the girl.

"Airlock fourteen, level three."

Campbell bolted from his chair and dashed for the nearest door.

Larry snapped, "Hook me into the intercom."

The girl nodded and did things to her keyboard. "Okay now, sir."

Leaning over her shoulder to speak into the microphone built into the console's face, Larry said. "This is the Chairman speaking. Dan Christopher has attacked a guard at airlock fourteen, level three. All search squads converge on that location. All guard units, remain on duty at your assigned posts." He started to straighten up, then had another thought. "Dan...Dan Christopher. Give up, Dan. You can't win. We want to help you. Give up and you won't be hurt."

But it sounded empty, even as he said it.

Larry fidgeted on the bridge for about a minute longer, then said, "I'm going up to that airlock. Relay any calls for me to that location."

He got there as the guard was being carried off to the infirmary on a stretcher. Campbell was standing inside the airlock, filling its cramped metal space with his formidable bulk. He had his hands on his hips.

Larry pushed past a dozen men and stepped through the airlock's inner hatch to squeeze in next to Campbell.

"Well, now we know where he is," Campbell said.

"What happened?"

Campbell jerked a thumb at the rack of pressure suits hanging outside the airlock, in the corridor. "He slugged the guard, took one of the suits, and went outside."

"What? You're sure?"

Nodding, Campbell answered, "Yep. Just checking the hatch here. It was open when we arrived a few minutes ago."

"He's outside?"

"He's committing suicide."

Larry thought it over for a few moments. "No. He's moving to a part of the ship where he wants to be ... My god! He can cut open bulkheads anywhere he wants to and blow whole sections of the ship into vacuum. If he does that in the living quarters ..."

Even Campbell's normal calm seemed shaken. "We'd better get all the living quarters on disaster alert. All hatches sealed ..."

Larry nodded. "And guards on every airlock."

"Right. Anything else?"

"Yes. Get a squad of volunteers together. We've got to go outside after him. And I'm going with you."

(16)

It was a strange, eerie feeling.

Larry had been outside the ship before, but never since they had taken up orbit around the planet. Its massive curving bulk hung over him, it seemed, close and beckoning yet somehow menacing. He felt almost as if it was going to fall on him and crush him.

He shook his head inside the suit's helmet. *You've got a job to do. No time for sightseeing.*

A dozen men had floated out of the airlock in search of Dan. A dozen men to cover the thousands of possible places where he might be lurking.

They worked with a plan in mind. They came out of one airlock at the first level, the largest of the ship's seven wheels. They spread out around the periphery of that wheel. The plan was for each man to search the area between connecting tubes. Then, if none of them found Dan, they would work their way simultaneously up each of the connector tubes to the next ring, search there, then on to the third ring. And so on, right up to the hub.

We could use a hundred men, Larry thought. Only twelve men qualified for outside work had volunteered. Most of the people aboard the ship had never been outside it.

Larry watched the man nearest him disappear over the curve of the ship's ring-like structure. He was alone now, standing on the ring's metal skin with magnetically gripping boots, looking down a connector tube, past the seven rings to the bulging plastiglass blisters of the hub.

The stars formed a solemn, unblinking backdrop, like

millions of eyes watching him. And behind him, Larry could *feel* rather than see the immense ponderous presence of the planet.

Campbell's voice crackled in his earphones. "Everbody ready?"

One by one, the eleven others answered by the numbers that had been hastily sprayed onto their suits.

"All right, everybody work to his left. Keep your guns loose."

Larry fingered the laser tool-turned-weapon at his waist. Sonic stunners wouldn't work in vacuum. If there was any shooting, somebody was going to die.

He began walking in a spiral around the big main wheel, his footsteps tacky in the magnetic boots. Around and around, spiraling like an electron in a strong magnetic field, curving from one connector tube to the next. There was practically no place for a man to hide here; the main level's outer wall was almost perfectly smooth, broken only by an occasional viewport.

Larry carefully avoided stepping on the viewports. Being plastiglass, they'd provide no grip for his magnetic boots. Larry didn't feel like slipping off the ship's surface. There were steering jets on his belt, but he preferred to stay in contact with the ship rather than try zooming through empty space.

At last he came to the next connector tube. He found that he was breathing hard, sweating, but feeling relieved. No sign of Dan. And that somehow made him almost happy.

At least I didn't have to shoot it out with him.

"Not yet," he heard himself mutter.

The others began reporting in. None of them had seen Dan.

"All right," Campbell said. "Every man goes along the tube he's at now. Stop at level two and report in."

It was taking too long, Larry realized. More than an hour had passed since they had first come outside. It would easily take another hour or more by the time they had checked out level two. It wasn't going to work. They'd have to go inside long before they could inspect level three. If Dan didn't show up soon, they'd have to call off the whole idea of searching outside for him. Unless they could get more people outside to help.

Larry always felt hot inside the suits. There was a radiator on the back of his lifepack, but it never seemed to get rid of his body heat fast enough. The air blowers whirred noisily, but he still found himself drenched with sweat before he was halfway up the tube to level two.

Around and around. Down was up, and then it was down again. He saw the planet swing by as he stolidly plodded along the metal skin of the tube. Stars and planets, turning, turning, turning. *Keep your eyes searching for Dan!* he warned himself. But where? He could be crouched behind that antenna; Larry checked it out carefully. No. He could be hovering no more than a hundred meters from the ship, and he'd be virtually invisible against the backdrop of stars. *We'd never see him . . . you'd have to be lucky enough to look in exactly the right place at the right time . . .*

And then Larry began to get the uncanny feeling that Dan was walking along behind him, following his footsteps, tiptoeing the way children sometimes do behind someone they're trying to surprise.

He knew it was silly, irrational. But the feeling grew. He felt a cold shudder go through him. *If he is behind me . . .*

Larry whirled around. It was a clumsy move in the pressure suit, and his boots left contact with the ship. *No one!* Then he realized he was drifting away. He slapped at the control unit on his belt, and the microjets puffed briefly and slammed him hard back onto the tube. His knees buckled momentarily, but he stayed erect.

You're getting spooked, he raged at himself.

He glanced at the oxygen gauge on his wrist. Still in the green, but a sliver of yellow was showing. When the yellow went to red, he'd have to either go inside or get a fresh tank.

His earphones buzzed. "Mr. Chairman?"

"Here."

"Just a moment, sir . . ."

Then Valery's voice said, "Larry? I think Dr. Hsai might have come up with something."

"What?"

"Wait . . . I'll put him on."

Larry kept plodding on, kept his eyes searching.

"Mr. Chairman," the psychotech said formally.

"Doctor," Larry responded automatically.

"I've been reviewing my records of Dan Christopher's case."

"And?"

"I believe I may have found something significant."

Larry fumed inside his helmet. "Well, what is it?"

But there was no hurrying Hsai. "Do you recall when Mr. Christopher was first placed under my care...just after his father died?"

"Yes. Go on."

"He was treated for a few days and then released. I tried to maintain contact with him, to follow up his case."

"I know. We put him under observation for a month." *And you found nothing,* Larry added mentally.

"Yes. Exactly so. But before then—just after he was released from the infirmary for the first time, I asked him several times to check in with me for follow-up tests. He refused."

"So?"

Dr. Hsai's voice continued smoothly, with just the barest hint of excitement. "At one point, he warned me that his job was too important to be interfered with."

"Warned you?"

"I have his exact words here...listen..."

Larry stopped moving and hung frozen on the skin of the tube. The ship's vast turning motion swung him majestically around, like a lone rider on an ancient merry-go-round. Then he heard Dan's voice, which startled him for a moment, until he realized it was one of Dr. Hsai's tapes:

"Our reactors are feeding the ship's main rocket engines," Dan was saying hotly, "on a very, *very* carefully programmed schedule. This ship can't take more than a tiny thrust loading—we're simply not built to stand high thrust, it'd tear us apart..."

"Everyone knows this." Hsai's voice.

Dan answered, "Uh-huh. This is a very delicate part of the mission. A slight miscalculation or a tiny flaw in the reactors could destroy this ship and kill everyone."

Click.

"Do you understand what he was trying to tell me?" Dr. Hsai asked.

Larry blinked puzzledly. "Frankly, no. What he was saying was perfectly true."

"Of course. But underneath the obvious truth, he was threatening to destroy the ship and everyone in it if he didn't get his way."

"What?"

"I believe that is what is in his mind," Hsai went on. "Of course, I am no psychiatrist, but I think such an action of self-destruction would be be consistent with Christopher's behavior pattern."

Larry instantly blurted, "The reactors!"

Val's voice came on. "Larry, do you think he'd do it?"

"We can't run the risk of *not* thinking it. Val, get the power crew on the phone and have them abandon level seven. Everybody out except a skeleton crew, and I want them in pressure suits. Quick!"

"Right."

Larry fumbled with the radio switches on his belt.

"Mort, this is Larry." *Do I have the right frequency?*

"You find something?"

"No. I just got a call from inside. Hsai thinks Dan might try to blow the reactors."

"Holy..."

"I'm jetting up there. You keep the search going, just to make sure I'm not on a wild-goose chase."

"Okay."

Larry pushed off the tube wall and touched the microjet controls. He felt tiny hands grab him around the waist and push him up toward the ship's hub. The rings of the ship passed beneath him: three, four, five, six.

There was a flash and a puff of what looked like steam, up ahead at level seven. Something cartwheeled up, a jagged shard of metal. Larry steered in that direction.

Level seven's only viewport had been blown apart. The lights inside were gone. Larry grabbed the jagged rim of the exploded port and hauled himself in through the hole.

If I turn on my helmet lamp I'll be a certain target.

Something heavy and metallic slammed thunderously in the distance and a gust of wind tore past Larry, cracking like a miniature thunderclap.

Safety hatch! He's opened the safety hatch between the offices and the reactor area.

Larry reached to his belt with both hands, turned on his helmet lamp, and pulled the laser pistol from its holster.

The office was a shambles. When the viewport blew open, air pressure inside the office gusted violently out into space, bowling over everything in its path. Chairs were overturned, desk fittings broken and scattered over the floor. Any papers that had been around were blown outside.

But no bodies. Valery's warning must have reached the technicians just in time.

Larry hefted the pistol in his right hand and took a deep breath. The suit air suddenly tasted good. He moved toward the safety hatch that connected the office with the reactor area. In the low gravity of level seven, it was easy to move around, even inside the cumbersome suit. But still Larry moved slowly, cautiously. He was only moments behind Dan. Maybe he could surprise him.

The safety hatch was open, and the reactor area was deep in darkness. For a moment, Larry thought about switching off his helmet lamp. But he couldn't. *Be blind without it.*

He edged toward the hatch. It opened, he knew, onto a metal catwalk that hung above the two main working reactors and the main electrical power generator.

He stepped out onto the catwalk, then immediately flicked off his lamp.

Down below, kneeling by the power generator in a pool of light from his own helmt lamp, was Dan. He had a laser pistol in his hand, and he was burning it at full intensity on some of the exposed wiring of the generator. Smoke and sparks were sputtering from the generator's innards.

With barely a thought about what he was doing, Larry clambered over the catwalk's flimsy railing and launched himself at Dan. It was like a dream, a nightmare. He floated through the twenty meters separating them like a cloud drifting across the sky. Larry raised his right hand and threw his pistol as hard as he could at Dan. It banged into Dan's hand, knocking his own laser skittering across the floor. There was no sound.

Dan turned toward him, his lamp suddenly glaring straight into Larry's eyes. Then they collided, hitting with a bone-jarring impact that carried the two of them up and over the generator and into a confused tangle of arms and legs onto the narrow floor space between the generator and one of the reactors.

It was like two robots grappling. In the low gravity, every strenuous move was overly done, and they fought clumsily, swinging, bouncing, rolling across the floor and flailing at each other. Noiselessly, except for the bone-carried shock of impact and the grunts that each man made inside his suit.

Larry's head was banged around inside his helmet a dozen times. His ears rang and he tasted blood in his mouth. Sweat was trickling stingingly into his eyes.

Dan was reaching up over Larry's shoulder, trying to grab his airline. Larry knocked his arm away and pushed Dan back against the smooth metal wall of the reactor. Dan bounced off, doubled over, and sliced Larry's legs, knocking him sprawling.

Feeling like a turtle on its back, Larry tried to scramble up again, but Dan was on top of him. Through the metal-to-metal contact of the suits, he could hear Dan faintly yelling something; it was unintelligible.

Dan had him by the shoulders now and was banging his head and torso against the metal floor plates. Each slam jarred Larry, blurred his vision. Either his suit was going to crack open or his head would; it didn't matter which one happened first.

He grappled his arms around Dan's torso, trying to hold on and prevent Dan from slamming him. But Dan just rode up and down on top of him, adding his own body's mass to the process of bludgeoning Larry to death.

Larry's hands grasped frantically and closed on a slim piece of tubing. *Airline!* His first instinct was to rip it loose, but instead Larry simply squeezed on it, grabbed it hard and hung on.

In a few moments Dan stopped the pounding. He tried to reach Larry's arm, but Larry was wrapped too closely to him for that. Dan rolled over onto his back, but Larry hung on. Squeezing, squeezing the airline, keeping fresh oxygen from Dan's lungs, letting him suffocate on his own carbon dioxide.

Dan went limp.

Larry hung on for a few seconds longer, then let go. He himself sagged, barely conscious, on top of Dan's inert form. *No. Can't...pass out. He'll be coming around...as soon as fresh air...gets into his suit.*

Dazed, bloody, Larry got to his knees. He knew he couldn't

stand up. He flicked on the helmet lamp and turned to look for the lasers. Dan's legs started to move feebly. Larry crawled on all fours, found one of the little pistols on the floor, and took it in his hands. He flopped into a sitting position, leaning his back against the generator, and pointed the pistol at Dan. With his free hand he worked the suit's radio switch.

"I've got him," he said weakly. "Reactor area."

[17]

The Council members all looked happy enough, but Larry felt nothing but numbness inside himself.

Even Valery looked pleased. She had just shown all her data tapes about the Epsilon Indi planet. It looked as much like Earth, from this distance, as Earth itself did.

"I would like to suggest," Dr. Polanyi said, beaming across the table at her, "that Miss Loring be accepted as a member of the Council *pro tem*—for as long as her father is unable to attend our meetings."

There was a general nodding of heads and approving murmurs.

"Any dissenting voices?" Larry asked.

None.

"Then it's done."

There was only one empty seat at the table: Dan's. Larry glanced at it, his mouth tightening with bitterness.

Adrienne Kaufman cleared her throat. "What about the data we've just seen? Should we consider heading for this new planet? If not, we have a huge task of genetic work ahead of us."

Larry glanced around the table. None of the Council members seemed willing to speak before he did.

"Actually," he smiled at last, "I don't see any reason to rush into such a decision. We're going to be here in orbit for many months, refurbishing the ship. Let's spend that time gathering more data about this new planet."

Valery said, "If we could build a bigger telescope, or improve the sensitivity of the instruments we have . . ."

"That could be done," Polanyi said quickly.

"Epsilon Indì is about the same distance from us as Alpha Centauri is from Earth," Larry said. "If we decide to go there, it will take another half-century."

"None of us will be awake for much of that trip," Polanyi said.

"If we decide to go," Adrienne Kaufman put in.

"Oh, I think we will," said the old engineer. "It looks too good to ignore."

The meeting broke up shortly after that. Valery got up from her chair and went toward Larry.

"They're putting Dan into cryosleep today. Dr. Tomaso says he can work on Dan's neural patterns much more easily when the nerve impulses are slowed down by the low temperature."

"I know," Larry said.

"He might be under cryosleep for years and years," she said.

He thought he knew what was bothering him, but he was afraid to mention it. Afraid she might tell him that his fears were correct.

She looked at him curiously. "I know what you're thinking."

"Do you?"

"Yes." Valery almost smiled. "You're wondering if I want to go into cryosleep too, and be awakened when Dan's cured."

He reached out and took her hand. "Do you?"

"No," she said. "Silly. When are you going to believe that you're the one I want?"

He grinned foolishly. "Any day now."

They walked together out of the conference room and down a long, curving corridor. They stopped at a viewport and stared silently at the golden planet outside.

"It would've been a lovely world...." Larry muttered. "So close...so close..."

"There's a better one waiting for us," Val said.

"But if we don't go into cryosleep," Larry realized, "we'll probably never see that new world."

She smiled up at him. "I know. But someone's got to keep the ship going, and raise a new generation of children who *will* see the new world. See it and live on it."

"Our children," he said.

"Human children," Val added. "Beautiful strong human men and women for the new world."

"For the new world," he echoed.

They smiled together and walked off down the corridor, arm in arm.

END OF EXILE

To Regina, with love and hope
for a better tomorrow.

Book One

[1]

The glass was cold.

Linc rubbed at it with the heel of his hand and felt the coldness of death sucking at his skin. His whole body trembled. It was chill here in the darkness outside the Ghost Place, but it wasn't the cold that made him shake.

Still he had to decide. Peta's life hung in the balance. And before he could decide, Linc had to *know*.

Wiping his freezing hand against the thin leg of his ragged coverall, Linc peered through the misty glass into the Ghost Place.

They were there, just as they'd always been.

More of them than Linc could count. More than the fingers of both hands. Ghosts.

They looked almost like real men and women. But of course no one that old still lived in the Wheel. The adults were all dead—all except Jerlet, who lived far up above the Wheel.

The ghosts were frozen in place, just as they had always been. Most of them were seated at the strange machines that stretched along one long wall of the place. Some of them were on the floor; one was kneeling with its back against the other wall, eyes closed as if in meditation. Most of them had their backs to Linc, but the few faces he could see were twisted in agony and terror. He shuddered as he thought of the first time he had seen them, when he had been barely big enough to scramble atop an old dead servomech's shoulder and peek through the mist-shrouded window at the horrifying sight beyond.

It doesn't scare me now, Linc told himself.

But still he could feel cold sweat trickling down his thin ribs; the smell of fear was real and pungent.

The ghosts stayed at their posts, staring blankly at the long curving wall full of strange machines. The strange buttons and lights; the wall screens above them were just as blank as the ghosts' eyes—most of them. Linc's heart leaped inside him as he saw a few of the screens still flickering, showing strange shadowy pictures that changed constantly.

Some of the machines still work! he realized.

The ghosts had been people once. *Real people, just like Magda or Jerlet or any of the others.* But they never moved, never breathed, never relaxed from their agonized frozen stares at the dead and dying machines.

They were real people once. And someday . . . someday I'll become a ghost. Like them. Frozen. Dead.

But some of the ancient machines were still working; some of the wall screens still lived. *Does that mean that the machines are meant to keep on working? Does it mean that I should try to fix the machine that Peta broke?*

His whole body was shaking badly now. It was cold here in the darkness. Linc had to get back to the living section, where there was light and warmth and people. Living people. Maybe it was true that the ghosts walked through the Wheel's passageways when everyone was asleep. Maybe *all* the frightening stories that Magda told were true.

It was a long and painful trek back to the living area. Many passageways were blocked off, sealed by heavy metal hatches. Other long sections were too dangerous for a lone traveler. Rats prowled there hungrily.

Linc had to take a tube-tunnel up to the next level, where he felt so much lighter that he could almost glide like one of the bright-colored birds down in the farming section of the Living Wheel. He stretched his legs and covered more paces in one leap than he had fingers on a hand.

Here in the second level it was fun. The corridors were empty and dark. The doors along them closed tight. There were strange markings on each door; Linc couldn't understand them, but Jerlet had promised long ago to someday show him what they meant.

He was alone and free here, soaring down the corridor, letting his muscles lift his suddenly lightened body for long jumps down the shadowy passageway. He forgot the ghosts, forgot Peta's trouble, forgot even Jerlet and Magda. There was nothing in his mind except the thrill of almost-flying, and the words of an ancient song. His voice had deepened not long ago, and no longer cracked and squeaked when he tried to sing. He was happily impressed with it as he heard it echoing off the bare corridor walls:

> "Weeruffa seethu wizzer
> Swunnerfool wizzeruv oz...."

Then he sailed past a big observation window and skidded to a stop, nearly falling as he braked his momentum, and turned to look through the broad expanse of plastiglass.

The stars were circling slowly outside, quiet and solemn and unblinking. *So many stars!* More stars than there were people down in the Living Wheel. More than the birds and insects and pigs and all the other animals down in the farms. More even than the rats. *So many.*

Was he right about Jerlet's teachings? It seemed to Linc that some of Jerlet's words meant that the Living Wheel—and all the other wheels up at the higher levels—were actually part of a huge machine that was whirling around and carrying them from one star to another. Linc shook his head. Jerlet's words were hard to figure out; and besides, that was Magda's job, not his.

Then the yellow star swung into view. It was brighter than all the rest, so bright that it hurt Linc's eyes to look at it. He squinted and turned his face away, but still saw the brilliant spot of yellow before his eyes, wherever he looked.

After a few moments it faded away. And Linc's blood froze in his veins.

For he saw stretched across the scuffed, worn floor plates of the passageway a vague dark shadow stretching out, reaching up the far wall across the passageway from the window.

His own shadow, Linc realized quickly. But that brought no relief from fear. For the light casting the shadow came from the yellow star.

It really is getting closer to us, Linc told himself. *The old legends are true!*

Keeping his back to the window and the yellow star, staring at his slowly shifting shadow, Linc felt panic clutching at him.

The yellow star is coming to get us. It's going to make ghosts of us all!

[2]

Linc had no idea how long he stayed, nearly paralyzed with fear, at the observation window. His shadow crept across the floor and up the far wall of the passageway, faded into darkness, then reappeared again. And again, And again.

Finally he pulled himself away, muttering, "If I tell the others about this, they'll go crazy. But Magda . . . I've got to tell Magda."

His voice sounded odd, even to himself. Shaky, high, and unsure. "I wish Jerlet was still with us."

He stalked down the passageway purposefully, no more playful lightweighted leaps. Into the next open hatch he ducked, then stopped at the platform that opened onto the long spiraling metal stairs of the tube-tunnel. Jerlet was upward, in the far domain where legends said there was no weight at all and everything floated in midair. Downward were the others, his own people, in the Living Wheel, where there was warmth and food and life.

And fear.

"Jerlet. I've got to find Jerlet," Linc told himself sternly, even though he had no idea of how far the journey would be, or how difficult.

Linc placed his slippered foot on the first cold metal step leading upward. But he heard a scuffling sound—faint as a brea.h, but enough to make him freeze in his steps.

Again. A faint rustling sound in the darkness. Something soft padding on the metal steps in the shadows below.

Rats? Linc wondered.

There hadn't been any rats in this tube-tunnel for a long time, although it had taken the death of four of Linc's friends to clear the tunnel of them. The little monsters fought fiercely when they couldn't run or hide.

Linc gripped the hilt of his only weapon, a slim blade that had once been a screwdriver. He had ground the working end down until it was a sharp dagger. Holding the plastic hilt in a suddenly sweaty palm, Linc peered into the darkness of the tunnel, looking down the spiraling steps for the glint of red, beady eyes.

If there's too many of them....

The shadows seemed to bunch up and take shape. A person.

"Peta!" Linc shouted, and his voice echoed off the tube's cold metal walls.

The kid jumped as if sparks from a machine had seared him.

"Peta, it's me, Linc. Don't be afraid."

"Linc! Oh, Linc...." Peta scrambled up the steps and grabbed at Linc's outstretched hand. He was breathless, sweaty, wide-eyed.

"What are you doing up here?" Linc asked. "I thought you were waiting for Magda to...."

"I've got to get away! Monel and his guards...they're after me!"

Linc thought of Peta as just a kid, although all the people in the Living Wheel were exactly the same age, of course. But Peta was small, his skin pink and soft, his hair as yellow as the star that was coming toward them. He looked more like a child than a young man. Linc, whose face was bony and dark with the beginnings of a beard, towered over him.

Linc held the slim youth by both shoulders. "Listen. You're supposed to be waiting for judgement by Magda. You can't run away."

Peta's hands were fluttering wildly. "But Monel and his guards...he said I'd broken the pump on purpose. He said they were going to cast me into outer darkness!"

"He can't do that...."

"But Magda can. He said Magda told him that's what she was going to judge."

Linc shook his head. "No, Magda wouldn't make up her mind before hearing your side of it."

Peta glanced back over his shoulder. "I was hungry. And tired. I'd been working in the tanks for a long time...everybody else had a chance to eat, but Stav said I couldn't stop until I finished weeding my whole tank."

"Stav knows what's right," Linc said. "He's fair."

Even in the shadowy light of the tube-tunnel, Linc could see Peta's normally pink face had gone completely white with fright. "I know...but I stuffed the weeds I had pulled into the water trough."

"Oh no...." Linc could feel the back of his neck tensing. "And they clogged the pump...?"

Peta nodded dumbly.

"And that's why the pump broke, and now half the farm tanks can't get water," Linc finished. "Half our food supply is ruined."

Peta's voice was a miserable whine. "Monel came to my compartment with his guards. They took me out...said they were taking me to the deadlock to...to cast me out."

"He can't do that!"

"I ran away from them," Peta babbled on. "I grabbed the stick that Monel carries and hit the guard that was holding my arm and ran away."

"You *what?*"

"I...hit...the guard." It was a tortured whisper.

"You hit him? You really struck him?" Linc sank down onto the metal step and let his head droop into his hands. Peta stood fidgeting in front of him, his mouth opening but nothing coming out except a barely audible squeak.

Looking up at him again, Linc asked, "How could you do it? If you had deliberately tried to break every rule Jerlet's given us you couldn't have done worse."

"They were going to push me into the deadlock," Peta cried.

Linc shook his head.

"Help me!"

"Help you?" Linc spread his hands helplessly. "How? Half the people will starve because you were lazy. Maybe I can fix the pump, but you know Jerlet's laws about touching the machines. And you *hit* a guard. Violence! All the tales about the wars and the killings...didn't they mean anything to you?"

"They were going to cast me out!"

"Not even Monel would do that without Magda's judgement," Linc snapped. "I'm no friend of his, Jerlet knows. There's a lot about him I can't stand. But he'd never hurt you with anything except his tongue. He and his guards were playing with you, and you were stupid enough to believe they meant what they were saying. Only Magda can give punishment, you know that."

Peta dropped to his knees and clutched at Linc. "Help me, please! They'll take me back for judgment. . . ."

"That's just what you deserve."

"No! *Please!* Hide me . . . help me get away from them."

Linc shook his head. "You can't hide away, all by yourself. You'd either starve or have to steal food; Monel's guards would catch you sooner or later. Or the rats would."

"Please Linc! Do something. Don't let them get me. They'll. . . ."

Linc pushed him away and stood up. "Come on, I'm taking you to Magda."

"Noooo," Peta cried.

"The best thing is to give yourself up. Maybe she'll make your punishment easier then. I'll ask her to go easy on you."

"Very well spoken!"

Linc wheeled around. From out of the darkness above him, Monel and three guards came down the metal stairs. Two of the guards held Monel's chair, grunting with each step they took. Another three guards appeared out of the shadows on the steps below them.

Monel was smiling. Once he had been as tall as Linc, but since the fall that ruined his legs and forced him to stay forever in his chair, his body had seemed to shrivel and dry out. Now he was a twisted, frail knot of anger and pain. His eyes burned in the darkness. His voice was as brittle-thin and hurtful as a bare high-voltage wire.

"Don't look so surprised, little Peta," he said in his thin, acid-bitter voice. "Once we saw you scramble into this tunnel it was a simple matter to set a trap for you."

Linc bent down and, as gently as he could, lifted the wordless Peta to his feet.

"I thought for a moment," Monel said to Linc, "that we would catch you in the trap, too. But you turned out to be a loyal friend of Magda."

Linc said nothing. He could see in the dimness a dark welt along the cheek of one of the guards. *Must be where Peta hit him.*

Monel's smile was blood-chilling. "Let's go see Magda now. She's waiting for her little Peta."

(3)

The meeting room was filled. All the people were there; many more than the fingers of both Linc's hands. More even than the knuckle joints on each finger.

Magda sat in the center of the meeting room, as she should. She sat on the old desk with its tiny, dead viewing screen and the pretty colored buttons alongside it. Everyone sat on the floor tiles around her, as they should. All eyes were on Magda. Even the empty shelves that lined the walls of the big room seemed to be staring at her. There were only a few ancient books left on the shelves, dusty and crumbling. They were being saved for an emergency, for a time when the cold seeped so deeply into the Living Wheel that even this last precious bit of fuel would be needed. All the other books had been used for warmth long ago, before Linc could remember.

Magda sat on the desk, her back straight, her chin high, her eyes closed. Her slim legs were folded under her in the correct manner for her duty as priestess. Her dark hair was carefully combed and glistened in the shadowless light from the ceiling panels.

She wore her priestess's robe, and although it was threadbare and patched in places, the strange signs and lettering on it still stood out boldly: ELCTRC BLNKT, 110 V, AC ONLY. In her right hand was the wand of power and authority, which the ancients called a sliderule; in her left was the symbol of justice and compassion, an infant's skull. Around her waist was the golden chain of the zodiac, with its twelve mysterious signs.

Linc sat at Magda's feet, close enough to the desk to reach

out and touch it. Which no one in his right mind would dare to do. The desk was sacred to the priestess, and not to be touched by ordinary hands.

He looked up at Madga's face, framed by the huge silver-gray wall screen behind her. When she was serving in her office as priestess and meditating, as she was now, Magda seemed to be unable to see anyone, so fiercely did she concentrate on her duty.

Still she was beautiful. Her eyes were darker than the eternal night outside the Wheel. Her face as finely cast as the most delicate tracings of the golden zodiac signs. Yet there was strength and authority in those high-arched cheekbones and firm jawline. And wisdom came from her lips.

She stirred and opened her eyes. The crowd sighed and shifted uneasily. Her meditation was ended.

Magda's deep black eyes focused on the people. She swept her gaze across the room and smiled.

"I'm ready," she said simply.

Monel started to push his wheeled chair forward, but Linc was faster and got to his feet. Peta, sitting flanked by two of Monel's guards, didn't move at all. He seemed petrified, too terrified even to tremble.

"We have a problem," Linc said in the time-honored words of custom. "Peta messed up his work at the farm tanks and one of the main pumps is broken because of his carelessness...."

A gasp went through the crowd. Most of them already knew about the pump's breakdown, but still the thought of losing half their food shocked them.

Magda glanced at Peta but said nothing.

"And then when Monel and his guards threatened him," Linc went on, "Peta hit one of the guards and ran away."

The crowd sighed again, louder this time. Whispers buzzed through them.

The priestess's face went cold. "Is this true, Monel?" she asked.

Monel wheeled his chair up to where Linc was standing and motioned his bruised guard to step forward. "The evidence is clear to see," he said. The guard turned slowly so that the whole crowd could gape at his bruised face.

"Peta was frightened," Linc said. "Monel told him they were taking him to the deadlock."

"A lie!" Monel snapped. "Peta was running away and we tried to stop him."

Linc shook his head. "Peta has decided to give himself up to your justice, Magda. Monel and his guards came on us in the tube-tunnel just as he agreed to return to you and ask for mercy."

Magda tapped her wand against her knee for a moment. "What do you have to do with all this, Linc? Were you there when it happened?"

"No. I was off duty." *No sense telling everybody about the Ghost Place. Or how close the yellow star's getting. It would only scare them.* "Peta and I met by accident in a tube-tunnel."

Monel edged his chair slightly in front of Linc. "Peta is a lazy clod. And stupid. His laziness and stupidity ruined half the farm tanks. Ask Stav if it's not so!"

"Are they really ruined?" Magda asked.

"Yes," came Stav's heavy voice from the rear of the crowd.

She looked down at Peta. "All that food—ruined. How can we live without food?"

Before the frightened youth could answer, Linc said, "I brought Peta to you for justice. And mercy."

She almost smiled at Linc. For an instant their eyes were locked together as if no one else was in the room with them. Linc could feel his own lips part in a slight grin.

"But worst of all," Monel shouted, "is that Peta is *violent*! He attacked my guard. He could attack anyone, at any time. Any one of you!" He waved his arm at the crowd.

They muttered and stared at Peta. He hung his head so low that no one could see his face. The guards alongside him tensed and watched Monel, not Magda.

"We all know the punishment for violence," Monel went on, still speaking to the crowd rather than the priestess. "Violence is the one crime we cannot tolerate."

"Cast him into outer darkness!" someone shouted.

"Cast him out!" one of the guards echoed.

"Yes...yes...." The crowd picked up the vibration.

Monel turned back toward Magda, his thin face flushed with success, his crooked smile triumphant.

Magda raised her arms for silence, and the crowd settled down to a dull murmur. She waited a moment longer, staring at the people, and they became absolutely still. Peta sat unmoving, his head sunk low.

"Peta," she said softly. "What do you have to say for yourself?"

He raised his face high enough to look at her. With a miserable shrug he let his head droop again.

"Peta," Magda said, but now it was a voice of command, "get to your feet."

He slowly stood up.

"Is it your fault that the pump is dead?" she asked.

He nodded dumbly.

"Did you strike the guard?"

"He . . . they said. . . ."

"Did you strike him?"

Peta's voice broke. He nodded.

Monel rubbed the wheels of his chair. "He admits it."

"He came here for justice and mercy," Linc said.

"The punishment for violence is to be cast into the outer darkness!" Monel raged. He turned back to the crowd again. "Everybody knows that. Right?"

Before they could respond, Magda raised her slim arms.

"The punishment for violence," she said in a steel-cold voice, "will be decided by the priestess, and no one else."

"Give me a chance to look at the broken pump," Linc said. "Maybe I can fix it."

"Fix it?" Monel almost laughed. "You mean—make it work again, so that the crops won't die?"

"Yes," Linc said.

"Madness! You know it's against Jerlet's law to touch such a machine. And even if you could, how would you fix it? It's not like a cut finger that can be healed. . . ."

"Or a bruised face that will be normal in a little while?"

Monel's face darkened. "That's something else again. But the farm pump is a *machine*. Once it's dead, it's dead. It can't be healed, or fixed."

Turning to Magda, Linc said, "Let me try to fix the pump. Maybe we can save the crops. I've fixed other things before . . . wires, some of the electrical machines. Maybe. . . ."

But Magda shook her head. "It's forbidden to touch that kind of machine. You know Jerlet's laws."

"But. . . ."

"It is forbidden."

And she closed her eyes for meditation. Everyone in the crowd did the same. Linc sat down on the floor and shut his eyes.

He tried to squeeze out all thoughts and let his mind float free. But he kept seeing the frozen ghosts at the Ghost Place. He shuddered. *The cold is getting worse; it's coming into the living section. Even some of the crops in the farm tanks are dying of the cold.* Then he remembered the yellow star approaching. *Strange that we'll all die in fire. If only we could use that star to warm us and drive away the cold. . . .*

But such thoughts were not helping him to meditate. Linc tried to get his mind free. *The world is only a temporary illusion*, he chanted to himself. *The world is. . . .*

"I have decided," Magda announced.

Everyone looked up at her.

She pointed the wand at Peta. "No one has committed the sin of violence among us since Jerlet left us, back when we were all children. We must ask Jerlet for judgment, because the punishment for violence is too heavy even for the priestess to bear alone."

Peta's thin chest was rising and falling in rapid, choking gasps. Magda touched the colored buttons on the desk top where she sat. The big wall screen behind her glowed to a silvery-shimmery gray.

Jerlet's face filled the screen, huge, dominating the whole assembly, bigger than Linc's own height, mighty and powerful.

He was old, far older than anyone in the Living Wheel. His face was strong and square, with deep creases around the eyes and mouth. His hair was long and thick, streaked with gray as it curled over his ears and down to his shoulders. His voice was a thundering command, saying the words of the law just as he always said them:

"I've tried to set you kids up as well as possible. The servomechs ought to last long enough for you to grow up enough to take care of yourselves. There's nobody left now except me . . . and all of you. I can't stay any longer, but I think you'll be okay. You can make it. I'm sure of it."

Most of the people sitting on the floor were mouthing the

ancient words along with Jerlet's image on the screen. Everyone knew the words by heart, they had heard them so often since childhood.

"I'll come back whenever I can to see how you're doing... and I'll watch you on the TV intercom. But I've got to get up to the zero *g* section now. My heart can't take any more of this load."

Linc had to shift his position on the floor to see around Magda. She sat transfixed on the desk top, her slim body a dark silhouette against the massive presence of Jerlet.

"Now remember," Jerlet was saying, "all the rules I've set down. They're for your own safety. Especially, don't mess around with the machines that I haven't shown you how to handle. Let the servomechs take care of the machines; that's what they're for. You'll only hurt yourselves if you touch the machines. It's going to be tough enough for you, alone down here, without fooling around with the machinery.

"And above all—don't hurt each other. Violence and anger and hate have killed almost everybody on this ship. You're the only chance left for survival. Don't throw everything away... everything that we've worked for, for so many generations. You have a tough road ahead of you. Violence will make it tougher... you could easily wipe yourselves out. So..." his eyes squeezed shut, as if he were in sudden pain, "...above all... don't hurt one another. Violence is the greatest enemy you face. Never hurt one another. *Never!*"

The image disappeared, leaving only an empty glowing screen. Linc heard a few of the girls crying softly in the crowd.

"Jerlet has spoken," Madga said.

"But...." Peta found his voice. "But, that's what he always says...."

Magda nodded gravely. "He has not changed his rules for you, Peta. There is no forgiveness for the sin of violence. You must be cast out."

Peta tried to scramble to his feet. The guards grabbed him roughly and he screamed out, "No! Please!"

Linc yelled at Magda, "Show him mercy!"

"He deserves none," Magda said, her gaze flicking from Linc to Monel and back again. Peta was standing now, no longer struggling, head down. The two guards had a firm grip on his arms.

"But," Magda went on, "we have never seen the sin of violence before, and it would take even more violence to cast Peta into the outer darkness. That is the nature of the sin; violence breeds more violence."

Linc wondered what she was leading up to.

"Therefore," she said, "Peta will not be pushed through the deadlock into outer darkness. Instead, he will be given enough food and water for three meals, and sent into the tube-tunnel to seek Jerlet's domain. Let Jerlet take him and make the final judgment."

The crowd was stunned. No one moved.

Magda uttered the magic words that made her decision final: *"Quod erat Demonstrandum."*

(4)

Slowly everyone left the meeting room, leaving only Magda and Linc there.

He walked up and stood beside her. She touched the control button that turned off the wall screen, then put down her symbols and let her robe slip off her shoulders.

Linc didn't try to touch her, even though she was now no longer acting in her office as priestess.

"Are you all right?" he asked.

Nodding. "Yes. . . ."

"For sure?"

"Well," she smiled and the room seemed to glow brighter, "it always shakes me when Jerlet speaks to us. His voice . . . I have dreams about it sometimes."

"That's why you're the priestess."

With the two of them alone in the big empty room, with no one and nothing there except the few remaining books on the bare shelves, Magda was less the priestess and more of a normal human being.

She looked up at Linc, her dark eyes questioning. "Are you angry with me?"

"Angry? Why?"

"You wanted me to show mercy to Peta."

Linc felt his teeth clench slightly. *Peta. I'd nearly forgotten about him. A few moments alone with her and I forget everything.*

"Jerlet will take him," Linc said.

"But you think I should have gone easier on him."

Is she trying to start a fight? "You could have, if you wanted to. Peta isn't really a violent person."

"No; I could see that he acted out of panic."

Linc felt puzzled. "Yet you sent him out into the tubes. He might never make it as far as Jerlet's domain. The rats, and who knows what else...."

"Do you know why I had to send him away?"

Linc shook his head.

"Because of Monel," Magda admitted.

"You thought he was right and I was wrong."

She laughed suddenly, and reached out to touch Linc's cheek. "No, you silly fool! And stop looking so grim. I wanted to let Peta go free. It would have been fun to watch Monel turn purple. And besides...."

Linc waited for her to go on. When she didn't, he asked, "Besides...?"

She walked away a few steps, toward the room's big double doors. "Besides, it would have pleased you."

Linc rocked back on his heels. Magda turned away from him and hurried toward the door.

"Hey...wait. Magda!" He raced across the worn floor tiles after her. His long legs gobbled the distance in a few strides, and he jumped in front of her, leaning his back against the closed doors.

"You wanted to please me?"

"Yes."

Truly puzzled, he asked, "Then... why didn't you? Why cast Peta out? Why ask Jerlet to speak? You knew he'd just say the same old things...he never says anything else."

Her smile faded and the troubled look returned to her eyes. "Linc...Monel wants power. He's a bully. I'm sure he frightened Peta terribly; why else would the poor boy strike one of his guards? Peta never harmed anyone in any way before."

"But then...."

She put a finger over his lips, silencing him. "Hear me. The *real* reason why I'm priestess is that I'm sensitive to the way people think. Monel wants to rule. He wants to be the leader and tell everyone what to do. He would make a terrible leader; he would hurt people. So I've got to stay ahead of him. I've got to make sure that he doesn't gain more power."

Linc felt as fluttery inside as he did up on the second level, where the gravity was lower. But now it wasn't a happy feeling.

"Monel wants...how do you know...?"

She shrugged her slim shoulders. "I know. I can hear him thinking about it. I can smell his hunger."

Linc muttered, "Monel likes to boss people around."

"He's made it clear that he'd love to have an alliance with me. I stay priestess and he tells me what to do."

In his mind, Linc saw himself facing Monel, and for the first time in his life he *wanted* to be violent.

"You're shaking!" Magda said.

He grasped her shoulders. "I haven't liked Monel since we were all children together and Jerlet lived with us. When he had the fall and his legs were crippled, well...I tried to forget that I didn't like him. But now...now...."

"It's all right," Magda soothed, stepping close enough to Linc to lean her cheek against his chest. "I know how to handle Monel. Don't fear...."

"It's not fear that I feel," Linc said tightly. His arms slid around her. Then a new thought struck him. "But...why did you do what Monel wanted? Why did you send Peta away?"

She pulled away from Linc slightly and looked up into his eyes. "Suppose I let Peta go free. And suppose somebody was attacked afterward? What then?"

"But Peta wouldn't...."

"No. But Monel would. And then say that Peta did it."

The breath nearly left Linc's body. "Now I understand."

"I couldn't let that happen; I couldn't take the chance. It would mean that Monel would take charge of everything and everyone—even me. *I will not have that.* I am the priestess and I'm going to stay the priestess, no matter what Monel tries."

"So Peta had to be sacrificed."

"Punished," Magda corrected. "He was lazy, and stupid, and violent. Showing him mercy would have been playing into Monel's hands."

For a long moment Linc said nothing. Finally, "I hope he makes it up to Jerlet's area. It's a long climb. And dangerous."

Magda turned slightly in his arms to glance at the wall screen. "Let's get out of here. I have the feeling that he sees and hears everything we do in here."

"Jerlet?"

"No. Monel."

They were walking down the corridor toward the living area when Linc told her about the yellow star.

"It's bright enough now to cast shadows. It's getting so close that you can't look at it without hurting your eyes."

"How long do we have?" Magda asked.

He shrugged. "Who can tell? Maybe only a few sleeps. Maybe so long that we'll all grow as old as Jerlet."

"No one could ever get that old!"

They laughed together.

Then Linc said, "Want to go up and see it?"

Magda hesitated only a moment. "Yes. Show me."

They were almost at the hatch that led into the tube-tunnel when one of the farm workers called out to them. Magda and Linc waited at the hatch as he hurried along the passageway toward them. The overhead light panels were mostly dead in this section of the passageway, so the worker flashed from light to shadow, light to shadow, as he approached.

"Magda," he puffed as he came to a stop before them, "Monel... wants to see you... right away."

"He can wait," Linc said.

"No... it's about the crops. Now that there's not enough food for everybody...."

Magda's face set into a tight mask. *Even so, she's beautiful*, Linc thought.

"All right," Magda said to the worker. "I'll speak to Monel about the food."

The three of them started down the passageway. Linc looked back over his shoulder at the hatch to the tube-tunnel. *That must be the tunnel they put Peta into. I wonder if he's all right? Can he get to Jerlet before he needs food or sleep? Does the tunnel really go all the way up to Jerlet's domain?*

Monel was in a warm little compartment that had a rumpled bunk, a dead viewing screen on the far wall, and a desk studded with push buttons—also dead.

But on the bare part of the desk he had strewn lots and lots of colored chips of plastic. *Where did he get them?* Linc wondered.

He and Magda stood by the door of the little room. Monel

sat behind the desk in his wheeled chair, his long skinny fingers toying with the plastic chips. Sitting on the bunk was Jayna, a girl who had worked as a farmer. Now, somehow, she seemed to work for Monel all the time.

"I've learned how to use these bits of plastic to solve our food problem," Monel said.

"And I helped," Jayna added.

"We're going to eat plastic?" Linc asked.

"Of course not!" Monel snapped. "But these plastic pieces can show us how to give food to the right people."

"The right people?" Magda echoed.

"Yes...look...." Monel touched a few of the chips, began lining them in straight files. "You see? Each piece stands for one of us."

"The yellow ones are for the boys and the green ones are for the girls," Jayna said, with a big smile of accomplishment on her face.

Linc watched Monel lining them up. "How do you know you've got the same number of chips as there are people?"

"That's what *I* did," Jayna said happily. "I picked out one chip for each person. I remembered everybody's chip...see, they're all shaped a little differently. So I can remember which chip belongs to which person. I'm good at remembering." She jumped eagerly from the bunk and bounced to the desk. "See? This one is you, Magda...it's the biggest green one. And this one is Monel, he's right behind you. Each chip *means* somebody!"

Monel seemed to be smiling and frowning at once.

"Very interesting," Magda said. It sounded to Linc as if she were trying to keep her voice as flat and calm as possible, and not quite succeeding. "But what does all this have to do with food?"

"Ahah!" Monel's frown vanished and he was all toothy smile. "Since Peta broke the pump, we have a problem: not enough food for everybody."

"Not yet," Linc said. "We have enough for the time being."

Monel shot him a nasty glance. "But when the next crop is harvested, we'll only have half of what we need. Somebody's going to go hungry...lots of people, in fact."

"We all will," Magda said. "We share the food equally."

"We always have," Monel agreed, "up to now. But that

doesn't mean we have to keep on doing things the old way. With these little chips, we can decide who should get food and how much he or she should get."

"But everybody needs food," Linc said.

Monel's answer was swift. "But not everybody deserves it."

"Deserves . . . ?"

"You know people are always doing wrong things." Monel said. "Not working hard enough, getting angry, not meditating when they're supposed to . . . my guards see a lot of wrongs being done, and so do you, if you keep your eyes open. With these chips, we can put a mark down on a person's chip whenever he does something wrong. The more marks he gets, the less food we give him."

Linc felt his jaw drop open, but before he could say anything, Magda's voice cut through the room like an ice knife:

"And who decides when someone's done something wrong?"

Monel smiled again, and it was enough to turn Linc's stomach. "Why, the priestess will decide, of course," Monel said. "Assisted by these chips and those who know how to work them."

"You can't. . . ." Linc began, but Magda waved him silent.

"And suppose," she asked, "that the priestess is unwilling to do this? Suppose that the priestess decides that this is an evil scheme, to deprive people of food deliberately?"

The smile on Monel's thin face stayed fixed, as if frozen there. Finally he said, "When the people get tired of having so little to eat, they will see that this scheme is better for them."

"Some of them."

"The good ones among us," Monel said. "Once they are convinced that this plan is better than letting everyone go hungry, they will decide that the priestess is wrong to oppose it."

"And then?" Magda asked.

"Then we will get a new priestess." He turned, ever so slightly, toward Jayna. The girl stared at Magda with bright eyes.

"It's wrong!" Linc shouted. "We've always shared all the food equally. This plan is just plain wrong. It's against the rules that Jerlet gave us."

"Then ask Jerlet what to do," Monel snapped.

For the first time, Magda looked shaken. Her voice almost trembled as she said, "You know that Jerlet doesn't answer every little question we put to him."

Monel said acidly, "I know that Jerlet *never* answers any questions that *you* put to him. He only says the same thing, over and over again."

"But if we had a new priestess..." Jayna whispered.

"...maybe he would answer her," Monel finished.

Linc suddenly felt rage. He wanted to smash his fists into something: the dead wall screen, the desk, the door... Monel's twisted smiling face. *Violence! Mustn't commit the sin of....* Yet his fists clenched, and he took a step toward Monel.

Magda grabbed at his arm. "Linc! Come with me. We've heard enough of this."

He stared at Monel with hatred seething inside him, but Magda's hand on his arm and her voice were enough to turn him. Without another word he followed her out of the room and into the passageway.

She pushed the door shut. It was cooler out in the corridor. Linc could feel the flames within him damping down.

"That's just what he wants," Magda said. "If you attack him he'll have you cast out. Now I understand what happened to Peta... Monel used him as a test. If he could make poor little Peta attack him, he knew he could get you to do it."

"I'll kill him," Linc muttered.

"You will not," Magda commanded. "If you even try, you'll be killing yourself; and me, too."

"Then what can we do?"

She let herself smile. "You were going to show me the yellow star. Let's do that."

"Now?"

"Yes. Now."

They stood together at the wide observation window, his arm around her shoulders, hers around his waist. They gazed out at the stars that scattered across the darkness in an endless pattern of glory. And when the yellow star spun into view, they turned their faces and watched their shadows creep across the floor and walls of the passageway.

"It's strange," Magda murmured. "The yellow star brings warmth... it drives away the cold. It feels good."

"Only for a while," Linc said. "It will get hotter and hotter. It will turn everything to fire."

"Too much warmth and we die," she said.

Linc nodded.

"Too little food and we die," she added.

He still said nothing.

"Linc . . . Monel is right, isn't he? I'll have to decide on his way about the food?"

"You can't do that," said Linc. "We've always shared everything equally. You can't just decide that one person will starve while another eats."

Her dark eyes seemed to cut right through him. "The priestess can decide such things," she said.

"It would be wrong. . . ."

"*I* decide what's wrong! No one else. Only the priestess."

"With Monel telling you what to do," Linc shot back.

She nearly smiled. "No one tells me what to do . . . except Jerlet."

The anger that Linc had tried to keep bottled up inside him came boiling out. "Jerlet never says anything new to you or anybody else. He always says the same thing!"

Magda remained icy-calm. "Of course. That's because he's told us everything that we need to know. Don't you see? Jerlet has given us all the rules we need. It's up to his priestess to use those rules wisely."

"By letting people starve?"

"If I find it necessary."

"If Monel *tells you* it's necessary!"

"Linc . . . there are so many things you don't understand. If I must decide that certain evil people must starve, and the people accept it, what's to stop me from deciding one day that Monel must starve?"

"You. . . ." Linc had to take a breath, and even when he did, his voice was still high-pitched with shock. "You would do that?"

"If I find that Monel is evil."

He stared at Magda, as if seeing her for the first time in his life. This slim, lovely girl was in command of their lives. "You'd kill him?"

Magda smiled. "It will never come to pass. Sometimes I can see into the future . . . well, maybe *see* is the wrong word. I get feelings, like a cold draft touching me. . . ."

"And?"

Turning slightly away from Linc, staring off into the

darkness of the corridor, Magda said in a strangely hollow voice, "I'm not sure . . . I don't see myself sentencing anyone to starve . . . not even Monel. I . . . it *feels* as if a miracle is going to happen. Yes, that's it!" She fixed her gaze on Linc. "A miracle, Linc! Jerlet's going to make the pump work again! He's going to bring it back to life!"

Linc couldn't pull his eyes away from Magda's brightly smiling face. But his mind was telling him, *Jerlet's not going to do a thing . . . unless you do it for him.*

(5)

They slept right there in the passageway, next to the big observation window, huddled together to keep the chill away. The yellow star's radiance wasn't enough to really warm them, but that didn't matter.

Linc woke first.

He sat up and watched Magda breathing easily in her sleep. Just like when they had been children together, and there were no worries or fears. Jerlet had been with them then, and he had strange and wonderful machines that did everything for all the children: kept them clean, even kept their clothing clean; fed them; taught them how to speak and walk; everything.

One by one, the machines broke down or wore out. A few of the cleaning machines still worked. Something Jerlet had called ultrasonics. You stepped in and a weird trembly feeling came over you for an instant. Then you were clean. But even those machines were wearing out.

Linc frowned at the memories playing in his head. He had fixed one of the cleaning machines once, a long time ago. It wasn't working right, and Linc poked into its strange humming heart one day when no one was looking. There was a lot of dust and grime inside. He cleaned it out and the machine worked fine afterward.

He never told anyone about it. It would have made Jerlet angry.

It's a strange rule, Linc thought. *Why would Jerlet give us a rule like that? If the machines don't work, we'll all die. But if we could fix them, fix the heaters and the farm tanks and the lights....*

He glanced down again at Magda. She was stirring, beginning to wake up.

If I could fix the pump, then Monel's game with the chips wouldn't be needed.

He had told himself that same thing a thousand times since Magda had spoken of a miracle.

If I can fix it.

And if I don't get caught.

Magda finally awoke and they went down to the Living Wheel together. People were up and about. Monel was hissing orders at everyone as they lined up for firstmeal. He browbeat the cooks and made sure that everyone stayed in line. He checked the worn and faded plastic dishes that each person carried, and made sure no one took any extra food. He made a general nuisance of himself.

But no one complained. A few smiled. A mild joke here and there. That was all. They were accustomed to Monel's fussing about. And afraid of his guards.

Then the workday began. Linc's task was in the electrical distribution center. He stood by a flickering wall screen, just as Jerlet had taught him to do when he had been only a child, and watched the colored lights flash on and off. There was little else to do. The screen flashed and flickered. Once in a whole a light would flare red and then go blank. It would never light up on the screen again.

Over the years, Linc had gradually figured out that each little light on the screen stood for different rooms of the Living Wheel, and even different machines within the rooms. Whenever a symbol disappeared from the screen, a machine went dead somewhere. It could be a heater, or an air fan, or a cooking unit . . . anything. *Which one stands for the pump Peta broke?* Linc studied the section of the screen that represented the farming chambers.

One of the biggest thrills of Linc's life had been the moment he realized that the straight lines on the screen stood for the wires that stretched along the passageways behind the plastic wall panels. The lines were even colored the same way the wires were: yellow, green, red, blue, and so forth. Once he had even fixed one of the wires; he found the trouble spot by noticing that one of the lines on the screen suddenly showed a flashing red light on it.

It had taken a long argument and nearly a day's worth of meditation by the priestess before she decided that a wire was not a machine, and therefore could be touched by human hands. Linc fixed the faulty wire the way he had seen Jerlet and the servomechs do it years before, and a while room that had gone dark and cold suddenly became light and warm again.

Can I fix the pump? he asked himself, over and over again, all through the long day.

At the end of the workday he was still asking himself. He wondered about it all through lastmeal... which was noticeably skimpier than most lastmeals. And Monel was still there at the food line, wheeling his chair back and forth, badgering everybody.

Magda was nowhere to be seen. Which meant she had retired to her shrine to meditate.

She's trying to reach Jerlet, Linc knew.

With Monel's voice yammering in his ears, Linc took his food plate back to his own compartment and ate there alone. In silence.

The lights dimmed for sleeping as they always did, automatically. Linc stretched out on his bunk and felt the warmth in the room seeping away; the heaters were turned down, too, at sleep time. But Linc had no intention of going to sleep.

Now the question he asked himself wasn't: *Can I fix it?* It was: *Will they catch me?*

He stayed silent and unmoving on his bunk for a long time, eyes staring into the darkness. *Jerlet didn't want us to tamper with the machines because we were just kids when he had to leave us. He left the servomechs to fix the machines. He didn't want us to hurt ourselves, or mess up the machines.*

Linc rose slowly and sat up on his bunk. *The servomechs were supposed to keep all the machines working. But they themselves broke down and died. So there's nobody here to fix machines. Except me.*

He went to the door of his compartment and opened it a crack. The corridor outside was darkened, too. No sounds out there. Everyone was asleep.

I hope! Linc told himself.

Swiftly, he made his way down the corridor that went

through the sleeping compartments, through the kitchen and the bolted-down tables and chairs of the galley, and up to the metal hatch that opened on the main passageway.

Magda and the others are wrong when they say Jerlet doesn't want us to tamper with the machines. He wouldn't mind if I tried to fix the pump. He wouldn't get angry at me.

Still, Linc could feel a clammy sweat breaking out all over him. Gathering his strength, he pushed the hatch open and stepped out into the main passageway of the Living Wheel. Down at the end of the passageway loomed the huge double doors of the farm area. They were called airlocks, although Linc could never figure out how anyone could lock up air.

So far, all you've done is take a walk. But if they find you inside the farm section, Monel will know what you were up to.

Then he pictured Monel's smug face with the plastic chips, smiling at Magda and telling her that she was a failure as priestess. Linc pushed down on the heavy latch that opened the airlock door.

The farms were fully lit, and the vast room was warm and pungent with green and growing smells. The air felt softer, somehow. Linc squinted in the sudden brightness and let the warmth soak into his bones. It felt good. The crop tanks stood there, row after row of them, huge square metal boxes glinting in the glare of the long overhead light tubes. The only sound in the vast high-domed chamber was the gentle gurgle of the nutrient fluids flowing through the crop tanks. The pigs and fowl and even the bees were asleep in shaded, shadowed areas across the big room.

Linc went straight to the pump that had been damaged. It looked completely normal from the outside: a heavy, squat chunk of metal with pipes going into it and out of it. But it was silent. The floor plates around it were stained, as if there had been a flood of nutrient fluid that the farmers had mopped up.

He clambered up the metal ladder to the rim of the nearest crop tank and peered in. Young corn was growing in the pebbly bed, together with something else green that Linc couldn't identify. Nothing seemed to be wilted yet, but Linc was no farmer. Stav had said the crops would die without the nutrients that the pump provided, and the troughs criss-crossing the plastic pebbles of the tank were completely dry. The crops' roots were sunk into those pebbles, and they were getting no nutrients.

Frowning, Linc clambered down again and stared at the pump. *All right, brave hero. Now how do you fix it?* Linc realized that he didn't even know how to get the pump's casing off so he could examine it.

Jerlet would know. But Jerlet never answered Magda's questions; he only spoke the same old words. Linc squatted down and stared at the pump. It sat there, silent and dead. Beyond it, on the far wall of the chamber, Linc could see a dead viewing screen. No one had used it since Jerlet had left them; it was a machine that only Magda could touch.

Linc focused his eyes on the distant screen. *Suppose I called Jerlet and just asked him how to fix this pump? If he didn't want me to touch it, he could tell me.* He frowned. Another voice in his head asked, *What makes you think Jerlet will answer you, when he doesn't answer the priestess?*

"If he doesn't answer," Linc whispered to himself, "that means he doesn't want me to touch the pump."

Yes, but to try to reach him means that you'll have to touch the viewing screen controls. That's just as bad as tampering with the pump.

Linc had no answer for that. He walked across the big empty room and stood in front of the wall screen. A tiny desk projected out from under the screen. It had three rows of colored buttons on it. Some of the colors on the buttons had been chipped away. *That's where Monel got his colored plastics!*

There was no chair at the desk. Linc looked down at the buttons, then up at the screen, then down at the buttons again.

"Jerlet wouldn't mind me calling him," he told himself. "Besides, if Monel can touch the buttons, why can't I?"

Still, as he reached out for the biggest of the buttons, his outstretched hand trembled. Swallowing hard, Linc jabbed at the button.

The screen glowed a pearly gray.

No face showed on it, no picture of any sort, nor any sound. But it was alive! It glowed softly.

"Jerlet," Linc blurted. "Can you hear me?"

The screen did nothing. It merely kept on glowing. Frowning, Linc called Jerlet's name a few more times. Still no response. Impatiently, he started pressing the other buttons, jamming them down in haphazard fashion. The screen flashed pictures, lights, swirling colors. But no Jerlet.

"Jerlet! Jerlet, answer me! Please!"

After a few frantic minutes, a booming voice said:

"UNAUTHORIZED PERSONNEL ARE NOT PERMITTED TO USE THIS TERMINAL."

Linc staggered back, startled. "Wha . . . Are you Jerlet?"

"UNAUTHORIZED PERSONNEL ARE NOT PERMITTED TO USE THIS TERMINAL."

"Jerlet! I need help!"

"UNAUTHORI. . . ." The voice stopped for an eyeblink. "WHAT SORT OF ASSISTANCE DO YOU REQUIRE?"

It didn't sound at all like Jerlet's voice. But it was somebody's voice.

"The pump . . . the main pump for the crop tanks," Linc said. "I need help to fix it."

The screen hummed for a moment. Then, "MAINTENANCE AND REPAIR HYDROPONICS SECTION: CODE SEVEN-FOUR-FOUR."

"What?" Linc said. "I don't understand."

The screen suddenly showed a picture of the buttons on the desk. Three of the buttons had red circles drawn around them.

"MAINTENANCE AND REPAIR INFORMATION FOR HYDROPONICS EQUIPMENT. PUNCH CODE SEVEN-FOUR-FOUR."

It took Linc a while to figure out what the strange words meant. He poked at the buttons indicated, and some even stranger symbols appeared on the screen. He told the screen that the pump was broken. The screen jabbered more meaningless words at him, then showed some pictures. Gradually, Linc realized that they were pictures of the pump: its insides as well as its outside.

It took a long time, so long that Linc was certain the workday would begin and the farmers would come in and discover him there.

In pictures, the screen showed him that the tools he needed were stored in a special wall panel. Linc found the panel; it hadn't been touched for so long that it was crusted over with dirt, but he pulled it open with back-straining desperation.

Some of the tools the screen's voice spoke about just didn't work. Something it called a "torch" stayed cold and lifeless, even when the pictures showed that a flame was supposed to come out of it.

Maybe I just don't know how to work it, Linc thought.

But the screen was patient, and staggered Linc with its flood of knowledge. With pictures and the steady, unhurried voice, it showed Linc how to unfasten the pump's cover, disconnect its input and output pipes, check the seals and screens and motor. Linc, sitting in the midst of scattered bolts, metal pieces, lengths of plastic pipe, found that the main inner chamber of the pump was clogged with weeds and dead leaves. He cleaned it as thoroughly as he could, then followed the screen's instructions in reassembling the machine.

"ACTIVATE THE POWER SWITCH," the voice said at last, and the picture showed a yellow arrow pointing to a tiny switch at the base of the pump.

Linc went back and pushed at the little toggle. The whole pump seemed to shudder and clatter for an instant, then settled down to a smooth steady hum. Above his head, in the crop tanks, Linc could hear the sudden gurgle of nutrient fluid flowing again.

He should have felt exultant. Instead, he merely felt tired. He managed a weak smile, went back to the screen, and said:

"Thank you, whoever you are."

The screen did not reply. Linc clicked it off, then turned just in time to see the first group of farmers entering the big, echoing room.

(6)

Linc's first impulse was to run.

But as the farmers noticed him there, sweat- and dirt-streaked, they seemed more surprised and curious than angry.

Why should I be afraid? Linc asked himself. *I fixed the pump. There's nothing to be afraid of.*

The farmers were walking up to him, slowly, looking puzzled.

"Linc," said a lanky girl called Hollie, "what are you doing here?"

"What's going on?" Stav's strong voice came from behind them. The broad-faced, sandy-haired leader of the farmers pushed past Hollie to stare at Linc.

Linc was so tired that all he wanted to do was sleep. He pointed to the pump. "I fixed it," he said. "I saved the crops."

"What? You must be crazy," Stav said. "Nobody can fix the pump. It's dead."

Linc grinned at him. "Go see for yourself."

A crowd of farmers was gathering around them now. With a good-humored shrug, Hollie said, "Won't hurt to look."

She went to the pump, bent down and listened, put a hand on it.

"It's working, all right!" she shouted.

Everyone rushed to the pump, leaving Linc standing alone. Stav clambered up to the top of the nearest crop tank. A few other farmers followed him, bumping each other in their haste to climb the metal rungs. Others dashed to other tanks.

"The nutrient's flowing again!" someone yelled.

They all rushed back toward Linc. Stav grabbed him in a

bear hug that almost cracked his spine. The others pounded Linc on the shoulders, laughing and shouting, congratulating and thanking him. They half-carried him toward the airlock doors.

"Hey, no. . . ." Linc objected weakly. "Let me go . . . all I want is some sleep."

They left him at the doors and turned back to their work. They were all smiling. One voice picked up an ancient work song, something about Hi Ho, whatever that was. Other voices joined the chant.

Linc smiled, too, as he headed down the passageway toward his bunk.

He was jolted out of his sleep when one of Monel's guards kicked his door open. Before Linc could get up from the bunk, they were on him, three of them. Two grabbed his arms and yanked him to his feet.

The third said, "Monel wants to see you. *Now*."

They pushed Linc out into the corridor and led him down to Monel's little room.

He was sitting at the desk, fingering the plastic chips. Jayna sat back in a corner, looking frightened, staring at Monel with big unblinking eyes. Monel himself seemed furious. He was flexing the chips in his fingers, bending them as if he wanted to break them into tiny bits.

For a long time Linc simply stood there, crowded against the doorway by the three husky guards.

Finally, Monel looked up at him. "You tampered with the food tank." His voice was pure acid.

"I fixed the pump."

"You touched a machine when you knew it was forbidden!"

Linc repeated stubbornly, "I fixed it."

"That's a crime! And you know it."

Stepping up closer to the desk and leaning his knuckles on it so that he loomed over Monel, Linc said, "I made sure that we'll have enough food for everybody. So you won't have to decide who's going to eat and who should starve."

"You committed a crime," Monel insisted.

"That's for the priestess to decide; not you."

Monel glared at Linc for a moment. Then a teeth-baring smile spread across his face. "Oh, she'll say it. Don't worry about that. She'll say it, and you'll be condemned to outer darkness. Or maybe you *both* will!"

They let Linc go back to his room while the workday wore on. After lastmeal everyone would gather in the meeting room to hear Magda's decision about Linc.

He sat on his bunk and stared at the wall. *Magda won't sentence me, she'll thank me. I did it for her. She'll be glad.*

But still he worried.

The time for midmeal passed. Linc didn't bother going out to the galley, and no one brought him any food.

But then he heard swift footsteps outside his door. The door slid open, and Magda stepped into his room.

He stood up and reached for her.

"How could you?" she whispered.

He blinked, confused. "What do you mean?"

"How could you cause all this trouble? Fix the pump! You know that it's forbidden to tamper with the machines."

"I didn't tamper with it," Linc said stubbornly, "I fixed it. I figured out how to use the wall screen in the farm section, and the screen told me...."

But her eyes were wide with horror. "Linc! Do you realize what you're saying! No one's allowed to touch the machines. You can't play with viewing screens."

"But the screens know how to fix the machines."

She covered her mouth with one hand and paced the length of the room in four rapid strides. Turning back to Linc, she asked:

"Have you told anybody about the screen?"

"No...I don't think so."

"Good. Now listen to me. When we meet after lastmeal, say nothing about the screen. Or—better yet, tell them Jerlet appeared on the screen without you touching it."

"I was trying to get Jerlet to speak, that's why I turned the screen on."

"*Listen* to me," she urged. "Don't say that you turned the screen on. I'll tell them that I was meditating and looking for an answer to our problem all through the night. Which is no lie. I was. And Jerlet must have seen me, or heard me...and fixed the pump for us."

"But that's not true," Linc said. "I fixed it. I did it by myself, with my own hands."

She shook her head impatiently. "Monel will destroy you . . . both of us, if we give him the chance."

"But I saved the crops. Nobody will go hungry."

"Which is why he's angry."

Linc pounded his fists against his thighs. "The people will be *glad* that the pump's working again. The farmers were singing!"

Magda glared at him. "Linc, people don't behave like machines. Don't you see what Monel will do? He'll say that it's a crime to tamper with the machines, yet you went ahead and did it anyway. This time it worked, but if you're left free to tamper again, you could destroy something and kill us all."

Linc sank down onto his bunk. "That's stupid."

"But that's just what he'll do. And then he'll tell me to get Jerlet to speak to us, and Jerlet will just answer with the same words he always speaks, and I'll have to condemn you. I'll have to!"

"I did it for you," Linc muttered. "You wanted a miracle."

Her look softened. "I know. But we've got to be careful about how we explain it to the people. You've got to say that the screen came on by itself, and Jerlet told you what to do."

With a frown, Linc said, "And how do I explain why I went into the farms in the first place?"

Magda bowed her head in thought for a moment. Then she came up smiling. "Oh, it's easy! You say that Jerlet came to you in a dream, while you were sleeping, and told you to go to the farms."

"But that's not true!"

She sat on the bunk beside him and put a finger to his lips. "Linc, you couldn't have fixed the pump without Jerlet's help. We both know that."

"But. . . ."

"We'll just *explain* his help a little differently from the way it really happened. It's not really lying; it's . . . well, it's bending the truth a little, so that the people won't get frightened."

"I don't like it."

"Trust the priestess," Magda whispered. "I want to help you."

With a shake of his head, Linc answered, "But you don't

understand what's really important. I found out that the screens . . . they know how to fix things. They show you what to do. We can fix all the dead machines. . . ."

"No!" Magda snapped. "You mustn't say that. You'll frighten everyone . . . you'll be playing into Monel's hands." She got up from the bunk and started pacing the floor again.

He looked at her. "Am I frightening you?"

From the corner of the tiny compartment she returned his stare. "Yes," she said at last, in a hushed voice. "Yes . . . a little."

He reached a hand out toward her, and she rushed over and sat beside him on the bunk. She gripped his hands hard, and her fingers were ice cold.

"Magda, we can fix everything. . . ."

"Hush." She bent forward slightly, squeezing his hands with a strength he never knew she possessed. She pressed her eyes shut, and began to tremble wildly.

Linc had seen Magda entrance herself before. She was searching the future, trying to see what would happen, what they should do.

She stopped trembling and eased up the pressure on his hands. She straightened up and looked into his eyes. Her own deep black eyes were rimmed with red and glimmering with tears.

"Linc . . . you're going to Jerlet." Her voice was a frightened whisper. "You . . . you're going to *see* him, talk with him. But before you do . . . you'll see Peta again."

Linc pulled his hands away from her. "That's what you see in the future, huh? All that means is that you're going to have me cast out, just the way you cast out Peta."

"No. . . ." she gasped.

He jumped to his feet. "I know how to fix the machines, but you and the others are too scared to see the noses on your faces!"

"You think I'm wrong?" Magda's voice went rigid; it was the priestess speaking now, not his friend.

"The screens can tell us how to fix everything. . . ."

"It is forbidden to touch the screens, or any other machine. You have committed sins and you're telling me that you're not sorry about it. You're telling me that you want to do even worse things."

"I want to save us! If we can learn how to fix all the machines, maybe we can\push the yellow star away."

"You'll make Jerlet angry at all of us."

"No, I want to save us all."

Magda walked past Linc to the door. She stopped, facing it. He could see from the stiff back, the way she held her head high, that every centimeter of her slim body was rigid with tension and anger.

She whipped around and faced him once more. "Linc, I want to help you, but you're going against everything we know. Everything we have. So you fixed one pump. That might have been luck or even a trap...."

"A trap?"

"Yes!" she insisted. "You think you know how to fix all the machines. Suppose Jerlet is just testing you, seeing if you'll tamper with more machines. *You're going against his rules*, Linc! I can't let you do that."

For the first time, Linc felt anger seething inside his guts. "You just don't believe that I can fix them. You believe all this stuff about not touching the machines, but you don't believe me."

"No one can fix them."

"You'd rather just sit here and let one machine after another break down until we're freezing and starving. You'd sit here and let the yellow star swallow us up, without even lifting a finger to *try....*"

"Jerlet's rules are...."

"Don't yammer at me about Jerlet's rules!" he roared. "I don't care about his stupid rules!"

Her mouth dropped open.

Forcing himself to take a deep, calming breath, Linc said more softly, "Magda, listen to me. Suppose this really *is* a test? Suppose Jerlet's trying to find out if we'll use the brains he gave us to find out how to fix the machines?"

"But his rules say we mustn't tamper with the machines."

"We were children when he told us that...so small we couldn't see over the galley tables. And all the servomechs worked then. Things are different now, and Jerlet hasn't said anything new about the machines for a long, long time." He felt a smile trying to work its way across his face. "Remember back then? Remember how I used to boost you up, so you could reach the top buttons on the food selector?"

She grinned and looked down, so that Linc couldn't see her face. "Yes. . . ."

"But then the selector broke down . . . and the servomechs broke down . . . all the machines are dying. Jerlet wouldn't want us to sit here and die with them. He wants us to fix them."

"Then why hasn't he told us so?" Magda asked.

Linc shrugged.

She came away from the door and sat on the bunk beside Linc. "And you've forgotten about Monel."

"Hmp! What about him? After I've fixed a few more machines he. . . ."

She touched his shoulder. "Linc, you might know about machines, but you don't know about people. Monel won't let you fix anything. I can see just what he'll do."

He took her hand, engulfing it in his own. "He won't be able to stop me if you're on my side. Together we can convince the people."

"No." Magda shook her head. "Not if you try to tell everyone that the screens speak, and you want to fix all the machines. It's too much for them to take, all at once. Monel will turn them against you."

"The farmers. . . ."

"The farmers are glad the pump's working again. But Monel can frighten them into casting you out."

"But if I just tell them the truth. . . ."

"If you tell them the truth, we'll both be cast out!" Magda's voice was iron hard now. "I want to save you, Linc, but you've got to help me. I will not allow Monel to become my master. I will not allow him to set up another priestess, I *must* be the priestess here! It's Jerlet's command."

Linc could feel the coldness of outside seeping into him. "You mean that you'll let them cast me out, rather than risk your position as priestess."

"It's what I have to do." Magda's voice was low, almost a whisper, but still unalterably firm.

"It's what you *want* to do," Linc answered bitterly.

Magda sat unmoving, like a statue. Even her face seemed to have gone hard and lifeless.

Finally, she spoke. "I *am* the priestess. I can see the future. I can see into people's minds. I must stay as priestess. No one else can be priestess in my place."

Linc said tightly, "So what happens now?"

Magda still didn't move. Her voice sounded as if it came from one of the ghosts. "You will be brought before me for judgment, because you tampered with the machine."

He said nothing.

"If you confess that you did it, and say nothing about the screen, and tell the people that you followed Jerlet's commands, I can show you mercy. Monel wouldn't dare insist on casting you out . . . this time. But if you try to insist that you can reach Jerlet by using the screens, and fix all the machines. . . ."

Her voice trailed off.

For a long moment there was no sound in the tiny compartment except the distant buzz of an air blower. Linc felt the wall hard and unyielding against his back, the softer foamplastic of the bunk beneath him. It all seemed unreal, strange, as if he'd never been in this place before. Yet he had lived all his life here.

"And your vision of the future," he heard himself ask, stiffly, as if he was talking to a stranger. "You said I was going to find Jerlet . . . and Peta."

Magda nodded slowly.

"That means I'm going to be cast out, just as Peta was."

Her voice was distant, as if it came from the farthest star. "Don't force me to do it, Linc. Please . . . don't make me do it."

He didn't answer.

After a long silent time, she got up and left him sitting there by himself.

(7)

He stayed alone on his bunk for only a few minutes.

Everybody's at lastmeal by now, he thought. He knew what he had to do. Suddenly, it was as clear as the instructions the wall screen had given him about the pump. *Magda's vision of the future was right. I'm going to find Jerlet.*

He went to the door and stepped out into the corridor. It was empty; everyone was in the galley.

Hurriedly, Linc padded down the corridor to his station at the electrical distribution compartment. He gathered a few tools: the knife he had made out of a screwdriver, a length of metal pipe, some coiled wire. They were the only things that he could vaguely imagine as being helpful on the long trek upward to the region of weightlessness.

He almost got to the tube-tunnel hatch without being seen. A couple was lounging in the recessed alcove that the hatch was set into, out of sight from the main walkway of the corridor, shadowed from the overhead lights. They were just as startled to see Linc as he was to find them there when he ducked into the alcove.

"Hey what. . . ." The guy jumped and yelled as Linc bumped into him.

"Oh . . . sorry," Linc said.

The girl was even more upset. "Why don't you watch . . . say," she recognized Linc. "Where are you going? There's going to be a meeting about you. . . ."

Linc pushed past. "I won't be there."

"You can't run away," the guy said, reaching out to grab Linc. "Monel wants you. . . ."

Linc brushed his hand away. "I'm not running away from anybody. I'm going up to find Jerlet. Tell Monel I'll be back."

They stood there, stunned, as Linc worked the hatch mechanism and swung it back. He stepped through. The last he saw of them was their shocked, wide-eyed faces as he slammed the hatch shut again.

It was dark in the tunnel. Linc stepped out across the metal platform and leaned over the railing. Up and up spiraled the metal steps, winding around the tunnel's circular walls until they were lost in blackness.

How far up did they go? *Can I really climb them high enough to reach Jerlet?* Linc wondered.

As he started up the winding steps, he told himself, *It must be possible. Magda wouldn't have sent Peta up this way if the steps didn't go all the way to Jerlet.*

With a sudden shock Linc realized that he had no food with him, and he had missed lastmeal and midmeal. He didn't feel particularly hungry; more excited and curious. *But suppose it takes a really long time to get up there? I could starve!*

He shook his head and kept on climbing. *No, Magda's vision said I'd find Peta and Jerlet. I won't starve.*

Sleep reached out for him before hunger did. Linc climbed for as long as he could, until his legs grew numb and his eyes gummed together. Then he tried to get out of the tunnel; he didn't want to sleep in this cold, dark, hollow-ringing metal tube. There could be rats here, or other things, unknown things, that were even worse.

The first hatch that he tried was jammed shut. Linc strained against it, but it refused to budge. He climbed up a long, spiraling level. The hatch there was shut, too, but there was a small window in it. Yellowish light slanted across the scene on the other side of the hatch. *The yellow star!* Linc realized. *Closer than ever.*

Then he focused on what the light was showing him. The passageway beyond the hatch was wrecked. Its walls gaped open, and Linc could see stars from outside peering into the shattered, twisted passageway. No one could live in there; it was all outer darkness, even in the warmth of the approaching star.

The hatch at the next level was open and Linc wearily stepped through. The passageway was intact; it was even warm. Rows of doors lined the walls. Groggy from sleepiness, Linc tottered to the nearest door and pushed it open.

It was a small storeroom of some sort, caked with dust and ages of filth. In the light from the corridor, Linc found the control switch on the wall beside the door and flicked it. The overhead panels glowed to life.

No one had been in this room for ages. The thick dust was undisturbed. Not even the tiny footprints of rats or other animals. Linc nodded, satisfied that it was safe. He shut the door, turned off the lights, and stretched out on the grimy floor. He was asleep almost instantly, in spite of the choking smell of dust in his nostrils.

A dream awakened him.

Linc sat bolt upright, sweating and trembling. He had been screaming in his nightmare, and his mouth was open now, but nothing came out except a strangled cough. The dream fled from his memory; the harder he tried to recall, the smaller and smaller it dwindled inside his mind until, within a few moments, it was lost altogether. All he could remember was the terror. Something had been after him and nearly got him.

Still coughing from the dust, Linc got to his feet and left the room. Within a few minutes he was back in the tube-tunnel, shuddering slightly from the coldness of it. He touched the curving metal wall; it was so cold that it hurt his fingertips.

Upward, ever upward. Spiraling around and around until he grew dizzy and had to stop and sit on the steps and catch his breath. Then the cold would seep through his thin coveralls and he'd be forced to his feet again. Exercise warmed him. But his belly growled complainingly. It had been empty too long.

Once when he stopped, he heard scrabbling sounds. Clawed feet scratching across metal. Lots of them. In the echoes of the tunnel he couldn't tell if the noise was coming from below him or above.

Linc pulled the length of pipe from his belt loop and hefted it firmly in his hand. But his hand shook, and not merely from the cold.

He climbed more slowly now, and paused often to listen. The sounds were always there, and seemed to be drawing nearer. He pounded the pipe against the steps, and the clanging frightened even himself. But within a few heartbeats, the scrabblings of the rats returned.

Linc had suffered an electric shock when he had fixed a faulty wire in the distribution center. He still remembered the feeling.

It was mild compared to the shock he felt when he saw Peta's body.

The boy was lying in a tumbled heap at one of the platforms in front of a hatch. His clothes were badly chewed up and caked with blood. Linc sank to his knees and stared at the dead body. There was a huge red gash across his forehead. His eyes were open, staring sightlessly at nothingness.

Linc lost track of how long he knelt there, not knowing what to do. *Did Jerlet do this? No, it couldn't be. This isn't the weightless domain. Jerlet's not here.*

That meant that something, or someone, had killed Peta.

Monel's guards? Did they track him all this way and kill him? Linc shook his head. *Impossible. Why would they? And even Monel's guards couldn't deliberately kill somebody.*

As he knelt there, a tiny tick-tick-ticking sound scurried across the platform. Linc looked down to Peta's bare feet. A pair of rats were sniffing there, their red eyes glittering in the darkness.

Linc swung his pipe at them but they scampered away unharmed and disappeared. The pipe clattered across the metal floor plates.

Can't leave Peta here!

Linc retrieved the pipe, then hoisted Peta's cold body to his shoulder. He worked the hatch open and stepped into the passageway on the other side.

For the first time he realized how little weight there was here. His own weight had been diminishing steadily, but he had been too sleepy and hungry, and too tired, to notice it. Peta felt as light as a bunk mattress, and Linc was almost tempted to try gliding down the passageway.

There's got to be a deadlock here someplace, Linc told himself as he tiptoed down the passageway. *Got to put Peta safely away into the outer darkness.*

The passageway seemed strange. The ceiling was lower than any Linc had ever seen before. There were doors only on one side of the corridor. And the floor curved sharply upward. It looked as if Linc were walking uphill, but it felt to his tired legs as if he was on a perfectly flat floor.

The deadlock was at the end of the passageway, blocking it completely, a huge, heavy metal hatch with the strange symbols that the ancients had put there.

Linc studied it for a long while, to make certain it was exactly the same as the deadlock in the Living Wheel. It seemed the same; as if it had been made by someone who couldn't possibly make two things differently.

He didn't like the idea of staying there any longer than he had to, but Linc worked the deadlock very carefully. He went exactly by the ritual Jerlet had taught them so long ago, for he knew that to deviate from the ritual would mean instant death.

Carefully he touched the buttons set into the wall alongside the hatch in the proper order and watched the lights inside each button turn on, just as they were supposed to. When the correct ritual had been performed, the inner hatch slid open, and Linc peered into the glittery metal chamber of the deadlock itself.

Strangely, he found that his eyes misted over and he was nearly crying as he gently laid Peta's body in the cold metal chamber. He looked so little, so helpless.

"Soon you will be outside," Linc whispered the words of the ritual, "with all the others who have ever lived. You will become a star, Peta, and you will never feel cold or alone again."

Linc went back to the keyboard to finish the ritual. The hatch closed and the red light over it flashed on. Linc could hear a faint hum and *whoosh* of the outer hatch opening and Peta's body taking flight for the stars. Then the humming stopped and the red light turned off.

It was done. Peta was launched into the outer world, as was proper. Yet Linc felt no happiness about it. He had done the correct thing, but it made him sad and somehow lonelier than he had ever felt before in his life.

Grimly, he made his way back along the passageway to the hatch that opened onto the tube-tunnel. Hunger and cold were his only companions now.

Except for the rats.

(8)

The tunnel was endless.

Linc pushed on, up the eternally-spiraling steps, eyes burning from lack of sleep, hands shaking from the cold. It was dark in the tunnel, the only light came from an occasional window. The starlight carried no warmth with it. Somehow the light from the yellow star never reached these windows; its warmth never touched the metal chill of the tunnel.

At his back Linc could hear the rats. At first they had been faint, distant. But now their scrabbling claws scratched clearly on the metal steps. Their screeching chatter came echoing off the curved tunnel walls.

Linc pushed on. His weight was getting lighter and lighter, but his strength was ebbing away fast, too, leached from his body by the cold and hunger.

Can't stop, he told himself. *If you stop you'll fall asleep. And the rats will get to you....*

He stumbled. He fell. He picked himself up. He spread out his arms and soared effortlessly. The tunnel was no longer spiraling up over his head. It was flat and open and there was no up or down. He laughed aloud, and heard a strange crackling harsh voice echoing off the metal walls of the tunnel.

He floated almost weightlessly. *Floating, floating....* Everything was dark around him. Impenetrable black. He was alone in the darkness, without even a star to watch over him. *Nothing...no one...alone....* Something deep inside Linc's mind was telling him to stay awake, but the voice was far, far away.

Alone...all alone...and cold.... It didn't make any difference if his eyes were open or shut. There was nothing to see. The darkness was complete.

Linc drifted, weightless. His eyes closed. The cold seemed to wrap him tenderly now. It didn't hurt anymore. His aching muscles relaxed. He floated on nothingness.

Nothingness.

Pain awoke him. Not a sharp stabbing pain, but a far-off dull kind of discomfort that comes when there's a lump in your slipper. Or when a rat begins chewing on a leg that's numb from cold.

Linc shook his head to clear it. He wasn't certain that he was awake....

And then he saw the red gleaming eyes, heard the chittering of thousands of rats, felt them crawling over his body. A warm furry blur brushed across his face.

He screamed and jackknifed, doubling over weightlessly and sending his body twisting madly across the dark tunnel in a cloud of equally-weightless rats. They screamed, too, and scattered.

Linc bounced off a bitingly-cold metal wall and felt around his waist for the pipe he had been carrying, the wire, anything he could use as a weapon. His hand felt warm sticky blood.

Thousands of glaring red eyes surrounded him in the darkness. He kicked out, flailing arms and legs as he edged his back along the burningly-cold wall.

The rats flowed back away from him. They chattered among themselves as if to say, *Stay clear. He's still strong enough to fight. Wait a while. He won't last long.*

Linc kept edging away from the malevolent eyes, his back to the wall. But in the dark and weightlessness he couldn't tell which way he was going. *Which way is up?* he sobbed to himself. *How can I tell?*

The rats hovered just out of his reach, waiting, chittering.

Linc's feet were still dangling in midair. His only contact with the tunnel was the wall at his back. He pushed sideways on the frozen metal with the palms of his bloody hands, reaching out with his feet for some solid contact.

The steps. His feet touched a step. The rats followed him, chattering, patient.

Sinking to his knees on the steps, Linc forced his mind to remember: *The railing. When you were going up the tunnel, the rail was on your left and the wall was on your right.*

He reached out with his left hand. Nothing. He peered into the darkness but he couldn't even see his own hand. He reached out farther. His hand bumped into the wall.

Suddenly Linc was sweating. It was a cold sweat trickling down his face and flanks like rivers of ice, making him shiver. He edged away from the wall and reached out with his right hand. It touched something warm and furry that shrieked. Linc yelled, too, and pulled the hand back. Tremblingly, he forced himself to reach out again. *Yes, there's the rail.*

Rail on the right. Wall on the left.

That means I'm turned around. I'm facing down the tunnel.

Something in him didn't believe that. Somehow he knew that if he turned around and started down the tunnel in the reverse direction from the way he was facing now, he would be walking into an endless fury of rats, heading away from Jerlet, going back the way he had so laboriously traveled.

He squeezed his eyes shut and tried to concentrate. He pictured all the times he had been in the tunnel, including the long journey he was on now. And he saw himself climbing up the spiraling steps with the rail on his left and the wall on his right.

No, the frightened voice within him screamed. *You're wrong. I know you're wrong.*

Linc opened his eyes. The rats were edging closer, glowering at him, saying, *Make up your mind. Either way, it doesn't matter. We'll get you no matter what you do.*

Every instinct in Linc's body was screaming for him to go forward, not to turn around, not to turn his back to the rats.

But his memory, his mind showed him clearly that he must travel with the rail at his left if he wanted to continue upward, toward Jerlet.

Forcing down a shaking shriek of fright, Linc slowly turned and grasped the rail firmly with his left hand. His feet floated slowly off the steps.

He took a deep shuddery breath, grasped the freezing, skin-sticking rail with both hands, and pulled himself into flight. He soared through the darkness like an arrow...upward toward Jerlet. *I hope!*

The rats followed, screeching.

But Linc could use his hands to pull himself along the spiraling railing, speeding along faster than the rats could follow. Hand over hand, racing faster and faster through the darkness, while the red eyes and evil voices dwindled behind him.

Even if I'm going in the wrong direction, Linc thought, *at least I'm outdistancing them*.

He was almost feeling good about it when he slammed into something utterly hard and unyielding. The darkness was split by a million shooting stars of pain.

And then the darkness swallowed him completely.

He awoke slowly.

And when he opened his eyes for the briefest flash of a moment, he wasn't sure that he had really awakened.

Dreaming, he told himself. *I'm dreaming*.

He cracked his eyes open again, just a slit, because of the brightness.

Squinting cautiously, he saw that he was in a room. A small room, not much bigger than his sleeping compartment back in the Living Wheel. But it was brilliant with light, light everywhere, white and clean and dazzling. And warm! The warmth flooded through him, soothing and gentle. Linc felt warmer than he ever had since he had been a tiny child.

Then the dream began to turn into a nightmare. He felt good enough to sit up, but found that he was unable to move. He could raise his head a little, but that was all. The rest of his body seemed to be paralyzed. He looked down at himself and saw that broad soft straps were holding down his arms and legs. Another strap crossed his middle so that he couldn't move his torso much.

There were some sort of coverings wrapped around his hands and feet. He was dressed in a clean, crisp white gown with short sleeves.

And there was a slim, flexible tube connected to his left arm, just above the inner elbow.

Suddenly frightened, Linc twisted his head around and saw that the tube was connected to a green bottle that was hanging upside down from a support on the wall. The other end of the tube was inside his arm. The place where it entered his flesh was covered by something white and plastic looking. Linc could *feel* it inside him, and it made his flesh crawl.

"What is this place?" he yelled out. "Where am I? What are you doing to me?"

Only then did it occur to him that he had no idea at all of who "you" might be. The ship was much vaster than he had ever imagined. There might be all sorts of people living in it. . . .

Linc let his head sink back on the bed. *Don't panic*, he told himself. *At least you got away from the rats.*

But the tight knot in his stomach didn't feel any better. Not for a moment. He glanced up at the tube going into his arm again, then turned his face away.

What are they doing to me?

He must have fallen asleep, because he was startled when the door banged open. Lifting his head as far as he could, Linc saw a shaggy, hugely fat old man push himself through the doorway, barely squeezing through. He floated weightlessly toward the bed, like an immense cloud of flesh wrapped in a gray, stained coverall that barely stretched across his girth.

"You finally woke up." His voice was as heavy and gravelly as his body and face.

"Who . . . who are you?"

The old man looked mildly surprised. "Don't you recognize me? I'm Jerlet."

"No you're not," Linc said. "You don't look anything like Jerlet."

(9)

A slow smile spread across the old man's craggy features. His face was shaggy with stubbly white hair across his cheeks and chin. The skin hung loose from his jowls and looked gray, not healthy. His hair was dead white and tangled in crazy locks that floated every which way in the weightlessness.

"Don't recognize me, huh," he said. He seemed amused by the idea.

He started unfastening the straps that held Linc down. "Don't move that arm," he warned, "until I get the I.V. out of you. . . ."

Ivy? Linc wondered. That was something that grew down in the farms.

The old man floated lightly over the bed, to the side where the tube was, his huge bulk blotting out the light from overhead as he passed over Linc.

"Yep," he muttered in a throaty deep rumbling voice, "it's been a helluva long time since I cut those training tapes for you squirts. You're practically an adult. . . . What's your name?"

"Linc."

"Linc . . . Linc. . . ." The old man's face knotted in a frown of concentration. "Hell, been so long I don't even remember myself. Got to look back at the records."

Linc was studying his face. The more he watched it, the more he had to admit that there *was* some resemblance to the Jerlet who showed himself on the screen down in the Living Wheel. But while the Jerlet he knew from the screen was old, this man seemed *ancient*. Even his hands were gnarled and covered with blue veins. Yet his body was huge, immense.

Those gnarled old fingers withdrew the tube from Linc's arm and covered the wound with a patch of plastic so quickly that Linc couldn't see the wound itself.

"The I.V.'s been feeding you since I brought you here...you've been out cold for nearly seventy hours."

"Hours?" Linc echoed.

The old man made a sour face. "Yeah, you squirts probably don't measure time that way at all, do you?"

Linc shook his head.

"Okay, see if you can sit up. Go easy now...."

Linc pushed himself up to a sitting position, then gripped the edge of the bed to keep from floating away. *Weightless...maybe this is Jerlet's domain, after all.*

"Guess I've aged a bit," he was saying. "Bloat like a gasbag up here in zero *g*. But listen, son—I am Jerlet. The one and only. Nobody here but me. Those pictures of me you see on the screens down in your area, well, those tapes were cut a long time ago. I was a lot younger then. So were you."

Linc was barely listening. He was staring down at his bandaged arms and legs. "You saved me from the rats."

Shaking his head, the old man said, "Nope, you saved yourself from them. I just saved you from bleeding to death, or freezing. You ran smack into my electrical fence and knocked yourself out. I had to come out and get you. Wasn't expecting visitors. But I'm glad you came."

"You...really are Jerlet?" Linc asked.

He bobbed his head up and down, and his tangled hair waved around his face.

Linc scratched at his own shoulder-length hair and realized that it too was floating weightlessly.

"Look, kid, I know I look kinda shabby, but I've been living alone up here for a lotta years...since you and your batchmates were barely big enough to reach the selector buttons in the autogalley."

"Why did you leave us?"

Jerlet shrugged. "I was dying. If I had stayed down there, in a full Earth gravity, my ol' ticker would've popped out on me."

"What? I don't understand?"

Jerlet smiled at him, an oddly gentle smile in that stubbly, shaggy face. "C'mon, I'll explain over lunch."

"What's lunch?"

"Hot food, sonny. Best in the world . . . this world, at least."

Jerlet led Linc out of the little room and down a narrow passageway that curved so steeply Linc couldn't see more than a few paces ahead. Yet it was all weightless.

"It's not really zero gravity here," Jerlet said as they glided along the passageway. "Just enough weight here to keep something down where you put it. But with your one *g* muscles this must seem like total weightlessness."

Linc nodded, not really sure he understood what the old man was rumbling about. *He must be Jerlet, all right,* Linc told himself. *But he sure doesn't look the way I thought he would!*

They passed a double door. Jerlet nodded at it. "Biology lab; where you and the rest of the kids were born. Show you later."

Linc said nothing. Jerlet's words were puzzling.

Jerlet squeezed his bulk through a doorway, and Linc followed him into another small room. But this one had a round table and several soft-looking chairs in it. One wall was covered with buttons and little hatches and strange symbols.

"A food selector!" Linc marveled. "And it works?"

"Sure," Jerlet answered heartily. "Look at the size of me! Think I'd let the food recyclers go out of whack?"

Linc studied the buttons and the symbols on each one.

Jerlet loomed beside him. "Go on! Pick anything you want . . . it all works fine."

"Uh. . . ." Linc suddenly felt stupid. "How do you know which button to push? I mean, back home we knew which button gave what kind of food . . . before it all broke down. . . ."

"Broke down?" Jerlet snapped. "You mean the repair servomechs didn't keep it going?"

"They broke down, too. . . ."

"Then how do you . . . you cook the food yourselves?"

Linc nodded.

The old man looked upset. "I didn't think the machines would fail so soon . . . the repair units, especially. I'm not as smart as I thought I was." He put a hand on Linc's shoulder. His voice sounded strange, almost as if he was afraid of what he was saying. "How . . . how many of you . . . are still alive?"

Linc shrugged. "More than both hands."

"Both hands? You don't know the number? You can't even count? What happened to the education tapes?"

Somehow Linc felt as if he had hurt the old man. "I can name everybody for you. Would that be all right?"

Jerlet didn't answer, so Linc began, "There's Magda, she's the priestess, of course. And Monel, and Stav...." He went through all the names of all the people. He almost said Peta's name, but left it out when he remembered.

"Fifty-seven of you," Jerlet muttered. He seemed shaken. He shuffled slowly from the food selector to the nearest chair and sat down heavily, despite the minuscule gravity. "Fifty-seven. Out of a hundred. Nearly half of you dead in less than fifteen years...." He sank his face in his hands.

Linc stood by the food selector wall, helpless, and watched the old man, his huge bloated expanse of flesh squeezed into the graceful little chair. A far part of Linc's mind marveled that the chair's slim legs didn't buckle under Jerlet's gross weight, despite the low gravity.

The old man looked up at last, and his eyes were rimmed with red.

"Don't you understand?" His voice was rough, shaky, almost begging. "I *made* you! You're my children, just as surely as if I was your father...I made you, and then I had to leave. Now nearly half of you are dead...my fault...."

Linc stared at him.

Jerlet pulled himself out of the chair and took a shambling step toward Linc.

"Don't you understand?" His voice rose to a roar. "It's my fault! You were going to be the beautiful new people, the best generation ever! You were going to reach the new world...raised in love and kindness.... BUT YOU'RE NOTHING BUT A PACK OF IGNORANT HOWLING SAVAGES!"

His voice boomed off the walls of the tiny room. Linc winced and backed a step, bumping into the selector buttons.

"Fifty-seven of you," Jerlet bellowed. "Stupid, superstitious savages." He took a couple of faltering steps toward Linc, then stopped, gasping, his huge body wracked with shuddering panting sobs.

"No...." he gasped. "Not now...." He seemed to be

muttering to himself. But then his eyes focused on Linc, and he could see that the old man's eyes were as red and burning as the rats'. But not with hate, Linc knew. Jerlet's eyes were filled with pain.

"You don't...understand...any of this," the old man puffed, his voice low and rasping now. "Do you? It's all...beyond you...."

Linc wanted to say something, to reach out to him or run away, do *something*. But he was frozen where he stood. Even his voice seemed paralyzed.

Jerlet waved a meaty hand, feebly, at Linc and staggered out of the room.

He's crazy, Linc thought. *Like Robar, when he tried to go through the deadlock with Sheela's body. What he says doesn't make any sense.*

Linc wondered if he should try to follow the old man. Then he noticed that some food had dropped into the selector's pickup bin. *I must have touched some of the buttons when I backed into the wall,* he realized.

The food was neatly packaged, sitting in little shining boxes on a tray. Linc looked up toward the door, then decided, *I'd better leave him alone. If he really is Jerlet, he'll come back to me.*

He picked up the tray and took it to the table. Unwrapping each box, he blinked at the strange sights. One box contained a liquid that was an odd color, almost like one of the colors used in the wiring back at the Living Wheel. It felt cold to his lips. The second box was an oblong metal container filled with something that looked almost like meat. When Linc peeled off the transparent film from its top, the stuff began to steam. Linc smiled. It *smelled* like meat.

The third box was also cold, and filled with something smooth and featureless and white. Linc dug a fingertip into it, and tasted the tiny sample. *Sweet!* He had never tasted anything like it before.

Without thinking about additional selections he might make, Linc sat down at the table. This stuff was strange, but it was good food.

So his first meal in Jerlet's domain consisted of orange juice, soyburger, and ice cream.

* * *

Linc slept right there in the eating room. The floor was soft and warm, so he stretched out and went to sleep almost immediately.

In his dreams he saw Jerlet and some of the people from the Living Wheel—Magda was trying to tell him something, but Monel got between them somehow. It was all mixed up and strange.

Then he was falling, in his dream, falling through darkness with the evil red eyes of the rats chasing behind him. But the eyes all merged into one single huge red eye with a great hollow booming voice roaring after him. Linc fell through the empty darkness, cold, alone, helpless. . . .

And woke with a shock. He was lying face down on the soft floor of the eating room. Soaked with sweat, hot, mouth open in what must have been a yell of terror.

He sat up.

He felt wide awake. The dreams quickly faded into the dark parts of the mind where forgetfulness covers everything.

Drawing his knees up under his chin, and wrapping his arms around his legs, Linc tried to concentrate and think.

Almost immediately he smiled to himself. "Magda, wherever you are, forgive me. I'm not going to meditate. I'm not going to ask for Jerlet to point out the way I should go. I have to think this out for myself."

It was funny, but in a bitter way. *Here I nearly kill myself to find Jerlet, and it turns out that he's crazy.* A new thought struck Linc's mind, and even his faint smile vanished. *Maybe he's dangerous! Maybe he'll try to hurt me . . . kill me. He sure looked angry at lastmeal. Sounded it, too.*

Carefully, Linc pushed the door open and peered down the narrow, strangely-curved passageway. No one in sight. He tiptoed down the passageway and tried several other doors. No sign of Jerlet, although he did find a couple of sleeping rooms, complete with sonic showers and bins full of strange-looking clothes.

All the machines worked up here! Linc saw that the lights were all glowing faithfully. He stepped into one of the bedrooms and the door slid shut behind him automatically. He tried the water tap, a shining metal faucet set above an equally-sparkling sink, and water flowed sweet and cold from it.

I'll bet the sonic shower works, too.

Locking the door to the passageway, Linc quickly stripped off the formless white robe Jerlet had dressed him in and showered. The tingling vibrations all over his skin made him feel better than he had since he'd been a child. *No standing in line. No worrying about the power running down before your turn comes.*

He examined the clothes that were stored in the bins next to the bed. They seemed too small for Linc to wear, but when he tried on one of the shirts, it stretched to fit his body exactly. The pants, too.

And there are different colors!

One of the wall screens was strangely shaped, long enough to reach from ceiling to floor, and so narrow that it was barely as wide as Linc's shoulders. And it was bright; it reflected everything in the room very clearly. Linc had never heard of a mirror before, but he automatically used this one as he tried on clothes of different colors.

He finally settled on a high-necked shirt that was almost the same shade of blue as his eyes, and a dark-brown pair of pants. He found slippers in another bin, and even they adjusted their shape magically to fit his feet snugly.

"Hello!"

Linc jumped as if an electric shock sparked through him.

"Hello!" Jerlet's rough, husky voice called again. "Can you hear me?"

It was coming from a speaker grill in the ceiling, Linc realized. There was a viewing screen on the wall facing the bed, but it was dark and dead.

"Look . . . I don't even remember your name, dammit. I, uh, listen son, I got very upset yesterday and I acted like an idiot. I'm sorry."

Linc saw that there was a small keyboard on the table beside the bed. Frowning, he wondered if he should touch any of the buttons.

"It won't do you any good to hide from me. You'll have to come out for food sooner or later," Jerlet was saying. "And I really want to help you, son. Really I do. The way I acted yesterday . . . well, I'll explain it if you'll give me a chance. At

least turn on one of the screens so I can talk to you face to
face... what in hell is your name, anyway. I know you told me,
but you mentioned all those other names, too, and now I can't
remember... guess I'm getting old."

Linc stepped across to the table where the keyboard buttons
glowed in their different colors. He felt as if his head was
spinning; not just from the low gravity, but from the effort to
decide what he should do. Slowly, reluctantly, he reached out
for the buttons.

"If you want to turn on a screen," Jerlet was saying, "just
punch the red button on any of the keyboards...."

Linc's outstretched finger touched the red button. Jerlet's
haggard, stubbly face leaped into view on the wall screen across
the room.

He was still saying earnestly, "I know I acted like a madman
last night, but I can explain... oh, there you are!"

Linc gazed straight into Jerlet's eyes. They looked sad now.
The pain was still there, but it was deeper, covered over by
sadness.

"Linc. My name is Linc."

Jerlet bobbed his head eagerly, making his fleshy jowls
bounce. "Yep, that's right. Linc. You told me, but I couldn't
remember."

Linc started to reply, but found that he had nothing to say.

Jerlet filled in the silence. "I see you've cleaned up and
changed clothes. Good! How about meeting me in the
autogalley? Got a lot of things to show you."

"The autogalley?" Linc asked.

"The eating room. Where the food selector is."

"Oh.... Okay."

"Do you know how to find it from where you are?" Jerlet
asked.

Linc nodded. "I can find it."

"Okay, good. I'll meet you there." The old man seemed
genuinely happy.

He was still smiling when he eased his bulk through the
doorway of the autogalley and glided toward Linc. He stuck out
a heavy, short-fingered hand.

"Linc, I dunno what kind of customs you kids have put
together down in the living section, but it's an old human custom

for two men to shake hands when they meet."

Thoroughly puzzled, Linc put his hand out.

Jerlet waggled a finger at him. "No, no . . . the right hand."

With a shrug, Linc raised his right hand and let Jerlet grasp it firmly. *The old man's a lot stronger than he looks,* he realized.

"Good!" Jerlet beamed. "Now we're formally met. Got so much to show you." He rubbed his hands together. "Let's start with the food selector. Show you how that works."

They ate well. Jerlet showed Linc all sorts of new foods and tastes that he had never known before. As the food began to make a comfortable warm glow in his middle, Linc found his worries and suspicions about Jerlet melting away.

Then they were up and moving through the nearly weightless world of Jerlet. The old man showed Linc the power generators, the mysterious humming machines that kept electricity going out to all parts of the ship. Then the master computer, with its blinking lights and odd sing-song voices. And a room full of servomechs, standing stiffly at attention, mechanical arms at their sides, sensors turned off.

"Are they dead?" Linc asked, his voice hushed.

"You mean deactivated," Jerlet replied in his normal booming tone. "Here . . . look, lemme show you." He took a tiny control box from a shelf near the door and touched one of the buttons studding its top. The nearest servomech came to life. Its sensors glowed; it pivoted slightly to face Jerlet, moving on noiseless little wheels.

"See?" Jerlet said. "They all work fine."

Linc shook his head. "Down in the Living Wheel they all died, a long time ago."

Jerlet snorted. "Well, we'll have to do something about *that*."

He took Linc down the passageway and through a set of double doors into a strange, dead silent room. It felt odd. Linc knew he had never been here before, yet there was a faint odor of something that made his spine tingle and the back of his neck go shuddery. The room was filled with strange glass spheres, long looping tubes, viewscreens, desks, other things of glass and metal and plastic that Linc couldn't even guess at.

"Genetics lab," Jerlet said. His voice sounded odd; half-proud, half-sad. "This is where you were born, Linc. You and the others down in the living section."

"Here?"

Jerlet nodded. "Yep. Took the sperm and ova from those cryofreezers, back behind the radiation shielding over there," he pointed to a heavy-looking dull metal wall, "and brought the fetuses to term in these plastic capsules. All very carefully done, very scientifically. Each specimen picked for its genetic perfection. Each resulting infant nurtured as meticulously as the psychologists could hope. A generation of physically and mentally perfect children. Geniuses... left to live in an idiotic environment."

Linc said, "I don't understand you."

Jerlet waved his pudgy hands about the laboratory. "I was in charge of the project. I made you. Right here. This is where you were all created. By me."

[1O]

Before Linc could ask any more questions, Jerlet swept him through the genetics lab and back out into the passageway.

"You haven't seen the best part yet," he said.

Totally puzzled by everything he'd seen and heard so far, Linc quietly followed the old man through a hatch into a tight little metal room. It felt cold and scary, like a deadlock. *But even if he's crazy, he wouldn't put us both in a deadlock,* Linc told himself. And a tiny voice asked back, *Would he?*

Jerlet's massive bulk seemed to completely fill the metal chamber. Linc couldn't breathe.

"Not too comfortable in here with both of us," the old man muttered as he fingered a complicated row of buttons. "Not very comfy in here by myself, come to think of it."

The top of the chamber swung open, and Linc realized it was another hatch. Jerlet grinned at him, then pushed against the sides of the chamber and floated up through the overhead hatch. Linc took a deep breath, glad to feel un-squeezed.

"Come on up and see the view!" Jerlet called. His voice suddenly sounded very distant and hollow.

Linc crouched slightly and sprang straight up. He shot through the open hatch and past Jerlet's floating obesity. . . .

And nearly screamed in terror. He was in the outer darkness! Surrounded by stars and the blackness of the outside where there was no air or warmth or. . . .

He felt a hand grabbing at his ankle and Jerlet calling, "Hey, whoa, take it easy." He realized that there *was* warmth and air to breathe.

Jerlet was chuckling as the two of them floated slowly in the star-flecked darkness. Yet it really wasn't dark, either. The stars glowed all around them, over their heads, below their feet.

"What is this place?" Linc asked. His voice seemed to float, too, strange and hollow and lost in vast distance.

"Used to be an observatory," Jerlet's voice came back toward him, echoing.

Slowly, Linc's eyes adjusted to the dim light. They were in a vast round room made almost entirely of glass: transparent plastiglass, actually, although Linc didn't know that yet. The splendor of the stars surrounded them—stars powdering the blackness of infinity with endless points of light. White stars, blue stars, red stars, yellow stars . . . stars beyond counting, and even swirls and loops of brightness that glowed with strangely cool blues and pinks.

Linc felt his jaw hanging open as he floated in true weightlessness, hanging in the darkened observatory dome, gaping at the enormity of the universe.

And then he glanced downward, toward where his feet happened to be pointing, and saw the yellow star that was so close. He closed his eyes against its glare, but still its image burned against the inside of his eyelids.

"We'll be there soon," Jerlet's voice sounded near to him.

Linc opened his eyes and saw the old man's face next to him, haloed by the after-image of the yellow star. "It's coming to swallow us," Linc whispered. "It will kill us all in fire."

Jerlet's booming laughter surprised Linc. It echoed all around the huge dome.

"You've got it just about entirely wrong, son," the old man said. "The yellow star isn't coming toward us, *we're* heading for *it*. And it's not going to kill us—it offers us life. Hope. If we can get to it before this bucket falls completely apart!"

Linc started to say, *I don't understand*, but it had become such an overworked line that he felt ashamed to use it again.

"C'mon down this way," Jerlet tugged at his wrist, "and I'll show you something."

They swam weightlessly through empty air down to a patch of shadows that were deeper than the darkness of the rest of the dome. A spidery framework took shape as they approached, and Jerlet reached out a practiced hand for it.

"Careful," he said to Linc. "Slow your speed or you'll hurt

yourself when you hit the deck. Just 'cause you've got no weight doesn't mean you've got no inertia."

He can never say more than three words in a row that make sense, Linc thought. *He always uses words I never heard before.*

The deck was made of cold metal, and Linc could see that several desks and odd-looking instruments were attached to it. The biggest loomed far over their heads; the cylinder of metal struts that Jerlet had grabbed a few moments earlier.

"Telescopes," Jerlet said. "Devil's own time keeping them aligned right. Our closing rate is outrunning the old computer program and I haven't figured out how to update it. Gyros must be wearing out, too."

Linc shook his head and said nothing.

Jerlet squeezed his soft body into a seat behind one of the desks. "Take a look at this screen," he said as he touched some buttons on the desk top. Linc noticed that the desk top seemed to be nothing but buttons, row upon row of them.

The screen lit up and showed a fiery yellow ball that seethed and shimmered and shot out tongues of what could only be pure fire.

"That's the yellow sun we're heading for," Jerlet said. "I tried for years to find out if the old generations had a name for it, but the tapes don't have their star catalogues on 'em. Not anymore, anyway. Or maybe I just haven't found the right tape.... Anyway, I've named it Baryta, in honor of its color and in memory of my long-lost education in chemistry. That's the name for our star: Baryta."

A tiny voice inside Linc's head began to whisper, *He's sounding crazy again.*

Linc watched Jerlet's face. The slanting light from the yellow star threw weird long shadows across his stubbly jowls and strongly-hooked nose. The creases under his eyes and around his mouth became deeply-shadowed crevasses. The glow from the little viewscreen where the blazing star smoldered wasn't enough to penetrate the shadows.

"Now my frightened-looking friend," Jerlet smiled up at Linc, "take a look at *this*...."

He touched another set of buttons, and the screen went blank for a moment, then showed a picture of a bluish-green circle. It was flecked with white spots. It seemed to be hanging in outer darkness, because all around it was nothing but black.

"The new world." Jerlet's voice was barely audible now, a low rumble of hope and awe. "It's a planet, Linc. A world that orbits around Baryta. I call it Beryl. It's the destination that this ship has been heading for, for who knows how many generations."

"A . . . world?"

"An open, beautiful, free world, Linc. With good air and clean water and more room than any of us could even imagine. Like the old Earth, except better: cleaner, freer, newer. It's our destination, Linc. Our new home. That's where we're going!"

Slowly, Linc began to learn.

With Jerlet as a teacher, and the ship's computer and memory tapes to help, Linc began to understand the who, the how, and the why of life.

The ship was incredibly old, so old that no one—not even the computer and its memory tapes—knew how long it had been sailing through space. Linc saw that the Living Wheel, the section where he had lived all his life, was actually the outermost wheel in a series of twenty concentric circular structures. The tube-tunnels linked them together like spokes that radiated outward from the central hub. The hub was Jerlet's domain, permanently weightless. The Living Wheel, turning endlessly on the widest arc of all the twenty wheels, was in a one g, Earth-normal gravitational condition.

The origins of the ship were shrouded in mystery, but the computer tapes made it clear that the ship's oldest generation was forced to leave Earth, sent away to roam the stars against their will. Watching the men and women who spoke from the computer's viewscreen, Linc saw that they regarded the Earth as evil and corrupt.

But when the history tapes showed pictures of Earth on the viewscreens, the pangs of ancient memories twisted inside Linc and made tears flow. All the old stories he had seen as a child, before the machines had died down in the Living Wheel: open skies of blue, bright soft clouds of purest white, mountains with snow on their shoulders, streams of clear water, grass and farms and forests that stretched as far as the eye could see. Cities that gleamed in the sunlight and sparkled at night. And people!

People of all ages, all sizes, all colors. By the uncountable multitudes. People everywhere.

Not everything he saw of Earth was good. There was sickness. There was death. There was violence that turned Linc's stomach—gangs beating people on city streets, strange machines that spewed fire, people lying dead and twisted on the streets.

Now I know why Jerlet warned us against violence, Linc told himself.

But even at its worst, it was clear to see that Earth was a beautiful world. It made the cold metal walls of the ship seem like a prison to Linc.

"Beryl's a planet that's very much like Earth," Jerlet said one evening as they watched the ancient tapes together. The viewscreen was showing a broad grassland with strange, long-tailed beasts thudding across the landscape on hooved slim legs. "It'll be even better than Earth. Untouched. Our new world. Our new Eden."

"When will we get there?" Linc asked.

"Not when, son . . . *if.*"

As Linc learned more of the history of the ship, he soon realized how badly the machines had fallen apart. Here in Jerlet's domain everything worked well, but that was only one tiny section of the vast ship. Most of the other sections were shattered, ruined, decayed beyond all hope of repair.

"Some of the machines are still working down in the Living Wheel," he told Jerlet.

"I know," the old man said. "We spent the best years and the best people we had among us to set you kids up in a strong, safe area. But it might not have been good enough. We're in a race against time."

Again and again Jerlet told him the story. How the ship had come to a planet almost like Earth. How the people aboard had decided not to stop there, but to look for a world that was *exactly* like Earth.

"Beryl is that world . . . but it might be too late for you kids. It's already too late for me."

Jerlet explained it all. Time after time. He kept talking about the ship's bridge, and how important it was to make the machines there work again. Slowly Linc began to realize that he was speaking of the Ghost Place, and the "ghosts" were Jerlet's friends and companions who had been killed in some terrible accident.

The old man taught Linc how to read and count, how to work the computers, how to understand the strange words that were needed to run the ship. And every night, during dinner and far into the night, until Linc nodded and fell asleep, Jerlet would tell his own story.

The ship was never designed to function for so long without complete overhaul and repair. Although the ancient generations had been very wise, still they could not keep the ship's machinery from slowly deteriorating.

As the ship cruised blindly through the depths of interstellar space, seeking the unknown world that was exactly like Earth, the machines that kept the people alive began to break down and die.

Whole sections of the ship became unlivable. The sections that remained intact were quickly overcrowded with too many people. Tempers flared. Violence erupted. And for generations the people of the ship lived in separate warring groups, each hating all the others, learning to fear strangers, to fight, to kill.

The cycle grew tighter and tighter. As more years passed, more and more of the ship's complex machinery broke down. It became a greater struggle to survive, to keep the air pumps working and the farm tanks productive. Bands of marauding killers skulked through the tube-tunnels, breaking into living areas to steal and murder.

"The most ironic part of all," Jerlet would say each night to Linc, "was that there was a scientific renaissance going on up here at the same time."

In the hub of the ship a few dozen people had established themselves in some degree of comfort. They had control of the ship's main power generators, and could turn off the supply of electricity—which meant warmth, air, life—to any group that displeased them. They tried to put an end to the roving bands of looters, but were never successful at it. On the other hand, the looters never tried to harm them.

The men and women who lived in the hub were scientists. Never more than a handful, they still managed to maintain themselves in relative peace.

"The things they learned!" Jerlet would always shake his head at the thought.

Their work in genetics reached the stage of perfection where they could, if they wanted to, create perfectly normal human children in their lab. The physicists probed deeply into the relationship of matter to energy, in an attempt to find a way to break free of the confines of the dying ship.

"They learned how to turn solid objects into a beam of energy, and then re-assemble them back into solid objects again, the way they were when they started," Jerlet said. "But it took too much power for anything we really needed. We couldn't get a rat's whisker off the ship and back to Earth. But when we get close enough to Beryl's surface, you'll be able to whisk yourself down to the planet's surface in an eyeblink."

"But us, the kids down in the Living Wheel," Linc always asked. "How did we come about? Why did you make us?"

And Jerlet would smile.

"We finally found a star like the Sun, and it had a few planets around it, although we were still too far away to see if any of the planets were truly like Earth. But we decided to take the risk. We *had* to... we knew the ship couldn't last much longer, no matter what we did.

"I was getting to be middle-aged when we started the program to create you in the genetics lab. A hundred perfect specimens, as physically strong and mentally bright as we could produce. A hundred supermen and women.

"Well, we did it. And we set you up in the living section down in the one *g* wheel, next to the bridge. Six of us stayed with you the first few years, to get you started right. The servomechs did most of the dirty work, of course. But still... it was damned noisy down there!

"Around the time you were learning to walk, some marauders got to us. We protected you kids, but it cost us the lives of two people. One of them was my wife...."

Linc knew that a wife was a fully-grown girl.

"None of us could live indefinitely in a one *g* environment. We had all spent too much of our lives up here, in zero *g*. I stayed the longest, and I worked damned hard to make sure that all the machines and servomechs would work right and take care of you until you were old enough to take care of yourselves. Meanwhile, the rest of my friends systematically finished off all the marauders on the ship. We weren't going to let them raid you again."

"And then you left us on our own?"

Jerlet would nod his head sadly. "Had to. Gravity got to my heart. I had to come back up here. Then, while you pups were still growing up, the rest of my friends died off, most of them in an accident down on the bridge. I'm the last one left."

Linc heard the story many times. But one particular night, as Jerlet wound up the tale, Linc said brightly:

"Well, at least you'll be able to come with us to the new world . . . if the ship makes it there."

Jerlet fixed him with a stern gaze. "It's up to you to make sure this bucket limps into orbit around Beryl. That's what I'm training you for, Linc. I spent a lot of years waiting for you kids to grow up and come up here and find me. You've got to keep this ship going until all you kids are safely transferred to the planet's surface."

For several minutes neither of them said a word. Finally, Linc nodded solemnly and said, "I'll do it. I'll get us all to Beryl if I have to go outside the ship and push it with my bare hands."

Jerlet laughed. "That'd be something to see!"

"I'll get us there. All of us. And that includes you."

But the old man slowly shook his head. "No, not me. I can't leave this zero *g* environment. My heart would go *poof* if I even tried to walk a few levels down the tube-tunnel, where the gravity starts to build up."

Linc said, "No . . . we'll find a way . . . something. . . ."

"Listen, son," Jerlet said calmly. "I'm an old man. I might not even make it to the time when we go into orbit around Beryl. That's why I'm pushing you so hard. It's all on your shoulders, Linc. You're the difference between life and death for all your friends."

Book Two

[11]

The inflated pressure suit stood before Linc like a live human being. But its "face"—the visor of its helmet—was blank and empty. Linc tested each joint for air leaks: ankles, knees, hips, wrists, shoulders. All okay.

He started to run his pressure sensor around the neck seal, where the bulbous helmet connected with the blue fabric of the suit. He smiled as he thought:

A few months ago I would have thought this was an evil spirit or a ghost . . . it would have scared me out of my skin.

Satisfied that the suit was airtight, Linc touched a stud on the suit's belt, and the air sighed back into the tanks on the suit's back. The suit began to collapse, sag at the knees and shoulders, held up only because the air tanks were fastened to the workroom's bulkhead wall.

Linc watched the suit deflate and found himself thinking of Jerlet. *He's been sagging himself lately. Losing weight. Slowing down.*

He turned to the tiny communicator screen mounted atop the workbench at his right, and touched the red button.

"Hello . . . Jerlet. I've finished with the suit."

The old man's face appeared on the miniature screen. It looked more haggard than ever, as if he hadn't slept all night.

"Good," he rumbled. "Come on up to the observatory. Got some good news."

Linc made his way out of the workroom, down the short corridor, and into the airlock. He moved in the ultralow gravity without even thinking about it now, and when he floated up into the vast darkened dome of the observatory he no longer panicked at the sight of the universe stretching all around him.

But he still thrilled at it.

The yellow sun was bright enough to make the metal framework of the main telescope glint and glisten with headlights. Jerlet sat at the observer's desk, wrapped in an electrically-heated safety suit. *But it's not that cold in here,* Linc told himself.

Obviously Jerlet felt differently. His fingers were shaking slightly as he worked the keyboard that controlled the telescope and other instruments.

Linc floated lightly to the desk and touched his slippered feet down next to Jerlet's chair. The old man looked up at him and smiled tiredly. His face was like a picture Linc had seen of old Earth: a beautiful river winding through a valley of scarred, ragged hills and bare, stubbly ground.

"Finally got the spectral analyzer working," Jerlet muttered without preamble. "Took all night, but I did it."

"You ought to get more rest," Linc said.

The old man shook his head. "Rest when we get there. Here...look at this."

He touched a few buttons and a view of Beryl flashed onto the main desk-top screen. It was blue-green and beautiful, a lovely gibbous crescent hanging in space, flecked with white clouds, topped by a polar cap of dazzling white.

"Now watch...." Jerlet touched more buttons.

The picture disappeared, to be replaced by a strange glow of colors that ranged from violet to deepest red. Squinting at the unfamiliar sight, Linc saw that there were hundreds of black lines scratched vertically across the band of colors.

"That's a spectrogram of the planet," Jerlet said. "A sort of fingerprint of Beryl."

"Fingerprint?" Linc asked.

Jerlet scratched at his craggy face. "That's right, you don't know what fingerprints are. Well...what's on the agenda for lunch?"

"We're supposed to go over the route I take to get back to the Living Wheel."

"H'mm. And dinner?"

"Nothing yet." He and Jerlet had a set routine for each meal. If Linc had any questions that required a lengthy explanation,

Jerlet used mealtime to explain them.

"Okay, dinner. The subject will be fingerprints. Might even tell you about retinal patterns and voice prints."

Linc nodded. He didn't understand, but he knew that Jerlet would explain.

"Now, about this spectrogram," the old man resumed. "It tells us what the air on Beryl is made of . . . what elements and compounds are in the air."

Curiosity knit Linc's brow. "How's it do that?"

Jerlet smiled again. Patiently he explained how the light from the planet is split into a rainbow pattern of colors by the spectrograph's prisms; how the spectrograph is fitted into the telescope; how each element and compound leaves its own distinctive telltale mark on the rainbow pattern of Beryl's spectrum.

Linc listened and learned. Usually, he only had to hear things once to remember them permanently.

". . . And here," Jerlet said, his rough voice trembling with excitement, "is the computer's analysis, together with a reference to old Earth's atmospheric composition."

He touched a button, and the viewscreen showed:

ATMOSPHERIC CONSTITUENTS

BERYL		EARTH	
Nitrogen	77.23%	Nitrogen	78.09%
Oxygen	20.44%	Oxygen	20.95%
Argon	1.01%	Argon	0.93%
Carbon Dioxide	0.72%	Carbon Dioxide	0.03%
Water Vapor: variable up to 1.8% abs.		Water Vapor: variable, up to 1.5% abs.	

Linc studied the numbers for a few moments. Then he looked back at Jerlet.

"It's almost the same as Earth . . . but not *exactly*."

"Close enough to be a twin," Jerlet boomed. "And as close as any planet's going to be. A smidge less oxygen and more carbon dioxide, but that could be because the planet's a bit newer than Earth. There's chlorophyll all over the place, lots of it. That means green plants, just like Earth."

"We can live there," Linc said.

Jerlet pumped his shaggy head up and down. His mouth was trying to form a word, but nothing came out for several seconds. Finally he gulped a strangled, "Yes, you can live there."

Linc saw that there were tears in his eyes.

"I'll have to tell the other kids about it," Linc said. "They'll be terrified by Baryta. They all think that the yellow sun is going to swallow us . . . burn us."

"I know," said Jerlet.

Linc went on, "I ought to get back to them as soon as I can. They've got to know about Beryl. I've got to stop them from being afraid."

Jerlet nodded wearily.

"If they think that we're all going to die, there's no telling what they'll do. . . ."

"All right!" Jerlet slammed his heavy hand on the desk top. It startled Linc, made him jump and drift away a few meters, weightlessly.

"I know you've got to get back to them, dammit." In the golden light of Baryta the old man's paunchy body glowed in radiance, his wild hair looked like a crazy halo. "I know you've got to go back. I . . . it's just that . . . I don't want to be alone anymore. I want you to stay here, with me."

Linc reached up for a handhold on the telescope frame and pushed back toward Jerlet.

"But I've *got* to go back," he said. "The bridge. . . ."

"I know," Jerlet grumbled. His face scowled. "But I don't have to like it! There's nothing in the laws of thermodynamics that says I have to like the idea."

Linc felt the air easing out of his lungs. He had been so tense that he had been holding his breath. But now Jerlet was grumbling in his usual way, and Linc could let himself grin. It would be all right. He would go back. Jerlet wouldn't try to keep him here.

The rest of the day went normally. Jerlet stayed in the observatory, studying Beryl. Linc went down to the workshop and studied the computer's memory tapes for information on repairing the instruments on the ship's bridge.

That's going to be the toughest part of the job, he told himself. *Clearing the dead crew out of the bridge and getting the controls working again.* Despite himself, he shuddered.

At dinner that evening Jerlet launched into a long explanation of fingerprints, retinal patterns, voice prints, and other aspects of detective work.

Linc felt confused. "But why bother with all that? Everybody knew everybody else, didn't they? Why couldn't they just ask who a person was?"

Jerlet guffawed, stuffed a slice of synthetic steak into his mouth, and then began to explain about crime and police work. By the time dessert was finished and the dishes flashed into the recycler, Linc was asking:

"Okay, but who figured out this business of fingerprinting? Kirchhoff and Bunsen?"

Jerlet slapped a palm to his forehead. "No, no! They worked out the principles of spectroscopy. The fingerprint technique was discovered by some policeman or detective or somebody like that. An Englishman named Holmes, I think. It's in the computer's memory banks somewhere."

Linc looked down at his fingertips and saw the swirling patterns of fine lines there. Then he looked up, Jerlet's face was dead white. Veins were throbbing blue in his forehead. Cords in his neck strained.

"What's wrong?"

"Ahhrg . . . hurts," Jerlet gasped. "Must've eaten . . . too much . . . too fast. . . ."

Linc pushed out of his chair and went to the old man.

"No . . . I'll be . . . all right. . . ."

Without bothering to argue, Linc pulled him up from his chair and propped him up with his shoulder. He wanted to carry the old man, but Jerlet's girth was too wide for Linc's arms to grasp, even though the minuscule gravity made him light enough to carry.

Linc walked him past his own bedroom and down to the infirmary. Jerlet was panting with pain as Linc eased him down onto the tiny medical center's only bed.

Turning to the keyboard that stood on a little pedestal beside the bed, Linc switched on the medical sensors. The infirmary was almost completely automatic, and Linc didn't understand most of its workings, but he watched the wall screen above the bed.

It showed numbers for pulse rate, breathing rate, body temperature, blood pressure—all in red, the color of danger. A green wiggly line traced out Jerlet's heartbeat. It was wildly irregular.

"What should I do?" Linc called out to the automated room. There was no one to hear or answer.

Except Jerlet. "Punch ... emergency input ... tell medicomputer ... heart attack...."

Linc did that, and the wall screen began printing out instructions for medicine and setting up an automated auxiliary ventricle pump. Linc followed the step-by-step instructions as they came on the screen. He lost all track of time, but finally had Jerlet surrounded by gleaming metal and plastic machines that hooked themselves onto his arms and legs.

Still the numbers on the wall screen glared red.

Linc stood by the bed endlessly. Jerlet lost consciousness, regained, drifted away again.

Linc fought to keep his eyes open. The only sounds in the room were the humming electricity of the machines, and a faint chugging sound of a pump.

"Linc...."

He snapped his eyes open. He had fallen asleep standing up.

Jerlet's hand was fluttering feebly, trying to reach toward him. But the machines had his arm firmly strapped down.

"Linc...." The old man's voice was a tortured whisper.

"I'm here. How do you feel? What can I do?"

"Terrible ... and nothing. If the machines can't pull me through, then it's over. 'Bout time, too. I...." His words sank into an indecipherable mumble.

"Don't die," Linc begged. "Please don't die."

Jerlet's eyes blinked slowly. "Not my idea, son. ... Just glad I held on long enough ... to meet you ... train you...."

"No...." Linc felt completely helpless.

The old man's voice was getting weaker. Strangely, the harshness of it seemed to melt away as it faded. "Listen...."

Linc bent his ear to the ragged, ravaged face of Jerlet. His breath was gulping out in great racking sobs that were painful just to hear. His whole bloated body heaved with each shuddering gasp. Linc felt the old man's breath on his cheek. It smelled of dust.

"You...you know what...to do...?"

Linc nodded. His voice wouldn't work right. His eyes were blurry.

"The machines...you'll fix...what they need...to get to Beryl...."

"I will." It was a distant, tear-choked voice. "I promise. I'll do it."

"Good." Jerlet's face relaxed into a faint smile. His body-racking gasps eased. His eyes closed.

"Please don't die!"

Jerlet's eyes opened so slightly that Linc couldn't be sure the eyelids moved at all. "You can...make it without me."

Linc clenched his fists on the edge of the bed's spongy surface. "But I don't *want* you to die!"

Jerlet almost laughed. "Told you...wasn't my idea.... I'm no...proud-faced martyr, son. Just get back ...away...machinery oughtta start...any second...."

"Back? Away?"

"Go on...'less you want to...be frozen, too."

Unconsciously Linc edged slightly away from the bed. He stood there for a moment uncertainly, watching the old man lying there. Jerlet's eyes closed again. All the numbers and the symbols on the wall screen began blinking red, and a soft but insistent tone started beep-beeping. The words CLINICAL DEATH flashed on and off again so quickly that Linc hardly had time to notice them. Then a piercing whistling note howled out of the machines around Jerlet's bed, as if in their mechanical way they were bewailing his death—or their inability to save him. Then the screen lettered out in green: CRYOGENIC IMMERSION PROCEDURE.

As Linc stepped farther away from the bed, the screen flashed numbers and graphs so quickly that only a machine could read them. The shining metal things around Jerlet's bed began to hum louder, vibrate, and move back. Linc watched, frozen in fascination, as Jerlet's entire bed sank down slowly into the floor. The machines went silent and still as the bed slowly receded through a trapdoor. As Linc stepped up for a closer look, the bed disappeared entirely and the trapdoor slid shut once again. A whisp of white steamy vapor drifted up just before it closed completely.

The machines rolled silently back to their niches in the room's bare white walls. The viewscreen went blank.

"Cryogenic immersion," Linc muttered to himself. His mind started working actively again. "He had this all set up for himself. The machines are going to freeze him, so that he can be revived and made healthy again someday."

Even though Linc knew that Jerlet was dead in every sense of the word, that he would never see the old man again because even if he were revived someday it would be so far in the future that Linc would never live to see it, even though he realized all this, Linc somehow felt better.

"Good-bye old man," he said to the empty room. "I'll get them to Beryl for you."

(12)

Despite all his training, despite all he knew, despite Jerlet's assurances, Linc was tense as he donned the pressure suit.

It was like being swallowed alive by some monster that was vaguely human in form, but bigger than any man and strangely different. Linc's nose wrinkled at the odors of machine oil and plastic as he stepped into the suit and eased himself into it.

And there was another scent now, too. His own clammy sweat. The odor of fear, fear of going into the outer darkness.

It's space! he fumed at himself. *Nothing but emptiness. Jerlet explained a thousand times. There's nothing out there to hurt you.*

"If the suit works right," he answered himself as he lifted the bubble-shaped helmet over his head.

Just as he had been taught, he sealed the helmet on and then tested all the suit's seals and equipment. The faint whir of the air fan made Linc feel a little better. So did the slightly stale tang of oxygen.

Slowly he clumped to the inner hatch of the deadlock. *Airlock!* he reminded himself. He reached out a heavily-gloved hand for the buttons on the wall that would open the hatch, and stopped.

"You could stay right here," he told himself, his voice sounding strangely muffled inside the helmet. "Jerlet left everything in working condition. You could live here in ease and comfort for the rest of your life."

Until the ship crashes into Baryta, he answered silently, *and everyone dies.*

"What makes you think Magda and the others will believe

371

you? You think Monel's going to do what you tell him? You think any of them will touch a machine just because you say it's all right to do it?"

But Linc knew the answers even before he spoke the questions. *It doesn't matter what they think or do. I've got to try.*

His outstretched hand moved the final few centimeters and touched the airlock control button. There was a moment's hesitation, then the heavy metal hatch slid smoothly aside for him.

He flicked at the other buttons, which would set the airlock mechanism on its automatic cycle, then stepped inside the cramped metal chamber. The inner hatch sighed shut. Pumps clattered. Linc couldn't hear them inside his suit, but he felt their vibrations through the thick metallic soles of his boots. His pulse throbbed faster and faster as he stood there, waiting.

The outer hatch slid open. Linc was suddenly standing on the edge of the world, gazing out at endless stars.

And smiling. All his fears evaporated. It was like being in the observatory. The beauty was overwhelming. The silence and peace of eternity hovered before him, watching gravely, patiently.

Linc stepped out of the airlock and for the first time saw the ship as it really existed: a huge set of wheels within wheels, starkly lit by the glaring yellow sun that was behind his back. Fat circular wheels, each one bigger than the one before it, stretching away from the central hub where he stood, turning slowly against the background of stars. And connecting them were half a dozen spokes, the tube-tunnels, seen from the outside.

One of the spokes was lit by a row of winking tiny lights. Jerlet had shown Linc how to turn them on. They were Linc's guidepath, showing him which tube-tunnel would lead back to the living area in the farthest, largest wheel, where the rest of the people were.

Linc plodded slowly along the lane of yellow lights, moving carefully inside the bulky pressure suit. He was fully aware that a mistake now—a slip, a stumble—could send him tumbling off the ship, never to return.

But Jerlet had trained him well. Linc could see that there were footholds and handgrips studding the outer skin of the tube-tunnel. The metallic soles of his boots were slightly magnetized, so that it took a conscious effort to lift a foot off the metal decking. The oxygen he was breathing made him a trifle lightheaded, but he felt safe and warm inside the suit.

The main trick was to avoid looking out at the stars. After the first few moments of awestruck sightseeing, Linc realized that the ship's spinning motion made it impossible to stargaze and walk a straight line at the same time.

So, shrugging inside the cumbersome suit, he kept his eyes on the winking yellow lights, on the handgrips and footholds that marked his way back to the Living Wheel.

Linc had no idea of how much time passed. He was sweating with exertion long before he neared the Living Wheel. He knew that he should feel hungry, because except for sips of water from the tube inside his helmet he had eaten nothing. But his insides were trembling with exertion and excitement. His only hunger was to reach his destination.

As he neared the outermost wheel, gravity began to make itself felt. The footholds turned into stairs that spiraled around the tube's outer skin. There was a definite feeling of *up* and *down* that grew more certain with each step. Instead of walking along a path, Linc found himself climbing down a spiraling ladder.

Abruptly, most unexpectedly, he was there. The last winking yellow light gave way to a circle of tiny blue lights that outlined the hatch of an airlock.

Linc stood there for a long moment, his feet magnetically gripping the ladder's final rung, one hand closed around the last handgrip. He studied the control panel set alongside the hatch. Out of the corner of his eye he could see the stars pinwheeling majestically as the largest of the ship's wheels turned slowly around the distant hub. He had come a long way.

With his free hand, Linc pushed the button that opened the hatch. He barely felt the button through the heavy metal mesh of his glove.

For an eternity, nothing happened. Then the hatch slowly edged outward and to one side. Nothing could be heard in the hard vacuum, but Linc could swear that the hatch creaked as it moved.

He stepped inside the cramped metal chamber of the airlock, and touched the buttons that would cycle the machinery. *What if it doesn't work?* he asked himself in sudden panic. *I'll have to go all the way back to the hub and fight my way down the inside of the tube-tunnel!*

But the machines did their job. The outer hatch slid shut and sealed itself. Air hissed into the chamber. The telltale lights on the control panel flicked from red through amber to green, and the inner hatch sighed open.

Linc clumped through into the passageway.

He was home.

The passageway was empty. *It usually is, down at this end,* he reminded himself. *After all, they call this the deadlock. It's not a happy place to be.*

He thumped up the passageway, heading for the living quarters. He felt oddly weary and slow, only gradually realizing that here in normal gravity his pressure suit and backpack weighed almost as much as he did himself.

But he was too eager and excited to take them off.

He was approaching the farming section when he saw the first people. A group of men were coming out of the big double doors of the farm area.

Linc wanted to run toward them, but his legs were too tired to make his motion more than a clumsy shamble.

"Hey . . . it's me, Linc!" he shouted and waved both arms at them.

They froze. Seven of them, sweat-stained and dirty-faced, stopped dead in their tracks and stared at Linc, open-mouthed and wide-eyed.

"Stav . . . Cal . . . it's me, Linc!"

Terror twisted their faces. They broke and ran up the corridor, away from Linc, screaming.

Linc clumped to a stop, laughing. *All they see is the suit!*

Slowly he pulled off his gloves and started to undo the neck seal, so that he could remove his helmet and let them see his face.

They probably couldn't even hear me, from inside this bowl, he realized.

Before Linc could get the helmet off, Stav and three others came creeping down the corridor, armed with lengths of pipe. They moved as slowly and quietly as they could, but there was no way for them to hide in the bare corridor. They saw Linc and stopped, crouched, wary, scared.

Linc held up both hands. Then, realizing that they wouldn't

be able to hear him even if he shouted from inside the helmet, he reached down and touched the radio control studs set into the suit's waist.

"I've come from Jerlet," Linc said. The radio unit amplied his voice into a booming, echoing crack of doom. He turned the volume down a little.

"It's me, Linc. I've come back. Jerlet sent me back to you."

One of the farmers dropped his weapon and sank to his knees.

Stav scowled at him and held his ground. "What kind of monster are you? What have you done with Linc?"

"Wait," Linc said.

He finished undoing the neck seal and lifted the helmet off his head.

"I'm not a monster at all, Stav," he called to them in his normal voice. "I'm Linc. I've come back to you. Jerlet sent me."

Stav and the others fell to their knees.

It took many minutes for Linc to convince them that he was just as normal and alive as they were, even though he was wearing strange garments.

The four farmers watched, goggle-eyed with a mixture of fear and fascination, as Linc slid the heavy backpack off his shoulders, unstrapped the support web beneath it, and finally pulled off his cumbersome boots.

Stav was the first to recover.

"You . . . you *are* Linc!" He slowly got to his feet. The others, behind him, did likewise. A bit shakily, Linc thought.

"Of course I'm Linc."

"But you went away. Monel and the others said you died," one of the farmers muttered.

"I didn't die. Did Magda ever say I was dead?"

They looked at each other, puzzled, uneasy.

"I don't think she ever did," Stav replied.

Linc was glad to hear it.

"I didn't die," he said. "I'm as alive and normal as any of you. I found Jerlet. He told me many things, and gave me this suit to protect me so that I could come back to you. And he also gave me good news. The yellow star isn't going to swallow us. It brings us life, not death."

The good news didn't seem to impress them at all. But at least they didn't look so frightened.

Stav walked up to Linc and put out a hand to touch him. He peered closely at Linc's face. A slow smile unfolded across his broad, stolid face.

"You really are Linc,"

"Yes, Stav. It's good to see you again. Can you take me to Magda?"

Nodding, Stav answered, "Yes, yes . . . of course. But I think Monel will be on his way here before we can get to the priestess."

Monel did arrive, almost breathless, with four more men behind him. They were all armed with lengths of pipe and knives from the galley.

Stav and the farmers had picked up the various pieces of Linc's pressure suit, their faces showing awe more than fear. Linc still wore the main body covering of the suit, and felt slightly ridiculous with his stockinged feet and bare hands poking out of the bulbous blue garment.

"It *is* you!" Monel's tone made it clear that he didn't want to believe what he was seeing.

Linc could feel his face harden toward Monel. "That's right. I've come back. Jerlet sent me back to you."

"Jerlet? You don't expect us to believe. . . ."

"I don't expect anything from you," Linc snapped. "I'm here to see Magda. I don't have time to waste on discussions with you."

Monel's thin face went red. He held up a hand, as if to stop Linc if he should try to move. The guards behind him tensed and gripped their weapons more tightly.

"You're not going to see Magda or anyone else until I'm satisfied that you're no danger to the people. . . ."

Linc smiled at him, but his words were dead serious: "There's only one danger to the people, and that's delay. Jerlet showed me how to save the ship. We're not going to die; the yellow sun isn't going to kill us. If we act quickly. There's a new world waiting for us, if we do the right things to get there."

Monel's chair rolled back a few centimeters, but he insisted, "Jerlet showed you? You mean you talked with Jerlet?"

"That's right."

"Then why didn't he come with you?"

"He died...."

A shock wave went through them. Linc could feel it.

"Died?"

"Jerlet is dead?"

"Yes," Linc said. "But he'll come back again someday. When we've reached the new world and learned how to live on it. Probably not in our lifetime, but our children will see him when he returns."

Even Monel was visibly shaken by Linc's words. "I don't understand...." His voice was almost a whisper.

"I know," Linc said. "That's why I have to see Magda. She'll know what to do."

Monel pursed his lips, thinking. The others—the farmers and Monel's guards—clustered around Linc wordlessly. One of the farmers reached out and touched the rubberized fabric of Linc's pressure suit.

"We're wasting time," Linc said to Monel. "I've got to see Magda."

He started striding down the corridor, and the others hesitated only a moment. The farmers fell into step behind Linc. Monel's guards shifted uneasily, eyed their sallow little leader, then looked toward Linc and the farmers.

"Don't just stand there!" Monel snapped at them. "Get me up there with him."

If anything, Magda was even more beautiful than Linc remembered her. She stood in the center of her tiny compartment, her dark eyes deep and somber, her finely-drawn face utterly serious, every line of her body held with regal pride.

"You returned," she said.

Linc stepped into her room, and suddenly the crowd of people that had gathered around him as he had marched down the corridor seemed to disappear. There was no one in his sight except Magda.

"Jerlet sent me back."

But Magda didn't move toward him, didn't smile. Her gaze shifted to the people crowding the doorway behind Linc.

"Leave us," she commanded. "I must talk with Linc alone."

They murmured and shuffled back away from the door. Linc

shut it firmly. Then he turned back to Magda.

"I knew you would return," she said, her voice so low that he could barely hear her. "Every night, every meditation, I knew you were alive and would return."

"You don't seem too happy about it," Linc said.

Instead of responding to that, Magda said, "I must know everything about your journey. Every detail. You really saw Jerlet? He spoke to you?"

Linc sat down cross-legged on the warm carpeted floor and leaned his back against the bunk. Magda sat next to him, and he began to tell her about his time with Jerlet.

He knew this room, had known it all his life, since long before Jerlet had gone away from them and the kids decided to turn to Magda for the wisdom and future-seeing abilities that had made her priestess. But the room seemed different now. Magda was different. Everything *looked* the same: the carpeting, the drawing on the walls that Peta had done, the glowing zodiac signs traced across the ceiling. But it all *felt* different. Strange.

Magda listened to Linc's tale without interrupting once. Her eyes went misty when he told her about Peta, otherwise she showed no emotion at all. The room's lights dimmed to sleeping level, and still Linc wasn't finished. On the ceiling, the Bull, the Twins, the Lion, the Virgin also listened in their customary silence. In the shadows Magda sat unmoving, straight-backed, as if in meditation. The only sign that she heard Linc was an occasional nod of her head.

"...And, well, I guess that's all of it," Linc said at last. His throat was dry, raspy.

Magda seemed to sense how he felt. "I'll get you some water," she said, rising to her feet. "Stay there."

She went to the little niche in the wall where the water tap was and filled a cup for Linc.

Handing it to him and sitting down beside him again, Magda asked, "Jerlet *wants* us to fix the machines?"

Linc could hear uncertainty in her voice. Disbelief.

"Yes," he answered. "The machines are our only hope. If we don't fix them and use them properly, then we *will* fall into Baryta—the yellow sun. And we'll all die. But with the help of the machines, we can reach the new world, Beryl. And we can live there."

Magda said nothing.

Linc reached through the shadows to grasp her arm gently. "Think of it, Magda! A whole world for us! Open and free and clean. No more conning walls. All the air and food and water we could want. All the room!"

"The machines," she said softly. "Jerlet told us long ago never to touch the machines. *Never*."

Linc smiled at her, even though it was too dark for her to see it. "That was when we were children. Babies! Of course he told us not to touch the machines then. We would have hurt ourselves or fouled up the machines."

She didn't move away from his touch. But she didn't move toward him, either.

"If Jerlet himself could tell us to fix the machines...."

"He can't. He's dead."

"Yes, you told me."

"He used the machines himself. All the time. Even when he was dying."

"They didn't save his life."

"He was old, Magda. Unbelievably old. And he'd been sick for a long time."

"But the machines still let him die," she said.

Linc answered, "He's inside a machine now. A machine is keeping his body safe until we—or our children, I guess—learn enough to bring him back to life."

He felt her shudder, as though a touch of the outer darkness's cold had gone through her.

Linc lay back on the carpeting and stared up at the softly glowing figures on the ceiling. The Ram, the Scales, the Scorpion. Once they had been strange and mysterious signs that had puzzled and even frightened him a little. Now, thanks to Jerlet, he knew what astronomical constellations were and how the art of astrology had begun on old Earth.

"Magda," he said, surprised at the tone of his own voice. "We're dealing with the difference between life and death. We can save the people, and reach the new world. But only if we use the machines. We've got to repair them and then use them. If we help the machines, they will help us. To live. If we don't do it, then we will all die."

"Jerlet told you that."

"Jerlet *showed* me the truth of it. He taught me. He put ideas and information into my mind. I know what we have to do. But the people won't do it unless you tell them to. You are their priestess. If you tell them that it's the right thing to do, they'll believe you."

"Monel thinks he's their leader."

"Monel!" Linc heard anger and disgust in his voice. "He can play at being a leader, but if *you* tell the people that we've got to fix the machines, they'll do it no matter how much Monel hollers."

"You're really certain...?"

"I know what we have to do," Linc said firmly.

For a moment, Magda said nothing. Then, "All right, Linc. I want to believe you. I don't think I even care if you're right or wrong. I want to believe you."

He smiled into the darkness. "Magda...."

"Where will we start, Linc? What has to be done first?"

"The bridge," he said. "We've got to get the bridge back into functioning condition."

"Bridge?" she echoed. "Where is that?"

He hesitated. "Um... it's what we call... the Ghost Place."

Magda sat bolt upright. "The Ghost Place?" Her voice was a horrified whisper. "*The Ghost Place?* Linc, how could you even think of that? It's impossible! You can't go there!"

"We've got to."

"No!" Magda screamed. "Never! That's a place of death. I'll never let you go there. You, or anyone else."

[13]

Linc got slowly to his feet.

"Magda," he said, forcing his voice to stay steady and calm, "this is something that I understand and you don't. I've been with Jerlet; I know what has to be done."

She stood beside him, fists planted stubbornly on her hips. "You don't understand anything! You can't go to the Ghost Place. It's death...."

"That's wrong. I know how to go there. I've got to clear out the bodies and fix the machines so that...."

"Linc, listen to me!" Her voice was more pleading than angry now. "I couldn't stand it if you died."

"I won't die."

"Jerlet died! You could, too." She took a deep breath. "Besides, if you go there it'll give Monel the chance he's been waiting for. He'll drive us both out."

"Monel?"

"I don't have the strength to fight him," Magda said. "He wanted to make Jayna priestess. But when I stopped fighting against him so much and let him have things his own way... he let that drop. I'm still priestess, but Monel tells everybody what to do."

Linc could feel his face pulling into a frown in the darkness. He couldn't see the expression on Magda's face, only the glint of highlights in her hair and the outline of her determined jaw, silhouetted against the fluorescent pictures on the walls.

"I'm here now," he said. "I'll take care of Monel."

"How?" she snapped. "By going to the Ghost Place? By killing yourself? Or by making everybody so scared of you and what you're doing that they'll listen to whatever Monel tells them?"

He reached out toward her. "Magda, it's got to be done, or we'll all die."

"No, I don't believe that. Jerlet wouldn't. . . ."

"Jerlet has no control over it! He never did! He was a man, an ordinary man. He couldn't even move out of the weightless area. He couldn't control the ship."

Someone knocked at the door. Two sharp raps, loud and demanding. Their argument ended.

"Who is it?" Magda called.

"Monel."

Before Linc could say anything, Magda answered, "Come in."

The door slid open and Monel wheeled himself into the room.

"No lights?" His voice was mocking, a thin knife blade of sound. "Are you two meditating in the dark?"

Linc couldn't see Monel's face, but his two guards out in the softly-lit corridor were grinning. He went over and closed the door with one hand, while palming the light switch with the other. The room brightened.

"You two have had enough time to walk around the Wheel," said Monel. "How about telling the rest of us what you're up to."

The rest of us, Linc thought, *meaning you*.

"Linc has been telling me about his time with Jerlet," Magda said guardedly.

"Yes? You must tell us all about it." Monel was smiling, but there was neither friendship nor warmth in his face.

"Jerlet sent me back to fix the machines," Linc said, "so that we can be saved from the yellow sun."

"And you say that Jerlet has died," Monel added, "so that he can't tell us what he wants us to do. We've got to learn about it from you."

"That's right."

"And we must trust that you're telling the truth about what Jerlet desires."

Linc felt his fists clenching. "Do you think that I'm a liar?"

"Did I say that?" Monel countered smoothly.

Long ago, when he was only a tiny child and Jerlet still lived with the kids, Linc saw a pair of cats getting ready to fight one another. They glared at each other, made weird wailing sounds, and paced stiffly around one another. It took a long time for them to actually fight, but they finally worked themselves up to it.

That's what we're doing now, Linc realized as he and Monel traded questions and demands. *Just like the cats; we're getting ready to fight.*

"I've got to repair the machinery on the bridge," Linc heard himself saying. "It's necessary, if we're to reach the new world."

"The Ghost Place," Magda added.

Monel didn't seem surprised.

"I've forbidden it," Magda said. "No one can go there and live."

"I can," Linc insisted.

"Jerlet told you how to do it?" Monel asked.

"Yes."

Magda shook her head violently. "It's wrong! You mustn't disturb the ghosts!"

"It's either that, or we all die."

Monel laughed. He threw his head back and laughed, a scratched, harsh, cackling laughter that grated against Linc's nerves.

"You really think anybody will believe you?" he demanded of Linc. "Do you think that the people will let you tamper with the machines—or go to the *Ghost Place*?"

"They will," Linc answered, "if Magda tells them it's all right."

He turned to look at her. She stared straight back at him, her space-black eyes hard and glittering. But she said nothing.

"Magda will say what I want her to say," Monel told Linc. And he wheeled his chair over to her. She stood unmoving as he reached an arm around her waist. "Magda is mine."

Linc felt the flames of anger flare within him.

But before he could say or do anything, Monel added, "And all you have is this crazy story about Jerlet. You have no proof. No one will believe you. No one at all."

Linc took a step toward the smirking rat-faced thing in the wheelchair. He wanted to silence Monel, wipe the evil smile off his face, close his ratlike eyes forever.

Magda stopped him with a word.

"Linc."

He stood there balanced on the balls of his feet, hanging between his desire to smash Monel and his desire to make Magda his own.

"Go in peace, Linc," she commanded.

And suddenly Monel's smile evaporated. He looked displeased, angry. *That's it!* Linc realized. *He wants me to attack him. Then the guards outside can come in and save him, and he'll have me for the sin of violence.*

Linc felt ice replacing the fire inside him. He stood there for an uncertain moment, then said to Monel:

"I know what has to be done. All you offer the people is death, but I bring the gift of life from Jerlet. And I'll show you—and all the people—proof of what Jerlet demands from us."

Monel's voice was low and ominous. "How will you do that?"

Linc ignored his question and said to Magda, "Call a meeting of the people. Meditate and ask for Jerlet's guidance. He'll answer you with the proof that we have a chance to reach the new world. He'll show you that world, and tell you what needs to be done to reach it." *If I can get back to Jerlet's domain and set up the proper tapes for the wall screens to show.*

"There'll be no meeting," Monel snapped.

"I'll tell the people about it. They'll want a chance to see the proof," said Linc. "The priestess can't deny giving someone a chance to be heard."

"That's true," Magda said. "If the people ask for a meeting, I can't refuse. It's my duty as priestess."

"After the next workday," Linc said. "Call the people together to see Jerlet's proof."

Magda nodded her head so slightly that Linc wondered if she moved it at all. Monel sat glaring, red-faced with fury.

Linc turned and pushed the door open. He strode past the guards and down the corridor to his own room.

It should be a simple matter to set up the back-up communications antennas, Linc told himself as he paced down the corridor. *Jerlet showed me how, and the computer has all the information I need to do it. Then I can beam the data about Beryl into the screens down here, even though the regular communications channels are broken.*

But sleep was making its insistent demands on him. By the time he got to his old room, he knew that he had to rest for a few hours, at least.

He was asleep as soon as his head touched the bunk. A deep dreamless sleep of exhaustion.

He awoke to someone shaking him by the shoulder.

"Linc...wake up. Please! Wake up."

He swam up through a fog, focusing his eyes slowly, with enormous effort. It was so good to sleep, to slide back into warm oblivion....

"Linc, please! Wake up!"

He flicked his eyes open. Bending over him was Jayna. She looked terribly upset.

"Wha...what's wrong?" Linc pushed himself up to a sitting position.

Jayna brushed back a wisp of hair. She was pretty, Linc realized. Golden hair and ice-blue eyes. Like the gold and blue of Baryta and Beryl, except that she was close enough to touch, warm, alive.

"What's the matter?" he asked again.

She glanced nervously at the door to the corridor. It was closed, but from the look on her face, she seemed to be afraid that someone could see her in here with Linc.

"You're in danger," Jayna said breathlessly. Her voice was soft and high-pitched, a little girl's voice. "Monel wants to cast you out."

"That's nothing new," he grumbled as he reached down for his slippers.

"No! You don't understand! He's going to do it now. This shift. Before the meeting."

Linc looked up at her. "What time is it?"

"Firstmeal's just starting."

He tugged on the slippers. "I've got a lot to do."

Jayna sank to her knees beside him. "Linc...*please* listen to what I'm saying. Monel is out to kill you. He won't let you get to the meeting. He wants you *dead*."

He stared at her. She seemed really frightened. "How do you know? And why...."

"I heard him telling his guards to find you and bring you to the deadlock. They're waiting for you at the galley. If you don't show up there, they'll come down here and get you."

He got to his feet. Jayna stood up beside him. *She's shorter than Magda*, he automatically noticed. *But softer*.

"We can hide in my room," she said. "They won't think of looking for you there."

A trap? Aloud, he said, "Grab that helmet. I'll get the rest of the suit." He picked up the various pieces of his pressure suit, limp and lifeless now without him inside it. The backpack with its oxygen tanks was heavy, but Linc hefted it over one shoulder, gripping it by the straps.

"Hurry!" Jayna urged.

"The boots . . . can you carry them?"

She scurried to the corner of the room where he had left the boots and picked them up, shifting the bulbous helmet under her other arm.

Linc eased the door open and peeked out. A few people were walking in the corridor, but none of Monel's guards were in sight.

"Come on," he said, and started down the corridor.

"My room's in the other direction."

With a shake of his head, Linc countered, "This way. Toward the deadlock. That's where we're heading."

She looked even more terrified, but she scampered along beside him. Wordlessly, they rushed down the corridor and made it to the lock without any interference.

Linc began pulling on the pressure suit. As he sealed the leggings and sleeves, he asked Jayna:

"Why did you warn me? I thought you were Monel's girl."

"I couldn't let him hurt you. And besides . . ." her little-girl's face looked hurt, almost teary, "he's not interested in me. Only Magda. He said he was going to make me priestess, but all he does is stay with *her*."

"Listen," Linc said. "You'd better get down to the galley for firstmeal. Act as if everything's normal. Otherwise Monel and his guards will realize that you've warned me."

The frightened look came back into her eyes. "Oh. I hadn't thought of that."

"Go on . . . I'll be all right."

"You're sure?"

He nodded. Then, as she hesitated, watching him pull on his gloves, she handed him the helmet that she was still holding.

"Thanks," he said.

Jayna suddenly threw her arms around Linc's neck and kissed him. "Don't let them hurt you," she whispered. Before Linc could answer she let go and dashed off down the corridor, toward the galley.

With a puzzled shrug, Linc cycled the airlock hatch open and stepped inside. *No sense hanging around out in the corridor where they might see me.* But he knew the airlock would be the last place Monel's guards would search for him. To them, it was the deadlock, the dreaded place where the dead were sent into outer darkness. No one went there unless they had to.

Linc put the helmet on, connected the oxygen and life-support hoses, and checked out the pressure suit quickly but thoroughly. Satisfied, he touched the buttons that put the airlock through the rest of its cycle. The air pumped out of the cramped metal-walled chamber, into the storage bottles that lay hidden behind the access panels lining the walls. The telltale lights on the tiny control panel shifted from amber to red, and the outer hatch swung open.

Once again Linc was outside the ship. This time, though, he hurried up the outer skin of the tube-tunnel, racing against time to get to the hub of the ship.

He had something less than ten hours before the meeting would begin, just after lastmeal. Less than ten hours to find the tapes he wanted and set them up on the back-up communications system.

I can do it, he told himself. *I know I can.* He kept repeating it to himself.

It seemed strange to re-enter Jerlet's domain. His months there were suddenly like a dream, something that had happened only in his imagination. *No wonder the others have a hard time believing it,* Linc realized. *I hardly can believe it myself.*

He took off the helmet, backpack, and gloves, then went to work.

It took hours. There were a few tapes where Jerlet's voice droned over the pictures of Baryta and Beryl. There were no tapes with Jerlet's picture. Linc found some old tapes in the computer's memory files, scenes from old Earth that would show the people where their ancestors had come from. A carefully programmed series of old Earth as seen from the ship, centuries ago, together with similar views of Beryl. *They* do *look alike*, Linc saw.

Finally he had the tapes he wanted, arranged the way he wanted them, and programmed them into the communications system.

Then, soaking with sweat, he went back to the airlock and donned the rest of the pressure suit and its equipment. Outside once more, he checked the back-up communication system's antenna. It looked all right. The test panel set into the ship's skin, along-side the two-hands-wide, bowl-shaped antenna, glowed green when Linc touched its buttons.

Now he fairly flew down the outside of the tube-tunnel toward the Living Wheel. He took great incautious leaps, spanning a dozen meters in a stride. As he got closer to the living area and the gravity built up, he had to slow down and use the stairs more normally. But still he hurried.

It took agonizing minutes to find the back-up communications antenna down on the first level. It was clear on the opposite side of the wheel from the airlock. Linc located it at last, activated it, and let his breath gulp out in a grateful sob when the panel light flashed green.

All set, then. Wall screens'll show them everything. All I have to do is get Magda to turn them on. When she calls on Jerlet for guidance they'll see the new world and everything else I've programmed.

Wearily, suddenly realizing how utterly exhausted he was, Linc clumped back along the Living Wheel's skin to the airlock hatch. He stopped for a moment and watched the stars swinging in their stately course as the ship rotated. *It'd be so easy to float off*, he knew. *So easy to forget everything and just drift away. Float among the stars forever.*

But as he gazed out at the swirling stars, his mind's eye pictured Monel and the way he held Magda. As if he owned her, possessed her. And she let him do it. *She let him!* She didn't seem to be happy about it, but she didn't try to stop him, either.

Linc felt confused. Magda and Monel...Jayna warning him...everything seemed upside down. No one stayed the way they were. Everything was changing.

As the ship swung on its ponderous arc, the yellow sun came up over the curve of the metal wheel. The faceplate on Linc's helmet automatically darkened, but he still had to squint and look away.

It can bring us death, he said to himself, *if we stray too close to it. But it can also give us life, if we act properly.*

And suddenly he knew that he could never let himself drift into the oblivion of death, even if it meant spending his final moments among the glories of the universe. He would fight for life. Fight with every gram of strength in him.

Doggedly, Linc pushed his tired muscles back to the airlock hatch. *There's still a lot to do. An awful lot to do.*

He opened the hatch and stepped inside the airlock chamber. For a moment longer he gazed outward at the stars. But then he reached up and touched the button that closed the hatch. The pumps hidden behind the metal walls clattered to life; Linc felt their vibrations through the soles of his boots. Soon he could hear air hissing around him. The control panel light went from amber to green, and the inner hatch slid open.

Monel and four of his guards were waiting there.

"Good evening," Monel said sarcastically. "I'm glad we didn't sit here through lastmeal for nothing. I was expecting you to return sooner."

Linc stepped out into the passageway and unfastened his helmet.

"Sorry to keep you waiting," he said, as he raised the helmet off his head. "I had a lot of work to do."

"You finished your work? You're ready for the meeting?"

"Yes. When does it start?"

"In a little while." Monel seemed to be enjoying the conversation. He was smiling broadly as he said, "Too bad we'll have to have the meeting without you."

"You can't keep me away from it."

Monel laughed. He raised his right hand and pointed it somewhere behind Linc.

Before he could turn around, Linc felt his arms pinned to his sides by the guards. Someone loosened the straps holding his life support pack and its oxygen tanks. It thudded to the floor.

Monel had Linc's helmet in his lap.

"It's going to be my sad duty to organize a search party to try to find you," he said pleasantly. "After all, when you don't show up at your own meeting, people will start to worry about you. We'll find this helmet here in the passageway, right beside the deadlock hatch. Someone will open the hatch to see if you're hiding in there. They'll find your body there. Too bad. But that's what happens to people who tinker with machines. It'll be a good lesson for everybody."

Linc was too furious to say a word. His voice gagged in his throat.

Silently, the guards opened the airlock hatch and pushed Linc inside. He fell to the floor in a heap. Before he could get to his knees, the hatch slammed shut.

The green panel light changed to amber. Linc could hear the pumps starting. The air was being sucked out of the chamber.

(14)

Linc scrambled to his feet and clawed at the control panel. No use. Monel had jammed it, somehow. But underneath the panel lights and the regular cycle control buttons there was a red button marked EMERGENCY OVERRIDE. Jerlet had explained to Linc that the override would stop the airlock's operation and fill the chamber with air whenever it was pushed.

Linc leaned on it. Nothing. The pumps kept on throbbing, the pulse in Linc's ears was pounding in rhythm with it.

He's tampered with the controls! Monel himself has tampered with the machinery!

But the realization wasn't going to help, Linc knew.

Already it was difficult to breathe. Linc staggered to the access panel where the pumps and oxygen bottles were hidden. He flicked the latches open and the panel slid to the floor with a crash.

An empty pressure suit was hanging limply inside the compartment. Linc grabbed at the helmet and quickly pulled it over his head. There was enough air in it to let him take one quick breath. Blinking away the dark spots from his vision, he saw that there were instructions printed on the wall of the compartment, under a red EMERGENCY PROCEDURE heading.

Blessing Jerlet for teaching him to read, Linc reached for the emergency oxygen line that connected to a green metal tank and plugged it into the collar of his helmet. The stuff tasted stale and felt cold, but it was breathable.

Linc quickly sealed the helmet, pulled the oxygen tanks and life support pack from the emergency suit onto his own back, and then disconnected the emergency oxygen supply line. He was fully suited up, able to face hard vacuum without danger.

He turned and saw that the amber control light was still on. As he lifted the access panel back into place, the light turned red and the outer hatch began to open.

If I stay here, they'll just take this equipment away from me and do it all over again, Linc thought. There was only one escape route: outside.

He clumped to the lip of the hatch and stepped outside once again. Grimly, Linc stood there and watched the hatch close.

He wished he could see the look on Monel's face when they opened the airlock and he was gone. Would they think he had been whisked away to outer darkness? Or would Monel guess that Linc had somehow escaped?

Either way, Monel would probably keep a guard or two at the hatch, just in case Linc should try to get back.

His earlier weariness was still tugging at him. But now he had the adrenalin-fueled fires of survival and hatred urging him on.

Carefully he paced along the catwalk built into the Wheel's outer skin. As Baryta "rose" from behind the curve of the Wheel, Linc could see in its golden light that the metal of the ship was pitted and streaked, marked by time and the vast distances the ship had traveled.

Here and there were larger holes, actual punctures, and Linc began to understand why some sections of the Living Wheel were closed off. *No air. It leaked out of the holes.*

In one place there was a gaping wound in the Wheel's side. He could peer inside and see an empty room; nothing in it except a few tables welded firmly to the floor. There were some viewing screens built into the tabletops.

And then Baryta's sunlight glinted off the rounded hump of an airlock hatch. Linc felt a surge of joy warm his innards. He shouted to himself and dashed toward the airlock as fast as he could.

It wouldn't budge. He pushed the buttons a dozen times, but the hatch refused to move. Then, remembering what Jerlet had taught him, he tried the long lever of the hatch's manual control. It too remained frozen in place.

Linc wanted to cry. He sank to a sitting position as Baryta

slid out of sight. The stars looked down impassively on the figure of a lone, exhausted, frightened young man as he sat and felt the warmth of life ebbing out of his body.

Then Linc remembered. *The hole in the ship. Maybe I can get through there.*

He backtracked and found the ragged hole again. It was barely big enough for his shoulders to squeeze through. Praying that he wouldn't rip the suit's fabric, Linc crawled through and put his booted feet down on the room's bare metal flooring. The tough suit fabric held up. His backpack stuck in the opening for a scary moment, but Linc managed to worm it through. He stood up.

I'm inside, but it's just as bad as being outside unless I can get past this room.

There were two doors in the room, Linc saw in the light of his helmet lamp. One of them looked as if it opened onto a corridor; it was heavy, airtight, as all the corridor doors were. But the other, on a side wall, looked as if it were made of plastic rather than metal.

Linc tried to pull it open. It refused to slide as it should. He leaned against it, and it bowed slightly. He backed off a step, then kicked at the door with the metal sole of his boot with all the strength he could muster.

The door split apart.

Linc stepped through the sagging halves.

Into the Ghost Place.

Despite himself he shuddered. *Inside!* The ghosts were mute and immobile, their faces frozen in twisted soundless screams of horror and pain. Their eyes stared; their bodies slumped or sagged; their hands reached for control buttons, the hatches leading out of the bridge, or just groped blindly. Most of the ghosts still sat at the bridge's control stations, in front of instruments that were mostly dead. Only a pitiful few of the screens still flickered with active displays, Linc saw.

He noticed that a couple of the ghosts were staring up overhead. Linc looked up and saw that several pipes were split up there, hanging loosely from broken brackets. From the faded colors, Linc knew that the pipes at one time must have carried liquid oxygen and liquid helium.

They must have been frozen where they stood, when whatever tore the hole in the next room broke the pipes.

Suddenly, they weren't ghosts anymore. They were people like himself, like Jerlet, like Stav or Magda or Jayna or any of the others. Real people who died at their posts, trying to save the ship instead of running away.

There was no fear in Linc now. But his eyes were blurry as he realized that these people had given their lives so that the ship could continue living.

Slowly, Linc made his way past the dead bridge crew, heading toward the hatch that opened onto the passageway outside. *They protected the bridge with airlocks, so that a loss of air outside wouldn't hurt the crew in here...and then the disaster struck from inside the bridge itself.*

The airlock hatch was frozen shut, of course. It took Linc several moments to remember that there were tools here on the bridge. He found a laser handwelder, plugged it into the bridge's power supply, and grinned with relief when it worked. He set the tool on low power and played its thin red beam across the hatch mechanism.

The metal creaked and ticked and finally, when Linc tried the handle for the eleventh time, clicked open. Linc stepped into the airtight compartment between the two hatches, closed the inner hatch and opened the outer one. Warm air from the passageway rushed in, making it hard to push the hatch open.

But it did open, and Linc stood out in the familiar passageway once again. He started toward the library, hoping that the meeting was still going on. He unsealed his helmet as he clumped along the corridor, after clamping the hand-welder to a clip on the side of his suit.

No one was in the corridor. That meant they were all in the library, at the meeting. Linc passed his own empty room, and a sudden idea came to him.

He ducked inside and looked at the tiny screen set into the wall above his bunk. Since he had been a child, it had been untouched. Was it workable?

He pulled his gloves off and touched the red ON button. The screen glowed to life. He tried several different buttons and got nothing but views of other empty rooms. Finally, just as he was about to give up, the screen showed the library, crowded with all the people.

"He still hasn't shown up," Monel was saying. He was sitting beside Magda, who held her rightful place on the central pedestal. "He's scared of the truth, scared to face us all with his wild stories."

The crowd was muttering, a dozen different conversations going on at once.

"How long are we going to wait for him?" Monel demanded of Magda.

She looked down at him from her perch and said, "It's not like Linc to run away."

If Monel felt any guilt at her remark, he didn't show it. He merely insisted, "Linc demanded that we ask Jerlet's guidance. I say we should call on Jerlet now, and see what he has to say. Either that, or call an end to this meeting. Linc isn't going to show up. He's afraid of Jerlet's truth."

Smiling in the glow of his viewscreen, Linc punched the buttons that activated the computer tapes he had programmed earlier. All the screens in the Living Wheel, including the huge wall screen in the meeting room, suddenly blazed into life.

A view of old Earth, brilliant blue and dazzling white, swimming against the blackness of space.

Jerlet's rough, unmistakable voice rumbled, "That's Earth, the world where we all came from originally...."

The view abruptly changed to show an ancient city on old Earth. And Jerlet said, "I'm not sure which city this is, but it doesn't make much difference. They all got to be pretty much the same...." The crowds and noise were overwhelming. The sky was dark and somehow dirty-looking. Millions of people and vehicles snarled at each other along the city's passageways.

Then the scene shifted to show mountains, rivers, oceans of pounding surf. And Jerlet's voice continued:

"This is the world of our origin, where our ancestors came from, where this ship came from. It was a good world, long ago. But it turned rotten. Our ancestors fled in this ship ... seems they were driven away by evil people, although they were glad enough to leave Earth; it had gone sour. They came out to the stars to find a new world where they could live in happiness and peace."

The scene changed abruptly once again, showing a telescopic view of Beryl.

"This is the new world," Jerlet said. "We can reach it, if we're lucky. But there's a lot of work ahead of us if we're going to make it there safely...."

Linc left his helmet and gloves on the bunk and strode out toward the meeting room.

(15)

For a moment, Linc felt silly as he approached the library, clumping along the corridor in the bright-blue pressure suit. He hadn't even bothered to take off the backpack. Only his gloves and helmet were missing.

But then he thought, *I'll need every bit of impact I can get. If the suit impresses them, so much the better.*

He checked to see if the hand-welder's power line was connected to the suit's electrical system. It was.

If Monel tries to send his guards at me, I'll burn the wheels off his chair.

He paused at the double doors of the library. Peering through the discolored windows he could see that everyone in the room—including Magda—was sitting with their eyes riveted to the big wall screen. Quietly, Linc pushed one of the doors open and slipped inside.

The screen was showing engineering drawings of the ship. Specific areas were outlined with pulsing yellow circles, as Jerlet's voice commanded:

"The key to the whole damned thing is the bridge. That's where the astrogation computer and all the necessary instruments are. Can't start making course corrections until you know exactly where you are in relation to Baryta and Beryl. And I mean *exactly*. Laser wavelength accuracies, son."

Linc smiled to himself. In his mind's eye he could see the old man's shambling figure, bloated and almost grotesque, and the intense glitter in his eyes as he tried to get his points across to Linc. *Hard to think of him as dead*, Linc said to himself. But it was still harder to understand how he could be frozen, like the

397

ghosts on the bridge, and yet someday be brought back to life.

"The rocket engines ought to be all right; we checked them and repaired them back when you pups were being hatched," Jerlet's voice rumbled on. The screen showed red arrows where the thrusters were located. "You'll have to make sure all the connections are still in place, so when the computer orders a burn the thrusters get the info. That'll mean some outside work...."

The pictures went on, with Jerlet's unmistakable voice explaining them, until they ended with another view of Beryl.

"That's the new world, Linc," the old man rasped. "Your world. Yours and the rest of the kids'. It's up to you, son. You've got to get them there safely. It's all up to you."

The wall screen went blank.

No one in the room moved. They all kept staring at the screen, open-mouthed with awe.

"I intend to follow Jerlet's command," Linc said as loudly and strongly as he could.

They whipped around to see him. Magda's hands flew to her face. A girl screamed. Monel sagged in his chair.

Slowly, deliberately, Linc walked through the shocked people sitting on the floor, up to the pedestal where Magda reigned.

He turned to face the people. "I'm not dead, as you can see. And I'm not afraid to face you. I've been with Jerlet, and he sent me back here to help us get to the new world."

Jayna was sitting up front, her face glowing. No one spoke; the crowd hardly breathed.

Linc went on, "You all saw the pictures on the screen. There's a new world waiting for us. A world that's open and free. A world where we won't have to worry about warmth or food or anything else."

"Is it... is it really true?" someone in the crowd asked.

"Can it be really true?"

"It's real," Linc said. "I've seen it myself. The new world really exists. Its name is Beryl. Jerlet named it."

"And we're going there?"

"We can get there—but only if we fix the machines."

"That's forbidden!" Monel snapped.

A few people muttered agreement with him.

"Not anymore," Linc said. "Jerlet forbade us from touching machinery while we were children, and too young to understand what we were doing. Now he wants us to fix the machines and save ourselves from death."

Monel pushed his chair up toward Linc. "How do we know that was really Jerlet speaking to us? We didn't see his face. And you said Jerlet is *dead!*"

A shocked murmur went through the crowd.

"He is dead, but he will come back to life someday. He left those words and pictures for us, to teach us, to show us what we've got to do."

"Why didn't he speak to us directly?" someone asked.

Monel added, "And all this talk about fixing the machines in the bridge. That's the Ghost Place! How can Jerlet expect anyone to go there? It's a place of death."

"I was there a little while ago, and I'm not dead."

They actually drew back away from him. Monel's chair seemed to roll backward a few centimeters all by itself. The crowd sucked in its breath in a collective gasp of surprise and fear.

"I'm telling you," Linc shouted to them, "that all this fear of the machines is stupid! Do you know what Jerlet thought of us? He called us superstitious idiots! He was ashamed of us!"

They muttered. They shook their heads.

"How do we know you're telling the truth?" Monel demanded. "Just because you *say* you've been with Jerlet, and you *say* you've been to the Ghost Place...."

Linc found that he had the welding laser in his hand. Its smooth grip felt good against his palm. His fingers tightened over it.

"This suit I got from Jerlet. None of you has ever seen anything like it, have you?"

A mumbled "No."

"And this..." he held up the welder so that they could all see it, "I took from the bridge—the Ghost Place. Watch."

He turned to one of the few ragged books left on the shelves and pulled the laser's trigger. A pencil-thin beam of red light leaped out. The book burst into flames.

The people *oohed*.

Linc eased off the trigger. He waved the laser in the general direction of one of Monel's guards. "Put the fire out before it causes some real damage," he ordered. The fellow hesitated a moment, then went over and smothered the smoldering book with a rag he pulled from his pocket.

"I have been with Jerlet," Linc repeated to the crowd. "I have been to the Ghost Place. Your fears are silly. It's time for us to stop acting like children and start doing what's needed to save ourselves and reach the new world."

"No."

Linc turned. It was Magda.

"You are wrong," she said. "Misguided. You may honestly think that you're doing Jerlet's work, but you are wrong."

"I *lived* with him!"

Magda's face was a mask of steel. "There is no proof. You tell us that Jerlet is dead, yet will live again. You say that Jerlet spoke the words we heard from the screen, yet he didn't show himself to us. You tell us to fix the machines, yet we have Jerlet's own words warning us that we mustn't touch the machines."

And she pressed the yellow button on the pedestal where she sat.

The wall screen glowed again, and now Jerlet's face appeared. Linc knew that it was the younger Jerlet, speaking to them when they had been only children.

"I've tried to set you kids up as well as possible," the tape began as it always began.

Linc watched the screen in sullen rage as the old tape unwound its familiar message. *How can I get it through their skulls?* he fumed at himself. *How can I make them see?*

"Now remember," Jerlet was saying, "all the rules I've set down. They're for your own safety. Especially, don't mess around with the machines...."

Magda turned from the wall screen to Linc. "That is Jerlet," she said. "He still lives. He speaks to us when the priestess summons him." Her mouth was tight and hard; her eyes burning with—what? *Is it fear? Or pain? Or hate?*

As Jerlet droned on, Magda raised a hand to point at Linc. "What you've told us is false!"

The laser was back in Linc's hand. Without even thinking of it, he fired at the screen. It exploded in a shower of sparks and plastic shards. The crowd screamed.

"You're wrong!" he shouted at them, waving the laser. "Superstitious idiots . . . Jerlet was right. Well, I'm going to the bridge. I'm going to repair those machines. By myself, if I have to. And don't any of you try to stop me!"

No one moved as he stomped out of the meeting room. Either to stop him or to help him.

(16)

Linc slammed the welder on the desk top in fury.

He was standing in front of the bridge's main data screen. The access panels of the computer behind the screen were open, and the computer's complex innards stood bare and revealed to him. They were a heartbreakingly hopeless mess. Something had smashed the plastic circuit chips, melted the metal tracings of the circuit boards, vaporized the eyelash-small transistors.

Hopeless, Linc told himself.

Two servomechs stood impassively behind him, waist-high cubes of metal with little domes of sensors atop them and tiny silent wheels underneath. Their mechanical arms hung uselessly at their sides. They couldn't handle this kind of work, although they had been invaluable to Linc on many other jobs.

He still remembered how everyone in the corridors had fled in terror when the first few servomechs came through the tube-tunnel hatch and into the main passageway, trundling quietly and purposefully toward the bridge, under Linc's radio command.

Now I'll have to send one of them all the way back to the hub for more spare parts, Linc told himself. In the past months, more than one servomech had failed to make it all the way through the tube-tunnels and back again.

Linc frowned. "Well," he said to the nearest of the little machines, "you're just going to have to try to get through. I hope there are enough replacement parts left in the storage bins."

For months now Linc had had no one to talk to except the servomechs. They weren't very good company.

He programmed the servomech and it obediently rolled out

to the hatch, snaked a flexible arm up to the control button, and let itself out of the bridge.

Linc arched his back tiredly. The bridge's main observation viewscreen was focused on Baryta. The yellow sun was no longer merely a bright star; it showed a discernible disk. Even through the filtered screen display, it was bright enough to hurt Linc's eyes. Close beside hung a bluish star: Beryl itself was now visible.

But no one came from the people to tell him that they saw Beryl, and that they now believed him.

"Let them meditate and frighten themselves to death," Linc muttered as he walked tiredly toward the room he had made the servomechs fix up for him. His voice sounded harsh and strained; he hadn't used it too much lately.

Starting to sound as ragged as Jerlet, he said to himself.

He glanced at the airtight hatch that let to the passageway as he walked down the long, curving length of the bridge. Once in a while he thought he saw someone peering through the tiny window at him, watching him. "Imagination," he snorted. "You want them to come to you, so you imagine seeing faces. Next thing you know, you'll start imagining the ghosts are real."

They had seen the ghosts, all right. When the servomechs, led by Linc, carried the long-dead crew to the deadlock, the people had watched, aghast. No one offered to help. After the first few shocked moments of watching, they had all run into their rooms and shut their doors tightly.

The window in the hatch was dark, as usual, when he looked at....

There *was* a face there!

Linc stopped in his tracks. He blinked. The face was there, staring at him. The window was too clouded to make out who it was. A hint of yellow hair, that's all he could see.

After a moment's hesitation, Linc stepped over to the hatch. The face didn't go away.

He reached for the hatch's lever and pulled it open. Jayna stood on the other side, an odd-shaped package in her hands.

"H . . . hello," Linc said, his voice nearly cracking.

She stood wide-eyed, frightened looking. But she didn't run away.

"I brought you some food." Jayna's voice was high and trembly.

She looks so scared, Linc thought. *Scared and little and helpless. And awfully pretty.*

"Thanks," he said, reaching out for the package.

"I've been here before, but you never noticed me."

"You should have rapped on the hatch."

"Oh no . . . I didn't want to . . . to bother you," she said.

"I would have welcomed some company. It's been pretty lonesome in here all by myself. Nothing to talk to except machines, and they don't talk back."

"Oh."

They stood awkwardly facing each other, on either side of the hatch's metal lip.

"Want to come in and see what I'm doing?" Linc asked.

An even deeper fear flickered across her face.

"It's all right," he said, smiling. "I've cleared away the ghosts and cleaned up the place." He reached his free hand out for her.

She hesitated a second, then took his hand. Her grasp felt warm and wonderful to Linc.

She stepped inside and Linc swung the hatch shut.

"Do Monel or Magda know you've come here?"

Shaking her head, Jayna answered, "No. But I don't care if they do. They're going crazy, all of them. Every time we see the yellow star it's closer and hotter. But they say if we work harder and meditate longer it'll go away. But it's not!"

Smiling grimly, Linc said, "It better not. It's our chance for life. Has anybody noticed the little blue star beside it?"

"Yes . . . a few. Monel claims it's not there. He says it's a trick, to fool us."

"Hmp. That 'trick' is Beryl. Our new homeworld, if we can reach it." He walked slowly back to the row of desks that lined the far wall of the bridge's length, and placed the food package down.

"A trick, huh? And who's playing this trick on everybody? Has Monel blamed anybody for it?"

Nodding, "Yes. . . . You."

Linc nodded back. "I thought so."

He showed Jayna the bridge, showed how many of the instruments and sensors he had already repaired. She watched in silent wonder as Linc made views of Beryl appear on the viewing screens that lined the bridge's curving length.

"The sensors are starting to bring us information on how far away we are, and what changes in our course we need to make to get to the new world," he explained to her. *But it's all useless if I can't get the astrogation computer working,* he added silently.

Linc showed the girl where he and the servomechs had repaired the hole in the ship's hull, and how he had fitted out the room next to the bridge—the captain's lounge, he had learned from the computer plans—for his own comfort. He kept the servomechs still while Jayna was near them; he didn't want to frighten her with machines that rolled around the floor and blinked lights and used mechanical arms.

She was silent all through the tour. Finally she said, "It's all wonderful! Linc, what you've done is wonderful! *You're* wonderful!"

"You're not frightened of me now?"

"No." She was looking up at him with those large, sweet blue eyes. "I was scared when I came in . . . I only meant to bring you some food. I didn't think I'd have the nerve to really come inside."

"There's nothing here to be frightened of."

She stepped close to him. "I know that . . . now." His arms circled around her automatically.

For a while they stayed together, holding each other, not moving. But finally, Linc gently disengaged himself.

"You'd better go back, before they find out that you've come here."

Jayna looked up at him, her eyes troubled. "Linc . . . let me stay here. With you."

"No." He shook his head. "You can't."

"Please."

His hands reached out to her, almost as if they had a life of their own and he had no control over them. But he stopped them and let them fall to his sides.

"No," he said firmly. "You've got to go back. If you stay, Monel will send his guards here to bring you back. It will be the excuse he needs to try to stop me."

"They'd be afraid to come in here," she said.

I want her to stay! Linc realized. But he said to Jayna, "You can't stay here. Go back to the rest of them. Tell them you've been here, if you want to. Tell them what you saw, what I'm doing. Tell them—all of them—that I'm going to save their lives whether they help me or not."

"I'll help you." Her voice was pleading now. "I want to help you."

"The best way for you to help is to go back and tell them."

Jayna looked as if she would keep on arguing. But abruptly, she pulled her gaze away from Linc, turned, and nearly ran for the hatch that led to the passageway. She didn't look back. Linc stood rooted to the floor plates, as if welded there, and watched her open the hatch and flee back to the rest of the people.

Idiot! he snarled at himself. *She doesn't know why you wanted her to leave.* After a moment's thought, he admitted, *And neither do I.*

Time became a meaningless, endless round of work. Linc slept, ate, and worked. He sent the servomechs back and forth from the bridge to the hub so often that he lost count. He learned what he needed to know from the computer's instruction screens; and a lot more besides.

Jayna returned for more brief visits. She always brought food, even though Linc assured her that he ate very well; the servomechs brought food down from the galley in the hub. She stopped asking to stay with him, but hinted subtly about it. Linc ignored her hints.

Beryl grew brighter, and Baryta became a blinding sphere of brilliance that he could watch only through the special filters of the telescopes and viewing screens. Linc finally got the astrogation computer working, and then faced the problem of checking out the controls and wiring that linked the computer's command system to the ship's rocket thrusters.

That's when Stav showed up.

He simply pushed open the airlock hatch and called in his heavy deep voice, "Linc? It's me, Stav."

Linc was at the other end of the bridge, studying a diagram on a viewing screen. It traced out the wiring circuits that led to the main rocket engines.

He rushed down the length of the bridge as Stav called again:

"Hey Linc. Where are you? It's me..."

Stav heard his pounding footsteps and turned to see him. Linc skidded to a halt.

"...Stav," he ended, his voice going soft.

For a moment, Linc didn't know what to say. "I...it's...it's good to see you, Stav."

His broad-cheeked, square-jawed face broke into a wide boy's grin. "Jayna told me she's been here and the ghosts didn't get her. I felt kind of silly, staying away."

"There's nothing here to be afraid of."

"Huhn...that's what Jayna said. Thought I'd come and see for myself."

Linc waved a hand at the curving line of desks and viewscreens that formed the bridge. "Sure...see for yourself."

Stav paced along, hands locked behind his broad back, and looked at the instrument screens. Nearly all of them were working now, showing views of Beryl, readout numbers and curving graph lines in different colors that reported on how the ship's power generators and other machines were working. Stav seemed especially fascinated by the computer and it's winking lights.

"You've got all the machines working," Stav said.

"Almost all of them," Linc replied. "It wasn't too tough to do. Most of them just needed minor repairs. Whoever built them made them to last."

Stav nodded heavily. He was impressed.

"I could use some help," Linc said.

Stav pursed his lips quizzically. "Monel wouldn't like that."

"Is he just as bad as when I left?"

"Worse."

"Oh."

"Every day the yellow sun gets closer, the people get more afraid, and Monel gets crazier. He's got everybody lining up in the morning for firstmeal. If he doesn't like you, you have to go to the end of the line. Maybe you don't get any food at all. His guards watch us all day long. It's not easy to do your work with somebody staring at you all the time. If you try to rest for a few moments they yell at you. And then you don't get any food at lastmeal."

"And the people are putting up with that?"

"What can we do? I almost wrapped a hoe around one guard's head, but then I remembered what happened to poor litle Peta. I don't want to be cast out!"

Linc frowned. "What about Magda?"

"We never see her anymore. She's locked herself in her room. Monel claims she's meditating day and night, trying to save us by pure mental concentration."

Linc looked away from the thick-armed farmer and stared at a viewscreen that showed green curving lines snaking across a gridwork graph. The background of the screen was black, and Linc could see his face reflected in it: tight, hollow-cheeked, thin-lipped, eyes scowling.

"Stav," he said at last, "meditating isn't going to save this ship. And nothing Monel can do will save us, either. But *I* can save us all. I know how to get us safely to the new world. Most of the machines are working now. I need help to get the rest of them in shape."

"You want me to help you."

"Not just you," Linc said. "All the people. Anyone and everyone. Go back and tell them that they can help me . . . and if they do, they'll be saving themselves."

Stav blinked his eyes. Like almost everything he did, it was a slow and deliberate movement. "Not everybody can come here. Somebody's got to work the farm tanks. . . ."

"I need all the help I can get. We're in a race against time. Everything's got to be ready *before* we get too close to the yellow sun. Otherwise we won't be able to pull away from it and land on the new world."

"All right," Stav said. "I'll tell the people. Monel and his guards, though. . . ."

"They can't stop you. Not if you all act together."

Stav nodded slowly, but he didn't seem convinced.

(17)

Linc paced slowly along the bridge, watching the viewscreens and the men and women sitting at their stations tending the instruments. He felt a warm glow of pride.

The ship works beautifully, he said to himself. *My ship. I brought it back to life. I made it work again.* He wished for a moment that Jerlet could see it all; how the machines hummed and clicked to themselves. How the people had come to him: Jayna first, then Stav, then two more, a handful, a dozen. Now he had enough people to do all the tasks that needed doing. They didn't even jump when a servomech trundled past them, anymore. The rocket engines tested out; the connections were solid. The computer had worked out a flight plan to put them in orbit around Beryl.

All that remains to do is to test the matter transmitter, Linc knew. *But even if it takes time to get it working, once we're in a stable orbit around Beryl we'll have plenty of time.* Already the main computer up in the hub was going over all the necessary data and working up a program that would tell Linc how to repair and test the matter transmitter system.

If Jerlet could only see this! He'd be proud of me. But Linc frowned to himself. He knew who he really wanted to see his accomplishments: Magda. But she had never once visited the bridge, his domain.

Monel had come.

Red-faced, thinner, and nastier than ever, he had come flanked by six of his guards and watched—angry and snarling—as more than a dozen people worked at the tasks Linc had assigned them.

"You'll get no food!" he screamed at them. "None at all! Don't expect to go against my orders and still get fed."

Linc countered, "We have food processors at the hub and other levels of the ship. The servomechs keep us well-supplied. We won't starve."

Monel spun his chair around and wheeled himself away from the bridge. One of his guards stayed with Linc, a fellow named Rix. "He's gone crazy," Rix said. "I'm better off with you."

Linc didn't tell everyone that the food processors couldn't feed a large number of people indefinitely. They would need inputs of fresh food eventually. *But by that time we'll either be in orbit around Beryl or dead.*

Monel was back a few days later, this time threatening to have the guards tear people away from the bridge by force, if necessary.

"Violence?" Linc asked.

"Justice!" Monel snarled.

Linc went to a desk top and touched a button. A servomech rolled up to Monel's chair and stood there, its dome sensors pulsing with a faint reddish light. Monel backed his chair away.

"Those metal arms," Linc said, "can inflict a lot of *justice* on your guards. Or you."

Monel left the bridge. He never returned. Neither did his guards.

And Magda never came at all.

I could go get her, Linc thought. But he shook his head at the idea. *No! Let her come to me. She's wrong and I'm right.*

Besides, there was Jayna and a dozen other girls who wanted to be with him now. *Let Magda sit in her shrine,* Linc told himself. *Let her meditate 'til she turns green!*

Most of the people came to the bridge to help him every day, then returned to their quarters for meals and sleep. Despite the threats and grumblings, Monel took no action to stop them. Stav and his farmers hardly ever showed up on the bridge, but Linc knew they were on his side.

Linc himself slept in the captain's lounge, next to the bridge. He ate what Jayna or some of the other girls brought him.

He spent most of his time working on the matter transmitter.

It was incredibly complex, and he didn't understand the first tenth of what he was doing. But the computer patiently showed detailed diagrams, gave him long lists of parts and instructions on where to find them and how to use them.

And each day the yellow sun grew brighter, bigger. It seemed to be reaching out for them.

Linc was squatting on the floor of the transmitter booth—a tall cylinder of transparent plastic that stood in front of the system's roomful of electronic hardware—when Hollie came running up to him.

"Linc," she called breathlessly, "the astrogation computer is starting to print out the final course corrections!"

Linc scrambled to his feet and wordlessly followed her to the bridge. Hollie was a slim, lanky girl, almost Linc's own height, and her long legs kept pace with him as they raced down the corridor from the transmitter station to the bridge.

More than a dozen people were crowded around the astrogation computer desk. They moved back when Linc arrived and let him slide into the seat.

Above the desk, the computer's main viewscreen had split into several different displays. One showed numbers: the exact timing and thrust levels of the rocket burns that must be made. Another showed a picture of their course, laid against a schematic drawing of the solar system that they were finally reaching. Thin yellow lines showed the orbits of the system's six planets: Beryl was the second-closest to the yellow sun. A glowing blue line showed the course that the ship would have to follow; it ended in a circular orbit around Beryl. A flashing green dot showed where the rocket burns had to be made.

Linc studied the numbers and nodded.

"Twelve hours," he said. "The first rocket burn has to be made in twelve hours."

They all clapped and laughed. They were excited, eager. Their long weeks of work were finally resulting in something they could see.

But Linc found himself wishing for more time. *I've got to be in a dozen places at once,* he realized. The matter transmitter wasn't ready for testing yet, and no one else could read or handle the tools well enough to be trusted with it. But he also had to be here on the bridge to make certain that the course-changing maneuvers were done exactly right. Otherwise everything was doomed.

And, he realized, he had to see Magda.

It was night. Everyone was asleep. Linc stood by the astrogation computer and watched all the unsleeping, hard-working instruments of the bridge. *The whole ship is at my fingertips. All mine. Just as though nobody else existed.*

In three more hours they would all be awake and clustered here at the bridge while the rocket engines roared briefly to life. A few seconds to thrust, that was all that was needed for this first course correction. A quick burn that would swerve them away from Baryta's glaring hot grasp.

The difference between life and death.

She won't come to see it happen, he knew. *She'll stay in her little shrine and wait for me to come to her.*

He paced the length of the bridge once. Then twice. Abruptly he strode to the hatch and pushed it open. For the first time in many months, he went back to the living area.

It seemed strange to be walking down the old corridor again. His home, for most of life. But now it looked old, worn, and tired, somehow different than Linc remembered it. The walls were stained and discolored. The floor was scuffed and dull.

He passed the big double doors of the farm section. How many lifetimes ago had he repaired the pump that Peta had damaged? How much had happened since then!

Linc found himself slowing down as he neared Magda's door. He glanced up and saw a long-dead TV camera's eye staring blindly out of the ceiling. *I could fix that and watch the corridor from the bridge*, he thought idly.

He finally got to her door, hesitated, then tapped on it lightly.

"Come in Linc," came Magda's muffled voice.

The room was the same. The walls glowed dimly. The strange sky shapes shone across the ceiling. Magda sat on the bunk, her face deep in shadow, as Linc stepped in and let the door slide shut behind him.

"How did you know it was me?" he asked. She pushed her hair back away from her face with a graceful hand.

"I'm the priestess. I can see things that other people can't see."

He didn't answer.

"Besides," she said, "who else would it be? I knew you'd come sooner or later. And probably while everyone else was asleep."

He crossed the tiny room in three strides and sat on the floor, at her feet.

"You don't sleep?" he asked.

"Not very much, anymore."

From this close he could see, despite the room's dimness, that her face was even more gaunt and hollowed than his own.

"I've got the ship running smoothly now," Linc said.

She looked down at him and let one hand rest on his shoulder. "Yes, I know." Her hand felt cold through the thin fabric of his shirt. She seemed tense, almost afraid.

"We'll be able to make it to the new world."

"Perhaps."

"You could help us...."

"I have helped you," Magda said.

Linc stared up at her. "You have? How? By meditating? A few hours with a screwdriver would have been more help."

"Don't joke about serious things," Magda said softly. "I've helped you by staying here and fasting, concentrating, meditating—and by preventing Monel from stopping your work."

"Monel couldn't...."

"Monel tried to rouse all the people against you," Magda said. "But Stav and his farmers refused to follow him. Thanks to the priestess."

Linc didn't understand. "What? Are you saying...?"

It was difficult to see her face in the shadows. Magda seemed to be staring off somewhere in the darkness. "Ever since you went to the Ghost Place," she explained, "Monel has tried everyday to make me say that you are evil, and you must be stopped. I have not said it. Stav asked me for guidance, and I told him that he should not fear you, or the Ghost Place."

"But you told me...." Linc didn't bother finishing the sentence. None of it made any sense to him.

Magda went on, "You are such children, all of you. You each

want to be the mighty leader, the one who gives orders, who decides what must be done. You *know* you're right. Monel *knows* you're wrong. At least Stav doesn't pretend to know everything, he asks the priestess for guidance."

Shaking his head, Linc asked, "I thought you believed...."

Her hand tightened on his shoulder. "The priestess is always in command. Monel thinks he's the leader; he's a fool. You think you can save us all from death; you're a fool, too. *I* am the leader here, and all of you do as *I* wish. I am letting you try to fix the machines because you might be right about them. I am letting Monel think he's giving orders to everyone because then I can make him give the orders that I want him to give.

"When you tried to overthrow everything we have believed all our lives, even the power of the priestess, I used Monel to balance your new power. When Monel wanted to stop your work in the Ghost Place and have you cast out, I used Stav to balance him. You men do all the struggling and I remain the priestess, the real leader, the one who brings Jerlet's wisdom into the lives of the people."

Linc felt stunned. "You've been playing us against each other?"

Magda's voice smiled. "Of course. I've been directing all of you ever since I became priestess. Before that time, even when we were children, I could make any one of you do almost anything I wanted to."

"But you didn't want me to fix the machines in the bridge."

"True. I was afraid for you. And afraid that if you succeeded, it would ruin my power and the people's belief in Jerlet. But when I realized that I couldn't stop you, I decided it was foolish to resist. This way, you counterbalance Monel's power. And Stav and his farmers have become a third power, in between the two of you."

Sagging against the edge of the bunk, Linc said, "I just can't believe it. You can't play with people's lives like that. No one can. You just think...."

"Why do you think you came here tonight?" Magda asked.

"Why do I think...? I came here because we're going to light off the rockets tomorrow for the first course change, and I'd like you to be there."

"No, that's not why you came." And her hand gripped his

shoulder hard. "Linc, I summoned you. I called you. That's why I knew who it was when you knocked."

He puffed out a disgusted breath of air.

"I know you don't believe me." Magda's voice was so quiet that he could barely hear her. "But you might at least ask why I called you."

"All right: why?"

"Because I have a terrible fear. Your rockets are not going to work tomorrow. We're all going to plunge into the yellow star and be burned . . . or . . . something terrible is going to happen."

"Don't be silly." But her hand was a claw biting into his shoulder now. "Magda, everything's checked out. The computer. . . ."

"Don't tell me what machines say!" she snapped. "I *know* something is wrong. And I need you to help me find out exactly what it is."

"Need me?"

She nodded and closed her eyes. "I have to touch you, feel your vibrations, to find out what's wrong."

He stared up at her. "You're serious about this, aren't you?"

But she was no longer listening to him. Her fingers were digging deeply into his shoulder. Her eyes glittered, but she was staring at empty shadows. Her entire body was shaking spasmodically.

Magda's mouth worked, tried to form words, but no sounds came out. Despite himself, Linc felt drawn into her spell. "What is it? What do you see?"

She didn't answer.

He waited. The minutes stretched tautly. Still she seemed possessed by something invisible.

Then she sagged and nearly collapsed against him. Linc got to his knees and held her.

"Magda, what is it? What's wrong?"

She was cold with sweat. "I . . . trouble. . . ." she gasped weakly. "Trouble with the engines. . . ."

"What kind of trouble? What will go wrong?"

"I don't know . . . couldn't see."

He held her tightly, his mind racing. *Foolishness! You're letting yourself get caught up in this whole superstitious nonsense.* But his own inner voice asked, *What could go wrong?*

Where could a failure happen? The answer: *Anywhere.*

"But what's the most likely way that a failure could happen?" he asked himself. And the answer flashed into his mind like an explosion. "If someone tampered with the engines...or the connections between the astrogation computer and the controls...or...."

Magda stiffened in his arms. She pulled away and stared into Linc's eyes.

"Monel," she whispered.

(18)

Monel was not in his room.

Linc and Magda raced down the corridor and banged on his door. When there was no answer, they pushed it open. No one was there.

"There's a hundred places he could be," Linc said.

"What should we do?" Magda's eyes were wide with fear.

He grabbed her hand. "Let's go to the bridge."

Linc tried to force himself to think calmly as they ran toward the bridge. But his mind was a hopeless jumble of fears, hatred, darting wild thoughts.

He didn't even realize that the bridge was totally new to Magda. He just made his way to the main computer desk and plunked himself down in the chair. With one hand he waved Magda to the empty chair beside him, with the other he switched on the computer screen.

"Show me the locations of the main rocket thrusters, the control systems, and all the links between them and the bridge," he commanded.

A series of diagrams flashed onto the screens that lined the wall above the curving desk. The areas that Linc asked about were circled with bright colors.

"How could Monel know where these are?" Magda wondered, staring at the screens.

"Somebody told him," Linc snapped. "Rix . . . the guard that stayed here to help us. A traitor. That overfed, rat-faced . . . he's been telling Monel everything, I'll bet."

Linc hauled himself out of the computer desk chair and hurried over to another station. He punched buttons madly and studied the pictures that the screens there showed: TV camera views of a half-dozen different parts of the ship. All empty.

He spun around and faced Magda. "We'll have to search everyplace where he might be."

"How much time do we have?"

Linc glanced at the computer's countdown timer. "A little more than two hours until the rockets fire."

"How can we search...."

But Linc was already at the communications desk. "Everybody...wake up!" he bellowed into the pin-sized microphone that projected from the desk top. "Stav, Cal, Hollie, get up and report to the bridge *at once*. Emergency! We need everybody up here right away."

In less than five minutes they staggered in, sleepy, puzzled, surprised. Linc quickly told them what had happened.

There were nearly four dozen people standing around as Linc said:

"I don't think he could get much farther than the second level, upstairs. The computer has shown us where the vital areas are. He must be in one of those places. We've got just about two hours to find him. I want you to move in teams of at least six people each. No telling how many of his guards are with him."

Magda stayed on the bridge with Linc. He checked every circuit, all the controls, using the computer and the ship's sensing equipment to tell him if Monel had damaged the rocket engines or their control circuits.

Linc showed Magda how to work the communications desk, and she began to keep track of the search parties. They could hear the people shouting to one another, thanks to the ship's built-in microphones and loudspeakers, as they tracked through the corridors and rooms of the first and second levels.

"Nothing in here."

"Hey, I thought I saw...naw, just a shadow."

"Look at this! Does this look like wheel tracks?"

"Where?"

"Right here. See, he must've rolled through that oil stain back there...."

Linc wished a thousand times each minute that he had fixed the TV cameras in all the corridors so that he could *see* what they were doing.

The countdown timer went past the one-hour mark. Forty-five minutes. Thirty.

"Up here, by the deadlock."

Linc hadn't moved from the checkout desk. The whole rocket system still seemed to be perfectly intact; no damage.

"Ask them where they are . . . the ones who're following those wheel tracks," he said to Magda, without taking his eyes off the viewscreens.

She said back to him, "The tracks go into the deadlock up on level two."

You mean airlock, he corrected silently. Then he realized that Magda was working the communications machinery without arguing or complaining and he was glad that he'd kept his mouth shut. *If she's scared to touch the machines, she's not showing it.*

"WE GOT HIM!" The voice was a triumphant shout.

"He was in the deadlock, hiding. We got him. We're bringing him back down to the bridge."

Linc realized that he should feel relieved. There was still more than twenty minutes to go before the rockets would fire. But somehow he still felt anxious. *What was he doing in there?* He glanced over at Magda. She looked apprehensive, too.

"Still worried?" he asked.

She nodded. "You?"

"I'll feel better when the engines fire okay."

Monel was his usual glaring, angry self.

"You think I'm crazy, don't you? All of you!" he shouted. He sat huddled in his chair, surrounded by the grinning men and women who had ferreted him out of his hiding place. They had also found all of his guards.

All except Rix.

"What were you trying to do?" Linc demanded.

"Stop you."

"By hiding in an airlock?"

Monel looked disgusted. "By getting your attention away from these damnable machines!"

The answer didn't satisfy Linc at all. But before he could say anything, Stav shook Monel by the shoulder roughly.

"Why don't you want us to get to the new world? You want us all to die?"

Monel pulled himself free of the farmer's heavy hand. "What makes you think that you'll be able to live on this new world? Because *he* says so?" He sneered at Linc. "We know we can live on the ship. But this new world of his . . . who's ever lived outside the ship?" His thin voice rose to a nerve-racking shrillness. "It's death to go outside, everyone knows that! The ship is life . . . everyplace else is death."

Linc stepped up in front of him, towering over him. "And what happens when the ship plunges into the yellow sun? That's *certain* death!"

"Who says we're going to fall into the yellow sun?" Monel snapped back. "You do! You claim Jerlet told you. But Jerlet never spoke to us about it."

Stav frowned down at Monel. "Everybody's afraid of being eaten by the yellow star. You are, too."

With an exasperated flap of his hands, Monel answered, "Of course I'm afraid! But I'd rather take my chances with the yellow star than deliberately leave the Living Wheel. We *know* it's death to go outside."

"Linc's been outside," said Jayna.

"In his special suit," Monel countered. "How long could he live out there? Well, Linc—tell them! How long could you live outside in that suit?"

Linc shrugged. "Many hours. A few days, probably."

"But you want us to live outside forever! Don't you?"

"Not in space," Linc said. "Not in outer darkness. On Beryl. On the new world. We'll live the way our ancestors did on old Earth."

"They had to leave old Earth, didn't they?"

"TIMECHECK," the computer's tape voice called out. "COUNT DOWN TIMECHECK: T MINUS FIVE MINUTES AND COUNTING."

Stav turned to Magda. "What do you say, priestess? Is Linc right or is Monel? Should we try to leave the ship and live on the new world, or should we stay here?"

Magda was standing halfway between Linc and Monel. All eyes turned to her.

"I've meditated on this for a long time," she said, her voice low but strong. "I've asked Jerlet for guidance, and tried to feel the inner truth of the problem."

"And . . . ?"

"Linc has shown that our old fears of the machines were probably wrong. He should be allowed to bring us to the new world."

The crowd sighed. A decision had been reached.

"If we were not meant to live there," Magda went on, "the machines will fail. Jerlet won't let us be led toward death. If the machines work as Linc says they will, then we will reach the new world safely and live there in happiness. But if they fail, we'll stay on the ship. All is Jerlet's will."

They seemed satisfied with that. Even Monel appeared to relax. But Linc shook his head. *Superstition. Nothing but stupid superstition.*

"COUNTDOWN TIMECHECK: T MINUS FOUR MINUTES AND COUNTING."

Time seemed to stretch out endlessly. Linc sat at the checkout desk, watching the displays on the viewscreens as they flickered past, showing every part of the rocket propulsion system. It all seemed perfectly normal, everything working smoothly.

Three minutes. Two. Sixty seconds . . . thirty . . . ten.

Linc suddenly felt as if he were somewhere high above the bridge, looking down on all the people standing there clustered around him, looking down on himself who stared solemn-eyed at the viewscreen displays, hands poised over the cutoff buttons, ready to stop the countdown if anything appeared to be wrong.

". . . THREE SECONDS . . ."

The fuel pump symbol on the viewscreen flashed from green to amber, showing that the pump had turned on exactly on schedule.

". . . TWO . . . ONE . . ."

Just at the count of ONE the pump symbol flashed red. Linc felt his jaw drop open. He jammed both hands down on the cutoff switch as the computer's toneless voice said:

"ZERO. IGNITION."

And an explosion tilted the bridge to a crazy angle, smashing Linc against the desk and sending everyone sprawling.

(19)

They were alive.

Through the pain that flamed through his chest, Linc realized that basic fact. He pulled himself up dizzily to his feet and looked around. The bridge seemed undamaged. There was no smoke, no fire. The people were dazed, but more from some inner turmoil than any outward fear. Hollie and one of the guards were helping Monel back into his chair.

He was laughing.

Linc glanced at the viewscreens. Everything seemed to be working, except that the astrogation display was flashing a red ERROR, ERROR, ERROR, sign.

Linc stepped over to Monel, who was laughing so hard that his eyes were squeezed shut. His head was thrown back and the cackling, screeching sound of his laughter was the only noise in the bridge.

Linc slapped him.

With all the fury in him, Linc slapped Monel's laughing face hard enough to knock him out of the chair.

No one moved.

"Get him out of here," Linc growled. "He's killed us all. Now get him out of here. All of you! Out! *Get out!*"

They grabbed at the sputtering Monel, his face striped with the white prints of Linc's fingers, and dragged him away. Someone pushed the empty wheelchair. They all scurried out of the bridge.

Linc turned and saw Magda standing in front of the communications desk, taut as a steel rod.

"He's killed us all," Linc said.

"You hit him."

"I wanted to kill him!" Linc pounded his fists against his thighs.

"You *struck* him."

"What difference does it make?" Linc shouted at her. "We're all dead. He's ruined everything."

She shook her head. "No, Linc. Nothing is ruined except your own inner peace. You'll find a way to get us to the new world, despite Monel. You'll make the machines do what you want. But you run the danger of turning into a machine yourself."

"Leave me alone," he snapped.

"I will. You're not fit for human company."

The machines told him what had happened. Someone had deliberately knocked the safety valve off one of the fuel pumps at precisely T minus one second, too late for even the automatic machinery to shut down the rocket firing. It turned out that it was Rix who had done it. Monel told him what to do, and he did it. The explosion wrecked one of the rocket engines and killed him. That much Stav found out, and came back to the bridge to tell Linc.

The computer told him more. The rocket's misfiring had still added thrust to the ship's velocity. Its course had been altered. Not in the precise way that Linc had planned, however.

He sat gloomily at the desk keyboard and watched the astrogation computer display the ship's new course. The blue line now swung wide of Baryta—they would not be roasted by the approaching star. But it also missed Beryl by a wide margin. No matter how Linc pushed buttons or coaxed the computer, there was no way for the ship to get into orbit around the new world.

He paced the bridge alone, refusing to see anyone, refusing food, refusing himself even the comfort of sleep. He checked the main computer about the matter transmitter.

Question: How close to Beryl must we be to use the transmitter?

Answer: TRANSMITTER EFFECTIVE OVER RANGES LESS THAN 5000 KILOMETERS.

To the astrogation computer he asked:

Question: What will be out nearest approach to Beryl?
Answer: 28,069.74 KILOMETERS.
Question: Can we get to within 5000 kilometers of Beryl?
Answer: WORKING. CALCULATED THRUST LEVELS REQUIRED TO ACHIEVE DESIRED DISTANCE FROM PLANET EXCEED STRUCTURAL LIMITS OF SHIP.

More pacing. Linc's body felt like a block of hard plastic. He buried the pain from the bruise across his chest, buried his fatigue and hunger. This was a problem he had to solve. Had to! And the machines couldn't solve it for him.

Why can't the matter transmitter work over a longer range? Because it would need more power, and there isn't any more power available for it.

Of course there's more power! Linc realized. *There's all sorts of power in this ship: lights, heat, all the power that runs the other machines....*

Back to the computer. More questions, more answers.

They all looked shocked when he showed up at the galley. It was lastmeal, Linc knew from the low level of the lighting in the corridor.

Jayna reached him first. "Linc! You look sick...." She took his arm. "Here ... sit down...."

"No. Not yet." He gestured to them all to sit down. Only a little more than half the people were in the galley. Magda wasn't. Neither was Monel.

"Listen to me. We've still got a chance to get to the new world. It'll be difficult, but we can do it. And if we don't ... then the ship is going to loop into a wide arc. We'll move away from Baryta—the yellow sun—for a while. We're already moving away from it. But inside of a year we'll fall back into it and get burned up."

They murmured among themselves. *They don't believe me,* Linc thought. *They're tired of hearing me.*

But Jayna asked, "What do we have to do, Linc?"

"Nothing," he answered. "There's nothing for you to do. Except ... when I tell you to move, you'd better all *jump.*" He snapped out the last word, startling them. "We're only going to have one tiny chance to make it—one chance for life. You'd better be ready to move when I tell you to."

He dragged himself back to the computer desk on the bridge and began programming it. *Every gram of rocket thrust... every erg of power... it's going to be all or nothing.*

Jayna brought him food. He took it without even speaking to her. He ate at the computer desk, while the screens flickered their messages at him. She stood behind him for a long while, not speaking, not interrupting. Linc could see her reflection in the screens, half a dozen Jaynas in half a dozen screens, all looking confused and worried. But she never questioned him.

He fell asleep at the desk. He awoke again and finished the programming. The computer digested all his instructions and questions, hummed and twittered to itself for nearly an hour—an incredibly long time for such a machine—and then reported with yellow block letters on its main screen:

"PROGRAM WORKING. ALL SYSTEMS FUNCTIONING AS REQUIRED."

Linc asked the machine, "How long before we reach the transfer point?"

The answer came immediately:

"76 HR 11 MIN 14.08 SEC."

"Start the countdown sequence at T minus three hours."

"ACKNOWLEDGED."

"How long will we be within transfer range?"

"53 MIN 12,64441 SEC."

"The matter transmitter will have to be cycled so that it can accept one person every fifty seconds or so. Can it do that automatically?"

"AUTOMATIC CIRCUITRY NOT OPERATIVE. MANUAL CONTROL NECESSARY."

Which means I'll have to stay aboard until the last person goes through the transmitter, Linc told himself.

He pushed his chair away from the computer desk and glanced at the countdown sequencer, a few desks down the row. Its central screen read:

"76 HR 10 MIN 06 SEC."

And counting, Linc added silently.

He spent most of the time up in the hub, away from everyone. He ate from the food machines and slept, a deep, long, restful sleep. Then he returned to the bridge to check the matter transmitter.

The machine didn't look as impressive as the long row of desks and controls on the bridge. There was a transparent plastic booth, big enough to hold a person. There was a gleaming metal console that housed complex electronic circuits snaking out of it. Linc had traced the power cables along the outside of the main tube-tunnel, straight into the fusion generators up near the hub. There was a control desk studded with knobs and switches. Linc would have to operate it smoothly, without a single wasted motion, if he was to save everyone aboard the ship.

He nodded to himself as he touched the buttons that activated the transmitter's self-inspection sensors. The checking circuit's green lights glowed at him. The machine was ready to function properly.

Linc frowned as he tried to fathom what fantastic powers must lie inside this machine. Jerlet had told him what the transmitter did: it transformed the atoms of whatever material was put inside it, changed them into energy that could be beamed like light for a certain distance. There was a receiving machine that had to be at the other end of the beam, which took the incoming energy and transformed it back to the original object. Put a person into the transmitter and he could be beamed instantly from the ship to the new world.

If there was enough power.

If the ship was close enough to the planet.

If the receiver was set up properly on the planet's surface.

If the person would actually take the risk of stepping inside a machine that would literally destroy his body completely.

We can get the power by shutting down everything else aboard the ship, Linc told himself. *And the remaining rockets can put us close enough to the planet for nearly an hour. The receiver's set to blast off by itself; it operates automatically.*

"That leaves only one problem," he muttered.

He went to find Magda. She wasn't in her room, she wasn't with Monel. She wasn't anywhere in the living area. Linc checked the library: empty. Then he realized where she must be.

He dashed up to the second level, soared with giant strides to the observation window.

She was kneeling on the floor, staring out at the yellow sun. Even through the heavy tint of the polarized window, Baryta glared bright and angry. Linc could see tongues of flame licking from the star's surface, beckoning to them, reaching for them.

"Magda," he called softly.

She looked up at him. "It's all right, Linc. I'm not meditating. Come sit beside me."

"What *are* you doing?" he asked.

"Waiting."

"For what?"

She shrugged and looked back toward the window. "For you. Or the yellow star. Whichever reaches me first."

"I'm here."

"You've found a way to save us."

"Yes."

She seemed neither surprised nor pleased. "I knew you would."

"There's something I want you to do," he said.

"What is it?"

"You've got to be the first to go through the matter transmitter."

She turned to him, her face perfectly serious, utterly calm. "I can't be, Linc. You know that. I can't use your machines . . . any of them. You see how we were punished when I tried to help you on the bridge."

A bright flash flared outside the window, and a long flaming streak dwindled off into the distance, heading for the tiny blue crescent that was Beryl.

"That's the receiver. It's in an automatic rocket that will land on Beryl's surface and wait for us."

Despite herself, Magda looked curious. "How did you make it do that? What did you do?"

He laughed. "The machines did it. They were built long, long ago by the scientists who lived in the ship. People who were old and gone before Jerlet was born."

"They made the machines," Magda said.

"Yes, and Jerlet showed me how to fix them so that they'll work properly."

She was still kneeling, her back rigid, her eyes dark and sad. "Linc, I can't touch your machines. I've been thinking about it, and meditating on it. I just can't. It would be wrong."

"It would be right for you to die?"

"Maybe."

"No maybe about it. And not only you—everybody on the ship will die, too. Because if you don't use the matter transmitter, nobody else will."

She closed her eyes. "I'm sorry, Linc. There's nothing else I can do."

He grasped her by the shoulders. "Listen to me! There's no choice for you. None at all. I'm going to destroy the ship. If you don't go through the transmitter, you'll be dead! Not maybe, not a year from now, but in just a few hours. This is for real. There's no other way. It's either go through the transmitter to the new world, or die here with the ship. The ship will be falling apart as we leave."

Her eyes were wide now. And angry. "You couldn't! No one would be able to destroy the ship . . . it's our home. . . ."

"Only for another few hours," Linc answered. "I had to do it, and it's already done. Just as that rocket took off for Beryl with the matter reciever, that's how automatically the ship is going to fall apart."

"You're going to kill us all!"

"I'm going to *save* you all!"

"You've gone crazy!" Magda screamed. "The machines have turned you into a monster!"

He stood up, grabbed her by the wrist, and yanked her to her feet. "Listen to me and listen hard. There's no more time to play your little games of balancing me against Monel. If you want to be a priestess to these people, then you'd better open your eyes to the truth. This ship is going to die in a few hours. Anyone left aboard will freeze, just like the ghosts."

Magda tried to pull her hand free, but Linc just held it tighter.

"If you really want to be the leader here," he went on, "then you've got to *lead*. If you don't step into that transmitter booth, none of the others will. We'll all die. You've got to lead us to life, Magda. If you're really our priestess, now is the time to set an example for everybody. Life or death! It's up to you."

(20)

Magda sat at the countdown desk, sullenly rubbing her wrist and glaring at Linc.

He was at the computer desk, staring intently at a display from the astrogation computer. The blue line that marked their course had several kinks in it, each kink jogging the line closer to the planet Beryl. A red flashing dot showed where the ship was at the moment. It was almost at the first kink.

"The main rockets will fire in another few seconds," Linc said to Magda. "That is, the ones that are still working."

He slid his chair over beside hers and touched a button on the countdown desk-top keyboard. The main screen continued to show the countdown for their transfer to Beryl. The lower left-hand screen of the group now showed a countdown for the rocket firing. It read: T MINUS 00 00 38.

"Hold on," Linc told her. "This might be a rough blast."

"More violence," she snarled at him.

"If you call what I did violence. . . ."

The bridge shook. It vibrated as if some giant's hand had grabbed it and was shaking it to see if anything inside would rattle out. Linc felt his teeth grating together and he gripped the edge of the desk to keep from falling off his chair. A deep rumbling growl filled the air: the giant's voice. Magda clutched at Linc, and he put an arm around her.

As abruptly as it started, the noise and vibration stopped. It didn't dwindle away; it *stopped*.

Magda pulled away from Linc immediately. Linc turned and looked at the astrogation display.

"Right on course." The flashing red dot was squarely on the

blue line, but now it was past the first bend.

"You should have warned the people about that," Magda said. "Somebody could have gotten hurt."

"There's worse to come."

"There's going to be more blasts like that?"

He nodded. Pointing to the screen, he said, "See? Two more. And then we're on a course that will sweep past the planet. As we fly by it, for a little less than an hour we'll be close enough to make the jump down to Beryl's surface. After that, the ship will swing out of range."

Magda said, "I'll go out and tell the people."

"No! You stay right here. You can talk to them on the loudspeaker . . . two seats down, the communications desk. You used it before."

Magda got slowly to her feet. She eyed the hatch that led out to the passageway. For a moment, Linc was afraid that she would walk out on him. Then she stepped over to the communications desk.

She stared at the keyboard for a long moment, then looked back at Linc.

"The red button next to the microphone," he said. "It won't hurt you. Just tap it with your finger."

She looked as if he was telling her to shove her hand into a flame. But she touched the red button, pulling her hand away from it almost before her finger reached it.

"Fine," Linc said to her. "Now all you have to do is sit down and talk."

Slowly she sat at the desk, frowning at the tiny microphone. Then she said, "This is Magda. Listen to me. Don't be afraid. The blast that we just went through was caused by the rockets firing. Linc has worked out a way for us to get off the ship and reach the new world. . . ."

As she spoke, Linc flicked the buttons on the computer keyboard that turned on the few TV cameras still working. Three of the screens in front of him showed people standing in the corridors, listening to Magda's voice. People came out of their rooms to hear her. Linc saw Stav and Hollie. He couldn't find Jayna in the crowd.

And there's Monel. Doesn't he look happy!

". . . Don't be afraid," Magda was repeating. "We can reach

the new world. The ship is dying, but Linc will bring us safely to the new world."

She turned to look at him. "I can't think of anything more to say."

"Tell them to stand by for my orders. I'll let them know when they have to move."

Looking worried, Magda relayed Linc's words to the people.

They began gathering at the bridge after the second rocket blast. Linc didn't like them clustering around him, but they came anyway.

Should have locked the hatch, he grumbled to himself.

But they didn't get in his way. They stood there silently, watching, staring at the screens that showed so many incomprehensible pictures, words, numbers. Linc could feel them at his back, breathing, waiting, wondering.

He glanced at Magda. She was sitting at the communications desk, her eyes closed and head bowed in meditation.

She's got to go into the transmitter booth when I tell her to, Linc knew. *If she doesn't, we're going to have a pack of crazy people going wild.*

The countdown sequencer gave off a warning whistle, and the crowd of people shrank back from it, gasping.

"Don't be afraid," Linc said. "It's just a signal that we're going to have another rocket blast in five minutes. This'll be the last one." *And the roughest.*

They stared at the countdown screens, fascinated by the ever-changing numbers even though they couldn't read them. A minute before the rockets were set to fire, Linc told them to lie down on the floor.

"Magda!" he called.

She raised her head and looked at him.

"Tell all the people who haven't come up to the bridge yet to get down on the floor or on their bunks. Tell them to keep away from anything that might fall on them. They've got . . . fifty-one seconds to the final rocket burn."

She spoke into the microphone. The crowd on the bridge lay down. Linc wedged his feet solidly against the desk supports and held onto the sides of his chair.

The giant spoke again. The roar was bone-rattling. The whole bridge shook as if it was going to come apart. Someone screamed. Linc realized he had squeezed his eyes shut. He opened them and tried to focus on the screens in front of him, but everything was shaking too much. All he could see was a jangled, multicolored blue.

Then it stopped. Linc leaned forward to stare at the astrogation display. *On course.* He didn't feel triumphant about it. Just grateful.

Magda was staring at him, watching him as intently as Linc himself watched the screens.

"Better tell everybody to start heading for the bridge. Now." As she turned back to the microphone, Linc said to the people who were getting up off the floor, "There's a short corridor on the other side of the hatch at the far end of the bridge. Line up there in single file. No pushing and no panic. Everything's going very smoothly, so let's not foul it up by getting excited."

A voice came screaming from the open airlock hatch that led to the passageway: "The farm tanks! Something's happened to the pumps. They've stopped!"

Linc glanced at the screens that told him what the electrical power system was doing. Lights were going out all over the ship. Heaters, too. *All on schedule.*

The people were lining up in the corridor that led to the matter transmitter. But fresh voices were coming from the passageway that led to the living area:

"There's no lights in the galley."

"The air fans have stopped."

"It's getting cold out here! The heaters...."

Linc went to the communications desk and reached for the microphone. It pulled out of the desk top easily, trailing a hair-thin wire.

"Listen to me!" he commanded. Magda pushed her chair back and stood beside him. "The ship is dying. We have only a little time to get off the ship and onto the new world. Line up here at the bridge and get ready. Bring whatever you can carry with you; we won't have time for anything else."

He handed the mike to Magda, who took it with only the slightest grimace of distaste. "My robe," she said. "My symbols...."

"No time," Linc snapped. "I've got to get the transmitter started. You keep the people calmed down as they come in here.

Get them in line. When I call you, you come. No arguments."

She started to say something, but let it drop. She nodded and turned away from him.

"Don't be afraid," she said into the microphone. And she forced a smile for the people who were milling confusedly around the bridge. "Let's line up now, down there where the hatch is...."

Linc hurried past the line of people and opened the door to the transmitter room. He sat at the desk and started working the controls. The lights on the bridge dimmed. Out of the corner of his eye, he could see a few of the display screens beyond the line of heads and shoulders in the corridor. The screens were starting to flicker and go dark.

Every erg of power....

Voices drifted in; Linc couldn't tell if they were from the corridor, the bridge, or the passageway outside.

"The machines are dying."

"Hey, I can see my breath...look it's like little puffs of smoke."

And Magda's voice. "It's all right. We'll all reach the new world safely. Don't be afraid."

"But it's *cold!*"

The lights on the control desk were all green.

Everything was ready. Linc got up, pushed through the people lined up in the corridor, and took a final look at the bridge's countdown screen. It was one of the few left alive. Its yellow numerals glowed in the shadowy half-light of the darkened bridge.

"Magda," he called. "Time to go."

She let the mike fall from her hand and followed him to the transmitter room. As they stepped into the room itself, she whispered:

"You've given us no choice."

"That's right," he said, leading her to the transmitter booth.

Magda hesitated for only an instant. As Linc swung the booth's transparent plastic door open, she straightened her back and marched right inside. The people at the front of the line watched, goggle-eyed.

"Smile at them," Linc whispered as he shut the door.

She put on a smile. To Linc it seemed obviously artificial.

He went swiftly to the desk, touched the controls, then let his hand hover over the orange ACTIVATE button. *What if something's wrong? What if the receiver landed in an area where we can't live? What if I kill her?*

"It's freezing out here," came a voice from the corridor.

Linc punched the orange button. The transmitter booth flared with a brilliant white-hot light for just an instant, then it was empty.

He stared at it for a moment, then turned to the people at the head of the line. They were staring, too.

"Did you see that?"

"She's gone!"

"It's magic!"

"All right," Linc called, suddenly unbearably weary. "Come on. One at a time. To the new world."

They did as they were told. There was no panic. A few of them were reluctant to enter the booth, obviously frightened. But the others in line jeered and joked at them. They all went in, with less than a minute between each one.

Linc operated the controls like an automaton, knowing that the real reason they all stepped blindly into the transmitter booth was not their faith in him or even in Magda. It was their fear of the obvious death of the ship. The bridge lights finally went out completely, leaving only the glowing fluorescent panels of the corridor and transmitter room to give a dim, eerie light. The heat ebbed away, and Linc's fingers began to go numb as he punched the buttons on the transmitter's keyboard over and over again. Twenty times. Thirty. Forty-five. He shuffled his feet and stamped them, sending needles of pain up his legs.

Monel! The thought hit him as he worked the controls. *Where is he? Why hasn't he shown up? It's not like him to be so quiet.*

Stav appeared in the line, and Linc waved him over. As the next man stepped into the booth and Linc worked the controls, he asked the broad-faced farmer, "Have you seen Monel?"

"Yes. He's at the end of the line. Him and his five guards."

"Why is he hanging back at the end of the line?" Linc asked.

Stav shrugged. "You want me to wait here with you? In case he tries to make trouble?"

Frowning, Linc shook his head. "No. Go ahead. I've kept you

here too long already. Get into the booth."

Stav grinned. "I wouldn't mind waiting. That . . . thing . . . it makes me scary. Big flash and *poof*, you're gone."

Linc smiled back at him. "That's right." He hit the orange button and a girl disappeared from the booth. "And *poof*, you're on the new world. Now get in there, you big potato brain, before somebody else starts admitting that he's scared."

Stav patted Linc on the shoulder and stepped around to the booth. Without a hint of fear he got in and waved to Linc as he flashed into nothingness.

Jayna showed up a few minutes later, smiling nervously. Linc nodded to her and sent her into oblivion also.

He realized that his mind was working against him. *I'm not sending them into oblivion. I'm not killing them. I'm giving them life, sending them to the new world.*

But still, all he saw was the people he had known all his life disappearing, one by one. Stepping into the transmitter booth—calm or frightened, grinning or tight-lipped—each of them stepping in and allowing him to utterly destroy their bodies.

His hands shook as he thought about it.

The timer on the control desk showed less than four minutes remaining when Monel and his guards came into the transmitter room.

"We're the last," Monel said. "There's no one left behind us."

"All right." Linc's breath puffed steamily as he spoke. "You have to get in one at a time."

"No," Monel said. "You've tricked the others, but you won't trick me."

Somehow, Linc had expected it. "Don't be an idiot. There's only a few minutes left."

But Monel wheeled his chair over to the control desk and leaned his thin, narrow-eyed face next to Linc's. "You think you'll keep the whole ship for yourself, don't you? Everything for yourself. Well, it won't work."

"The ship is dead," Linc said. "There's no way. . . ."

Monel smiled. On him, it wasn't a pleasant thing. "Do you think for an instant that I believe Jerlet would let this ship die?"

"Jerlet's dead. . . ."

"So you told us. But you said he would return to us some day.

How can he do that if the ship dies?"

"He can't," Linc admitted. "He'll plunge into Baryta with the dead ship. There's nothing I can do about that."

"I don't believe you."

Linc jabbed a thumb at the timer. "Look! We've got slightly more than three minutes to get the seven of us through the transmitter. That's barely enough time...."

Monel cut through with, "I want you to start turning on the machines again. I want the light and heat back, and all the machines to...."

"I can't!" Linc said, watching the timer click off the seconds. "Nobody can."

"You will. None of us are going through that machine. You're not going to get us to leave."

Linc looked up at the five guards. They seemed to be solidly agreed with Monel.

"All right," he said. "Then I'm going... you can have the ship if you want it so badly." He started to get up.

"You're not going anywhere!" Monel snapped.

Two of the nearest guards pushed Linc back into his chair. *Three minutes... two fifty-nine....*

"There's no way to bring the ship back to life," Linc shouted. "I had to dump every bit of power aboard into the transmitter. If we don't get out of here in the next two and a half minutes, we're all going to die!"

"You're bluffing," Monel said.

Linc clutched at his head. "*Bluffing?* Look around you, you stupid rat-brain! The machines are already dead. Nothing's working except the transmitter."

"You can fix the machines."

"Don't you realize how long it took me to fix the bridge? Months! We don't have months, we only have seconds! The air fans aren't working anymore. It's a race to see if we'll freeze before we suffocate!"

Monel started to shake his head, but Linc pushed himself up out of the chair. To the guards he said, "If he wants to kill himself, that's fine with me. But he's killing us, too."

They shifted on their feet, looked at each other.

"There's hardly more than a minute left! In one more minute we're all dead men."

The guard nearest the transmitter booth started to say, "Maybe...."

"No!" Monel snapped. "He wants to keep the ship for himself."

Linc pointed to the guard who had started to speak. "He's crazy. He wants to die, and he wants to kill us with him. Get into the booth, at least I can save one or two of you."

The guard hesitated a heartbeat, then grabbed at the booth's door.

"Don't you dare!" Monel screeched.

But the guard got inside and swung the door shut. Linc leaned over the control desk and started touching the buttons. Monel screamed and grabbed at him, but Linc pushed him away.

"Keep him off me," he growled.

With one hand he banged the buttons in the proper sequence and hit the orange ACTIVATE button. The booth flashed.

"No, it's a trick, don't let him...." Monel raged. But two of his guards lifted him out of his chair and dragged him to the hatch. They dropped him there in a huddled heap.

All four of the remaining guards tried to jam into the booth at once.

"No! Stop that!" Linc commanded. "The first two ... inside. You others wait for a few seconds." *The transmitter will handle two of them ... I hope!*

He sent them on their way with a soundless flash and the other two guards squeezed into the booth. The timer read 00 00 24 when they disappeared.

Linc punched buttons and hit the delay switch that would give him ten seconds to get into the booth before it activated again. He stepped away from the desk and reached for the booth's door.

Monel was lying at the edge of the hatch, staring at him with hate-filled eyes.

"You wanted the ship, it's all yours," Linc said.

Monel reached out a bony hand. His voice was a thin, high-pitched whine that Linc had never heard before.

"Please ... don't leave me...."

The timer read 00 00 07.

Linc flung the booth door open, stepped over, and scooped

Monel up in his arms. He was strangely light, frail, like a little child. He was whimpering. Linc dove into the booth and somehow managed to swing the door shut just as the whole universe exploded into blinding painful unbearable brilliance.

(21)

It was neither a long time nor a short time. It was no time at all. As if time didn't exist. Total blankness. Nothing to see, feel, hear, taste, smell.

I'm dead, Linc thought. *This is what death is. Absolute nothingness.*

He wasn't even sure that he was thinking. The blankness was so complete that even existence itself was doubtful. Totally alone, without sensation, as if his body and its organs no longer existed. Nothing but memory. Neither desire nor fear. Nothing but awareness, and the faint remembrance of....

The light hurt his eyes.

Squinting, Linc realized that he felt the weight of Monel's frail body in his arms. He felt his feet standing on solid flooring. He was breathing. His pulse throbbed in his ears.

For some reason his eyes were blurred with tears. He blinked a few times, and saw them.

The people were clustered around, all of them. Stav was yanking open the door of the receiver booth, grinning like a fool.

They grabbed at Linc, pulled Monel out of his arms, pounded him on the back, lifted him onto their shoulders. Laughing, shouting, all their voices raised at once, all of them looking up at him.

"Hey, wait...."

But they were jouncing him around on their shoulders, shouting over and over again, "You did it! You did it! We made it! We made it!"

Linc looked around and saw the new world.

It was green, not blue. That surprised him. The ground was

covered with soft green grass that waved slowly in a warm breeze. The sky was pale blue, fading almost to yellow near the horizon. Hills and trees, and a sparkling stream of water....

Everything was so open!

The world just went on and on, open and huge and green and warm. *Warm!* Linc twisted around slightly and saw that Baryta was no longer a fiery danger but a warm smile upon the land.

The landscape was open and beautiful. Gentle hills rolled off toward the horizon. A stream glinted in the sunlight. Trees dotted the open grassland, and farther off clustered into a thick forest. Something sailed through the air gracefully, effortlessly, on outstretched wings that were ablaze with color.

Finally they put him down, let him touch his feet on the grass of their new home.

"It's a good world you've brought us to," someone said.

"Not me," said Linc. "We all did it, together ... with Jerlet's help, and the machines."

"What do we do now?"

Linc saw that they were all looking at him, waiting for him to tell them what to do.

He shook his head. "We need a leader ... someone who can make wise decisions and help us learn how to live in this new world."

Before they could say anything, Linc stepped up to Stav and put an arm around the farmer's broad shoulder. "Stav should be out leader. He knows more about farming than any of us, and that's the kind of wisdom we need now."

They all shouted agreement. Stav actually blushed, but he didn't argue. Linc edged away from him as the crowd cheered their new leader.

Then he noticed Magda standing beside him.

"The people will still need a priestess," she said.

Linc nodded. "Probably they will. And they'll need machines, too."

"All the machines are on the ship."

With a grin, he said, "I think I can figure out how to make a few things ... like a windmill, maybe. Or a wheelchair for Monel. Maybe even a power generator, if we can find the right metals."

She reached a hand out toward him, and he took it in his.

"We both have a lot to learn," Magda said.

"We sure do," Linc agreed.

They lifted their eyes toward the sky, as a bright swift-moving star raced across the blue.

"The ship," said Linc.

Magda looked sat. "It's carrying Jerlet away from us."

Linc grinned. Remembering that shaggy, sloppy, wild-haired, booming-voiced old man, he said, "He accomplished what he set out to do; he got us here safely. And we'll always remember him."

A soft breeze tousled Magda's long hair. She nodded and smiled at Linc as the melodious song of a bird filled the morning air.

ABOUT THE AUTHOR

BEN BOVA began his career as a journalist in Philadelphia, went on to be the technical editor for project Vanguard and then the manager of marketing for Avco Everett Research Laboratory. During that time he wrote and published several short stories and novels. In 1971, following the death of then-editor John W. Campbell, Bova became the editor of the influential Analog Magazine. He won the Hugo Award for Best Editor every year from 1971 through 1977 for his work at Analog. He also wrote and published many novels during that period, among them MILLENNIUM, THE STARCROSSED, THE MULTIPLE MAN and COLONY. In 1978, Bova left Analog to become the Fiction Editor for the newly-founded OMNI Magazine, and shortly thereafter made the move to his current position of Executive Editor of OMNI. His newest novel, VOYAGER, will be published next year.